Praise for Sloan Parker's Books

"Sloan Parker is an amazing writer. Her work is beautiful and touching and emotional. If you haven't read any of her books, I suggest you run out and do so!"
—*Sadonna at The Armchair Reader*

"They are super sexy together, but also so sweet and loving... loved that sweet vs kinky contrast between them."
—*Joyfully Jay on MORE THAN JUST A GOOD BOOK*

"...I loved everything about this story—especially the level of intensity and connection that crackled between Grady and Mateo. I'd sum up my reading experience with this book in one word—unputdownable!"
—*Hearts on Fire Reviews on I SWEAR TO YOU*

"...I have loved every one of Sloan Parker's books and this one is no different. ...exciting, suspenseful and most importantly, romantic. The love story between Walter and Kevin is so sweet and real. They have a connection that can't be denied by either one of them."
—*Literary Nook on HOW TO SAVE A LIFE*

"I loved both of the heroes... and found myself easily rallying for their relationship to grow from being best friends to developing a loving, romantic relationship together that lived long within my heart long after the story was over."
—*Night Owl Reviews on TAKE ME HOME*

"So sweet and romantic and incredibly well done in such a short format."
—*Joyfully Jay on SOMETHING TO BELIEVE IN*

OTHER TITLES BY SLOAN PARKER

Breathe
Take Me Home
How to Save a Life (The Haven Book 1)
More Than Just a Good Book
Something to Believe In
I Swear to You
The Break-In
Swept Away
A Lesson in Truth

More
(More Book 1)

SLOAN PARKER

Wishing you much love and happiness!
Sloan Parker

MORE (More Book 1)
Copyright © 2010 by Sloan Parker

Revised Print Edition: 2014
Originally released in e-book format in 2010

All rights reserved. No part of this publication may be reproduced, stored in a retrieval system, or transmitted in any form or by any means—electronic, mechanical, photocopying, recording, scanning, or otherwise—without the prior written permission of the publisher.

ISBN-13: 978-1-4776359-9-5
ISBN-10: 1-4776359-9-8

Cover Design: Copyright © 2012 by Sloan Parker, Revised 2014
Cover Photos: licensed through shutterstock.com

This is a work of fiction. The names, characters, and incidents are either the product of the author's imagination or have been used fictitiously. Any resemblance to actual persons or incidents are coincidental.

Published by
Sloan Parker Press
www.sloanparker.com

DEDICATION

To Rosie. Thank you for the love, the laughter, and the dream.

Chapter One

I hadn't seen any sign of my stalkers. They'd either gotten worse at finding me or better at hiding. Eight months, and I hadn't spotted a single man following me. The longest stretch since my early twenties.

They'd find me, though. Given enough time and enough money, it was inevitable.

"Man, you sure you want to get out here?"

I nodded at the cab driver and glanced out the window at the five-story building with graffiti and faded, chipped bricks camouflaging the exterior. In the six months I'd been coming to the club, the facade had never changed. "This is the place."

I scanned the street and sidewalks around the cab. The late hour limited my view. An alley across the street was the worst of it. Every time I came, I had to worry about that damn alley. And it wasn't the three fire escapes climbing the sides of the abandoned buildings or the dumpster full of tied trash bags containing more used condoms than even I cared to think about. It was every dark corner where they could hide.

"Hope you know what you're getting into," he said.

"Wouldn't have taken the risk if I didn't." I paid him the fare and jumped out of the cab. He sped off the moment the door shut, and I shook my head and smirked.

If he only knew.

But he wasn't the type. My gaydar was right on the money most days. Probably lived in the suburbs with his wife, 2.5 kids, and dog named Riley, and spent his weekends at soccer games, peewee football practice, and Sunday morning services at Christians United or whichever flavor-of-the-week church he was into. He'd piss his pants walking into a gay sex club. I'd met my share of straight guys who assumed by just talking to a gay man that everyone they'd ever known—right down to their first grade teacher—would then assume they were gay too. Classic homophobia.

I strode to the unmarked doorway. The rush overwhelmed me. My body knew what the night would bring. The touch of another. The shattered control.

I scanned my ID card, gave one last look over my shoulder, and stepped inside. The combined aroma of blended aftershaves and liquor erased any concerns about who might have followed me there. After the bleak downtown street, the Haven, with its leather chairs, starched table linens, and ornate wood trim, offered a promise of decadence.

And I was more than ready for it.

Men packed the lounge, the dining room, the bar, and my anticipation mounted with each step through the crowd. The music pulsed in a low throb that hinted at dance music but wasn't near the beat required for anything more than a slow grinding of hips to hips. Foreplay. Like a primal mating ritual of young tribesmen, slicked and painted, ready to strike.

The lighting in the bar was dim but bright enough to make a search of the prospects without strain. I appreciated that. I came to the club for one reason. And drinks, dinner, and dancing had nothing to do with it.

I claimed an empty stool at the bar. Several members I hadn't been with yet caught my eye, but having seen them week after week, they screamed of redundancy—even if I hadn't yet glimpsed their cocks. I needed someone new. I wanted at least one of the men who'd fuck me to be someone I'd never laid eyes on before.

And I wanted to be tied up. I wanted to beg for it.

A shiver crawled over my skin. The decision to be with two men, and the way I wanted them to take me, heightened my need.

I didn't always spend the night with more than one man at a time, but it happened more often than not. And I never played with the same men more than once.

No exceptions.

Not that I let myself get propositioned for more. I'm an asshole to most guys I sleep with. Just not while we're in the sack. There, I'm generous. I return favors and all that. I like giving head. I like touching dick. I like getting fucked. But after, in the quiet, when we're catching our breaths, I'm out the door before he has a chance to ask me to become his next fuck buddy or for a number he can call when he gets to needing something.

What I didn't know then was I'd already followed that rule for the last time. The next two men I'd sleep with were going to ask me to break every damn rule I ever lived by.

Change wouldn't come easily, though. Not when you factor in my own resistance, and my father, of course.

The man had always been an asshole. A lot of fathers are. Mine also happened to be a US senator. Being an asshole may have been a requirement for the job. Who knew? My father never introduced me to his colleagues. He sponsored loads of legislation to strip away my rights. He understood if people knew about his gay son, they'd view him as a mean old bastard. Which, of course, he was. But I knew him in ways few did. I'd seen him point a loaded gun at my face and smile. And that had been when he still spoke to me.

Sitting at the bar in the Haven, I had no clue what I was about to do would be the catalyst for everything. I merely wanted to get fucked in the way I craved.

A half hour later, the turnout looked downright dim. I wasn't ready to give up. I'd find someone. I always did.

As if on cue from some spiritual guide for horny gay men, my gaze captured a young man. He wove in and out of the crowd, heading my way. I'd often considered approaching him, but each time, we'd already found our hookups.

The night was looking up. I'd caught him on his way in.

He had to be somewhere in his early twenties, but his youthful face gave him the look of someone younger. The slight bounce of each step and his wavy, dark hair added to it. He wore tight leather pants that showed off lean leg muscles with each step and a loose white dress shirt. The clothes, the hair, the face, every ounce of him was sexy as hell.

I wanted to be with him, had wanted it for weeks. Things were definitely looking good.

The kid sat on the stool next to mine, and in response to his silent nod, the bartender brought him a glass of club soda. He smiled his thank you and swallowed half his drink in one lift of the glass. His full lips held my attention as he spoke, the words whispered more to the glass than me. "Are you available tonight?"

With his question, I was halfway to getting what I needed. The Haven wouldn't disappoint. It never had.

"Yeah," I said.

He downed another gulp of the soda. The swipe of his tongue wet his lips, and I couldn't peel my eyes from his mouth.

"I'd like us to find another," I added.

His head bobbed twice. "That's fine with me." He spun the glass with two hands and watched the ice swirl and melt in the bubbly liquid.

I cracked a smile. I didn't usually go for his type. Not at the club, and not when I wanted someone to fuck the hell out of me, but something about the kid was inspiring. I ached to find out what he'd be like once we locked the door behind us.

"Let's get a table," I said. "Check out the clientele."

He nodded. The club soda continued to hold his interest.

I stood and heard him jump off the stool to follow. I made my way to a nearby table and turned to face him. He stared at his feet and stopped just short of ramming his forehead into my chin. Dramatic, dark eyes flashed up at me. They asked for something, begged for it. Yet they gave me an innocent, naive look as if he hoped I'd tell him what he needed.

Reading people wasn't my forte. Neither was waiting.

I drew in a long breath and stepped back. He moved by me and brushed the length of his arm along mine. The simple gesture jerked my prick awake. Or maybe it was him. He smelled of a crisp, spicy cologne and toothpaste. Had the bartender given him a mouthwash shot with his soda? Who knew that minty smell could alert my dick to the possibility of some action?

I sat across from him. "The name's Luke."

"Matthew." He held out a hand. Once he leaned back in his chair, his eyes found mine. "Can I ask how old you are?"

"You got an age requirement?"

"Nah. Just curious." He ran a hand through his dark hair. The strands straightened and snapped back into waves, the movement smooth. *What would that hand feel like wrapped around my dick?*

I let out a ragged breath. Waiting could be hard. Damn hard.

"Thirty-three," I said.

"How often are you here?"

"Friday nights. Some Saturdays. A few weeknights when I need it. It's hard to pass up a guaranteed fuck, you know?"

"I suppose so." The color rose in his cheeks. He dipped his head and ran a thumb along the edge of the table. "How come we've never done this before?" His gaze drifted between the tabletop and me.

"Don't know. Seems every time I considered it, you were already with someone else. Guess you're too popular."

He smiled, and his eyes shone as he stared at me. He had a great smile.

Waiting could be nearly impossible.

I scanned the room again. A few men who hadn't been in

attendance earlier caught my eye. No one I wanted, though. Then I saw him. He sat alone at a table on the far side of the dining room.

"Matthew, I think we have our third."

Chapter Two

Matthew peeked over his shoulder. "Oh, man. I've never seen him before."

"Me neither," I said.

"Maybe he's new." Matthew whipped his head around. "I mean, you're here a lot more than me."

"That's what I need."

He frowned and tilted his head to the side.

"I want someone I've never seen before tonight. He and you are going to be exactly what I need."

Matthew's lips spread. He bit at his bottom lip before releasing it and giving in to the full grin. *Damn.* That smile was sexier than any other.

I forced my attention across the room. The large man was strolling toward us. He had to be a little older than I, but not much. Tall, broad, and all muscle. Nobody would push him into a dark alley and holler "faggot" as they kicked him to the ground.

He wore dress slacks and a crisp blue shirt. Each hung from his body in a precise way. He carried a glass of wine in his hand and walked with a firm step. No hesitation. No worry over his large body's interference with the world around him. He stopped next to Matthew.

The younger man's gaze floated up the vast physique. He craned his neck to catch every last inch. I waited for the drooling to begin. Not that I could blame him for staring.

"You two want to be alone?" our potential third asked. The voice fit the man. Deep, low, powerful.

"No," Matthew and I said in unison.

"I didn't think so." He grabbed the back of a chair from the nearest table, swung it around, and sat in one quick movement. "Richard." He set his glass on the table and held out a hand. The large hand engulfed

Matthew's. They reminded me of a bear and a rabbit shaking hands. I kept the visual to myself. No sense offending right off the bat.

"Hi. Uh, Matthew." The younger man licked his lips.

Richard smirked. "You're cute, kid."

Matthew's face flushed. His pale skin hid nothing.

"Oh, this should be fun," Richard added with a laugh.

I skimmed the large man's body in a slow sweep. I couldn't agree more. He held out a hand to me.

"Luke."

The moment his hand connected with mine, a flush crept under the surface of my skin, and my cock hardened, giving me the ache I craved. I'd never been one to get worked up from a few words and a handshake, but never had someone's touch cranked my arousal up like his.

The Haven never let me down.

"Good to meet you both," Richard said, his voice even lower.

He and Matthew stared for a moment, the look they exchanged curious and intense, as if they said something to each other I couldn't hear or understand.

They broke the stare and Richard glanced my way. "What are you looking for?"

"Right now? I want to be tied up, and I want to be well used. No S&M. Condoms all the way around, even for blowjobs. And I won't change my mind, so don't even ask."

He revealed a slow grin. "That fits what I'm looking for. How about you, Matthew?"

"I, uh…" He looked at me, and back to Richard. His head snapped from point to point. "I don't mind helping you tie him up."

Richard threw me a look I took to mean we'd sealed the deal.

Matthew's gaze drifted to the wineglass. His brow furrowed, and his full lips pursed into a thin line. He grasped the edge of the table. "But…no drinking."

"Okay," I said, since he wouldn't look at either of us.

Richard motioned to a server. "No drinking, then. I've had two sips of wine. I'll stop." He handed off the glass.

"Thanks." Matthew's dark eyes shone again. He smiled and bounced a little in his seat.

"Just to be clear," I said. "I'm not looking for someone to fuck more than once. Tonight. That's it."

The big man spoke without a moment's hesitation. "I'm not after someone who wants a repeat."

"Good." I caught Matthew's frown out of the corner of my eye. It didn't last long. It transformed into a playful grin, like a mask he'd assumed many times before. I eyed the younger man with curiosity. What did he want? All I could give him was a guarantee to spend the night exchanging orgasms. It was a hell of a lot more than most men got on a consistent basis. "Want to head up, then?"

Richard led the way to the staircase at the rear of the dining room. I followed with Matthew close behind. We paused at the reservation desk at the top of the stairs. The club was efficient, and it didn't take long for Richard to have a key card in hand.

He selected a basic hotel-style room that included a few bondage supplies, as well as a large four-poster bed positioned in the center of the room, a full bathroom, and a small bar lined with miniature bottles of liquor. The pillows, the chairs, the bed linens, the walls, and the carpet all had an absence of color. Nothing dark or illicit or unseemly. Enough white draped the room, it screamed virginal, which was worth a laugh. Despite my numerous nights at the club, the room was a first for me. I gravitated toward men who preferred the darker side of the Haven.

I didn't care either way. The room's decor was not my priority.

Richard closed the door and gathered Matthew into his arms. Their lips and tongues connected, the kiss deepening with every second. Matthew moaned into the taller man's mouth. His arms wound around Richard's wide shoulders. His groin pushed against a thick thigh. Richard's hands wandered through Matthew's hair, down his back, over his ass.

God, they look great together. They mesmerized me. I inhaled a raspy, guttural sound and rubbed my hand over my firming bulge. Nothing could have stopped me.

"I couldn't get a room without alcohol," Richard said without letting go of Matthew. "All of them have it except for the S&M ones. I don't use those rooms. Ever."

"It's okay." Matthew held on to the larger man's shoulders.

"You sure can kiss, kid. Those lips and that tongue should come with a warning."

Matthew dropped his hands to his sides and swiped his palms over his thighs. "Thanks."

Richard took Matthew's hand in his and led him to me. He snaked his other arm around my waist and tugged me close. I lost my footing and gripped his biceps. Damn, he was strong. The heat of his skin leaked through his shirt. My fingers dug in as though they could sink through the fabric and get to his flesh.

Richard's kiss was soft when it landed on my lips, but once his mouth opened, it became fierce. He attacked my tongue with his, that muscle as strong as the rest of him. He tasted of breath mints. Had he popped a mint to wipe out the taste of the wine since Matthew asked him not to drink?

No. Guys didn't do that kind of courteous shit for each other.

Matthew's lips skated over my earlobe and traveled down. His hot breath warmed my already heated skin. I shuddered.

Richard released me and headed across the room.

Where the hell was he going? I wanted more of that kiss.

Matthew's hand cupped my neck, and he brought his mouth to mine. I swiped my tongue over his lower lip in a slow taste. He spread his lips and traced my tongue with his. That was all it took. Richard hadn't exaggerated.

I'd never been big on kissing. It wasn't the connection I was after. That could have been because I'd never been kissed by anyone like them. From Richard's hard, passionate kiss to Matthew's sweet, sensual exploration, I was appreciating the act in a new light.

The heat of Matthew's mouth made my own saliva seem cool. He eased up on the kiss, and I shoved against him harder. I wanted a fuck, but I wasn't ready for his lips to leave mine. He was too damn good.

He moaned. His hands explored my neck, my shoulders, my back. His fingers worked to learn every line, every curve of my body through the clothes. I ached to feel those hands on my skin. He moved and rubbed against me, his leather-covered cock dragging over me. He wanted this, needed it. I appreciated that. Matthew exuded sex, but there was more to him. He worked my mouth and body with more than a desire to get off. He consumed me. When I finally drew back, he pouted.

Richard chuckled, the sound low and tense with need.

I regarded our third partner for the night. He sat on the bed, his legs parted, gliding his large hand over the front of his pants.

"Are you going to join us?" I asked.

"I'd like to watch you two first, before we get to the tying you up part. If you don't mind." He stood. When he reached Matthew's side, he pressed his lips to the other man's ear. "Get him going for us, kid. Get him hard and ready to pop. And get him naked." He licked the length of Matthew's ear, walked away, and leaned against the far wall.

Matthew grasped my arm with a trembling hand and encouraged me to the edge of the bed. Was he nervous?

"Take it slow," Richard added.

Matthew nodded without detaching his gaze from me.

"You aren't going to watch all night, are you?" I wanted them to touch me, to give me pleasure in ways one man couldn't. I wanted to feel them—both of them.

"Hell, no. Want to enjoy the view is all." Richard stroked himself through his pants again.

I wanted to see his cock, breathe in the scent, watch it pulse in his hand, see the beads of his desire form at the tip, knowing it'd be in my ass eventually that night. It took all my willpower not to march over and grab a hold of him.

"Good," I said. "Sooner rather than later, huh?"

"Don't worry. I won't leave you hanging." His chest heaved as he stroked faster.

Matthew's hands steered me to his lips again. The touch was soft and wet and warm and…damn, could he kiss. I turned and rubbed my cock against his. A tremble seized my body. Even through the clothes, the contact sent me spiraling out of control.

I worked one hand through his wavy hair, grabbed his ass with the other, and pulled him against me. I needed more of him. I had to get us naked. I had to get inside him.

What the hell was he doing to me?

His fingers were nimble as they worked on my shirt. One button popped open after another, and his hands discovered my chest. He swiped a finger over a nipple, then pinched and tugged. I groaned. The sound of it surged in and out with the movements of his mouth over mine. Our lips parted and he smiled.

I wanted his mouth back on mine, our tongues tangling.

He shed his shirt, and his hand slid over the front of my jeans. I gasped as he worked the top button open. I wanted him to dip his hand inside. I needed his touch. I ached for it.

Matthew was perfection, but everything was moving slower than my usual evenings at the club. Especially since one of the night's participants still stood against the wall and touched only himself.

Matthew kissed me again, distracting me. I pressed my naked chest to his. His hands slipped inside the back of my jeans. He shoved my pants down and cupped my ass. The firm grip was nothing I expected from the kid I'd met in the bar.

My erect dick worked free of the fabric. A low sigh spilled out of Richard. *Man likes what he sees.*

Then why wouldn't he touch me?

Matthew's mouth followed his hands, proceeded lower and lower, explored my body until he paused before my dick. He stared at it, licking his lips while he removed my shoes and pants. *You want a taste, don't you?*

I coiled his dark hair around my fingers.

Without warning, he leaned in and lapped at my balls. My head spun. My breath came in short pants. What I would have given to take my dick in my hand and shove it into his mouth, condom be damned.

He moved on before I lost all reason and gave into the temptation.

Matthew ran his tongue along my stomach and up my chest until he sucked in a nipple. He sent me flying faster than I'd ever gone without someone around my dick or in my ass. I threaded my fingers through more of his hair, but I forced my palm to stay open as he licked and flicked my sensitive skin.

I threw my head back. "Yeah, like that, Matthew." I wasn't into talking to my sexual partners, but I couldn't hold back.

He hummed in response. He stayed at it for another few licks and sucks before he stepped back and worked his pants off. I admired the sight of his cock. Seeing a man's dick hard for me always turned me on more. I wrapped my hand around the shaft, kept the touches light, ran my thumb along the side until reaching the head, and squeezed. He groaned. His hips snapped. And he never stopped watching me.

Most guys closed their eyes once I touched their dicks. Most guys busied themselves with enjoying my body.

Not Matthew. He leaned in slowly and kept watching me until our lips met again. The kiss almost distracted me from the warm breath that painted the back of my neck. Richard wound his arms around my waist and stroked my dick in a slow grope. At that moment, nothing could have distracted me.

I leaned back and savored the muscular flesh. I wasn't a small man like Matthew, but Richard could lift me and fuck me against a wall without my feet ever touching the floor. A shiver spread throughout my body. He rocked against me, and his hard shaft grazed the top of my ass.

"Good man," I said, "getting naked for us."

His lips swept over my ear. "Loved watching you two. Thank you. On the bed, Luke. Time to get you ready."

With something that felt like regret, I drew my hands away from Matthew. I wanted to lie down to get fucked and still hold on to him. No one had ever felt so damn good in my arms. No one had ever spent so much time in my arms. I was all about the blowjob, or the rimming, or the connection of dick to ass.

I stretched out on my back and was awarded another striking vision of them. Matthew stood on his toes, and Richard was hunched over, his mouth on Matthew's, his red, swollen cock smashed against the smaller man's stomach.

I watched their mouths move together, watched them draw the desire out of each other. They kissed and touched as if they had all the time in the world and only the two of them to worry about. Had it not been such a turn-on, I'd have been annoyed. Instead, I sat and stared and stroked my dick as the erotic show played out before me. I'd never come to the club to spend time watching before. Seemed like a waste of the membership dues.

Their kiss ended, leaving both men breathless.

Richard's fingers brushed at the swollen flesh of Matthew's lips. "Damn. Why don't you go suck him and I'll tie him up."

"Oh, yeah. Okay." Matthew scrambled to the bar. He grabbed several condoms and small tubes of lube from a bowl and bounced his way to the bed. When he landed, the mattress bounced with him. His mouth formed a perfect circle, and his eyes widened. He laughed, his wavy hair swaying with the chuckles. The joy and ease of the sound was contagious, and I joined him.

I'd never laughed in a room at the Haven before.

Matthew crawled forward. He licked my body as soon as he reached my thighs, humming and rubbing against me, exploring my body with his tongue.

How could he go from laughing to deep need again that fast?

More importantly, how could he get me right there with him?

He knew more tricks with his mouth than I'd ever experienced. He'd also touched more of me in the past few minutes than all of my sexual partners at the club ever had.

And yet, I wanted more.

I heard Richard open the supply cabinet. Part of me wanted to know what he'd use to bind me, and part of me wanted to wait until the restraints made contact with my body.

Matthew trailed eager kisses toward my cock. He licked the line where hip met leg. I arched into it, and my head fell back. I heard him tear the condom wrapper open.

I lifted my head. "Kiss me again." *What the hell? More kissing?* But I couldn't take it back. I wanted his mouth on my lips again, his tongue connecting with mine.

He shot up. "Yeah. Yeah." He straddled my thighs, and his lips brushed against mine in a short, chaste kiss. "I love to kiss."

"I can tell." I wrapped my hands around his neck and encouraged him to kiss me again. He rocked in unison with the movements of our tongues, and a familiar swell surged through my dick. "Fuck. I'm gonna come from just kissing you."

"No. No, not yet. Let me—" He slid down, rolled the condom on, and sucked me all the way in.

Holy crap.

Not too many guys could go down that far.

His lips dragged over my shaft, and he sucked the sensitive head for a moment before pulling off. "You're sure? About the rubber?"

"I said—"

"Yeah. I just—most guys—I like giving head. I don't mind."

"I won't return the favor."

"It's okay."

"Just stop talking and put your lips over the damn condom."

He bit his lip, then drew me back into his mouth.

"Yeah, kid—ah fuck." He sucked harder. My pelvis rocked. The action pushed me deeper inside him. I twisted my fingers in the sheet and flattened my body to the bed. Matthew knew his shit. He'd take care of me.

But when did I leave it all up to the other guy? I said what I wanted. I took what I wanted.

"He that good?" Richard's breath tickled my ear. How long had he been kneeling next to the bed? Watching us?

"God, yes."

Richard ran a hand along my jaw, his bright green eyes fixated on me. I tilted my chin and drew his finger into my mouth, sucking in time with Matthew's pulls of my cock. Richard watched my mouth work him, and he gulped down a stiff swallow.

He slid his finger from my mouth and lifted my right arm over my head. He wrapped a rope around my wrist, stretched my arm taut, and tied off the rope, then restrained my left arm in the same way. My heart pounded. Knowing I couldn't get away from them heightened every sensation.

"You tell me if anything hurts," he said.

"Yeah. Okay."

Matthew moaned, and my cock vibrated in his mouth. Was it the idea of me tied up, or was he that turned on from sucking me? His hard prick rubbed along my leg. I loved it when a man could get off from a little sucking and humping.

Matthew pulled off. "Don't hold back." He took me in deep again. His head bobbed in a quick rhythm that threatened to pull me into oblivion before too long. His hands found my ass, encouraged me to thrust.

I didn't argue with him. I heaved off the bed and into his slick, hot mouth. The movement was awkward without the use of my arms—or my legs, since Matthew still pressed down on me—but I kept moving. And he took it all.

Richard's voice penetrated the haze fogging my brain. "Damn, you two look good together." He joined us on the bed and lay at my side.

The warmth of his body tempted me. I wanted to reach out and caress his hard pecs, feel the power, the flex of muscle. The ropes kept it a distant wish that almost had me pissed I'd asked to be restrained. A man like him deserved to be explored, touched, tasted.

I took a good look instead. Toned body, broad chest. He had a strong face, his nose a little crooked. The slight dusting of chest hair was as blond as the hair on his head. I wanted to run my tongue through it. Taste his flesh.

That's when I noticed it. A wide, raised scar from his right nipple to his left underarm. It was faint, but that could have had more to do with the passage of time than the wound itself. The damage had been bad when it was fresh. Painful. Bloody.

My mouth opened. What the hell could I say? His past was none of my business. I had my own scars—though none were what he could see—and I sure as hell wasn't going to share with some guy I met at the club.

Then I didn't give it another thought.

Matthew shoved a wet finger in my ass. I thrust one last time. My upper body left the bed, jerking the ropes tight, and I cried out as I came, the shrill sound nothing like me.

It was all what I wanted.

But I needed more. I wanted Richard to fuck me, take me while I yanked at the ropes, while I felt the push, the burn, the surrender.

Matthew rested his head on my thigh and exhaled heavy pants that mirrored my own. When his breathing slowed, he knelt between my legs. If the ropes weren't holding me back, I'd have taken him in my hand. His eyes, half-closed and hazy with need, studied me. He brought his lips to mine. The kiss was slow and tender. How could he hold back like that when he was so close to the edge?

Richard knelt behind him. I missed the warmth of him, the touch of his solid body at my side.

Matthew leaned back against his chest. "Dang, you feel good."

"Yeah? How's this feel?" Richard drew his hand across Matthew's chest and teased a nipple. The other hand pumped his cock. The massive fist spread precum over the shaft.

Matthew's hips moved. His head rolled from side to side. "Yeah.

That…that's…your hands are huge and…talented." He wrapped his fingers around my cock and pulled in rhythm with Richard's hand on his own.

Before long, sensations overwhelmed me, my dick willing itself back to full interest. I'd never had such a quick turnaround. Not even at Matthew's age. Those hands and kisses were like nothing else.

Matthew turned his head and kissed Richard. The younger man's light skin and lean body were a fascinating contrast to Richard's darker skin and ripped muscles.

But I wasn't into watching. I wanted to touch, to fuck, to suck, or to be the one getting the same. Yet there was something about them—the size difference, their noises, the way they moved together as Richard rubbed along Matthew's back.

I arched off the bed. "I want… I need… Fuck." I wanted to feel them. I yanked at the ropes. I needed the touch, the warmth. They were driving me crazy.

"Uh-huh." Richard eyed me over Matthew's shoulder. "I'm going to fuck you, Luke. And you're going to suck Matthew."

"That's… I won't argue with that."

"Yeah," Matthew said. He scurried up my body and straddled my chest.

Was it just sex, or was he that eager about everything in life? Did he still run for the tree and presents after he shot out of bed on Christmas morning? Fifteen years since I'd left home, and the only time I celebrated anything was when I got a promotion at work. And that had been a celebration for one with a six-pack.

Richard stroked my thighs. I quivered at the simple touch. *They're just hands. What the hell's the big deal?*

"I left your legs untied," he said. "I want to feel your legs wrapped around me."

"Good. That's…um…good." The sight of Matthew's prick pushing through his own hand distracted me from forming more words.

Richard handed Matthew a condom.

"Bring that here, kid," I said. "I want you in my mouth."

"Uh-huh. I haven't had a blowjob in forever."

Forever? How long was that? Before him, I hadn't had one in five days. And that had been a long stretch for me.

He rolled the condom on and shifted until his knees settled on each side of me. The scent of leather and his crisp cologne flooded my nostrils. Not overwhelming. Subtle and soothing. It made me want him more. Did he slather his dick and balls in the stuff as some sort of aphrodisiac?

He brought his cock to my lips, and I opened for him, sucking the tip until he dripped with my saliva, then taking in more of him.

Richard lifted my legs and angled my hips. Slick fingers brushed over me, stroking again and again before finally pushing in. I moaned around the cock in my mouth.

Matthew's head jerked back. Open and responsive, spread over me, he was one of the sexiest men I'd ever seen.

Richard pressed his big fingers in more. Teased. Twirled. Fucked me. My ass clenched around him.

How many men had touched me there? And not a single one had ever made it as good, had ever spent so much time. The pleasure went on and on. He should write a goddamn book. An instruction manual on that touch alone.

I couldn't see him work me from behind Matthew's body, and that turned me on even more. Desperate again, I didn't know if I'd be able to wait to come until he got inside me. When the hell was the last time that happened? With no one touching my dick?

Another press. Another swirl. How long could he keep me on the edge?

Then his fingers were gone, and I was empty, anxious for his touch again. I sucked harder on Matthew, needing him to come as much as I needed the same release.

The head of Richard's slick, sheathed cock rubbed along my ass. "Ready, Luke?"

With my mouth busy and my arms tied to the bed, I used the one way I had to let him know how much I needed him inside me. I rocked my hips, and the tip of his dick drove into me.

"God, yes." Richard growled with the words. "Luke." His first thrust came slow, but went deep. Persistent. Determined. He repeated the motion, and I tugged and moaned, the sound muted by Matthew inside me.

They were satisfying my ache. I felt them everywhere.

Matthew's noises grew louder. I tried to concentrate on the blowjob while Richard offered me what he had to give, but the big man knew what he was doing, and the distraction made thinking difficult at best. That was always the problem with the execution of a threesome. Too many distractions. Or perhaps just enough.

Matthew bent forward and thrust, his movements shallow. His eyes met mine, his stare intense. He didn't just watch me. He looked inside me.

Too intimate, too personal, too connected.

I wanted to turn away, but I couldn't. I saw something I liked in his gaze. Something in the way he needed me right then.

His hands gripped the headboard, and he went deeper with each shove into me. His words no longer made sense, but he didn't let up. His screams and moans grew louder than anyone I'd ever heard before. *God, he loves sex.* Worth the wait. His hips jerked, and he pushed farther inside my mouth as he came. When his dick finished pulsing, he rolled off me and onto his side with a whimper. I breathed deep and ignored the usual surge of loss.

Richard slammed into me harder.

I tightened my legs around him, loving the power in his movements. A fine mist of sweat covered his upper body. Several beads dripped, and I felt it when every drop struck my sensitive skin. His pelvis slapped my ass harder. A bolt of pleasure zipped through me.

"Yes! More." I arched, and the ropes tightened.

"Luke." He kept at it, kept moving in me, grunting with each shove.

Matthew kissed me. His body pressed close.

"I have to—" I said. His hand covered my cock.

"Not yet, kid," Richard said.

The hand left my dick in a flash, and Matthew's fingers traced my nipples. I lifted my arms, and the restraints caught me. The usual pinch and burn didn't plague my wrists. My hands didn't go numb. Richard knew his shit.

He snapped his hips faster as he dragged his dick in and out, over and over again. I groaned and closed my eyes, focusing on every touch stimulating me.

"Open your eyes," Richard said.

I heard his words, but my body didn't react.

He stilled, his cock hanging half out of me.

My eyes flew open. "What the fuck? Why are you stopping?"

"Don't close your eyes. Look at me."

"Don't stop. Need to come..."

"Watch me." He moved again, slow at first, then picking up speed. The muscles of his arms flexed, and his fingers dug into my hips. I wanted to run my hands over his thick muscles, bury my nose in his chest, and devour his scent. My hands twitched from their self-imposed prison.

With each thrust, my toes curled. My legs shot higher and squeezed around him. My eyes rolled, and I let them fall shut.

Everything stopped.

"Fuck." My voice cracked. I opened my eyes wide.

"I'm trying to, Luke." Richard's voice sounded as strained as mine, but his eyes teased. He held still for a moment more. Then he shoved into me with a long, hard plunge.

"Yes, don't stop."

Matthew giggled. The sound was low and sexual, but it was still a giggle.

Every time my eyes closed, Richard stopped moving, stopped driving into me. As soon as I made eye contact with him, he started again. His hips slammed faster than before. The sound of our bodies coming together and the groans and hums from Matthew filled the room.

The frustration built. This wasn't a quick fuck to get off like many of my nights at the club. This was a slow buildup of need. And deep down, I liked it. I needed it.

After I held Richard's stare for a few more slaps of balls to ass, he spoke again. "Kid, stroke him."

Matthew didn't play around. He worked my cock with his hand until pleasure flooded my shaft. I stared at Richard as I shuddered and rode out my orgasm. Only at the end of my spasms did my eyes close and my head tilt back.

Richard was too far gone to care. Between his clenched teeth, the word "Christ" slithered out like a hiss. His body rocked with pleasure until he collapsed onto my chest, my legs still in the air.

Matthew's hand sped over his own dick, and warm cum spilled over my leg. His forehead landed on my arm. Maybe he thought I was the pillow.

Richard's breathing sounded as labored as mine. "Damn. That…that was great." He lifted up and planted a long, deep kiss on my lips.

What the fuck?

I wanted to push him away. We'd already come. I didn't need him to kiss me. But I didn't stop him. I opened my mouth and caressed his tongue with my own.

He gave one last soft press of his lips to mine, leaned to the side, and kissed Matthew.

I couldn't take my eyes off them.

I loved that Richard's prick was still buried in my ass while he kissed Matthew. I loved that he hadn't rolled off and gotten dressed as soon as he'd finished fucking me. And what the hell did that mean? I was always the first one out the door after the cum went flying. I shifted, trying to give him a clue.

Richard held Matthew's gaze for a moment before he gripped the condom and withdrew. He stood and unfastened my restraints, checking each wrist and rubbing each hand. "Are you okay?"

I swallowed and searched for my voice. "Yeah. You know what you're doing." *God, does he know what he's doing.*

He grabbed towels from the cabinet and sprawled across the foot of the bed, tossing each of us a towel. "I don't like to cause any pain. That's not my thing."

Matthew lifted his head from my arm and rolled onto his back.

I settled my hands behind my head and relaxed into the sated warmth, feeling calm, comfortable, alive.

The fact that a sexual experience had caused the feeling gave me pause. Sex was for pleasure. During the act I wanted to fly, feel a loss of control, a release. But when it was done, it was over. It wasn't supposed to make me feel so damn secure.

Matthew rose onto his elbows and stared across the room. The question came out in a hurry on the trail of a long breath. "Are either of you going to be back anytime soon?"

I'd just gotten my brains fucked out, but I was pretty sure I'd given them my usual remarks about keeping it to a one-time thing.

"Maybe," Richard said.

I slid to the end of the bed, stood, and threw on my pants and shoes.

"Matthew, you can use the shower if you want," Richard said. "You look like you could use it."

Matthew stood and shifted from one foot to the other. "Yeah, okay. Thanks." He raked a hand through his sweat-covered waves. The remnants of cum shone on his fingers, and his hair slicked back with it. *My cum looks good in his hair.* I pictured him on his knees, me jacking myself, then shooting on his hair and face.

I need to get the hell out of here.

Matthew never glanced away from me as he traveled the distance from the bed to the bathroom. "In case you aren't here when I get back, that was great. Worth the wait, you know?"

I nodded but couldn't keep my gaze level with his. Once he slipped into the smaller room, I wrestled my shirt on. Richard lay back and watched me.

I went to the door. My back to the room, I didn't plan on speaking, until the words were already in the air between us and I had no way to take them back. "Thanks. I needed that." My hand gripped the doorknob until my knuckles turned white.

"Me too," he said.

I stepped out in the hall and jerked the door shut.

What the hell? I didn't thank anyone. Not for something as simple as fucking.

Chapter Three

The walk down to the main floor of the club was never as anticipation filled as the walk up, but it didn't bother me. I didn't mind anyone knowing what I'd been up to in a room upstairs. I liked the idea some things were that uncomplicated.

The bar was as crowded as before and would remain that way until the place closed. Some men wanted to keep the night going, even if they'd already taken a walk up the stairs. One quick drink and I'd head home. I never stayed long after the sex, but something wouldn't let me walk out. Something in me wanted to hold on to the night a little longer, hold on to the lingering sensations of them all over my body. No three-way had ever had me so undone.

I slumped onto a stool.

One of the regular bartenders approached. "Hey, Luke. Mr. Simon wanted you to know he's in tonight."

"Thanks. He been waiting long?"

"Not long. He's at his usual table."

A delighted smile hit my lips. Walter Simon was the one man who could elicit such a response without the anticipation of sexual follow-up. He was also the only club member whose last name everyone knew. He no longer frequented the club on a regular basis, but he'd been a member since the day the place opened.

Walter sat on the other side of the room, his legs crossed, an arm draped over the back of his chair, a glass of whiskey in his hand. His gaze swept over the dancing crowd. The gray at his temples dusting into the dark hair gave him a distinguished demeanor. As a cop, he'd kept in shape his entire life. Even his years as a detective and his early retirement hadn't softened him. There was a hard edge to his build. Yet his demeanor fit his current job, the CEO of his own security tech company.

He was the first man I'd fucked at the club, and was the only member I called a friend. I would've considered the man the closest to a father figure I knew as an adult, but since I'd sucked his cock, I kept the analogy in check.

I sat at his table. "I didn't see you when I came down."

Walter gave up on the crowd and smirked. "I noticed you were preoccupied." He tipped his glass at a young waiter by the table. "And a beer for my friend." Walter's gaze followed the young man's retreat to the bar behind me.

"He's cute," I said.

Walter met my stare and gave a shallow nod. "It's good to see you. Haven't talked with you in a while."

"Checking up on me?"

He tilted his drink my way. "You usually need checking up on."

I huffed out a short laugh. "I've been okay. Work's keeping me busy."

"It's good to see you taking time off. Then again, you wouldn't miss a Friday night at the Haven."

"Not a chance."

"That's why I'm here," he said. "I wanted to talk to you. Something came up with Vargas."

The waiter returned with our drinks. Walter sipped his new whiskey before saying more. "I met with him on a few security issues. He asked me to speak with you."

"Did I do something wrong?" I took a long swig of my beer.

"No." Walter set his glass on the table and rubbed the side of it with the pad of his thumb. "He received a call about you earlier this week."

My beer bottle clanked onto the table. "About me?"

"The man didn't give a name. Just asked how long you've been a member. How often you're here."

An invisible vice gripped my chest. "And what did Vargas tell him?"

"Nothing, of course. Vargas has managed this club too many years to risk upsetting his clientele. He doesn't discuss club members with anyone, especially an anonymous caller. He wanted you to know someone was asking about you." Walter sipped his whiskey again and scrutinized me. "Your father?"

"Who else?" Whether my father had made the call himself or not wasn't the point. It didn't bother me the man knew I was a member of a gay sex club. What bothered the hell out of me was he'd discovered where I played. My stalkers would be following me on the way home.

"Eventually someone's going to push the topic of his son," Walter said. "No one knows anything about you. You can't be in politics for long and hide your family, hide the fact that—"

"Your son's a queer?"

"I take it he'll blame you for any fallout with his conservative constituents?"

"That's an understatement. Everything wrong in his life is my fault."

Walter knew my father hurt me years ago, but he knew few details. He didn't press the topic. Most of the time he knew when to push. And when not to.

"So, who were you with tonight?" Genuine and direct. No bullshit with Walter. It was part of the reason I liked him.

"Richard and Matthew."

"Matthew? Maybe twenty, twenty-one, with dark hair?"

"Yep."

"I know several Richards."

"He's got a scar across his chest." Why the hell did I choose that quality to mention?

"That wouldn't be the blond with a body that makes the rest of these guys look like they're at play in the schoolyard?"

I lifted my beer for another swig and smirked before the bottle hit my lips. "That'd be him."

"Ah. Quite the night, then."

"You know them? The way I just knew them?"

He laughed. Our banter relaxed me in a way little else did. That was until I'd found myself upstairs with the two men we were discussing. And that bothered me—more than when I'd been in bed with them.

"No," Walter said in a long, drawn-out groan. I wasn't used to hearing that tone from him. "The kid's far too young for me." He shook his head. "I haven't played in years." He waved his hand at the crowd of dancing men as if the idea of being with any of them was absurd. He seized his drink and raised it to his lips again. The whiskey lingered in a long, slow sip. Walter watched me over the edge of the glass.

"You've made exceptions on occasion," I said.

He tipped his head back and laughed again. "That I have. Matthew, huh? I've heard a few things. He's…enthusiastic."

A snort escaped. "You can say that again." I signaled to the waiter, and he brought me another beer.

"And Richard," Walter said when we were alone again, "well, he hasn't been in the club in some time."

"I hadn't seen him before." Thinking about them was awakening my cock again. I shifted in my seat. I had to get my ass home and my mind off the club.

"The last time he was here on a regular basis was more than five years ago. And before you ask again, no, we never hooked up. Last time I saw him, we were both on to something more serious."

"Serious?" I lifted my beer again in an attempt to appear casual, but the question wasn't at all. Why was I interested in Richard's past? I definitely needed to get home.

"He and his partner didn't come to the club once they were exclusive."

I nodded my understanding and downed another mouthful of the beer. At the rate I swallowed it, I'd have trouble getting my ass to a cab if I stayed much longer.

Walter stilled the hand holding his drink and regarded me with a long stare. He leaned back in his chair. "I think he might be just what you need."

"I already had him. So"—I whipped a hand through the air—"that was it."

"Right. Your rule. Was it a one-night thing for him too?"

"Yep."

Walter studied me for another moment before his gaze traveled over the crowd of men. He wasn't about to pick any of them up. His scan was more amusement than intention.

The silence disturbed me. And that was odd. Walter and I didn't talk every moment we were together. In fact, most of the time we didn't talk much at all. It was another reason I liked him.

I sighed. "What is it you think I need?"

He didn't respond. I followed his stare to a couple near the far corner of the bar. They danced—or a better description might be embraced, or made love with their clothes on. Their lips didn't touch, but every other part of their bodies did. My eyes narrowed. Not many men at the club came together with such heat and familiarity. It seemed futile. Why would two men ever think they could succeed at long-term? The passion they exuded would never last. Not if they continued to patronize the Haven with its stream of available men.

"To trust yourself enough to put yourself at risk," Walter said.

I surrendered my judgmental stare. "I take risks all the time." I laughed at my own words.

"I meant for you to risk more than your body." He leaned forward and whispered. "Your parents aren't the only people in the world who can love you."

"Yeah. And they aren't the only ones who can fuck you over." Walter might have been the one person I could let go in front of and still be able to look at myself in the mirror the next morning, but I wasn't about to test the theory.

He continued to probe me with his stare. I found myself pondering what the man must have been thinking. Why did I let my parents have control over my life? Why did I let what they thought about me garner much import when it came to how I lived? And why the hell did spending more than one night with a guy scare the shit out of me?

"All right. Enough," I said. "Quit looking at me. I've got a lot of things I'm fucked up about. I know that. I don't need you to remind me. This is who I am. I'm enjoying my life."

"You could have more, you know. More than fucking at the club."

I scanned the slew of men surrounding our table. "I happen to like fucking at the club." As the words left my mouth, Matthew walked by the bar. His damp hair stuck out every which way, the waves returning. He wore a broad smile, and the man had a definite spring in his step. I smirked.

"I know you do," Walter said. "But trust me, one day you'll be old like me and you won't be able to sit alone in the silence for more than five minutes at a time. Your life will suffocate you."

Concern for him welled in my chest. I had no idea what to do about it.

Walter's shoulders slumped as he sank into the chair. "I wouldn't have traded my time with Gary for anything in the world. I have a past I can look back on. It's what I hold on to when I'm lonely. You have no past and no future. Your misery will encompass you until not even your random sexual encounters will be able to make it all go away."

I spotted Richard as he stepped down the stairs. He stopped and scanned the bar, and his gaze stilled once it landed on me. I expected him to walk past and leave the club.

He didn't. He strode toward me.

Walter stood. "I've got to go."

"Don't run off."

He waved a hand in the air. "Call me when you get a chance."

"I didn't mean to rush your friend off." The voice was as husky and strong as it'd been when he'd first spoken to me.

I stood. "It's fine."

Richard stepped closer, his gaze fixated on me. The stare was intense, like maybe he thought he'd imagined the entire escapade upstairs until he saw me in the bar. "I wanted you to know I had a great evening."

"Yeah, the best I've had in quite a while." I could have kicked myself. What was it about him that made me say things I'd never admit to anyone, not even myself?

He lifted a hand and stroked the side of my neck, grazing my chin with his thumb. The touch was more intimate than anything he'd done to me upstairs.

A swell of nerves gathered in my gut. Was I enjoying his touch that much?

"I'm glad," he said. "I must admit I haven't been to the club in a while. It far exceeded my expectations."

I smiled at him before he dropped his hand and walked away.

I'd completely lost my mind.

* * * *

I awoke the next morning hard as hell and pissed off.

I couldn't get them out of my head. I heard the grunts and moans, mine and theirs. Felt Matthew's tongue in my mouth. Heard Richard's groan as he came. Tasted his lips. Felt his dick slide in and out of me.

It was odd and disconcerting and hot as hell.

I pushed them out of my mind, threw back the sheet, and planted my feet on the bed. I grasped my dick in my hand and gave a few good strokes. It never took much to find my release.

Until then.

I bolted out of the bed and headed for the bathroom. The shower caddy had lube, and the heat of the water relaxed me in a way little else did.

The water turned tepid, and I still ran my hand over my dick.

The hot water in my cheap-ass apartment was for shit. There was never time for fancy jerk-off sessions. Normally that didn't bother me. I never had so much damn trouble getting off.

I concentrated on the slide of my hand and quickened the pace. I squeezed harder, ran my thumb over the tip, and jerked my hips. Finally, my body tightened, and I slapped the shower wall with my free hand as I came. I washed and got out before the water could go from cold to frigid.

Dressed and ready to focus on anything else, I headed for the kitchen to make a pot of coffee. My apartment was small. One bedroom with space for a bed and not much else, the bathroom, a kitchen that accommodated a three-legged folding table leaning against the wall, and a small living room I'd set up as an office, complete with a battered particle board desk that smelled like petrified glue. I poured a cup of coffee and took a seat at the desk. The folding chair creaked under my weight. The damn thing was bound to break, but it was the best of the set. It should last until I moved again.

The only other furniture in the room was a tattered, stained orange couch that smelled of sweat and dope and had too many places where the springs rubbed my ass. I hadn't bothered replacing it. I'd do as someone else did when I acquired it—leave it and the table and chairs for whoever rented the shithole apartment after me. I moved too much to care about the furniture I kept. I still had boxes of clothes and computer programming books stacked in the corner. I spent my money on what I had sitting on top of the desk—the computer and digital video equipment.

I didn't fear my father. But I didn't like giving him the satisfaction of knowing where I lived.

It had become a game. He'd spend resources and time tracking me. I'd spend my money and wits knowing when he was close and getting the hell out before his men could figure out I'd made them.

I swallowed a gulp of coffee and hissed with the burn.

It was going to be a long day.

I reached for the keyboard and entered my password. Two monitors flashed on. I checked the video feeds from the night before and knocked back the rest of the coffee. Several interior and exterior views of my apartment displayed on the screens. The previous eight hours replayed in fast forward.

Nothing. No movement. No unexpected guests. The extra precautions on the way home the night before had paid off.

One more day in Shangri-la.

I stared at the current video feeds, but I no longer saw the screens before me, or the apartment around me. The dimly lit room from the previous night glided into view. I felt Richard's hands upon my hips, his cock deep inside me, Matthew's lips on my dick, his sucking and swirling that brought me to my first of two orgasms.

I was getting hard. Again.

Determined not to take the matter in hand after the morning spent fighting for an orgasm, I reset the hidden cameras and the computer password and logged off the system. I grabbed my laptop bag and stepped out into the hall to complete my usual routine: triple-check the lock and add the translucent tape at the base of the door. Not a sophisticated system, but it allowed me to know before entering if there was a chance I wouldn't be alone.

The challenging part of my day was getting to and from work without being followed. I backtracked more than once and never took the same route twice in one week. The same procedure I followed to get to the Haven.

I ran a hand through my hair as I made my way down the stairwell. The swell in the front of my pants rubbed against the tight fabric with each step.

It was going to be one hell of a long day.

Chapter Four

I stormed into my apartment four hours later, the earliest ever on a Saturday. I slammed the door shut and hurled my keys onto the desk. By the time I entered the bathroom, I had every button of my shirt undone. I pushed the fabric off and onto the floor.

My pants were next. I undid the zipper and shoved my hand inside. My ass hit the sink.

"Fuck." I hadn't been so desperate while all alone in a long time.

I wrangled my pants off, turned on the shower, and stepped under the spray. A quick grope in the shower caddy produced the lube. I clicked the lid open one-handed and squeezed the contents over my dick and the hand working it. The cool lubricant ran down to my balls.

I pressed my forehead to the shower wall. The tip of my cock brushed at the cool fiberglass wall with each stroke. I imagined my hand was Matthew's mouth and the wall was the back of his throat as he took me deep.

"God, Matthew."

It might have been the first time I'd ever talked out loud to an imaginary partner while I was doing myself alone, but I didn't care. My hand felt amazing. And it wasn't just my talent in pleasuring myself. It had more to do with the vividness of my pretend participant. His fictional mouth and tongue slid over my shaft, licked the slit, and sucked me long and hard.

"That's it, Matthew. Swallow it. Swallow me."

I came fast with a loud moan. My body shook under the warm water. I leaned against the wall until breathing didn't require every cell in my body, then washed up and fondled myself. My dick twitched like I hadn't gotten off yet. I cranked the water off and moved my private party to the bedroom.

Before getting in the bed, I rummaged through the closet and seized the bag of toys tucked in the bottom of a lone box. I dug inside and sighed when my hand met the large dildo, the realistic type complete with balls. I hadn't wanted to use it—needed to use it—since before I joined the club.

I set the dildo next to the lube on the bed and crawled on top of the blankets. I stroked myself, pinched my nipples, and rolled my balls until I was hard again, panting and wanting more. I slicked my fingers and rode them. But it wasn't me. It was Richard filling me. First with his wide fingers, and then, when I slammed the dildo in, it was his cock pounding into me.

My hips rocketed off the bed. A fierce gasp exploded out of me.

I lay with my chest heaving for several minutes, long after I removed the dildo and wiped away the evidence of my pleasure. I hadn't come that hard by myself since college, since I'd last thought about any man in particular when I jerked off.

I wanted to sleep and put distance between myself and the sexual fantasies. Sleep wouldn't come though, and my thoughts wandered to those long-ago college days.

I spent the last two years of school with one man after another. It was then I first experienced a threesome—two nameless men torturing me with pleasure.

That was after my father took everything from me. After I'd last slept with the same man more than once. After I'd lost the only person I ever let myself fall for.

I rolled over, buried my face in the pillow, and gave myself permission to remember the last time we made love.

* * * *

"Luke, love you. God, love this."

"Tim."

He pushed in. His cock drove past the tight ring of muscle in a slow move that always left me writhing and begging for more. I lifted my hips off the bed, arched to meet him, tugged at him with my legs, clutched at him with my hands.

I couldn't get close enough. I wanted to feel him everywhere. I wanted to breathe in his scent. Memorize every muscle, every hair on his body. Show him who he was to me.

His eyes met mine. I didn't have to show him anything. He already knew how important he was to me.

And I was the same for him.

He pulled back and thrust in again. His hips collided with my ass. The force wasn't meant to hurt me, but to get him as close to me as he could.

I squeezed my eyes shut. "Tim. Don't stop."

"This will go on, Luke. I won't let it stop."

I opened my eyes at his words. Did he mean them the way they sounded? I didn't get a chance to ask.

The strong scent of a familiar cologne washed over me. At first, my brain couldn't reconcile the vision. It was in such contrast to what my body felt.

But there he was. My father stood next to the nightstand.

I retreated up the bed and dragged Tim with me.

Tim stared down at me, his face contorted in a mix of passion and confusion until he caught sight of my father. His dick slipped out of me, and he scrambled to my side.

My father whirled his arm upward. He jammed a cool, metal object against my face. A handgun. The barrel dug into the flesh of my cheek.

"Don't move, son."

* * * *

I awoke an hour later, my father's long-ago words still ringing in my ears.

"You start living a decent life or I swear to God, I will track you down and take away every lover you ever have. I'll make them see who you are. I'll make them hate you. I'll make your life a living hell."

Goose bumps formed at the base of my neck before I opened my eyes. I shot off the bed and didn't bother with clothes. I charged down the hall and lunged for the computer.

I entered the password three times before I hit the correct keys. My fingers tapped the edge of the desk as the video program opened. The playback started, and I clicked several times to advance the screens faster, scanning for any sign of my stalkers. The video playback caught up to the current time.

Nothing.

My breathing slowed. It was the first time I'd forgotten to check the tape on the door or the cameras.

The phone on the desk rang. I stared at it for four rings before I answered. No one had the number to my land line. Work had my cell number. The apartment wasn't in my name.

"Luke Moore?"

I straightened and pressed the phone closer to my ear. "Yes."

"My name's Mark Summers. I'm a reporter with *The Washington*

Times. I'm doing a story on your father and wondered if you'd be able to answer some questions."

"How'd you get this number?"

"I'm looking to do a human interest piece—about the man, his family, that sort of thing. I'm not out for dirt."

I banged a fist on the desk and hit the edge of the keyboard. Three keys popped off. They scattered and bounced on the floor. I watched as the letters *M* and *N* and *B* randomly surfaced over and over like the balls spinning around in a bingo cage. The tiny pieces of plastic clicked as they collided. They sounded like they were snickering at me.

I tried to keep my voice calm, neutral. "I asked you a question."

"I'm not going to be the last call you'll get. At some point, you'll have to answer questions. No one knows about his family."

"Why now?"

"Seriously? He's a big name these days. His energy bill saved a lot of jobs in this country. People want to know the man behind the name."

"Trust me. You don't want to know him." I slammed the phone down as I stood and kicked the flimsy chair backward, scraping a bare heel.

"Goddammit."

I cradled the injured foot in my hands and hopped around naked. I tripped over the busted chair and plunged onto the couch. The springs jammed into my hip. Pain exploded down my leg and mixed with the throb in my foot.

The crumbled, destroyed chair lay sprawled on the floor, mocking me. A reminder the time to move again was close. I stood and hobbled to the bedroom.

One place would make me feel better.

* * * *

I arrived at the Haven a few hours later—the earliest ever—dressed in leather pants, a burgundy dress shirt, and a cocky smirk on my face, determined to put all thoughts of my father, my past, and any other emotional crap behind me.

The Haven was my place to play. My place to feel better about my life and how I lived it.

I wanted to fuck the shit out of someone. I wanted to dominate, to take charge and possess someone, deny him an orgasm until I wanted him to come.

My expectations of what the night would entail affected my demeanor, and I stood taller. I eyed the room for a candidate before taking a seat. The hurried manner in which I went about the task would have bothered me on any other night. Not now. I had something to prove—to myself and to the voice of my father.

Yet, as I surveyed the room and sat on a bar stool, the image of one man assailed my thoughts—a grinning, licking, groaning Matthew.

Shit. I slammed a clenched fist on the bar.

"Something wrong, Luke?" the bartender asked.

"Uh, no. Nothing. Glass of water, please."

I raised the water to my lips and kept swallowing until I sucked in air instead of the cool liquid. I shoved the glass aside with the back of my hand. The scratching in my throat continued with each gulp of air.

I closed my eyes, and the daydream of Matthew and me slid into view. Richard soon arrived. He pushed into me with abandon while I continued to fuck Matthew.

I rubbed the back of my neck with an open hand. The gesture created more tension instead of easing it. Sex with the same men more than once wasn't the experience I wanted. Not that night. Not any night. It was too expected, redundant, reliable, and complicated. I wanted none of it.

Except I did want them. I couldn't deny how much I wanted to feel them in my arms, to touch them, to kiss them again.

I forced a glance around the room and took note of several men in the thick crowd. I gestured for another glass of water and forced a languid drink.

Then I spotted him, seated at a table in the middle of the dining room. I set the glass on the bar and whirled around.

His face was hidden, but the dark waves were unmistakable. Matthew lifted his head. He didn't look at me. He focused his attention on two others. The tall, bulky, leather-clad men strolled across the room and straight for his table. His head and gaze lowered the closer they came to him. The men sat without a word.

I'd been with both of them. They were a longtime couple and were heavy into bondage and toys as their only means of sexual contact—but not to do to each other. They wanted to play with someone else.

Would Matthew like to be bound? He seemed to be an entirely sensual man who wouldn't want to be with someone whom he couldn't explore with his hands, his lips, his tongue.

But I didn't know him. Or did I? I envisioned him tied to the bed with the large men using all manner of objects to touch him, arouse him. Initially, I found the image erotic. Then it turned into a scene I didn't care for as Matthew's frustration built the more he tried to move his hands for a single touch of his lovers, desperate for a kiss, for contact.

"Hello."

I lowered a foot and swiveled the barstool until I faced the voice's owner. The young man had been in the club a month before, but I hadn't been with him yet. I smiled. The expression required force. *Damn, kid. Get out of my head.*

"My friend and I are looking for someone tonight. Someone who might want to…take control. You interested?"

"Could be," I said. "Where is he?"

"Restroom. He saw you before he left. He's quite taken with the idea of the three of us."

I was too, until I caught sight of another man. He passed the bar and sat alone at a table. I wasn't aware I'd been staring until brilliant green eyes connected with mine.

I clutched at the bar.

Richard continued to stare until another man approached his table. The man had dark hair like Matthew's but was more my height and build. He was younger than I, though, and better looking, more fit. Why the hell did all the new guys at the club look like extras just off the set of *Queer as Folk*? The two talked, and Richard gestured to an empty chair. The other man dropped into the seat straight away. Of course, who wouldn't be anxious for a chance at Richard?

I forced my attention back to the man next to me. My prospect's tall friend joined us. He wrapped his arms around the seated man's shoulders. "Is this fine man interested?"

"I think he is." The seated man closed his eyes and leaned into his friend. They entwined their hands over his chest.

A relationship.

I'd separate them. Tie one up. Make him watch from across the room while I claimed and inspired his lover's body.

"Should we head up?" the tall man asked.

Unable to stop myself, I glanced in Richard's direction. His eyes were on Matthew. The frown and furrowed brow illustrated his opinion of the other man's partners for the night. Without looking away from Matthew and his new friends, Richard spoke to the man at his table. The man gave a curt nod, stood, and returned to the lounge, already on the prowl for someone else.

Richard didn't falter. He ignored every other man in the place and proceeded to the bar, to me.

The tall man straightened. "Hey, we're talking here."

Richard leaned an elbow on the bar. "Have you already found what you want tonight, Luke?"

I shook my head.

"Can I entice you again?"

"I think you already have." The words flew out without regret. I wanted to feel his hands on me. I wanted to wrap my lips around his tongue, my thighs around his hips.

Richard gripped my arm, and with a tug, he encouraged me off the stool. "Let's go rescue the kid. Yeah?"

"Okay. He'll want us again?"

He hesitated with his next step. "Were we in the same room last time?"

"Right."

We crossed the dining room, my arm in his hand, and with a slight slow of his gait, Richard spoke. "You coming, Matthew?"

Matthew's eyes widened, and he followed in a flash. Richard no longer held my arm. The decision to be with them for the second time in two days was under my own control—or lack of control, as the case may be.

More and more air left my body with each step. Breathing wouldn't come easily by the time we reached a room. I stopped at the base of the stairs. "Wait."

Richard halted. Matthew kept going. He made it up four more steps before stopping.

They couldn't be what I wanted. I wouldn't allow myself to break that rule.

"I think Luke needs a minute to adjust his game plan," Richard said. "Why don't we have a seat?"

Matthew barreled back down the stairs, and Richard pointed to a nearby table where they sat. I joined them, my lungs filling with air.

"What do you want tonight, Matthew?" Richard asked, his eyes still considering me.

Matthew smoothed out the linen tablecloth with his palms. "It was a great night last time. I think I'm already getting what I want—a second chance with both of you. I'm open for whatever you guys are up for."

Richard's large hand stroked the younger man's cheek. "I think you need more than one blowjob this time around."

Matthew whimpered and leaned into the touch.

"How about you, Luke?" Richard asked.

"No bondage. I'd like to bury myself in someone while someone else is in me." I no longer needed control over another. I wanted the same outcome they'd given me the night before. I wanted to feel alive. I wanted to be overwhelmed by them.

"I like your frankness," he said.

"There's no point in keeping what you want a secret. Not here."

"No, there isn't. Does that work for you?" he asked Matthew.

Matthew's nod said it all. The man vibrated. His fingers tapped at the table in rapid succession. His gaze shot to the stairs and back. If we didn't get moving soon, he'd come in his pants. The joys of being in your early twenties.

A lump formed in my throat. I should have been standing, walking away. "I thought you weren't looking for this?"

"What?" Richard asked.

"Repeats."

"I wasn't, but—" He leaned forward. "Do you know how hard I came jerking off today? Thinking about how we were last night? I'd like to think we'll be as good together tonight."

"I don't do this more than once...with anyone."

He scrutinized me for another moment and gave a quick nod. "Fair enough." He stood and looked around the room, searching for someone else, but he didn't move from the table.

A bluff. It had to be.

A young man not much older than Matthew with black eyeliner circling his eyes and purple tips at the ends of his spiky dark hair stalked toward the table, Richard in his sights. It didn't take long for men at the Haven to read someone's availability.

Richard gave his answer with a sweep of his head from side to side.

The man ran his index finger down Richard's arm in a last appeal as he passed by the table.

Richard shook his head one last time, his eyes on me. He smacked a palm on his thigh. "Damn." He regarded Matthew. "Since Luke won't play, if you still want me, I'd like to be with just you tonight."

"Okay." Matthew stood, his dark eyes hopeful as he watched me.

I pictured them fucking each other alone. "Wait." I glanced around the packed dining room but saw nothing—no one else. Richard inhaled an uneven breath. Matthew's spicy cologne wafted across the table. "Once more."

"I think we can manage more than once for you tonight," Richard said.

"Oh, yeah. I think so too." Matthew bounced while standing in place.

A laugh flew out of Richard as he stepped away from the table.

Matthew slipped his hand in mine and persuaded me to stand. "I'm glad you changed your mind." He didn't let go of me.

I'd never held hands with another man. My entire body tensed.

Then his thumb caressed the back of my hand, and I didn't want him to stop.

Chapter Five

The door closed behind me. Richard mashed his groin against my ass and wrapped his arms around me. Even through his pants, there was no denying his cock was on fire. Need raced from every point of contact straight to my balls. I rotated my ass over his groin.

He grabbed my shoulders, swung me around, and kissed me. Whether or not I should have been in a room with them no longer mattered. I clutched at his biceps and pressed against his frame. His strong body didn't shift an inch.

Matthew plastered himself to my back, his hands on my hips. I reached back and gripped his ass, needing more contact, more of them. Matthew let go of me and stepped away. The loss of him nearly had me crying out. Then he pressed his lips in close. I opened for him and his tongue combined with Richard's in my mouth. The smell, taste, and touch of both men surrounded me.

My first kiss with two men at once. Even after all the multiple partners I'd slept with. No one had ever been as sensual, as eager as Matthew.

The kissing continued. One man on my lips, in my mouth. Then the other. Over and over.

My pants were unbuttoned. Matthew's small hand freed my dick and teased the head. Richard gripped the base. They stroked me, hand over hand, touching every inch of my cock, leaving nothing to the air.

The slow slide of their hands, the warmth of their flesh on mine, the lingering stares that unraveled something deep inside me: it was exactly how I remembered them.

Richard's green eyes examined me, watching my every reaction as if I were a puzzle he had to solve, only he wasn't sure he'd find the answer he wanted. What was he looking for?

They stopped fondling me and started undressing me. I helped with their clothes, needing to touch more of them. Our frantic hands worked on buttons and zippers, and tugged out limbs until flesh touched flesh. Matthew and Richard kissed again.

I licked down Richard's body and headed for a nipple. I paused before it, unsure what the hell I was doing. I licked to the right and followed the line of his scar with my tongue and lips.

He seized the back of my head with his hand. I stilled and waited for him to force me away. He held me in place then encouraged me to continue. I sucked and licked along the scarred path to his armpit and back. He tasted salty and a bit sweet, and it lingered on my tongue. I drew the nipple into my mouth and slowly worked the sensitive nub. I tugged at it with my teeth, and Richard's hips bucked. His thick cock slapped against me. I wanted nothing more than to grab his dick and shove it in my mouth.

That's how it always was with me. One look at a hard cock and my reaction was oral. It's how I finally accepted I was gay. Nothing about a woman garnered the same effect.

But it'd been a long time since I'd done it without a rubber in the way.

Before I talked myself out of it, Richard's fingers dug into my hair. He wrenched me away from his chest and wrapped one hand around my arm and the other around Matthew's. He hauled us to the bed. "I cannot remember ever wanting anyone as much as I want the two of you. Can't get enough of you."

I groaned in response, unable to stop myself.

Richard pushed me onto the bed, and I sprawled out before them.

"Hey, kid." Richard tugged Matthew close until the smaller man's back flattened to his chest. His mouth brushed Matthew's ear as he whispered words I couldn't hear.

Matthew's eyes widened. "Uh-huh. I can do that." He slunk up the bed toward me.

"What did he tell you?" I asked.

"That I should make sure you're ready for him. Get you slick and open. Begging for him."

"Oh, fuck."

"That's right," Richard said. He stood at the end of the bed and stroked himself. I wanted his hand on me and my mouth on him.

Matthew gave me a soft kiss and slid down my length. My skin tingled where his hard nipples scraped. He held the stare between us until he lay with his head over my groin. He wrapped his hands around my legs and lifted my knees to my chest, spreading me wide. His tongue slid over the back of my thighs, my ass. He licked at my opening and the flesh surrounding it. Swirling, nipping, plunging. My cock throbbed on my lower abdomen. I moaned, begged, gripped at my own legs as he worked me over.

He pushed his slick fingers into me, gentle and firm at the same time. My eyes rolled back. *Fucking hell.* I groaned, the sound part moan, part whimper. Before Matthew and Richard, touch had never been such a big part of my sexual encounters.

Then it was Matthew who made noises—loud, gasping, erotic sounds. I lifted my head. He had his ass in the air and Richard was kneeling behind him.

"Matthew needs to get fucked this time," Richard said. "You're doing him, and I'm going to push you into him. Ready, Matthew?"

"Oh yeah." Matthew scrambled up the bed and landed on his knees. He displayed his ass in the air before I could move out of the way. "Want you both so much. Been thinking about it all day."

I got on my knees behind him and stroked the taut curve of his ass. I liked the look of his pale skin under my hands, the feel of his heated flesh. The sight of him bent over in front of me had me ready to go off. The skin of my dick stretched tight.

Richard handed me a condom. My hands trembled as I opened the rubber and slipped it on my dick. I added lube, and my balls drew up from my own touch. I wasn't supposed to need someone that much. I wasn't supposed to be out of control.

I leaned over Matthew and licked and nipped the back of his neck, savoring his taste, his scent—my brain already equating that smell with physical pleasure and sated bliss. The responding moans and sways of his body would have made anyone think I'd already entered him.

He needed me as much as I did him.

I lined up, the head of my dick pressing at his opening.

"Hold there," Richard said. His deep voice cut through the surge of desire, and I stilled. He forced my legs apart.

His cock slammed inside me with a fast thrust that drove my body forward into Matthew. I gasped. He knew when to take it easy and when to ram it in.

And just like that, I was fucking the same men as I had the night before. Only, I wasn't freaking. All I felt was them.

The combined pleasure made me lose concentration fast. But it was okay. They had me, held me between them—bodies swaying together, need and hunger taking over as they rocked and thrust.

The room filled with our noises. The bed creaked under us. Skin slapped against skin. Three men groaned as we soared, high on one another.

Matthew's fingers were twisted in the sheets before me, gripping so tight he'd rip the fabric. I reached around him and enjoyed the sleek, firm touch of his prick as it slid in my hand. His body writhed and quivered. His mouth screamed delicious words and sounds I was beginning to love.

Then he screamed my name, and that did me in. I came while he clenched around me. Unable to stop my sated body, I settled on his back. Richard thrust again and again until he jerked with his own release. He let out a low, contented murmur as his body melted over me.

We collapsed on the bed in a mix of legs, arms, and bodies.

"Damn." The word escaped my mouth mingled with a rush of air. I waited a moment to catch my breath, then got rid of the rubber. "That's the fourth time I got off today."

Matthew lifted his head. "Oh, man. Did you spend the day at the club or what?"

"No. I worked this morning and then went home. Alone." For some fucked-up reason, I felt it important to clarify that last point.

"I think our friend here was as turned on today as I was," Richard said. "Did you have fun by yourself, Luke?" He patted my hip and shifted to lie next to Matthew.

"Not as much as tonight. That's for damn sure."

"Me neither." Richard's hand cupped my jaw, and he steered my mouth to his, Matthew pinned between us. He kissed me soft and slow, not demanding more, not pushing me toward anything but the simple touch.

Matthew moaned at the sight of us. Damn, he had such great responses. What would he sound like when he was the one doing the fucking?

Did he top?

The image of Matthew topping Richard played over and over as Richard's tongue sought out mine. I pressed into the kiss, needing more all of a sudden, not sure if it was the sensation of his kiss or if it was the image of a lithe, groaning Matthew taking Richard that did me in.

When we parted, the words spilled out of my mouth. "Sometime I'd like to hear what he'd sound like fucking you."

The smile of victory spread across Richard's face.

What the hell am I doing?

"That'd be something," he said. "That sound good to you, kid?"

Matthew whimpered. With his body pushing in close, he couldn't hide the shake. Out of anticipation or trepidation? I took the cue and changed the subject. Why the hell was I still lying beside them, talking to them, anyway?

I rolled onto my back. "How long you been coming here?" I asked Richard.

"Years. I took a break for a while when I was in a relationship." He went into the bathroom and returned with a couple of towels. He stretched out next to Matthew again. "I was a bit older than you, kid, when the club opened. I joined not too long after."

"Wow." Matthew lifted his head and cocked it to the side. "There were other gay men all the way back then?"

Richard slid a hand under him and pinched his ass. "Funny."

Matthew giggled and smacked at Richard's arm. "Was the club like it is now?"

"No, it was a bit different back in the *Stone Age*." He rolled his eyes. "It was in a smaller building with three open rooms. The sex was less private. The entire club was more casual, less official. And it was all about the sex. Now a lot of members are into playing one game or another." Lost in some memory, his gaze fixated on a spot at the foot of the bed. On the end of a long exhale, he faced us again. "How about you, Luke? You new here?"

"Six months ago."

"Where'd you play before?"

"Not at a club." I stretched out and curled my arms under my head. "I made my way through the gay bars, hoping to find what I wanted. Most men were looking for a quick fuck, but some wanted more. Or they wanted to know you before they'd be up for anything physical. I wasn't getting what I needed. A guy I'd been with a while back told me about the club, said he was on a waiting list. I knew this place was for me the first night. The bar, the dining room, the lounge, all filled with men I'd never seen before."

"You keep up with your no repeats thing," Richard said, "you'll need a new club before long." The laugh after his words didn't fit how he'd said them.

I took it as the joke he'd made it out to be and shrugged. Anxious at my own comfort level with them, I wanted to get up and leave the room. I chose to move away from conversation. Maybe having more of them would help me get them out of my head.

It gave me some comfort to think I might be able to get over the foreign, intense desire I felt for them.

I leaned over Matthew and kissed Richard, trying to use my tongue in the same manner they'd used theirs on me. We traded kisses with each other, then with Matthew, our hands roaming, our lips lingering in a sated, slow rhythm that seemed to have nothing to do with sex. I had no idea how long it went on. The club may have closed for the night for all I knew. I took their dicks in my hands, trying to will their bodies back to an interest in screwing, trying to convince myself I didn't enjoy the drawn out way we touched and moved.

When the kissing turned desperate, I knew they were ready. I had officially kissed them more than any other men in the last fifteen years.

"So in all seriousness," I said to Richard, "you only top, or are you going to let me fuck you?"

He smirked. "I definitely need a man in me from time to time, and tonight"—he grasped my dick in his hand—"I want you inside me." He pumped a tight fist over my shaft.

Matthew moaned and rocked against my body. It seemed everything we did or said turned him into a pile of sexual mush.

I swung off the bed in search of more condoms and lube.

"C'mere, Matthew." Richard growled the command in a low voice. "I'm gonna suck you till you scream."

"Oh, God." Matthew froze. Richard had to help him slide over.

I handed Richard a condom, and a moment later, he swallowed the man's shaft.

Matthew's head flew back. His body arched. His hips rolled.

The sight of Richard's head between Matthew's legs and the sound of loud pants and moans triggered an ache in my balls. I didn't need any more encouragement to move in and join them.

I helped Richard to his knees as I massaged and cupped his ass, admiring the solid muscles, the dark skin, the fine brush of masculine hair. I didn't take too much time to get him open but, for a moment, I did wish for something I never thought about—fucking bare.

I clutched at the bed beside me for the condom. When my hand came up empty, I cursed and groped around until my fingers clasped the rubber. I sheathed my dick and lubed it. The contact of my cock against Richard nearly triggered my release. I needed inside him. I couldn't wait one more second.

It all reminded me of the first time I'd had anal sex. A goddamn teenager again.

I plunged into him. He must have pulled off Matthew because his low groan couldn't have made its way out around the dick in his mouth. He rocked back onto me a few times before he returned his attention to the blowjob.

"Yeah, yeah, Richard. Please." Matthew's voice sounded hoarse.

Richard's ass gripped me with a fierce clench. When had anyone last taken him? I didn't want to hurt him, but I couldn't still my movements. He felt unreal around me, tighter than I'd had in a while.

A husky groan exploded out of Matthew. His writhing beneath Richard had me coming faster than I wanted, but nothing could have stopped me. I fell onto Richard's back as my breath slowed. I pressed a light kiss to his shoulder and forced my mind blank before I could evaluate the action.

"Fifth," Matthew said. A giggle slipped out.

I lifted my head. "Huh?"

"That's your fifth today."

Richard moaned.

"I think someone still needs to come." I moved off him.

"Uh-huh." Matthew scooted forward under Richard. He wrapped his hand around the man's cock and gave his mouth a fierce kiss. When the kiss ended, Richard sat on his heels. Matthew slid closer and cupped a second hand under his balls.

Richard swatted the hands away. "Ride me?"

Matthew's eyes widened. "Oh. Oh, yeah."

"Want to know how you feel around me." Richard hauled Matthew to him. "Wanted it since I first saw you. Couldn't stand the thought of those other guys with you tonight."

"Me either," I said and clamped my mouth closed. *Shut the hell up.*

I reached for a condom and handed it along with the lube to Matthew. His hands shook as he worked open the wrapper and rolled the condom on Richard's thick cock. He added lube over it and his own body. My breath caught in my chest when he touched himself.

Matthew's cock had filled again, and droplets slid over the tip by the time he straddled the other man's thighs. He gasped as he lowered himself over Richard, and when he settled on the man's lap, a low sigh escaped him.

"He fills you up good, doesn't he?" I asked.

"God, yes." Matthew clutched at Richard's shoulders. He waited until his body stopped shuddering before he rose up and rammed back down.

"Kid!" Richard screamed. "Do that again."

He did. Again. And again. And I watched with utter fascination.

Matthew didn't stop with words or sounds the entire time he rode Richard's lap. He bounced, skin smacking, his ass swallowing the thick cock with each downward plunge. If I hadn't come so many times, my prick would have been coming back to life at the sight of them together. Matthew's lean leg muscles flexed with each lift. I ran a hand over his thigh as he dropped onto Richard again.

Why the hell was I touching him there?

I repositioned myself behind Matthew and slid my hand between them. With a few strokes, he came, a loud chorus of "yes, yes, yes" ringing out. He collapsed, his arms wrapped tight around Richard's neck.

Richard grunted through his last pushes upward, and once he stilled, he petted Matthew's back, the touch soft as he swept his fingers over the pale skin. The way I remembered petting my childhood dog, not something I ever did to another person.

I leaned forward and my chest pressed Richard's hand harder against Matthew's back. "Three," I whispered in Matthew's ear. "You've got me beat, at least in this room."

"Yeah. Uh-huh." Matthew's strained voice was barely audible. His breathing evened out as he came back to us from the far-off sated place he'd gone.

"Damn," Richard said. An exasperated sigh clung to the word.

"What?" I spread out with my head on the pillows. What the hell could be wrong after all that?

"Matthew still didn't get to fuck me."

"Oh." Matthew's body shook, his voice raspy.

Richard laughed. "Hey, kid, how long you been coming here?"

"Almost four years." Matthew slipped off Richard's lap and unfolded beside me.

My jaw dropped.

Richard stood and grabbed more towels. He settled across the bed, leaned forward, and brushed the cloth over Matthew.

Matthew gasped at the touch of cotton to skin as if the towel didn't separate them.

"Were you even legal then?" Richard asked. He threw the towels toward the bathroom.

"Yeah. I may not look it, but I'm twenty-two, been coming here since I turned nineteen." He shrugged. A blush crept over his cheeks and down his neck. "I applied nine months after I graduated from high school. I wasn't on the waiting list for too long. At my interview they said they usually don't accept members under twenty, but I must have made an impression with my enthusiasm for all things sex."

"Did they ask for an audition?" Richard asked. "'Cause that could explain it."

"No." Matthew frowned. His eyebrows drew in.

The look didn't sit right with me. Not on him.

"Oh wait. I did blow the guy." He laughed, and his face lit up.

Richard dropped his head forward. "Man, you are too much fun. And sexy as fuck."

"I am?"

"Hell yes."

Matthew stretched his arms over his head. "I'd like a shower." He leaned over to me. "Wanna join me?"

Every muscle in my body tightened.

Richard snorted. "Now, now, you've scared the skittish thing. And after all this talking, which I'm pretty sure our friend here isn't used to doing after sex. On top of the fact he's here with us again even though he's *never* with the same guys twice."

I threw him a challenging stare. I wanted to prove something to him, but why did I care what he thought of me? "Come on, kid. I can go for a shower."

Matthew jumped off the bed and followed me.

"Good for you, Luke." Richard stretched out on his back. "You two wore me out. I'm going to lie here for a while longer."

Matthew bounded back to the bed and planted a kiss on him. Richard's hands found Matthew's ass and tugged him onto his large body. They lingered over the kiss, hands groping, skin sliding over skin.

I leaned against the bathroom doorjamb and watched Matthew's ass move, watched his balls sway as he gyrated with the kiss. If he kept it up, he'd have Richard hard again in no time.

When they finally parted, Matthew made his way to the bathroom with a bounce in his step. He rubbed the back of his hand along my thigh as he slid past me.

I followed him in, turned on the water, and held the shower door open. He stepped under the spray, a new bar of soap in his hands. I stood back for a moment and admired his lean, smooth body and the way his wavy hair straightened under the weight of the water. I hadn't showered with anyone else in such close proximity since high school gym class.

I stepped closer and reached out. Matthew turned to me, and I halted my hand in midair. Wanting to touch him had nothing to do with getting off, returning a favor, or trying to convince him to go to bed with me. I simply wanted to touch his skin, feel his warmth under my fingers, and follow the dip and rise of each lean muscle as it fanned out from his middle.

Matthew watched me with his dark eyes. His chest heaved with each breath, the rest of his body still, waiting for my touch to connect us again.

My fingers danced in the air as if they'd already made up their minds, but the rest of me held them back. I inched my hand closer and trailed my fingers over his abdomen, traced the thin line of dark hair leading to his crotch with the pad of my thumb. He stepped into the touch. My hands explored around his cock, his sac, his thighs, and back up his body. He raised his hands to me and lathered the soap up my arms and over my shoulders.

He touched every part of my body and rotated between washing me and himself. Light, playful contact. My spent cock was just coming back to life when he turned the water off and got out of the shower.

I stepped out behind him. "I guess I can add tease to your list of qualities." Although, hadn't I teased too?

Matthew grinned and wrinkled his nose. He wrapped a towel around his waist and moved toward the door. I grabbed a hold of his wrist. His body came to mine with ease. We touched from shin to chest, the embrace more personal than any I'd known with another man, and we still had the towel between us.

I didn't think. I buried my face in his neck. "You smell good." He tilted his head, and I licked and sucked on his skin.

"It's the soap. They have nice soap here."

"Uh-uh. It's you. I thought it was your cologne, but now I know it's you." I kissed him. Why the hell couldn't I let go? And why was I telling him anything at all?

His fingers glided over my back. My skin quivered from the feathery touch. Right when I couldn't stand it any longer, he scraped his fingernails down my back and over my ass.

Without warning, he broke off the kiss. "Luke. I like the way your body moves when I touch you. It's like your skin wants to be closer to me. Like I'm making it feel special."

"No one's touched me the way you do. You and Richard."

"Speaking of..." Matthew backed up, holding my hand until he found the doorknob. He sashayed into the main room. "Shit."

I followed him out.

Richard was gone.

"I thought he'd stay."

I snatched up my pants. "Why would you think that?" The words came out more pissed than I intended. And I didn't want to admit it wasn't Matthew who had pissed me off. I'd just had some of the best sex in a long time, and I should have been enjoying the high, not angry over some guy who left the room before I did.

Matthew didn't move. "To at least say good-bye."

I stared at him, unsure what to do.

He turned away and slipped on his clothes before I had my shirt buttoned.

"Will you be here next weekend?" he asked without looking at me.

"I usually am." I couldn't bring myself to remind him I'd only agreed to one more night together.

He stepped close, his dark eyes focused on me. "I'll be here...you know, if you are...and if you want to..." He swiped his tongue over my lower lip. He left before I thought of anything to say.

I stared at the door as it closed behind him. I'd never been the last one left standing in a room at the Haven.

Chapter Six

I trudged into my apartment, dropped my laptop bag, and slammed the door shut with both hands. My sweaty palms stuck to the cheap paneled door, and my head fell forward. The flimsy fiberboard rattled, adding another sensation to the throb in my temples.

I'd lost my concentration on the trek home from work for the third time in as many days. Minutes had ticked by, and I hadn't been focused on anyone around me. The half hour walk had turned into an hour-and-a-half debacle.

A week had gone by since I'd last seen Matthew and Richard, and I couldn't stop thinking about them, wanting them. It interfered with everything. My work. My routine. My life. And it had to stop.

I logged on to the computer and fired up the video feeds. When the playback showed no signs of my stalkers, I plopped onto the couch.

A night at the Haven would help. I hadn't been to the club all week. Time to get back on the horse. As soon as my headache eased up.

I spread out on the couch. Richard's low voice and Matthew's giggle rose up around me. Matthew rode Richard's cock for several minutes before I forced myself to stop the vision.

I did not fantasize about what I already had, or sex that didn't include me. I pushed off the couch and headed for the kitchen. Dinner and get to the club early.

Best-laid plans.

Two steps from the couch, I saw it.

"Fuck." I spun around and stormed out of the apartment. I fished my cell out of my pocket, charged through the stairwell door, and called the first number on the speed dial.

"Simon."

"Walter, it's Luke. Someone's been in my apartment."

"When?"

"Today while I was at work."

"Did you get a good look—"

"No. They tampered with my cameras. I'm about to head back inside to check it out now."

"You're sure? Someone was there?"

"They moved the phone on my desk. You got anything I can use to figure out if they planted something?"

"Yeah. I'll stop by the office. Be right over."

* * * *

"Thanks for asking me over to watch the game." Walter stood at my door clutching two large duffle bags.

I grabbed a bag and held the door open for him.

There was more than one reason I liked Walter. He was smart as hell. I didn't know why he took early retirement, but it had to do with not wanting to do the job any longer, not that he couldn't.

"No problem," I said and set down the bag. I went to the desk. Since I didn't own a TV, I logged on to my work laptop and loaded one of the live college football sites I'd heard about. I entered my credit card number to order a subscription and picked any game about to start. I waited until a football field filled the screen and turned up the volume. "You want a beer?"

"I think I need one," he said.

I grabbed a couple of beers from the fridge and handed one to Walter. He took a swig and gathered his bags. "Who do you think's going to win?"

I glanced back at the computer screen to catch the name of at least one of the teams. "Ohio State."

Walter opened the first duffle bag and extracted a plastic case. He removed four separate metal pieces and assembled them into a long wandlike device. "Yeah, you're probably right. They've got a solid offense this year."

He opened the other bag and hauled out a large box with a computer screen and keypad attached to it. He placed the computerized device on the folding table and sat, raising his eyebrows as the table teetered with the extra weight. When it stilled, he flipped a switch and waited for the screen to turn on.

Walter kept talking like it required none of his thought to assemble his gear and begin checking my apartment. "Did you see it's supposed to snow all week? I hate the damn cold." He keyed in a command on the keypad. His fingers tapped with no sound. "I've been thinking about moving south, somewhere warmer before next winter."

The device's screen flashed off and came back on displaying a few lines of text. A list of the device types it had located nearby. Walter held up four fingers.

I looked around. Four goddamn listening devices planted somewhere in my small apartment. What the hell was my father up to?

"You going to move your business?" I asked.

"Maybe." He stood and reached for the wand. The phone on the desk was his first stop. He held the wand over it and an indicator light lit up. "I can run the business from anywhere." He squatted next to the desk and lifted the phone.

Did our sham conversation have any merit? "You know you're not that old."

Walter squinted up at me. "What?"

"Moving for the weather. Seems like something old guys do. They pack a camper, wear Hawaiian shirts and sandals, and move someplace where they can't catch a draft. You're not that guy."

Walter laughed and went back to work on the phone. "No. I guess I'm not. Someday, maybe." He used a screwdriver to pry the cover off the handset and removed a small device from inside. Then he detached several of the tiny wires and placed it into a metal box he'd brought with him.

"I'm going to find you a date," I said.

His brow furrowed and he stared at me for a moment before moving on to scan the wand over the computer equipment on the desk. "I don't need a date."

"The hell you don't. You're talking about bingo and shuffleboard."

He stilled and met my gaze. "I am not."

"It's too fucking cold here? You want to try for someplace warmer? Sounds like two steps away from the senior bus tour that travels to a different casino every weekend."

"Fuck you."

"No, I'm thinking it's you who needs a fuck."

He snorted. "Had a great lay six months back. Turned into a fine friend, but now I'm thinking he's a punk who should shut his mouth."

I held my hands in the air. "Ease up."

Walter went back to work. The sound of the game covered the silence between us. He located two more of the devices. One hidden under the desk, and another under the lamp in the bedroom. He searched the kitchen last and scanned for several minutes before the unit lit up over an electrical outlet. Walter retrieved the last device, deactivated it, and placed it inside the case. "Should be it."

"You're sure?"

He pointed to the computer on the table. "That's our latest creation. It can even find experimental devices, off-the-books type stuff. After 9/11, the government's willing to pay me good money, so I deliver the best. There's no way he's got anything else in here."

I paced the living room and dragged a hand through my hair. "Whoever my father has working for him this time is good. He knew to check the tape on the door, and that shit's impossible to see. He deleted today's video feed and restored yesterday's in its place."

"Smart." Walter eyed the computer. "You keep any personal info on there?"

"No. It's for surveillance. And my laptop was with me all day."

"Good." Walter walked back to the kitchen and peered into the small room. "Is anything missing?"

"Not that I can see." I shrugged. "I don't have much."

"This isn't a robbery, Luke. They weren't here for a TV and your DVDs. They may have taken something small, something with personal shit on it."

"I don't keep that kind of stuff."

He went into the kitchen and returned with two new beers. He handed me one. "What's he up to this time around?"

I swallowed a long gulp. The cool beer took the edge off my nerves. "I don't know. Somehow, he lets me know when he's found me. He wants me to know he can always find me. This time"—I shook my head—"he has another agenda."

"What are you going to do?"

"Move. Again!" I threw the half-empty beer. It smashed against the wall. Shards of glass and foaming beer ran down the surface in streaks.

Walter didn't flinch at my outburst. He scrutinized my impromptu work of art. "Has he ever told you why he has you followed?"

"No."

"Have you thought about leaving the city? Maybe he'd—"

"I won't let him run me off. Anyway, it's different this time. A reporter called here the other day."

Walter lowered the bottle from his lips. "Not good."

"I know. If in a couple of days, I haven't found a place—"

He raised a hand in the air. "You don't even have to ask. Just come on over. For as long as you need."

"Thanks. I'm sorry about before. I'm not used to... I don't know how to..." I shrugged.

"Care?"

"I guess."

"Thanks for the concern. I'm fine. You take care of yourself. I have a feeling he might become dangerous."

I met my friend's gaze. "He's always been dangerous."

We stood in silence for a few minutes. Walter fetched another beer from the kitchen and held it out to me. "So I haven't talked to you since last weekend. I take it Saturday night went well?"

I reached for the beer and winced. There was no way I was getting out of admitting whom I'd been with. "Fucker."

Walter took a seat on the couch. "Yep. So it was them again, huh?"

I sat on the edge of the desk. "I couldn't stop myself."

"Why should you?" He shifted on the cushion. "This couch is one uncomfortable piece of furniture."

"I'll leave it here when I go. Maybe this time I'll find a nicer place, get some real furniture." I tapped the beer bottle against my thigh. "Maybe I should stop trying to run from him and see what the hell he's going to do next."

"You can't run forever."

I took another swallow of beer, held it in my mouth, and let the cool liquid warm between my cheeks. Something I used to do with my milk as a kid. My father hated it. He'd sit across from me at the dinner table and demand I swallow. Milk wasn't to be drunk warm.

"Will I see you at the club tonight?" Walter asked.

I choked down the beer and wiped my mouth with the back of my hand. "You'll be back again already?"

"I might be. There's this guy—who doesn't get involved with anyone twice—who's taken to going upstairs with the same two men. I have to see who he ends up with next."

"Very funny."

"No, it isn't funny at all."

I regarded him with a questioning stare.

"Matthew's energetic, but he's honest, responsive. I think his energy will be a nice change for you. Richard is a good man. He's strong and confident. They are fine men."

I ditched the beer on the desk. "Hold up. Just 'cause I'm with the same guys twice in a row doesn't mean I'm about to start a relationship."

"Would that be the worst thing?"

"It just might be." I stood and headed for the door. I stopped short, my back to Walter. "What happened to him?"

"Who?"

"Richard. His scar."

Walter didn't answer. I faced him. The smug grin pissed me off.

Apparently, he didn't care. The damn grin widened. "I think that should be a question for him."

"Right." I'd likely never speak to Richard again. Then why the hell did I care about his past?

Walter stared at me as if he waited for me to share more. What did he want to hear? Then he spoke. "You're going through men as if you're looking for something, only you aren't sure what it is you want."

"I haven't been looking for anything. I'm just trying to enjoy life."

"I don't think so."

"How the hell do you know what I want?"

Walter stood and covered the distance between us. "You forget I've fucked you." He placed a hand on my shoulder. "I've seen men there for the pleasure. That hasn't been you since the first moment I met you." He embraced me. "Good luck tonight, Luke."

"You're an asshole, you know that?"

"That I am." He smirked and walked out the door.

I jumped in the shower, and his comments rolled around as only the observations of a friend could do. I was dressed and ready to go when I accepted he'd hit on a truth.

What the hell was I looking for?

I wasn't sure. But deep down, in a place I tried hard not to listen to, I knew I'd found it.

For that reason alone, I was determined to get to the club and look for two men I'd never been with before. Getting back to my usual play would help me shake off the thoughts of the past week—thoughts about my father, his stalkers, and my college years.

And most importantly, thoughts about the only two men I'd ever broken my rule for.

Chapter Seven

"Hello, Luke." The voice was low and deep, but unfamiliar.
The disappointment was hard to ignore.
I set my drink on the bar and inspected the man on the stool next to me. He could have stepped right off the pages of *GQ*. Every feature was a work of symmetry. The five o'clock shadow did nothing to hide the strong cleft chin. He had to be forty, but his skin showed no signs of age or any other abuse. Perhaps he pickled himself every night.
"Do I know you?" I asked.
"No, but your reputation precedes you. I've been wanting to make your acquaintance for a couple of weeks."
"Should I be flattered or concerned?"
"It's all good, I assure you. As am I. You won't be disappointed."
What he didn't know was I'd already had the best fuck of my life. It'd be hard for anyone to measure up. I glanced around the room and spotted another man. The one beside me no longer mattered. Whether or not I wanted to admit it, I'd found what I sought for the night.
Without taking my eyes off my find, I said, "I appreciate the offer, but I'm unavailable tonight."
"Really? You've been here alone for half an hour now, and I hear you never play with anyone more than once."
"You hear right. I don't play with just anyone more than once. But he"—I pointed across the room to a smiling Matthew—"isn't just anyone." I returned the smile before I knew what I'd done.
"Man, he's cute. Are you looking for another to join you? I'd enjoy that." He pressed the last of his words against my ear. His lips grazed my skin, and a layer of spit clung to me.
I jerked away and stood. "If you'd asked me that question last week, I'd already have your ass upstairs and naked by now. Tonight, I need something else." I stepped away from the bar, and before I thought too much on what it meant to be with someone for a third time, I made my way to Matthew's table.

If I had any doubt about his interest in me, the smoldering look in his eyes as he tracked my movements told me all I needed to know. I sat across from him. We stared for a few breaths before we looked away.

"Not sure he'll be here tonight, kid."

"I'm thinking we could wait...maybe for a little while. To see..."

"Yeah, that's fine with me. Even if he doesn't show, I want you." The last three words left my mouth in a low rumble I couldn't control. The way he stared at me, his eyes heavy, his mouth parted, and his bottom lip quivering as he ran his tongue over it, surprised me. And it stunned me more how much I liked seeing that look from him.

"I want you too, Luke." His dark pupils expanded. It gave him a wild, vigorous look.

Forcing myself not to look at him again and not to pay attention to the growing throb in my lap was the best option. I ordered a water and a club soda from the next waiter by the table. We waited twenty minutes before we said much more, but we made promises every time we glanced at each other.

"God, Luke," he said when his gaze caught mine again. "Don't know about waiting."

"Let's go. We can always catch up with him another night."

"Yeah?"

"If he ever shows again." *Great.* I was agreeing to a fourth time before we even started for the night. I had lost my goddamn mind.

Matthew stood. His tight pants did nothing to hide his erection. I groaned. I wanted to take his cock in my mouth right there in the middle of the dining room.

Matthew dropped his hands in front of the bulge. His face flushed, and he chewed on his lower lip. With the way he worked it, he'd be bleeding by the time I got him upstairs.

I requested a room from the desk and avoided Matthew while we waited. I couldn't look at him again without grabbing a hold of him, taking him in my arms, and pressing my lips to his. A minute later, I had the key card in my hand. I gripped the plastic so tight I'd likely crack it on the way to the room. I eased up. No way in hell would I head back to the desk again. If the card broke, we'd just have to screw in the hallway. Fuck the membership policy on public sex.

"Let's go." I seized his arm and lurched for the elevator.

A low hum escaped his throat. I wasn't the only one having a problem with waiting.

Inside the elevator, he leaned against the far wall, his hands clasped behind him, his head bent. The dark hair obscured his eyes.

I could smell him. Not his usual scent of spice and mint. He was as ready to pop as I was. I wanted to tear off his pants, bury my face in his groin, and breathe in more of that scent, taste his balls and lick the length of his dick.

I shoved my hands in my pockets and faced the door. What the hell was happening to me? I wanted Matthew like I'd wanted no one else. The elevator chimed, and relief flooded my chest. I stepped out and led the way to the room.

Who the hell cared? I was about to get his mouth on me. His hard, lean body under me. Nothing else mattered.

Except I wanted Richard. I wanted his hands on me. I wanted him in the room with us.

I ignored the disappointment. I was going to have Matthew. I was going to fuck the shit out of him and beg him for his mouth, his touch. That was something, more than something.

Not that I'd need to beg. Matthew was a bottle of sexual energy, and the minute we got in the room, the lid came off and he poured it on with fervor. His energy collided with my body as he crowded me against the closed door. His lips met mine, and his tongue spread pleasure over every part of my mouth again and again, reminding me how much he wanted me.

He wrapped his arms around my neck and pulled me closer. Our tongues dived deeper. I grabbed his ass and mashed our groins together. The moan that leaped from his mouth to mine sounded desperate, wanton.

I spun us around and slammed his back against the door, never breaking the kiss, crushing my pelvis against him. When our clothed cocks connected again, Matthew gave up on the kiss and arched into the contact.

"Yes. God yes, Luke." He put his hands on my face and forced me to look at him. The expression was similar to the lust-filled one he gave me in the dining room, except I could see something more there. What the hell was it?

Matthew breathed deep and ground more slowly against me. "Damn, you drive me crazy. I want you so much, I can't think about anything else. Just you and Richard."

"Yeah, Matthew. I need this, need you."

I hauled him away from the door, and we worked our way to the bed.

He sucked on my neck as we went. "You taste good. Can I leave marks on you?"

"Hell, yes. Just not where they'll be seen at work." I didn't care if anyone saw them, but the idea of hidden marks left by Matthew was maddening. I'd be able to see them days later. Remember him. His touch.

I laid him on the bed. Since neither of us was letting go, I went down with him. His legs wrapped around me.

"I need your clothes off," he said. He clawed at my shirt. I lifted to give him room to open the buttons, and then I raised his shirt over his head. We put off removing our pants as long as we could, his legs still tight around me.

"Need to get at your dick," I said.

"Uh-huh." His legs dropped to the bed.

"I'm going to screw your brains out, Matthew."

"Yeah. I want that, want you."

I unbuttoned his pants, then started on my own. He slid his off in an effortless motion, never moving with any awkwardness. My pants and underwear tangled at my feet with my shoes, and I had to give a few good kicks to get them off and onto the floor. Next to him, my writhing and kicking made me look like a finalist for the ten thousand dollar cash prize on *America's Funniest Home Videos*. Beautiful was the best word to describe him.

Once we were naked, our bodies connected again in a rush, like sex-crazed teenagers given the go-ahead on prom night, diving for each other. Six days must have been too long for either of us to wait to be together again. How did I think I was ever going to give him up? Either of them?

The idea of never having Richard again twisted my gut into a rigid knot. When he came back to the club, we'd hook up with him again.

We had to.

Matthew kissed me. Our cocks slid together as we humped at each other. His precum glided on my dick. When did I ever get that close to another man without a condom on? I was all about the fucking and not so much the crazy need to touch, rub, and connect with someone.

I looped my fingers through his hair and deepened the kiss. He moaned and hummed. I heard nothing but him and our bodies slapping together. Until I heard another sound: a brief but firm knock on the door.

Everything stopped.

We lay still, staring at the closed door.

Matthew's body tensed under mine. "You think?"

"How would he know we're in here?"

"Didn't you notice everyone watching you walk up the stairs? I guess you with me three times in a row is a real surprise." Matthew gave me a teasing smile before he slid out from under me and bounded for the door.

"I thought this club was discreet," I called after him.

He stopped, his hand on the doorknob, and smiled back at me again. Then he yanked the door open.

Richard stood in the hallway, his large form leaning on the doorframe. He scanned Matthew's naked body and paused at the straining cock. "Did you two get started without me?"

Matthew tugged him inside the room, threw the door shut, and kissed him. Richard's hands went straight to Matthew's ass and hauled him close. His fingers pawed the pale flesh.

"I didn't know if you'd come back," Matthew said.

"I didn't get either of your mouths on my dick yet."

Matthew whimpered and kissed him.

"And you didn't get to fuck me yet," Richard added.

"Uh—yeah, I didn't." His mouth covered Richard's again.

I headed for the door and the two bodies crashing together: one man still clothed, and the other naked.

"Good to see you here," Richard said when I stood beside him.

I reached out. The heat of his skin tempted me. I didn't clutch or pull. I massaged the back of his neck as I kissed him. It only took a moment for Matthew's tongue to tangle with mine, and together we tasted Richard.

"Clothes off," Matthew said as he parted Richard's shirt. I helped him get the big man naked.

Matthew's ass met the sheets first. He spread himself out before us. His body trembled. It begged for our touch. Richard lowered himself onto Matthew and pulled me alongside them.

We kissed, caressed, fondled balls, stroked cocks. Our moans and groans drove us forward as need and desire tore away at any semblance that what we were up to was a casual fuck. We all needed one another too much.

"Want my mouth on you?" Matthew whispered in Richard's ear between kisses.

"Yes. Been waiting for that." Richard rolled over onto his back. "Luke, fuck me?"

"You wanting me in you again?"

"Yes. You in me. Matthew's mouth. Been thinking about it all week." He kissed me. "Can't stop thinking about you two."

"God, me either." Matthew's words clung to a low groan.

"Uh-huh," I said. "Can't get enough of you." I was no longer worried about what to say or what not to say. That part of my brain had gone on a sabbatical. Desperation and desire had taken residence instead. I shifted to kneel between Richard's legs. He spread his thick thighs. "Damn, you look great like this."

He nodded. Maybe words had left his brain too. He tangled his hands in Matthew's dark hair, and they kissed again. I sat back on my heels. I'd never seen anything like them.

I managed to find lube and worked Richard's ass, telling myself it didn't mean anything how quickly I was trying to get inside him again. I got a condom on, handed one to Matthew, and lifted Richard's legs over my arms. I pushed into him with slow, shallow movements, never going all the way in. Every nerve ending in my body settled in my dick, the incredible pressure reminding me yet again how little the man must bottom.

"More, Luke. More." Richard's pleas set me to a faster pace.

I appreciated the close view of Matthew's mouth stretched to wrap around the thick cock. It amazed me how much he could take in. Richard wasn't small in any way, and Matthew worked it like getting the big man off was the only thing in the world that mattered.

"Yes, Matthew. Damn...where did you..." Richard reached for the headboard. His words stopped making sense as Matthew bobbed faster. I thrust again, pushing all the way in.

A few more movements of Matthew's mouth, and Richard screamed louder, writhed more. "Matthew! I can't...can't hold out." He came with a shout, his head thrown back, his eyes squeezed shut. For a brief moment, I wanted to force him to open them, tease him as he'd done to me on our first night, but I was enjoying his clenching ass too damn much to stop.

Matthew pulled off Richard and landed on his back, breathing heavily. I bent for a kiss. First from Matthew and then Richard. Their lips and tongues couldn't do anything with real coordination, but the kisses were still better than any I'd ever known.

What the hell? Since when did I need to kiss in the middle of a fuck?

I jerked back and shoved everything I had into Richard. The familiar sound of a hand moving over skin signaled Matthew's need.

"Kid," I said, "get over here."

His hand froze. His entire body went stiff. He parted his lips, but he didn't make a sound.

"Come on, Matthew. Fuck me."

He didn't move.

I stilled, my attention on him. "Don't you want to?"

"Um, yeah. I-I'd like that. I don't always get to, you know?"

"Yeah? Tonight you do." I leaned toward him and lowered my voice. "I want you inside me. Been thinking about it. Dreaming of it." Damn, the things I was telling them.

"Oh. I—" He advanced and kissed me. Not his usual kiss. It was rough, harsh, and fierce. His teeth scraped my lips. He pulled back with as much force and shifted to kneel behind me. I drove into Richard again.

"Yes," Richard said. "Don't stop. Getting hard again. Already. God, what you two do to me."

I kissed him and spread the words over his lips. "Not going to stop. Going to make you come again, going to make you feel it."

"Yes!" he cried out.

Matthew pressed down on my back, pinning me to Richard. His slick fingers brushed over me and made their way in.

I slammed into Richard again and stilled when the familiar swell built. "Close. Too close."

Matthew yanked his fingers out, and a moment later he buried his cock inside me. He pulled back and shoved in again, tentative at first. But after a few shaky thrusts, his movements came harder, faster.

"That's it," I said.

He licked at my back, nibbled at my shoulder. Then he gripped me with his teeth and sucked on my skin.

Holy shit. I was close again. My ass clamped around him, and Matthew cried out. His noises became louder than any I'd heard from him before.

I rose to angle myself better, and Richard groaned with the change. His hips rolled, and his ass rose to meet me with each slap of our bodies. His large hand sped over his own shaft. Matthew made fast work of catching the rhythm, and the three of us soared together.

It wasn't just sex. There was something more to our play. We were fending off our orgasms as if we were reacting to the idea it might be our last night together. How many times would the three of us find ourselves in the same room?

Hell, I'd almost missed out on it because of my own damn fears. The thought distracted me from keeping my release at bay. My balls drew up tight. Bright streaks of colors flashed behind my closed eyelids, and my body jerked through the intense pressure shooting out my cock.

Richard came for the second time. His ass gripped me in the vise his body had become. Matthew followed. I'd never been in a threesome where we all came in such rapid succession.

Matthew whispered his thanks in my ear, pulled out of me, and landed on the bed next to Richard. I groaned as my body protested the loss. My chest tightened when my own dick slipped out of Richard. I had to think for a moment before it came to me.

Disappointment.

I yanked the condom off and fell onto the bed, my hand draped over Richard's chest, my legs mingled with his. I was relaxed, soaring, at peace. And still touching him. I was losing complete control. But I couldn't stop myself. I didn't want to leave the warmth of them. I didn't want to go back to thinking anything I'd done was a mistake. I grazed a hand over his chest hair. My fingers brushed the scar.

"Goddamn." Richard's loose voice didn't quite form complete syllables.

I lifted up and looked down at him. "Good?"

"Beyond good."

"Uh-huh," Matthew said. His signature laugh followed.

I fell back onto the bed. "Hey, kid, you go by anything other than Matthew? Matt?"

"Nah. Guess I don't seem like a Matt. I've noticed you two like to call me 'kid' more than anything else."

Richard lifted his head. "No one else at the club's ever called you that? You're one of the younger ones here."

"Nope. Just you two." Matthew studied the ceiling. "No one else really calls me anything. I mean…I can't remember the last time someone might have said my name in bed."

Richard leaned over and pressed a kiss on his lips. "Matthew." He spoke the name in a drawn out tone. "You have rocked my world these three nights together. You and Luke."

Matthew gripped his lower lip with his teeth.

Richard sprawled out on his back again and crossed his arms behind his head. "Damn. I still didn't get the kid in my ass."

Matthew gasped.

"Maybe next time, huh?" I said.

Richard lifted his head again. "Yeah?"

I sighed. "Yeah." Whether or not I understood it yet, I wasn't done with either of them. I'd already broken my basic rule to be with them more than once. Pushing the line a little further didn't seem the sacrifice it once had.

Richard sat up and leaned against the headboard. "Well, then, I have a proposition."

Chapter Eight

Richard sat taller. "I'm reluctant to mention it. It's not always what guys at the club are looking for. Not when playing in a threesome."

Matthew rolled onto his stomach and stared at him.

Richard reached out and cupped Matthew's cheek in his hand. "I think you might agree. I like your eagerness, your curiosity. You hold nothing back. I worry you're too young." He glanced around the room before his gaze settled back on Matthew. "Three men—won't be easy. I don't want to see you get hurt."

"I can take care of myself."

"I know that. It's who I am. I worry, especially about those who mean something to me."

Matthew rose onto his elbows. "I mean something to you?"

"You're starting to. Both of you." Richard looked to me. "You'll want to get dressed and run out of the room the minute I mention my idea. I don't want to see you leave before you give us a chance."

I did want to get the hell out, and he hadn't given any details.

"I'd like to see you," he said, "outside of the club. I'd like to see if we can be more than what we have been."

Matthew's mouth gaped open. He bounced onto his knees, his head tilting, his wavy hair falling over one eye. "Are you asking us out? Both of us?"

Meeting at the club again—I might have agreed to that. But a goddamn date?

I leaped off the bed before Richard finished his nod.

"Dammit." He scrambled to the edge of the bed.

I threw my pants on, shirt and shoes in hand, and bolted for the door. He grabbed my arm and shoved me against the wall.

"How well I know you already." His voice was full of mockery. Yet, there was fear in his eyes, and the look enticed me. The man didn't want me to leave.

I tossed the reaction aside. "Let me go." I shook my arm free.

"But I don't think you want me to."

"You have no idea what I want."

"I think I do. If you'll give me a chance to show you."

Matthew placed a hand on my shoulder. "Give us both a chance."

"Then you'll agree?" Richard asked him.

"I'll try it."

"That's all I'm asking for." He kissed the younger man.

I didn't bother to hide the shock from my face. "You said you didn't want a relationship."

"I know what I said. I wanted to avoid getting close to anyone again. Three nights with the two of you, and I can't avoid it any longer." He spoke the last of his words to the floor. "I don't do well alone."

"You lied."

"No! I came back to the club the second night to find someone else, to get you out of my head. It took me all of two seconds when I saw you to realize I didn't want anyone else. And I sure didn't want to see either of you walk upstairs with other guys."

I turned away. I didn't want him to see it'd been the same for me.

"But now," he said, "I wish to explore what we're doing here. See if we can make this more than sex at the club."

Matthew lowered his head to where his chin rested upon his chest. "It's been fun, the club, the guys, you two, but I don't want it to always be like this."

Richard lifted the man's face. "I know." He caressed Matthew's cheek. With his large hands he could be gentle, tender, and could give so much in a caring touch. Even if I'd wanted to, I had no idea how to give that to someone.

Richard pulled the smaller man into his arms until Matthew's head lay on his chest. I stared at them, uncertain for a moment what was odd about their posture. I focused in on every point where their bodies touched.

Hugging. With no intention of it becoming anything more.

Richard reached for me with his other hand. I flinched. Fucking, sucking, getting off in any way he wanted—even kissing and touching—was one thing. I couldn't let him hold me.

His arm fell to his side. "I want us to get to know each other and explore our wants and needs together."

I stared at the arm he had draped over Matthew's shoulders. "Three guys can't—"

"Look at me."

I took a deep breath and lifted my gaze to his.

"They can. We can. I like you both. I want to get to know you. I want to see if what I've been feeling could be something."

"I told you I don't...I don't do this." I let my head fall back to the wall behind me. "I keep trying to figure out what it is about you two that's better than the men I was with the week before and the ones the week before that."

"It just is. We all feel it."

Matthew nodded.

Richard's gaze scanned mine.

"Can I think it over?" *Shit.* What was I going to agree to?

"Of course. Take some time. We can meet up again. But I won't sleep with you again until you decide." He spoke the words with kindness despite the statement they made. "I'm not going to keep having sex with you. Not when it's going to start meaning something to me and not to you."

"We go on a date or the fucking's off limits?"

"Yes. I want you, Luke. All of you."

He stepped back and let go of Matthew in the process. The smaller man watched Richard pull away from him, his large eyes confused, lost. Would he keep away from Matthew if I didn't agree?

I reached out. My hand found Richard's hip with no hesitation. Even with my mind protesting what it could all mean, I tugged him to me.

An open palm hit the wall beside my ear as he pressed in close. The scent of sweat and cum and his musky cologne overpowered me.

"Or maybe you can answer now? Can you give it a try, Luke?"

My fingers dug into his hip. I tried to settle on one rational reason why I shouldn't agree. The reasons would come later, of course, at home alone. But at that moment, I had nothing to say in protest. I wanted to keep fucking them, which was reason enough for me to leave the room and not look back, but the idea of not being with them again kept me from seeing any of the reasons why I never got serious. Kept me from thinking about my father and the ways he could hurt me—or them.

"What the hell am I doing?" I exhaled. "All right."

Relief flooded Richard's face. "You still in, Matthew?"

"Have you taken a look at you guys? I'm in." He laughed.

Richard and I stared at each other for another moment. What was that look? Nervousness? Excitement? Fear? I glanced at Matthew, and he grinned.

I planted a kiss upon his lips. "You're sweet and addictive." I could not shut up.

"I agree," Richard said.

Matthew wrinkled his nose and pouted. The expression didn't look right on him. I cupped his balls. He squeezed his eyes shut and gripped my arm. His soft moan and the twitch of his cock were enough to get my own dick back in service.

Richard had other ideas. He strolled across the room and sat on the bed. "Does tomorrow night work for you guys?"

My head hit the wall behind me, and I groaned.

Matthew rubbed a hand up and down my arm. "It'll be okay, Luke. It'll be like tonight, only we'll eat food and talk before the sex." Matthew raised his eyebrows and bobbed his head. He bounced to the bed and sat on the edge. "I'm free tomorrow night."

"Good. Luke?"

"Can we make it late? I've gotta look at new apartments."

"You're not moving to get away from us are you?"

"Shut up."

Richard huffed out a short laugh. "Late's fine by me. If you want, we can have dinner at my place. I'll cook."

I retreated from the wall, grabbed an armchair from near the bar, and sat. "That's fine with me."

"Me too," Matthew said. "Might be easier than going out somewhere. You know…three guys…might look weird."

"I don't care what we look like," Richard said. "But for a first date, you might be right. I'll give you my address before we leave. Say nine o'clock?"

Matthew agreed.

These two were crazy. A threesome? Dating?

"Sounds fine," I said.

Richard watched me. "I have one more thing I'd like to add."

What now?

"If we're going to try this, I need you both to agree—no sex outside the three of us. I won't date you unless I know you're not doing someone else. That's not my thing. Also, if this does work out, I'd like to be able to fuck you bare someday, and I need to know you haven't been sleeping around."

I never played bareback. Never. And I had no experience being faithful to anyone. Not since college. Since Tim. Could I do what Richard asked? And did I want to? I craved them, more than anyone I'd met in the last fifteen years, but could I say no to sex?

Matthew's dark hair swayed with the enthusiastic nod. For a moment, it didn't seem like his head would ever stop moving.

A throb built in my temples. My eyes blurred a bit with the pain. I stared at the floor in front of my chair. Specks of muted color seemed to dance and squirm in the light-colored carpet. Maybe they were the sperm of previous occupants, still writhing around in the hope of fulfilling their biological destiny. Gay sperm probably had no clue when they shot out of the body their fate was much less noble than creating life—yet, far more satisfactory, in my opinion. A laugh leaked out, like a balloon losing air in a slow hiss. The fictional sperm halted.

I was still laughing when I looked up. Richard's brow was furrowed, his elbows on his knees, his hands clasped before him. Matthew bit at his lip again. His face was angled down, but his eyes watched me.

Right. Serious discussion.

"You think you can just give up other men?" I asked. "No more nights at the club? No more blowjobs?"

"I've done it before," Richard said. "And who says I'm giving up blowjobs? I'm expecting a lot of those."

Matthew laughed.

Richard looked his way and nodded, a huge smirk on his face.

"All right," I said. "No outside sex."

Well, fuck. I was as surprised as they appeared to be. Maybe with the verbal agreement, I could keep my word.

Maybe.

Richard leaned back. "Good. Tomorrow night. My place. Dinner. Conversation. Nothing to stress about." His thick cock rested on his leg. Not hard, but not soft either. "I believe we already know we go nicely together in the sack, so there won't be any surprises there." He flashed a wicked grin.

"Uh-huh." I stood, chucked my pants, and took a few steps toward the bed. "But I'd be willing to test that again tonight." I'd just agreed to give up sex with anyone else. I had no qualms admitting how much I wanted them. I didn't wait for an answer.

Without another discussion point or another word, we came together. Richard's groans and Matthew's pleading words filled the room, surrounded me, and only then did I realize how much I'd missed hearing them.

The sex wasn't a heated exchange of lust. It was a slow confirmation of the arrangement we'd made—we were flying, floating, coming, and landing together as one, not three.

And that didn't scare me, not while in bed with them, no matter how intense the sex had been.

What did scare the shit out of me was what I'd be doing with them the next night.

Chapter Nine

I rang the doorbell of the town house.

A date. There was no way it was going to go well.

Except I wanted it to. A part of me I'd hidden for a long time had surfaced, a part that hadn't cared for the last fifteen years of my promiscuous life.

The door opened, and Matthew smiled at me. "Come on in. Richard's in the kitchen."

"Sorry I'm late. Had a few apartments to look at." *And I had to take three different subway routes to be sure I wasn't followed.*

"Don't worry about it. Richard's still cooking. I don't think he does it all that often." Matthew laughed. "He's dropped like three pans since I got here. And burned the first round of garlic bread. I'd be cursing and stuff, but he keeps at it."

Matthew led me into a dining room. It reminded me too much of my parents' with the long, solid wood table, a sideboard covered in crystal stemware, and a low-hanging brass chandelier. Formal. Polished. Stuffy. I wanted to turn around and leave. Matthew waited across the room. I went to him, my body anxious for him again. No way was I leaving while I was so close to him.

The smell of charred bread greeted us as we stepped into the kitchen. The smaller room reminded me nothing of my parents' home. Their kitchen had been large and impersonal. Richard's was comfortable and inviting. A small table sat off to one side, and a long counter sported bar stools for close conversation with the cook. His home was impressive. Nothing like my place.

I was more impressed with the large man bent over, peering into the oven, his firm ass encased in denim.

Richard straightened. Oven mitts covered his hands. He held them in the air like a doctor who had scrubbed for surgery. A long black line of burned fabric streaked one side of a tan-colored mitt.

"Luke." He wrapped his arms around my shoulders and kissed me.

The mitts pressed into my back. Soft and billowy, not like his warm, firm grip at all. Did people kiss at the beginning of a first date? Maybe when you'd already fucked. He stepped back. "You made it."

"I guess I did. You've got a nice place."

"Thanks. I bought it for the location. Not too far from my office downtown, but the neighborhood makes it feel like I'm in the suburbs. Have a seat. Dinner will be up in a minute." He shed the oven mitts and tossed them on the counter. "I hope you guys like Italian. Want a soda?"

"I'm not picky," I said. "A soda's fine." A beer sounded good, but I assumed I'd never have another with Matthew nearby. Richard handed me a bottle of soda, and I took a seat on a stool.

"Did you find a new apartment?" Matthew asked as he sat next to me.

"Not yet." I'd looked at four places available immediately, and none of them offered the necessary locations to hide any security cameras outside.

"What are you looking for?" Richard leaned against the counter behind him. "My business has a lot of real estate investments. Apartments. Condos."

"You own the business?" I asked.

"I do."

"Does it pay for this place?"

"It does."

"Then the kind of apartment I'm looking for is way below your radar."

Matthew chuckled.

"This place must have set you back," I said.

"I do okay. I didn't invite you here to show off."

"I didn't say that. I just…" I was already fucking up. "I don't like to spend a lot on where I live. I doubt anything you'd invest in is what I'm hoping to find."

"Fair enough." He crossed his solid arms over his chest.

We glared at each other. Had I pissed him off, or was he working something out in his own mind?

Matthew's voice broke the silence. "I know what you mean. I've been looking around and everything is expensive in this city."

Richard checked the bread in the oven again. "You're moving too?"

"I need to. I'm…" He picked at the label on his soda. "I live with my mom."

Richard stepped across the kitchen. He laid his palms on the counter in front of Matthew and lowered his head until eye level with him. "There's nothing wrong with that. Everyone's gotta start somewhere."

Matthew shrugged. "She needs the rent money I give her. She's a great mom, real supportive of me. I have to be able to afford a place and still help her. It makes it harder to leave, you know?"

"That's nice of you," I said.

"It is," Richard said. "You'll work it all out. You'll find a place."

Matthew nodded. He plucked away at the label on his soda.

Richard leaned back against the counter again. "So, Luke, can I ask why you're moving?"

I gulped down half the soda. "I can't stay where I'm at. I've gotta be out in a week."

"Doesn't leave you much time."

"Yeah. I'll figure something out."

A timer on the stove chimed. "Bread's up." Richard gestured to the table behind us. "Have a seat." He dished out heaping plates of garlic bread and penne pasta covered in a thick tomato sauce before he spoke again. "I realized the other night I don't know your last names. Since we aren't at the club anymore, I'd like us to come clean. My name's Richard Marshall."

Matthew smiled at Richard. "Matthew Stewart."

They turned my way.

I hadn't given my last name to any man I'd fucked in years. Couldn't we have started with something like my favorite brand of beer or action flick? But this wasn't a make-some-small-talk-till-you-get-in-his-pants conversation. This was a date. "Luke Moore."

"Well, Matthew Stewart and Luke Moore, dig in. I hope you like the pasta." He took a bite and groaned in approval of his own effort. "So, tell me about yourselves."

No matter what, there were things I wouldn't tell them. Hell, I couldn't think of one thing to say. I stuffed a large forkful of the pasta in my mouth and gave Richard a favorable nod.

Matthew hadn't eaten yet. He looked between me and Richard as if waiting for me to answer or for Richard to encourage me in some way.

"Matthew, where do you work?" Richard asked.

Matthew settled an elbow on each side of his plate. "I work part-time at Champion Music. It's in the Southview mall. I manage the inventory and cover the register when I'm needed. I don't make a lot but enough for now, I guess."

As each word passed over his lips, I relaxed into the chair.

"I'm thinking about going back to college," he said, "but I need to save the cash first. I sorta got into some trouble my first semester and I, uh...I had to move back home. I never went back to school." He shifted in his seat.

"Where do you live?" Richard asked.

Matthew ran a hand through his dark hair. "On the south side near Chesterfield Park."

"You go pretty far to get to the Haven."

"Yeah. It works for me. I make the time to get there."

"I'm glad."

Matthew ducked his head.

Richard watched him for a moment more, then looked my way. "What do you do?"

I drew in a shaky breath. They had to have heard it, but I couldn't have prevented it. I breathed deep again and did what I had when I was seven years old and went swimming for the first time at my parents' country club. I squeezed my eyes shut and jumped in before the fear stopped me.

"I'm a developer at Knox Consulting. It's an IT consulting firm." I shoved the food around on my plate. A solitary piece of pasta stuck to the end of the fork as I twirled the utensil around in the thick sauce. I shook the fork to free the pasta from its prison. It wouldn't budge.

"A rather prestigious firm," Richard said.

I lifted my head. "Huh? Oh, yeah, they are. It keeps me busy."

"Not too busy, I hope." He smirked and took another bite. His tongue snaked out and caught a bead of sauce that lingered on his bottom lip. He winked.

I shook my head. The man never let up.

"Are you a programmer?" Matthew asked.

"Yeah. Mostly Web-based applications for corporations."

"Cool. The Internet rocks." He smirked. "I mean, it's how I learned a lot of stuff. I can't imagine what you all did for gay porn when you were teenagers."

Richard about choked on his food. He downed most of his soda and laughed out loud once he could breathe.

"Well, kid, back in the Stone Age, we had to carve dirty pictures on the cave walls and hope our parents were too busy hunting and gathering to notice."

Matthew giggled. "You really have your own business?"

Richard wiped his mouth and laid his napkin across his lap. "I do. I started it ten years ago. I own and manage a number of investments, mostly development and real estate holdings." He looked my way.

"Despite what my house looks like, my work is important to me because I want to succeed, not because I want to be rich." He smirked. I took it to mean I hadn't royally pissed him off. "I know I'm jumping into things here, but I'd like to ask you guys about sex, if you don't mind."

"Why the hell would we mind that?" I said.

"I should have known it's the subject you'll speak of more easily than your personal life."

I nodded and took another bite of the pasta. Sex was less complicated.

"We don't know each other all that well," Richard said, "and we're agreeing to meet outside the club. I want to know what you expect." He swallowed another gulp of his soda and eyed us. The look reminded me of one chess players hid behind. A mix of repressing a reaction and reading the other player's next move. His game face. "I think it'd be best if we put our cards on the table and see what each person wants and needs from this."

Matthew waved a hand in the air and picked up his fork. "I'll go along with whatever you two decide." He took a bite. "This is really good."

Richard shook his head. "No, Matthew, you won't. You don't know what sorts of things we're into. You could get hurt—emotionally or physically—if we were to do something you didn't want. And I'm not only talking sex here. I want to see more of you. I want to get to know you. I don't want to take a chance I'll do or say something to hurt you."

Matthew cocked his head to the side. "Isn't that what dating is? Taking risks? Seeing if someone is compatible with you?"

Richard leaned back in his chair. "I don't take risks. Not in my personal life."

"Okay. Let me think about it. Maybe you or Luke can talk first."

Richard remained still for a moment more, his game face back in play. "I've already said what I think about you guys sleeping around. I'll add one other thing. This is a little different than anything I've been involved in before. Three guys. I think we should consider a rule about sex as a group. Two of us can play at any time, but no actual sex—and I mean penetration—unless the three of us are together in the same room. Later, we can all agree to change that if we want. For now, if it's two of us, we can rub off, exchange blowjobs, or whatever, but no fucking. It leaves something for us to do together."

Well, hell. He sure liked his rules, and every one of them was in direct conflict with my own. I glanced at Matthew. He had a forkful of pasta paused three inches from his mouth, his large eyes staring at Richard.

It didn't seem like Matthew was going to say anything, so I spoke. "Can I ask why?"

"Trust takes time. Time we should spend together. We are three people, not two. It may not be conventional, but it's what I want to try to make work. I don't think it's reasonable to suggest we do nothing at all. I can agree to getting off without fucking. That way when I get stuck at work late when we're supposed to get together, you two don't have to go it alone. We can all get some release when we need it."

I looked to Matthew again. A blowjob would be a great diversion.

A diversion? Since when did I need a diversion when it came to sex? Did I want to make this work enough?

"Okay," Matthew said.

I rolled my eyes. "Sounds like a good plan."

"Okay, Luke, what are your rules regarding sex?" Richard asked. "What would you agree to? What do you want to avoid in terms of the three of us?"

All of it. But that answer didn't sit right with me. Not any longer.

I'd never set the rules for anything more than one night of sexual play. My mind filled with all the things I should mention. What I would do. What I wouldn't do. But it all seemed unnecessary. A conversation of strangers. They were beginning to feel like anything but. "Condoms all the way around for sex and blowjobs—even if you want to have tests done or whatever—until I say differently."

"Sounds good," Richard said. "Trusting what we say about not playing around isn't easy to take on faith. For any of us. If this works out, I'd like us to get tested, but I'll agree to condoms until the last person says they go."

Matthew grabbed his soda and plucked away at the label again.

Richard eyed the younger man. "Matthew?"

"I, uh...I blow guys all the time without a condom, but I...I've never agreed to sex without one. I'm not sure I'll know when to go that far. I don't really know you. I'm ah...I'm afraid I'll take a risk when I shouldn't."

"You won't. You'll either know we've been tested and that you trust us, or if you aren't sure, we'll still be using the rubbers. Plain and simple."

Matthew ripped off a section of the soda's label and sat back in his seat, folding the jagged piece until it would fold no more.

I continued. "I'm not into the D/s or S&M lifestyle. Some

bondage—as you know—but that's it. I'm not into the power or pain thing."

"What you've said fits my tastes." Richard ate the last bites of his dinner. "I want equal partners."

Partners? Were he and I having the same conversation? I rushed to say the rest before I changed my mind and walked out of his house. "As for anything else, we're all used to the club scene, discussing sex openly. If one of us has something in mind, he asks."

Richard set his fork down. "At least I know you will. You'll probably describe where you want our hands, mouths, and cocks each time we fuck."

I laughed. "Probably."

Richard gestured to Matthew. "Your turn."

Matthew unfolded and refolded the plastic label as he talked. "I agree with what Luke said. I've done some of the BDSM stuff, and it wasn't for me. I shouldn't have tried it. I knew it wouldn't work out, but I liked the guy. I don't care to be tied up. I get frustrated, and I don't like feeling restrained. I like to touch, to move. And the pain stuff...it hurt, like a lot, and I wasn't in the mindset to enjoy it, so...well, it sucked all the way around. When he finally stopped hitting me and fucked me, I couldn't even come."

Someone had hurt him instead of taking him to places he could enjoy. I glanced at Richard. The skin of his forehead was puckered together in a series of vertical lines.

Matthew wasn't paying attention to either of us. "I should've used the safe word, but I sorta freaked. That was my fault, not his." He set the scrap of label on the table and dropped his hands to his lap. "I know I asked at the club, but I don't like it when people drink alcohol around me. If we're hanging out and you two wanna have a drink together, I can get lost."

Richard leaned in like he wanted to ask the younger man why he had an issue with alcohol.

Matthew looked away from him.

Richard settled back in his chair. "You got it, kid."

"That's fine with me," I said.

Matthew bit at the edge of a thumbnail. I figured he was done talking.

Richard watched him and made no move to speak or eat. The faint hint of a smile formed on his lips. He was waiting. For what?

Matthew lowered his hand. "I guess I have one other thing that might come up. Not really about sex, but sometimes...a lot of the time...when I'm laughing, I—hell, I giggle. It's annoying. And it drives most guys nuts."

Laughter bubbled up. I tapped the side of a fist to my mouth to stop it. "You giggle? I hadn't noticed."

Matthew whipped his head in my direction. His brow furrowed and he nodded. So goddamn serious.

I kept laughing.

Matthew's gaze swung back to Richard.

"I like your laugh," Richard said. "If I found it the least bit annoying, I wouldn't have invited you here."

Matthew slapped a hand to his forehead. "Oh, God. You already heard it."

I laughed harder. Tears threatened at the corners of my eyes.

Richard nodded. "The first night."

Matthew smacked his forehead again. "Oh God."

I reached for his arm and lowered it to the table. "There is nothing wrong with your laugh."

"He's right," Richard said. "We wouldn't have dragged you up the stairs that second night if you bothered us in any way." I was glad he was there. I had no idea how to reassure.

Matthew shook his head and smiled. Despite our words, he held back on the laugh.

I wanted to bury my face in his neck and hear him laugh while I nipped at his skin. But if I started there, I wouldn't be able to stop. I cleared my throat. "As I've said, this isn't my thing. For whatever reason, I can't seem to give you up yet. But dating, a relationship..." I shook my head several times. "That isn't something I do. I keep telling myself I can always walk away."

"Of course you can," Richard said. "Any of us can. If you want out, all you have to do is say so. That's how dating works, Luke."

"Shut up."

That time Matthew laughed.

The rest of the dinner passed with little conversation. We'd already talked more than I imagined most guys did on a first date. But it seemed to be Richard's way. I liked that he cared to understand what I wanted from them. I just wish I knew what the hell that was.

When we finished eating, Richard carried an armful of dishes to the kitchen. He set everything on the counter and stared into the sink. He didn't move or speak. He didn't turn on the water or scrape off the plates.

Matthew glanced over at me, the confusion evident.

"Richard? Something wrong?" I asked.

"Why don't you live here? Both of you."

The soda bottle in Matthew's hand dropped to the table, and its carbonated contents fizzled and bubbled up.

I stood. "What?"

Richard stepped around the kitchen counter. "Let me explain. You need a place to stay. Matthew said he wanted to get out of his mom's place. I've got the extra rooms upstairs. I understand this isn't what you're used to. You can stay until you find someplace else. We'll have a good time. No strings attached." The bulk of his body seemed to grow with each step closer to the table. He lifted one arm, then the other, and tucked the ends of his fingers into the pockets on his jeans. Each bicep flexed with the movement. He heaved a deep breath, and his chest puffed out. "Imagine all the ways we can get to know each other."

He had experience negotiating for success, and he was using his finest assets.

"We don't have to live together to fuck and get acquainted," I said.

"Right. But it helps in the way we like to live."

My eyes narrowed.

"You like to fuck two guys at one time, right?" he said.

"I believe we've all demonstrated we like it."

Richard snorted. "I don't believe you want to be at the club every weekend for the rest of your life." I opened my mouth to deny that, but he held up a hand and stepped closer. "My point is, you can keep on playing the field and have your fun, or you can try to make something work where you can live every day in the lifestyle you're drawn to. No more waiting to hit the club to find what you need. You'll come home, and there we'll be. Ready to fuck you, suck you, tie you up, and do all those little things you're quick to tell us you need each time we've met you."

He knew how to push my buttons like no one I'd ever met at the club, or anywhere else in my life.

I stole a look at Matthew. He stared up at Richard like he saw the answer to a prayer but couldn't believe it was being offered. He couldn't be expecting anything long-term. He'd been around the block. He had to know how these things worked.

"This is ridiculous," I said. "Guys don't move in together—not like this." I gestured between the three of us.

If I stayed, there'd be no way in hell I'd know when my father's men found me again. I wouldn't have my cameras. I wouldn't be able to watch my back all the time. It couldn't work.

But I needed to move anyway, to get my father's men off my ass for a while. I couldn't let my father have his victory. Richard's was as good a place as any to hide for a few weeks. At least I'd be getting the best sex of my life.

Oh God. "I've got reasons why I live alone."

Richard stood still. He focused in on my face as if he needed to burn my image into his memory. Maybe he thought he'd have to give my description to the cops someday.

I stared into his green eyes. What would it feel like to fuck him first thing in the morning? To go down on him in the shower? To wake up next to him? My breath quickened. I couldn't stand there and continue on. I'd hyperventilate before long.

I grabbed the bottle of soda from the table and took a long series of gulps. When I set the empty bottle down, I realized I'd grabbed Matthew's. I opened my mouth to apologize. "It'll just be for a few weeks."

"However long you need." Richard leaned into me. His lips brushed my temple.

The affection without any sexual intention was new for me. I expected to freak over it, and when I didn't, I was more confused than ever.

"How about you, Matthew?" Richard asked.

Matthew gawked at him, his eyes wide. "Why?"

Richard crouched next to his chair. "I'm offering my place because I want to. I like to help when I can. Luke needs a place to stay. And I'd like you to be here too. I think we'll have a great time together." He wrapped his hand around Matthew's neck and drew him in for a kiss. "I'd like you both to stay for as long as you need or as long as it works out."

"I can't stay here. I mean—we'd have to talk about money and stuff."

"Why can't you stay? I thought—"

"I can't afford to pay you for this place and help my mom."

"I'm not asking you to pay anything."

Matthew's stare met the far wall.

"Kid."

"What do you want from us? What are you expecting from us?" Matthew looked at me as if he wondered if I had the same question.

Richard straightened, his hands on his hips. "I'm not expecting anything, not in the way you're implying. I offered my place because I wanted to." He paused and rubbed a hand over the back of his neck. "I have no interest in keeping you around for my own amusement." He sighed and dropped next to Matthew again. "Listen, let's not talk about money. We'll see how this goes first. See how long you guys can stay, or want to stay. For now, you're crashing at my place. All right?"

"I guess that sounds okay."

"Then you'll stay?"

"I'll stay."

A loud, uncontrollable laugh spilled out of my mouth. "What the hell are we doing?" I slumped into the chair beside Matthew. "God, I lose all ability to think when I'm with you two."

Richard raised an eyebrow. "I'm beginning to understand that's a good thing, Luke."

Matthew laughed. The sound eased my nerves. I was already addicted to that low giggle.

Hell, I was already addicted to both of them. Maybe I needed to sign up with a twelve-step program before this got out of hand.

Chapter Ten

I left Richard's house unsure how I'd gotten into what I'd agreed to, and why the hell I'd agreed to it in the first place.

I was pretty far gone in lust when he'd suggested Matthew and I stay. If he'd asked me at the Haven before he'd fucked me, I'd have laughed until I puked. But having the man's dick up my ass did things to me. Combine that with Matthew, and I had no control left.

My attraction to them was powerful, and it hadn't waned since I'd met them. And it wasn't just the sex. I liked them. Matthew was funny. His good mood rubbed off on me. And Richard knew how to work me and push me like no one else. He was the take-control kind of person. I'd never have guessed I would agree to live with a man like him. Not considering the father I'd been on the run from most of my adult life.

The best sex of my life had seriously fucked with how I liked to live.

We'd exchanged phone numbers, and Richard promised he'd check his schedule before he called to tell us what time to be at his house on Friday night.

In less than one week, I'd be living with them. Two men I hardly knew. Two men I'd already slept with. Two men I'd spent the night with, talking, laughing, eating, with not one ounce of cum spilled.

It was all too much to contemplate.

In spite of that, a smile emerged on my face as I hailed a cab. What would my father say if he knew? It would drive the man crazy.

But when the hell had I ever done anything to either please or piss the man off? Never. I did what I wanted to do. I played by my own rules.

Then why the hell am I breaking all of them? To be with a man whose thick cock filled me like no one else's? Or a guy—not much more than a kid—who could keep a man hard after a long blowjob?

No, it was more than that. Was I ready?

I stopped off at a bar a block from my apartment. After three beers in less than fifteen minutes, I felt no concerns at all and laughed at how I'd have to pack my shit by the next Friday.

By the seventh beer, the bartender cut me off. Never did hold my alcohol all that well.

I'd just taken a swig of coffee when a man sat on the stool next to mine. I watched him swallow a gulp of his beer. Dark hair complemented his high cheekbones and bronzed skin. He set the bottle on the bar and glanced my way. He looked familiar. Had I slept with him before?

Even though the bar was usually heterosexual when it came to pickups, I was convinced the man was going to ask me for what I'd just agreed to give up—a quick fuck in the men's room or a back-alley suck.

"You're pretty drunk," Mr. Not-So-Innocent said.

"Uh-huh."

The heat of his body washed over me as he closed the distance between us. "You need help to find your way home?"

"Nope. Got it covered." My words slurred. I was fucked. Even in a non-inebriated capacity, it'd be hard to turn the man down.

It wasn't like my dick controlled me, but some reactions were hard to ignore—especially when you hadn't had to do so for fifteen years.

His stare pierced me. It unnerved something deep in my chest. I forced myself to look away. I needed to finish the coffee, let a few minutes pass since my last drink, and hit the street. I didn't need to be sober to make it to my apartment.

"Your father wouldn't want anyone to see you like this."

His words sent a chill up my spine before my brain managed to capture their meaning. I whipped my head in his direction, and my sobering mind put all the pieces together.

Barry Fowler. He'd worked for my father as an assistant since I was in high school. He'd also managed my father's senatorial campaign. And obviously still worked for him, doing dirty little tasks like following the man's gay son into a bar. But he had never been one of the men following me before. *Why now?*

"Fuck you, asshole." I managed not to slur any of those words.

"No, I don't play for your team. You won't be getting a fuck from me." The man's voice had changed. It contained the same level of contempt my father's held when I last heard the man speak to me. The tone made his next words sound odd at best. "I want to make sure you get home safely. Get you out of here before someone sees you."

"No one knows who the hell I am. Leave me alone."

"I'm taking you home." His hand clutched my arm and yanked me off the stool.

"Don't touch me." I jerked away. Unsteady on my drunken feet, I stumbled two steps and groped for the barstool.

"I know it isn't far, but I'd prefer to help you get there before you do anything embarrassing."

"Embarrassing for me or my father?" I threw enough cash on the bar to cover my bill and stumbled toward the exit. I heard his steps behind me. I spun around. "Are you the one who was in my apartment?"

He crowded me against the wall.

"Did you find anything you liked? I have a dildo in the closet you should try. Although it might be too big for your tight ass."

"Shut up. Let's get you home." He yanked on my arm again.

I shoved him away. "Why does he always need to know where I live? Why does he have me followed?"

"I'm not here to answer your questions. I'm here to make sure nothing hurts your father."

"I'm not doing anything to him."

"You're entire life is a threat to him. Don't you get that? I've seen you. Every night you go to that club, I watch you walk off with man after man. You barely know them and you're up the stairs, getting your ass fucked all night. I should give the senator more details than he's asked for. Then maybe he'd stop playing these games. Then maybe he'd do what he needs to."

"And what's that?"

Fowler smirked.

I turned away and stormed out of the bar. I didn't look to see if he followed. There was no point. He and my father knew where I lived—and where I played.

Not for long.

In less than a week, I'd be playing and living at Richard's. If I was careful, they wouldn't find out for a while. Maybe long enough for me to get Matthew and Richard out of my system.

I staggered into my apartment and slammed the door closed. I headed straight for bed, and for the first time since I'd met Richard and Matthew, I didn't fight the images. I allowed myself to relive the moments of my nights with them—the touching, the kissing, the fucking, and even the talking.

Before I drifted off to sleep, I planned out several ways to get from my apartment to Richard's again without being followed. Neither

Richard nor Matthew had asked for any problems. They didn't deserve to be fucked with in that way.

And if the need arose, my father would fuck with them in all the horrible ways he was capable of.

Chapter Eleven

"You're moving in with them?"

The shock in Walter's voice confirmed he hadn't heard about my self-imposed, ill-conceived fate. Hearing someone else say the words aloud was worse than the repetition of it in my own mind.

I switched the phone to my other ear. "I think my brain melted. I guess that's what happens when you spend a night with the best fuck and the best suck you've ever had."

"Three nights," he said.

"Yeah. That's where I went wrong."

"I wouldn't say you've gone wrong, Luke. I told you I think they'll be good for you. But I had no idea it would have progressed this far already."

"I know. I mentioned needing a new place to live, and he asked me to stay for a few weeks. Then Matthew said he'd move in too. I don't know how it happened."

"How long can you make this work?"

"You mean how long until my father finds out? Or how long until I mess it up?"

"I meant your father."

"I don't know. Until I find a new apartment. I can't risk it for long."

"Decent of him to offer. Surprising, though."

"Yeah. I couldn't have hooked up with a guy who wanted to date for years before becoming exclusive, could I? No. I have to get with someone who not only asks me to keep it in my pants unless I'm with him and the kid but also wants me to move in with them."

"He asked for exclusivity?"

"Oh, yeah. And I agreed. We'll be getting tests and everything."

"You play it safe until you get those results, you hear?"

"I'm not an idiot. I won't be doing anything bare until I say it's okay. Forget any tests."

"Good for you, but...don't hold back on everything. The sex is one thing. That's your physical safety. But the emotional shit—getting to know them. Open yourself to some of it. Don't make it all about the sex. It isn't why he asked you there."

I knew that. And it had me reeling. If it was him being a nice guy and giving me a place to stay, or about a guaranteed, live-in fuck buddy, Richard's invitation wouldn't have concerned me, at least not as much. It was something else.

"Walter, I've agreed to give it a try. Yeah, mostly I've agreed to because I don't want to give up sleeping with them, but I'm at least going to try. That's all I can do."

"Yep. Just don't forget to try, Luke."

Asshole. I needed to find a friend who didn't know me so well.

* * * *

The next call came Tuesday night.

I carried a stack of briefs and socks from my bedroom into the living room and set them on the couch next to the ragged suitcase with duct tape securing its corners and clothes piled high inside. Another suitcase, in worse shape than the first, sat empty on the floor. I should've splurged on new bags, but I couldn't bring myself to give that much import to the move.

I went into the kitchen and removed the leftover pizza from the oven. My cell rang. I chucked the pan onto the stovetop. "Yeah."

"Luke?"

"Hi, Richard." I headed back to the living room, my dinner forgotten.

"I guess it's a good start you can recognize my voice with just your name."

"I haven't known anyone with a voice as deep as yours. It sort of does something to me." *Flirting.* I was flirting.

"I can talk all night, Luke." He laughed when I didn't respond. "I hope you don't mind, but I've already called Matthew. If you haven't noticed, he has a bit of a self-esteem issue. I thought it'd be good for him to know I called him first."

I plopped onto the couch next to the suitcase and draped an arm behind my head. "Very perceptive of you. Of course it doesn't bother me."

"I knew you'd understand. I have an early dinner meeting on Friday. I should be home by eight. I told Matthew to come at nine. Will that work for you?"

"Sure."

"Have you packed anything yet?"

"No."

"I thought not. You sure you don't want me to rent a truck?"

"I don't have much. I'm going to stash most of it at a friend's." I didn't bother to tell him I'd spent thirty minutes earlier convincing myself to take more than one change of clothes to his house. I considered the two suitcases a huge step.

"Matthew said he'd just bring a few bags too. I've got pretty much everything else you'll need here." He paused. "Okay, then. I'll see you at nine on Friday. And Luke? I'm looking forward to this."

"Uh...yeah."

He laughed with a deep bellow. "Okay. See you on Friday."

I hung up and shoved at the open luggage. It fell on the floor and spilled its contents.

I paced the living room like a caged animal searching for the weakest link in the fence. After twenty minutes, I hadn't found any way to get out of what I'd agreed to with Matthew and Richard. And I wasn't sure I wanted to find it even if it did exist. Instead, I returned to the suitcases and struggled to accept what my life would become.

Only I had no concept of what that was.

* * * *

I stopped at a clearance table in front of Desert Island Books, a bookstore boasting "the best collection of books to be stranded anywhere with." I stared into the reflection of the store window and scanned the crowd behind me. The busy plaza was host to an odd mix of people. Tourists sporting bag after bag of souvenirs from shops like City Skyline Gifts. Teenage boys with the dangerous combination of no money to spend and time to kill. And the occasional suburbanite family shopping for anything they couldn't get outside the city limits, like a basket of twenty-eight gourmet cheeses that no one in their right mind would eat.

None of them were whom I needed to see. I picked up the nearest book in a practiced shopper's move. Who'd spend $9.95 on a self-help book titled *Live Today Like it's Your Last* anyway? Maybe not the best book to read when you're stranded alone on a deserted island. Shouldn't there be something like *How to Survive on a Deserted Island*?

I dropped the book, picked up another, and scanned the crowd in the window's reflection again. A man sitting alone on a bench reading a newspaper caught my eye. He lowered the paper and glanced around the plaza, his gaze sweeping over my back along with everyone else. He raised the paper again, hiding more of his face than before.

Bingo.

I set the book down and hefted my laptop bag higher on my shoulder. I'd gotten pretty good at dodging them. It wouldn't take long. Except...my stalker was smiling, his paper folded on his lap, his arms out. A young boy ran toward him.

"Daddy!"

He scooped the small boy into his arms and gripped him in a bear hug. A woman trailed behind the boy, an infant cradled in her arms.

What were the chances my father hired an entire family to stalk me? Did I want to know?

I turned and watched them walk by. The family made their way to the end of the plaza and into an all-you-can-eat seafood joint. My gaze lingered on the boy's small hand tucked inside his father's.

I almost missed the man I needed to see. Thankfully, Tony's Seafood kept the large glass windows clean. There, under the neon sign indicating Tony's had the freshest fish in the city, was Fowler's reflection. He was leaning against the doorway to a souvenir shop behind me. He sported dark sunglasses and watched my back as intently as I watched him in the restaurant's window.

I'd left my apartment an hour earlier with the two suitcases in hand and my laptop bag over my shoulder. I'd already dropped off everything else I owned to Walter's the night before. As I stepped out of my place, I gave one last glance at the apartment. It looked identical to the day I'd moved in—minus one cheap folding chair. How had I spent over eight months in a place and not left any sign I'd been there? If I dropped off the planet, would anyone notice? Would anyone know I'd ever been alive? I shook my head and closed the door behind me. When did I get so maudlin?

I'd spent most of the week trying to figure out if I could take my surveillance cameras. And if I didn't, how long I'd even last at Richard's before my father's men or another reporter found me. I settled on ditching the cameras and taking a chance for once. A short-term plan. And despite that I usually did everything in those terms, it surprised me I didn't like thinking of Matthew and Richard as temporary. I'd taken one hell of a chance to start down a new path, and I wanted to give it a little time before I bailed. I also wanted to take every precaution I could manage.

I glanced at the table of books again as I pulled out my cell phone. Usually I'd weave in and out of stores to shake my tail, but I was running late. I still needed to get my bags from the hotel where I'd paid the cab driver to drop them off. And Fowler seemed a cut above my father's other men. Time for something more sophisticated. No sense taking a chance right off the bat.

All you had to mention to get someone stopped was a possible explosive hidden under a jacket and a public place like the Erie Street Market. I gave Fowler's description and hung up. I grabbed another book. *Love After 50: Learning to Love Yourself, Extra Baggage and All*. What kind of baggage did people living on a deserted island have? Jesus, were there this many screwed up people in the world? When did we stop making decisions without the advice of complete strangers? And when the hell did love gain such a rosy picture? Life after love sucked more than life before it. I should write that book. How long before it'd find its way onto the 70 percent off table?

Quick footsteps sounded farther down the plaza. I tossed the book onto the clearance table and faced him. Fowler didn't duck behind a nearby shopper or sales rack like so many of my father's other men did. He stared back at me. I threw him a smile and winked before heading into the bookstore.

An official sounding voice echoed in the plaza behind me. "Halt. Stand still and put your hands over your head."

My smile grew as I headed for the bookstore's rear entrance.

Chapter Twelve

Richard's house didn't seem near as large as it had the week before. The closer I got to it, the more it shrank in size. How could three men live together and not kill one another?

My hand hesitated over the doorbell.

For the past six months, I sat on a barstool at the Haven every Friday night. How had I gotten myself into packing a few bags and moving into another man's house instead? Only the fact that I was pretty sure I'd be getting laid regardless helped to ease the tension.

The door swung open. Richard wore a huge grin. "I thought Matthew'd beat you here."

"Me too. He sure is an excited shit."

"I think he might be too much for even the two of us to keep up with."

"Speak for yourself, old man."

"Hey now," he said, but his gaze told me he looked forward to all Matthew and I could dish out.

The anticipation of more sexual interaction with them calmed me, and my cock filled at the mere thought of how the night would go. Would Richard mind that I stood at his door sporting a hard-on? Not likely. He was as into fucking me as I was him. I was clear on that. Even if not much else about what we were doing made sense to me.

He motioned for me to step inside and relieved me of one of the suitcases. "Leave your stuff by the door until Matthew gets here. Then I'll show you around. You didn't get to see the whole place last time."

I slid my laptop bag off and set it with my suitcase. We stood a few feet apart and stared at each other.

He clasped his hands behind his back. "I'm glad you came." The words were low enough to qualify as a whisper.

The doorbell rang.

"That'll be our eager shit now," Richard said.

Matthew sported a broad smile. His wavy hair was windblown,

more scattered than usual. His cheeks were pink, flushed from the cool night air—or excitement. Did I want to know which?

Richard grabbed two of Matthew's bags, and the small man stepped inside the house. He didn't move to touch Richard in any way, and his rigid stance surprised me. Richard placed his hand upon the younger man's shoulder and patted him.

"Hi," Matthew said. His smile dimmed. He didn't make eye contact with either of us.

Fuck this shit.

I traversed the distance between us and sealed his lips with a kiss. My tongue explored as I moved us backward until his back hit the wall behind him. The bag slung over his shoulder dropped to the floor with a loud thud, and then his hands were all over me. Richard came in close and gripped my hips.

This is more like it.

I wrenched my mouth away from Matthew's and groaned at Richard's touch. Matthew snaked his hand around me, and he pulled Richard in, pinning me between them. The two kissed over my shoulder. Damn, they looked best up close.

"God, kid," Richard said. "I missed your kisses." He licked a line down my neck.

"Yeah," I said. The word spread out longer than normal for a one-syllable word. I rocked between them.

Matthew smiled at me, the look vulnerable with a hint of something more I hadn't ever seen from any other man. Or maybe I had. I just didn't want to remember what it meant or admit Matthew looked at me like that. I ran my thumb over his cheek. He focused his eyes on mine.

He leaned forward and kissed me again.

Yeah, this is better.

Much better.

It was exactly what I needed.

I threw my head back on Richard's shoulder and skimmed my hands over his thick thighs. His muscles twitched.

I breathed deep. He smelled clean, crisp. I wanted more of that scent, more of them.

Richard let go of me and stepped away. "Glad you're here. Both of you."

Matthew tilted his head back to the wall. A low giggle floated out on his next breath. "I love moving day." He leaned in and placed a chaste kiss upon my lips. I tensed. Something snapped inside me, a realization fifteen years of sleeping alone hadn't prepared me for. This wasn't just sex. I was spending the night with them.

Matthew laid a hand on my arm. "What's wrong?"

I shrugged him off. "Nothing." I turned toward Richard. "So I take it we're waiting on the sex for later."

Matthew laughed again, and Richard replaced his serious expression with a slow, delighted grin. He moved out of the foyer and gestured for us to follow. "Let me show you around the place. We'll start in the basement." He threw us a coy smirk and headed into the kitchen.

When I didn't move to follow, Matthew glanced at me. "You coming?"

"He's really giving us a tour?"

"I think so."

"I haven't lived anywhere requiring a tour." Not since my parents' house with its five baths and two dining rooms.

Matthew laughed. "Me neither."

Richard popped his head around the corner. "Come on. You don't want to miss this."

* * * *

He directed us down a set of stairs just off the kitchen. The staircase opened to a large finished basement. A laundry area, weights, and a treadmill occupied one side of the space. The other half was divided off from the rest of the room with walls. Richard opened a door, and we slipped inside.

A double bed with a slatted headboard sat in the middle of the room. Chains hung from two slats. Each had leather-lined handcuffs affixed to the ends. On the small bedside table sat a jar full of condoms and lube. A few feet away from the bed was a long black bench with several rings for gripping or restraining. I knew it could be used as a spanking bench—the club had similar pieces—but there was no sign of whips, crops, or floggers.

Richard opened a cabinet door and revealed ropes and an assortment of silk ties. He pointed to several metal loops secured in the walls and floor—great locations for tying someone up.

Matthew sat on the bench. He grinned and slipped his hand into one of the upper rings.

I ran my fingers over the chains, the handcuffs, the loops. My cock filled with each touch of metal and leather.

Richard's breath struck the skin behind my ear. "You like it? I set it up special. It seems Matthew and I love to restrain you when we play." He cupped the front of my pants. "Hold that thought. There's more of the place to see." He backed away.

Matthew's fingers tightened on the metal loop, and he smiled at me again before following Richard out.

We moved through the house and into the living room. Spacious, tidy, and stark. The only adornment on the walls was a considerable painting hanging over the fireplace. A sea captured at night during a storm. The raging, choppy water stretched out over half the picture. A tall lighthouse filled the other half and poured a beam of light onto the dark, stormy waters. It reminded me of one of those pieces sold at the traveling art fairs advertised on TV between an infomercial selling plastic gloves that peeled potatoes and an episode of the original *Knight Rider*. Something he bought to fill the space, nothing more.

Matthew flopped onto the couch. "Comfy."

I spotted a small bar in the corner of the room. No booze, no glasses, the shelves bare, the cabinet doors locked shut. When Matthew wasn't looking, I raised an eyebrow at Richard. He shrugged and moved through an open doorway that led to his office.

A large desk sat in the middle of the room and dominated the space. I stepped around it and stopped at the picture window behind the desk. No curtains or other window treatments hindered the impressive cityscape. The view alone had to increase the value of the house.

"I work here when I can," Richard said, "but most days I go into the office downtown. If I'm not home, I want you both to treat the place like it's yours."

"You're not worried about us being here without you?" Matthew asked.

"Nope, not at all." He gave Matthew a brief pat on the ass before he led us through the living room to the stairs.

We walked the hall of the second floor and peeked in doorways. "There are two baths," Richard said. "Three bedrooms. You can each have one of the extra rooms."

I glanced inside the closest room. "There's no bed."

He leaned over my shoulder and peered in. "Said I had the rooms. Just didn't think through the rest."

"Sure you didn't."

"You're seeing right through me, aren't you?"

Matthew laughed from where he stood across the hall.

"I always have a plan." Richard's hand landed on my hip, and he closed the distance between us, bringing my body to him. "I want you in my bed." He stepped away and sauntered down the hall to the master bedroom. Matthew trailed after him without hesitation.

I let a smile form and fade before following them.

"Since we can't all fit our clothes and shit in this room, you can use the others. But I'd like for us to sleep in here together. Are you okay with that?"

Matthew nodded several times. He went still and sank to the bed.

I surveyed the room. There were no clothes thrown about. No books or magazines tossed next to the bed. A lone gold watch lay on one nightstand, a clock radio on the other. The king-size bed seemed small in terms of fitting the three of us—an assessment more about me sleeping in such close proximity to two other people, something I'd never done, rather than any real measurement of the bed versus the three of us.

The silence reached me. Richard sat on the bed. A troubled stare contorted his features. Matthew's expression was just as pronounced, his head cocked to the side.

"Oh yeah," I said. "I assumed as much when you offered your place."

Richard's expression relaxed. "You're gonna keep surprising me, aren't you?"

"I'll try if that's what you're into."

Matthew dropped his head as he held back yet another laugh.

I stepped into the bathroom doorway. The walk-in shower and oversize bathtub weren't a real surprise considering the rest of the house. "Nice tub."

Richard moved to stand beside me, brushing his hand along my hip. "I do enjoy a good splurge now and then. We should all fit."

Matthew made a small sound with his exhale from the other room.

I ran my hand up Richard's side and said, "I think he likes the idea." We had to be done with the tour. My fingers swept over the front of his shirt. The muscles of his abdomen quivered beneath the fabric.

"I think he does." His hand cupped my groin. I wasn't as hard as in the basement, but I was getting there. My cock knew where the night would end, and it was just waiting to get the right signal that it was time to play.

Richard kissed me, pulling me firm against him.

Yep, that was the signal.

I gripped his hips and mashed us together. He shoved me back against the doorjamb. A dull pain shot up my spine, but I didn't bother to move. His hard body on mine was enough to wipe out anything else. Anything except the intense feeling I was missing something. Someone.

Matthew.

I pulled away from Richard and glanced into the bedroom. "Jesus, kid."

"Shit," Richard said.

Matthew lay on his back, naked, his knees bent, his feet flat on the bed, his hard cock lying against his lower abdomen. One hand was cupping his balls. The other was wrapped around his prick, not tugging, but teasing the tip with his thumb.

Richard twisted his fingers in the fabric of my shirt and dragged me with him to the bed. "You are one hell of a sexy man, Matthew."

Lust flooded Matthew's voice. "You two are incredible. I could come just watching you kiss." He stroked his cock. "I want you."

I removed clothes as I spoke. "You're going to get us."

"Yes, you are," Richard said. "What do you want tonight, kid?"

My cock stiffened more with Richard's usual question.

Matthew propped himself on his elbows and spread his legs wider. "I want the weight of both of you pressing down on me. Both of you filling me, pushing into me. I want you to fuck me harder than ever."

I spared a quick glance at Richard. He was undressed and was eyeing Matthew like he could devour him in one move.

"Go get him, Luke. I'll get the condoms." Richard dashed to the nightstand and fished out a handful of condoms and lube. He threw his prizes near Matthew's head.

I crawled up the bed and lowered my weight onto Matthew. He looped his calves over the backs of my thighs. The fine coat of his leg hair grazed along my own. My groin pressed down, his pressed up, and his mouth met mine. His hands clutched, groped. He needed me, needed us. I moved lower and ran my tongue over his chest. I took a nipple in my mouth and his balls in my hand. Richard joined me, and we worked him together.

Words poured out in between licks and bites. "He's right, Matthew. You're so damn sexy, lying here all ready for us."

"I want you, need you, Luke. You and Richard."

I tugged at his nipple again.

He bucked and cried out. "Harder."

"What? Did you say you want us to stop?" I withdrew my mouth and hand. Richard got in on the game and jerked away too. A deep chuckle spilled out of his chest.

"God, no. Please don't stop." The distraught sound of Matthew's voice almost made me give up on the teasing. Almost.

"Oh, you want this harder?" I wrapped my hand around his dick and yanked the nipple with my teeth. Richard followed suit on Matthew's other nipple.

"God, yes. Need…"

"Need us to what?" I asked. "Need us to go get your bags so you can unpack? Need us to make you something to eat? What do you need?"

His hips rose off the bed. "Please, Luke, fill me."

I didn't know what possessed me to do it, but the words were out, and I didn't want to take them back. "Yeah. Well, if Richard gets his way, I'll be filling you with all of me someday. Shooting into your tight ass." I didn't let the words bother me. My cock was leading the show, and it needed to get inside him. I'd worry on the promises I made later.

Richard moaned then, a low rumble deep in his chest. I traced up the muscles of Matthew's body with my mouth, planted a last kiss on his lips, and knelt before him. Richard handed me lube and a condom, and then he straddled Matthew's chest.

"Going to get inside you now," I said.

"Yeah, please. God. Never wanted anyone the way I want you guys." Matthew's words tightened my chest. It wasn't the stiffness of nerves but of something I couldn't describe.

I worked the lube into him and watched his body take my fingers in. He moved down and fucked himself deeper. I eased back. I wanted him to be dying to have my dick plunge inside him, fill him better than the tormenting fingers.

I glanced up. Richard had one knee beside Matthew's head, and his other leg stretched out straight in a straddle that wouldn't crush Matthew with those sturdy thighs. Matthew hummed as he licked and sucked Richard's dick.

I took his hips in my hands. Once my cock slid all the way in, Matthew wrapped his legs around me, begging me for more, but I didn't move. I watched Richard's ass in front of me. When he began shallow thrusts into Matthew's mouth, his ass clenching as he moved, I followed suit and relished the heat and pressure of Matthew surrounding my dick.

What would he feel like with nothing in the way? The idea of fucking bare had never been a possibility before. I never even considered what it would feel like, or whether or not I'd want it. It wasn't to be.

Damn. Now I want it. Can't stop thinking about it.

Then I couldn't think about anything other than the overwhelming sensations of my body. I pushed harder, trying my best to give Matthew the fuck he'd asked for.

I took him in my hand, loving the slide of him over my palm, the slight twitch and swell as I worked him faster. A few more pulls and a brush of the head and he came. His body tightened around me with each shiver of his pleasure, and the pressure finished me off fast.

"Matthew!" I screamed and plunged deep into him one last time.

It keeps getting better. How is that possible?

I wanted to fall forward and collapse onto him, but Richard still straddled him. I breathed deep and took in the scent of our combined release and the sound of Matthew's slick mouth working Richard's cock.

Richard gasped and his body stiffened. After a few deep breaths, he rolled off and lay on his back. "Damn."

I ducked under Matthew's leg and dropped to the bed.

"Matthew, are you okay?" Richard asked. "Did I hurt you?"

I lifted my head. What the hell could be wrong?

"I'm fine," Matthew said. "You didn't hurt me."

"I try not to push in so hard. Not into someone's mouth. My dick isn't the biggest, but it isn't small."

"Not complaining here. It's a beautiful dick."

"Thanks. You didn't gag like most do, but I should have some self-control. You just melt me. You should teach a class or something."

"Yep," I said. "I believe I said he's addictive."

"And sweet," Richard said. "Don't forget sweet."

I laughed through a satisfied sigh, the sound like nothing I'd ever heard from myself.

Matthew got out of the bed and headed for the bathroom. "Fuck you." I couldn't look away from his tight ass, his lean hips.

"No, Matthew," I called after him. "You didn't fuck anyone. We fucked you. Pretty damn good too if I do say so myself." Richard laughed with me. The sound of running water was the only response from the bathroom.

Then the water stopped, and Matthew stepped out with a smile on his face. "Yeah, you did."

He bounced across the room and climbed into the bed. For a moment, I found myself positioned between the two men.

Panic surged.

Matthew kissed me, then crawled over me to offer the same to Richard. He settled in between us like there was nowhere else he wanted to be.

Richard spoke his next words in the softest tone he'd used yet. "Hey, Matthew?"

"Yeah?"

"That was the first time you told us what you wanted in bed."

"Yeah?"

"Yep. I'm glad you're here. You too, Luke."

"Thanks," I said, the panic gone. A relaxed contentment had replaced it. And I didn't care what had caused it. I was glad to accept it.

I'd seriously lost my mind.

Chapter Thirteen

I woke up with someone else in bed with me for the first time in fifteen years.

Since college.

Since Tim.

Matthew lay curled between us, asleep on his stomach where he had landed the night before, one arm draped over Richard's chest, one of his legs tangled with mine.

I had figured the first morning would be awkward, but until the moment my eyes opened, I hadn't a clue how strange it'd be.

It wasn't my bed. Not my apartment. Not my usual life.

I needed to get my ass into the office. I wasn't going to change my Saturday routine for anyone. I spotted the alarm clock on the stand next to Richard. 5:45 a.m. I had some time. I dropped my head to the pillow and listened to the rhythmic breathing beside me.

The rock of the mattress woke me. I hadn't fallen back asleep in the morning in years.

I should check the time, get up, and—

A warm hand lifted my cock. I drew in a sharp breath as one of my balls was captured by wet heat.

My eyes shot open wide. The blankets covered the figure working me over. I checked out the other side of the bed where Richard still lay on his back, sound asleep.

Of course. I should have known Matthew's technique.

He released me and squirmed up the bed until he popped his head out from under the blankets. "Can I suck you?"

"Do you always ask so many questions?" I reached for a condom and handed it to him.

He smiled, ducked back under the blankets, and rolled the condom over my dick. Pressure and heat engulfed the crown as his steady hand jacked the base.

"Matthew. Feels good."

He moaned in response. I snaked my arm under the covers and rested my hand on his head, needing to connect with him more, my palm sliding over his hair with his every move.

Richard stirred and rolled to his side. His gaze switched between my face and the blanket-covered head bobbing over me as his own hand moved under the blankets in a quick stroke.

"Kiss me," I said. He slid over without delay. His mouth crashed against mine. Our spit mixed, tongues tasted. Richard's hand flew faster and faster. I brought my free hand to his cock, and he moved his out of the way without complaint, thrusting into my touch.

I had no idea of the time, and it didn't matter. I couldn't have cared less if I made it to work that day or any other. Spending the morning in bed with them was the best Saturday in a long time.

Richard came first. His dick pulsated in my hand, the smell of his cum strong even from under the blankets. I kept touching him, spreading his cum over his cock, working him through every last twitch. Matthew's head bobbed faster. He sucked harder. I released Richard and arched. "Yes!"

Matthew brought me back down with slow swirls of his tongue even as his hips pumped against me when he came. He crawled up the bed and straddled me, smiling when his head popped out from under the blankets.

"Why did you do that?" I asked.

He shrugged. "I wanted to."

"Why me and not Richard?"

Richard sat up. "'Cause he knows you're the most likely of us to freak and bolt first thing this morning, bags in hand. Might as well show you what you'll be missing if you left so soon."

Matthew blushed and nodded. Then he rolled onto his back in the middle of the bed and laughed. I'd never been with a man who laughed in bed the way he did. It was a good sound to hear first thing in the morning.

* * * *

Matthew and I carried our bags up the stairs—managing everything in one trip—and paused at the top. Richard appeared at the end of the hall as naked as when we went to bed the night before. He waved us forward. "C'mon. I left you some drawers in here. You can put the rest in the spare rooms."

I selected the room farthest from the master bedroom and closest to the stairs. I took a more careful inventory than I had the night before: a closet, small desk, dresser, chair, and bookshelf. All of it nicer than anything I'd had since I lived with my parents. I deposited my bags and unpacked the items I needed for the day.

I walked back into the bedroom carrying my clothes and shaving kit to find Matthew on the bed with Richard. The two were sharing a lazy kiss.

"Should I use the bathroom down the hall?"

"No," Richard said, "you can use the one in here." He returned his attention to Matthew. "Your mouth is a fantastic way to start the day."

"You should feel it on your dick when you wake up," I said over my shoulder.

I heard Matthew say, "Maybe tomorrow," before I shut the bathroom door.

The showerhead was decadent and the hot water like a massage. Better than any shower at my apartment. Well, any shower not involving an imaginary blowjob from Matthew.

I shook my head under the spray. I could probably have that fantasy come true since I lived with the man. Funny how my life had changed from fantasy to reality in a flash. I didn't let the thought linger. No part of my current situation was a wish fulfilled. Was it?

I stepped out of the shower, shaved, and was ready to head out when I spotted a new bottle of cologne on the counter. Before I could stop myself, it was in my hands and the lid was off. What the hell was I doing? The stuff smelled good on him, but did I really need to be standing in the man's bathroom sniffing his personal hygiene products?

But one whiff and that thought vanished.

Not what Richard had worn the night before. The shit smelled like my goddamn father.

I wrenched the lid back on and shoved the bottle to the far end of the counter. I opened the bathroom door, a towel wrapped around my waist. Richard sat alone on the edge of the bed.

"Sorry to keep you waiting for your own bathroom."

"Not a problem. You live here now too. At least for now." He winked. "Matthew's using the shower down the hall. I'm in no hurry to get going. I just need to get to the office for a few hours to prep for a meeting."

He stood and approached me. His naked body came in close, but no part of his skin touched mine. "I thought about stepping in to join you, but I'm trying to keep my desire for all things intimate in check. I know this is new for you. It wasn't easy for you to wake up with us."

"You seem to think you know a lot."

"I can sense a lot. I'm hoping someday you'll feel relaxed here." He moved past me.

The slide of his arm along mine had my skin tingling. Need settled in my balls. My nostrils flared. Why did the simplest of his touches drive me crazy? I smelled the remnants of the past twelve hours all over him. Semen and sweat and the cologne from the previous night. "Can I ask you a favor?"

He turned to me. "Sure."

I pointed to the bottle on the counter. "Is that new?"

"It is."

"Don't wear it around me."

"Bad memories?"

"No. Just…you want to think of your dad when you're having sex?"

"Got it." He grabbed the full bottle and threw it in the trash.

"Thanks."

He gave a nod and stepped into the shower.

I dressed and headed to the kitchen, relieved to find a fresh pot of coffee already brewed. I opened cabinets in search of a cup and sat on a stool at the counter.

Matthew strolled in wearing jeans and a tight-as-hell black T-shirt with *Linkin Park* scrawled across his chest in gray lettering, his hair wet and somewhat straight. He spotted my coffee and headed to the pot. I pointed to the cabinet.

He fetched a cup and sat next to me. "You hungry?"

"I'll grab something on the way to the office. My Saturday morning ritual."

"You work far from here?"

"Yeah. I used to walk from my apartment. It was closer, and I don't have a car. I guess I'll hit the subway."

"I can drop you at the subway," Richard said, "or at your office." A clean, woodsy smell floated in with him. Simple, intoxicating. The same as the night before. And nothing like the bottle I'd found. He was dressed in slacks and a dress shirt, reminiscent of the first night at the club.

"Thanks," I said. "I like to walk for the exercise, but today, I'll take the ride to the subway. Not sure how long it'll take me to get there on foot."

"I'll find out," Matthew said. "I have to go to work for a couple of hours this afternoon. I'll let you know tonight."

"Thanks, kid."

Richard filled a travel mug with coffee. "Before we get going, I've got something for you." He fished an envelope out of his pocket and removed two keys. He handed one to each of us. "These are for the house. They work on the front and back doors."

Matthew ran a finger over the silver key and was quiet as he set it on the counter in front of him.

"You don't have to do this," I said.

"What? The keys?"

"Yeah. We don't know how long we're staying."

"If the three of us work out, I'm not going to kick you out of my house. You can stay as long as you need."

"Okay." Arguing with him seemed pointless. I dug in my pocket for my own keys and added the new one to the ring.

"I'll be ready to go in ten minutes," he said, and left the room with a grin plastered on his face.

I stood. "Have a good day, kid."

Matthew shifted in his seat. "You too." Then he smiled, his dark eyes focused on me.

Fuck if I couldn't get used to that look every morning.

* * * *

The bang of pots and pans greeted me as I stepped into Richard's. I followed the sounds and paused in the kitchen doorway. Matthew had his arms buried in soapy water, the suds climbing up past his elbows. Soap bubbles floated in the air over his head. How much detergent had he used?

He seemed lost in his own world, unaware of my presence. I leaned against the doorway and watched him fish out a bowl and rinse it.

I had stayed at work a few hours later than I expected. The recent distraction of lust had me further behind schedule at work. The added precautions on the way home didn't help.

It also didn't help that I spent two hours scanning Google results for one reporter named Mark Summers. Mostly his bylines with *The Washington Times*. The man's reporting habits didn't surprise me. He had found me when few people knew I existed.

Summers had a knack for locating dirt on anyone of import. Actors, politicians, sports personalities, Fortune 500 CEOs, basically the top 1 percent of the income bracket. It seemed like a sleazy way to make a living—pulling out people's hidden skeletons, no matter how old the bones, no matter how genuine the layers of dust covering them were.

The next question: Did he already have something on my father?

Any thoughts of Summers or my father were gone, though, as I watched Matthew. My gaze traveled to his ass. I didn't want to scare him, but I wanted to touch his fine body. Wasn't that one of the benefits Richard mentioned? I stepped close and pressed along his length. He sighed and leaned into me.

Right. Matthew wouldn't be startled by physical contact.

I ran my lips up the side of his neck. My nose grazed his skin. "You smell nice. Like cinnamon and sugar."

"Luke." His voice embraced a low moan with the sound of my name mixed in. Matthew wrapped his arm around me and cupped my ass with a wet hand. "I made apple pie for dessert." He rotated his ass and squeezed mine. "You like herb chicken and roasted potatoes?"

I crushed my groin to his ass and wished like hell I could do more. But he'd made food. I stepped back and sat on a stool. "Sounds good. That was nice of you."

"Nah. It's no big deal. I like to cook."

"Where is he?"

Matthew nodded toward the hall. "Working in his office. He had some calls to make."

"What was it like when he came home?"

Matthew dried his hands on a towel and leaned his forearms on the counter before me. "Weird. I felt like a wife meeting my husband at the door." He let out a giggle. His head shook with the laughter. "And then I didn't know what to talk to him about. At this point, I know more about what he likes in bed and how his dick feels in my mouth than I do about him. Don't get me wrong, I'm happy to be here. I'm just not sure how to get over the weirdness."

"I guess we'll either get over it or this won't work out."

Matthew straightened and frowned.

I wanted to reach out and distract him with more touching, but I didn't want him to think all I expected from him was sex. "I'm gonna head upstairs to change."

"Okay. Food's almost ready. I'll give you a holler if you aren't back in time." He returned to the sink and fished out another bowl from the soapy water.

"Leave the dishes. I'll help after we eat." I didn't wait for a response.

When I returned a few minutes later, Richard sat on a stool at the kitchen counter. He was watching Matthew check the contents of the oven. I joined him, unable to look away from the smaller man. Matthew moved with energy and coordination I never possessed at any time in my life. I wasn't accustomed to spending so much time out of bed with two men whom I wanted with such ferocity. My dick was having a hard time understanding the delay.

Matthew turned, threw a paper towel in the trash, and smiled at us, his expression surprised, horny. "Food's ready. Uh, should we eat here again or in the dining room?"

Richard stood. "Here's fine." He pulled three glasses from the cabinet. "You guys want water? Milk? Soda?"

I pushed aside the craving for a cold beer. "Water's good."

The food tasted delicious. Better than the frozen chicken nuggets and corn chips I'd had the night before.

"This apple pie is fabulous," Richard said. "I haven't had anything so good since my mom's."

I saw the hint of a smile before Matthew stuffed another bite into his mouth.

As we ate the dessert, Richard asked Matthew about his day, and the two made conversation easily. Matthew talked about how much he despised his new boss and the inventory glitch at work where they'd received three hundred Britney Spears bobblehead pens instead of her new CD. Richard added his own comments about a business deal he was working on to purchase real estate along the lakefront.

It was the longest we'd sat together without discussing sex. Richard and Matthew were interesting, and together they were a comfortable blend of refined authority and lighthearted exuberance. The awkwardness faded away with the food.

Once we polished off the pieces of pie, I helped Richard clear the dishes.

Matthew sat at the counter while we worked. "Richard?"

"Yeah?"

"Thanks for letting me cook."

"Thank you for doing it."

"How long have you lived here?"

"A year. I used to have a house on the north side near the river, but I had to sell it. I needed a change."

"Did you grow up around here?"

I handed Richard the last two plates and sat next to Matthew. His curiosity astounded me.

Richard closed the dishwasher and hit the start button. "No. I'm from New York. I moved here after college. I head back to visit my parents and my sister's family on holidays when I can. My dad and I are pretty close. He taught me a lot of what I know about business, how to work with people."

"Any other family?"

"No one I'm close to. How about you? Just you and your mom?"

"Yeah. I've got an aunt and uncle in Texas, but I haven't seen them in years. My mom's great. I came out to her right before my dad ran off. She's been real supportive of me. Always asking if I'm gonna get a boyfriend. At first, I thought me getting serious with someone scared her—like she didn't mind I was gay as long as she didn't have to see it." He ducked his head and straightened a stack of paper napkins on the counter. "Then I realized it was that I might never find someone that bothered her."

I envied the innocent love he showed for his mother. I'd never know the feeling again, and the reminder hit me hard.

Richard watched Matthew and said, "I'm glad you have her."

"Thanks. How about you, Luke?"

I was quiet for a moment. "My parents live here in the city. I don't speak with either of them—or, I should say, they don't speak to me. They couldn't accept I was gay, and they chose to ignore me rather than change themselves."

Both men sported pity-filled expressions.

I thumped my knuckles on the countertop. "Don't worry about it. I'm not the first gay man to lose his family over the issue of where he likes to stick his dick."

"That's still a shitty way for family to treat you," Richard said.

Matthew reached out and touched my arm. "Yeah. Some of my friends have had to deal with that. It pisses me off."

"Thanks."

Richard stepped around the counter. "Do either of you have plans for the evening?"

Matthew gave his usual silent shake of his head.

"You got something in mind?" I asked.

Richard grinned. "Want to try out the basement?"

Matthew stood so fast the wooden stool wobbled behind him. Its feet tapped the tiled floor. He reached back and steadied it.

"I think Matthew says yes. Luke?"

"Fuck, yes."

* * * *

We stepped into the makeshift bedroom, and I wandered around the bed to the opposite side of the room, unsure what the festivities would include or what I wanted, which was odd. I could normally define my sexual preferences in great detail at any moment.

Matthew sat on the bench. His fingers traced the metal handholds, his gaze darting between Richard and me.

Richard didn't ask his usual question about what we wanted. He strode across the room and had me in his arms before the door swung shut behind him. His lips were a mere inch from my mouth when he spoke, his guttural whisper loud enough for Matthew to hear. "I want you tied up again."

I groaned my approval and rocked my pelvis against him.

"Only this time," he said, "I want to watch Matthew do it. I like to watch him move."

"He does have a fantastic way with his body."

"God, yes."

I glanced at Matthew. His mouth hung open. He didn't move a muscle until he swallowed. Did he like the idea? Did it bother him to tie me up?

He stood. "I can do that." He gripped my hips and pulled me to the bed with him. Our mouths and tongues collided as he unbuttoned my shirt. Even beneath the garlic and rosemary lingering in his mouth, the taste of Matthew was strong. His touch, his sounds, his tastes were becoming a familiar addiction.

My shirt fell to the floor. He undid my pants and yanked them off. Then he gripped my arms and shoved me onto the bed. The breath caught in my chest. Matthew making such a forward move was erotic as hell. I closed my eyes, and the anticipation flowed through me.

Chains clinked. He lifted a handcuff, pressed my wrist into the leather strap, and slid the buckle in place until the cuff sat snug against my skin. He clicked the small lock shut and said, "I hope you have the key."

My head flew up.

Richard leaned against the far wall, much like he did our first night at the club. "In the cabinet. Don't you worry, Luke. We'll take care of you."

I settled back and enjoyed the grip of leather on my flesh and the sound of steel jangling near my head as Matthew finished securing me.

His small hand glided down my chest, along my thigh, and then left me. I heard kissing and clothes rustling. I lifted my head again.

They were shirtless, one leaning down, the other reaching up. Richard's right hand was twisted in Matthew's wavy hair. His other hand was down the front of Matthew's pants and was rubbing him mercilessly. The kissing ended, and they removed their clothes in a matter of seconds. Richard bent his knees and rocked his pelvis. Their cocks slid together. Matthew gripped Richard's arms and threw his head back.

Damn sexy kid.
I could still smell his saliva on my lips. I needed him in my mouth again. His tongue, his skin, his cock. Anything.

Richard whispered in Matthew's ear. Matthew nodded and came back to the bed. He straddled my body. His hands explored me everywhere. His tongue ran over my skin and licked at my nipples.

"Luke, your body is amazing." He moved farther down and dipped his tongue into my navel. His breath swept over my dick with each word. "I wanna taste you."

"Someday," Richard said.

"God, Matthew. I can't wait to shoot into your mouth." And I meant every word.

Richard stretched out beside me. "Can you imagine it? Nothing in the way of all that hot, wet suction."

"Uh-huh," I said. "Can you—" The mouth in question lapped my balls, fucking with my concentration. "Can you kiss me?"

Richard's mouth devoured mine with tenderness and slow swirls of tongue over tongue. He always kept me off guard. I never knew if his kiss would consume me or caress me. There was no monotony to him, his touches, or the way he fucked me.

"Matthew's right," he said. "You've got a great body. We're going to make you feel good."

I needed to touch him, to feel him. I lifted my arms, and the chains clanked as they wrenched against the bed frame. Frustration overwhelmed me, but I wanted it. And I wanted more. "The cuffs aren't tight enough."

"They'll have to do. Matthew is going to fuck you. And then I am. Sound good, Matthew?"

Oh, God. One then the other. How did he always know what I needed?

Matthew removed his hot mouth from my body and shot off the bed. Richard kissed me, keeping me distracted until Matthew's slick fingers pushed into me. I spread my legs farther and let him have all he wanted. He moaned, and the sound mingled with my name.

"Matthew, hurry."

He raised my legs over his thighs and slowly pressed inside me. The cuffs gripped me tighter as I made a fist with each tug. Richard kept touching me, kissing me, never letting me get too comfortable with any one sensation before moving on to another part of my body.

Matthew's speed and strength built with each thrust. He came before I was ready to have it end, his face strained with pleasure and relief. Being inside me did that to him. I wanted to come with him, but my neglected dick had other ideas. It wanted a touch, a mouth, something to give it pleasure.

When Matthew's body stilled, Richard encouraged him to lie down. "Luke, flip over onto your hands and knees." He swatted at my hip and helped me turn and slide up the bed.

With the slack in the chains, I crossed my arms in front of me. My head down and my ass in the air, my body shook with need and hunger.

"Hang on." Richard petted my ass before leaving the bed.

Matthew kissed my back and licked along my spine in a sated, relaxed performance. I moaned and rocked with his touch. I ached. "Matthew, so hard."

"Yeah, Luke. Richard's going to help you." His hand rubbed in circles on my back. A fire ignited every place he touched.

Richard returned and wrapped a rope around one of my ankles. He draped it over the edge of the bed and tied it off using a metal loop on the floor. He gave my other ankle the same treatment until he had me tied open.

My legs shook as they held my weight. I needed more. "Tighter."

Richard knelt behind me. I heard him opening the rubber. "They're tight enough." He ran a hand along my back from my ass to my shoulder and back down, smearing the sheen of sweat that clung to me. "I won't hurt you."

Matthew whispered in my ear. "You're sexy as hell, Luke. No one's ever let me fuck them the way you do." His words both thrilled and angered me. He'd been with too many goddamn selfish lovers. He made a great top. If he had wanted to, he should've been given the opportunity more than he obviously had in the past. I'd have told him how good he was at it, if only they hadn't stolen my voice as Richard entered me and Matthew slid his hand under my body and gripped my cock.

I drifted between them, my body on fire, their touches spot on, hitting all the right places, moving with the right speed. Had they crawled inside my goddamn head and read my mind?

With a few more strokes, I came. My legs trembled. It was all I could do to hold myself up.

Richard's hot breath blew over the base of my neck as he came. He fell forward and said, "I didn't know—I didn't know it'd get better."

I shuddered. My body needed to stop betraying me.

A moment later, Matthew's hands worked at my ankles while Richard retrieved the key and unlocked my wrists. I shook more as they freed me. Richard caught me and lowered me to the bed. He spread out next to me, and Matthew crawled up and landed on him.

I sank into the mattress and enjoyed the blissful moments between the end of sex and my conscious awareness of what I should or should not be doing.

Warm. Calm. Relaxed. At peace.

I didn't want to move. I wanted to lie there until someone dragged me out of that room.

"Luke, don't fall asleep," Richard said. "We have a huge bed upstairs."

Matthew sat up and patted my stomach. "Come on, sleepyhead."

Richard's large arms enveloped me, and he helped me off the bed. I was wrecked. I had no memory of the walk upstairs. I'd never been so out of it after sex. I drifted toward sleep as soon as I hit the sheets. Richard's low, husky whisper roused me.

"I think we should get tested. Since you'll be staying for a while, huh? We could at least get rid of the rubbers for blowjobs. Then maybe later…" He didn't finish.

"Uh-huh. Okay." I'd freak later. For the moment, I wanted it all.

Richard smiled and planted a kiss on my lips. "Tomorrow, then. Test should be back in a week or two."

"Any place open on Sundays?" Matthew asked.

"I think so," he said. "I know a place we can call."

Their voices trailed off as I floated away. All I could think about was taking a taste of something I hadn't had in a long time.

Chapter Fourteen

"I hope you don't mind me using the number you left."

Monday morning was half over and I was busy reviewing lines of a program that wouldn't run when the phone rang.

I couldn't help but smile when I heard Matthew's voice.

"Not at all," I said. "Is something wrong?"

"No." He hurried to say the rest. "Richard called, said he's got a last minute dinner meeting. I thought I'd give you a call, find out what you might want to eat tonight."

"How about we order in? I have a feeling you'll be cooking more than me. Let me treat you."

"Oh, okay."

"What sounds good?" I asked.

He didn't respond.

"It's just dinner. Anything you'd like."

"Okay. Um, Italian? There's a great place on Madison. Dominic's. They have the best ravioli."

"Yeah, I know it. I'll pick it up on my way home."

"Thanks, Luke."

"See you tonight. And Matthew?"

"Yeah?"

"You can call me whenever you want to."

"Oh, okay. Thanks."

I hung up and stared at the phone for another minute, the smile lingering too long.

The weekend hadn't gone badly.

In fact, it'd been the best time I'd had in a hell of a long time. We'd continued with the amazing sex the three of us seemed destined to have. I'd come more times than I ever had in one weekend since I'd joined the club. Hell, since I was fifteen. And I'd enjoyed the time out of bed as much as the time in it.

Even the damn tests hadn't freaked me, at least not yet. I couldn't bring myself to tell them no. Matthew and Richard's excitement radiated. They didn't say anything, but the sex when we returned home from the clinic had said it all. I was nearly as incoherent as I'd been the night before. We slept with Matthew between us, his head on Richard's chest, his arm draped over my waist.

I still hadn't freaked.

It would come. When the results came in, I'd be expected to follow through and do something I never planned to give to anyone. Not ever again.

Until then, I let them distract me.

I hadn't even given my father much thought. I still surveyed my surroundings when I went anywhere. I still planned out different routes to and from work. I just didn't let it consume my every thought.

Right after my concentration recalled where I'd left off with my code review, the phone rang again. The stupid, blissful grin spread across my face. I didn't even glance at the caller ID. I had the phone in my hand in a flash. "Did you change your mind on the ravioli?"

"Excuse me?"

I held my breath. That voice. Not Matthew's. It held more familiarity. Even if I hadn't heard it in years.

"Luke, is that you?"

I gulped in a mouthful of air and forced myself to take in another before speaking. "Yeah."

"How are you, son?" His tone belied the concerned words.

"Fine."

"Let's not bother with the small talk, shall we?"

"Why are you calling? I already know your men were in my apartment."

"I'd like to see you. Today. For lunch."

"Why?"

"Can you come or not? Believe me, I won't keep you long."

Believe me, I won't stay long. "Where? What time?"

* * * *

I arrived at Seymour's Diner fifteen minutes early. My father wouldn't be there yet. The man never arrived anywhere before the arranged time—being early was for the insecure. He was never a minute late—being late was for the inept.

I gave my name to the hostess, and she seated me in the back. My father had chosen well. I counted nine patrons scattered about the retro metal tables and red vinyl booths. Most were elderly men and woman—divided into duos by fate or boredom or stupidity—who scrutinized their coffee cups and not much else. Perhaps they'd talked themselves out or covered every last possible topic years ago.

I ordered a cup of coffee and picked up a menu. Food wasn't an option, but my hands wanted something to do. I glanced over the choices and the diner lingo—items like *Zeppelins in a Fog* and *Dough Well Done with Cow to Cover*—amused me. Did people really order that way? Or was it all for show?

I tucked the menu behind the napkin dispenser, leaned back, and eyed the front of the diner.

My father strolled through the door at twelve-thirty. He skulked his way around tables and chairs and sat without a nod or word of hello. The scent of his cologne drifted across the table. Fifteen years and he still wore the same damn shit, the same style of suit, the same stupid look of arrogance.

But the man had aged. White hair—instead of the dark brown he sported when I'd last seen him—edged a pale, gaunt face. Visible lines surrounded his eyes. His legs didn't bend as they should with each step. The stiff walk gave him the look of a man who didn't trust the ground under his feet.

Did the old man sitting before me represent what I'd look like someday—hard and ragged, an empty shell of a man?

I opened my mouth, and he raised a hand to silence me. Two men in suits cleared a nearby table of an elderly couple. It took several minutes for the old man to help his wife slide across the booth and swing her legs out from under the table. Once she had her feet under her, my father's men shuffled them off to a booth farther away.

"Let's be frank, shall we?" he said.

"Fine by me."

"I need to know what you've been up to. To be ready to deflect any negative press."

He wasn't asking about my work or my voting record. He wanted to know about my sex life. I pressed my shoulder blades into the seat and folded my arms across my chest. My fingernails burrowed into the shirtsleeves covering my biceps. "Why now? You've been in Congress for how long? Why am I an issue now?"

"Answer the damn question. If the press was to investigate your life, what would it find?"

"Oh, Dad, the stories I could tell you. Well, this weekend, I was chained up in a basement and fucked by two guys."

"Jesus, Luke." He raked his fingers through his hair, and his face paled more. He glanced around the room. "I don't even want to know if that's true."

I shrugged. "You asked. I thought you wanted to know what might cause negative press. Wouldn't me tied up, begging for sex from two guys I barely know give you cause for concern?"

"I can see there are things in your life I have to be worried about. Tell me, do you go to any clubs or other sex places? Where people might see you? Take pictures?"

"Wouldn't you love to see pictures? I could probably arrange something."

"Don't be a shit." He banged his fist on the table. The two sets of neatly arranged silverware momentarily took flight and clattered as they landed in disarray. The coffee in my cup sloshed and spilled over each side. "Tell me what I'm up against."

"Well, you're the one who's having me followed. What have you learned?"

"I wouldn't have to have someone watch you if I thought you could be trusted to live a civilized life. I know about that disgusting place you go to. I know you haven't been home in several days. Do I even want to know where you've been staying?"

"Do you think I'm going to tell you? No, Dad. You couldn't understand my life if you tried. Don't worry. I'll stay off the radar. I won't talk to the press. I won't come to see you or Mom. Hell, I won't even vote in the next goddamn election."

"I would expect nothing less. I'm more worried about something getting out you have no control over."

"If I have no control over it, then you don't either."

"We'll see. I warn you, son, do not mess with me. Or I'll make your life miserable."

"How am I messing with you? I don't talk to you. I don't see you. I'm living my own life."

"And the way you live is what will cause me problems. I know you all too well. You don't do anything you have to take too seriously. You're all about living in the moment and having your sick, perverted fun. You do not know how to commit to anything. How could you understand my dedication to serving this country?" He paused and made eye contact with me for the first time since he entered the diner. "Can't you leave the city? Live away from your mother and me? Try to live like a normal person? Try to have a goddamn normal relationship?"

My hands clenched around my biceps. "I'm not going anywhere." My voice was loud enough for the customers at several tables past his circle of henchmen to hear. He shifted in his seat and scanned the room. "Look at me," I said.

He glared at me.

"I have a life here. A life that isn't made up of any kind of filth, and I'm not going anywhere."

He squinted. Deep lines formed at the corners of his eyes as if he'd made the same judgmental expression a million times before. "You have one shot to make this work. For you and me. You quit going to that club or you'll see what kind of monster the press can be. And it won't just be me they tear apart." His palms slapped the table and he stood. "I won't be having you followed anymore for reasons that are my own business, but if I find out you're doing anything to make me look bad, you'll regret it." He threw a twenty on the table and left the restaurant, followed out by his protectors.

I stared at the crumpled bill and felt like a whore who'd been paid for one of the worst fucks of his life.

I banged my fist on the edge of the table and didn't miss the fact that my father had just done the same thing. A jagged piece of trim framing the metal tabletop dug into the flesh. Blood seeped and streamed down my wrist.

I grabbed a napkin and swiped at the blood over the gash of torn skin. No stitches needed, but bad enough. I focused in on the bite of the pain. Only, the pain didn't irritate me or disturb me or make me angry. It was unavoidable. A physical reminder of the conversation with my father. A necessary token. And I accepted it. I could never let myself forget the man's hatred of me.

I stood and headed for the door. I wasn't going back to work. For once, I could go home and find what I needed.

* * * *

I shook with rage and desperate need as I stepped inside the house. I set down my bag and keys and called out for Matthew.

From the time it took me to get to the subway, ride to my stop, and walk to the town house, I'd managed to work up to pissed off. I was done letting my father push me around. Done letting his game drive me into hiding and force me to move over and over.

I took a deep breath and waited for Matthew's response. I didn't mind being wound up with need, but I didn't want to bring any anger into a moment of pleasure with him. He didn't deserve that.

When he didn't answer me, I moved down the hall toward the kitchen and heard their voices.

"It sucks." Richard. Strained. Angry. But not aiming it at Matthew.
"I can imagine. After all your hard work." Matthew. Calm. Caring. He caught sight of me as I rounded the corner. "Hey, Luke. What ya doing home early?" The two were sitting across from each other at the kitchen table.

"I…uh, had a bad day. I thought I'd head home after lunch. Sorry about dinner. I can stop another night."

Matthew gave me a smile. "That's okay."

"Am I interrupting?" I asked.

"No," Richard said. "Just telling Matthew about my shit day. Got out of a meeting and cancelled my afternoon, including the dinner for tonight. Then I reminded myself if I came home early, I wouldn't be alone." He smiled at Matthew then grew serious again. "I lost the lakefront deal."

"Sorry." I shoved my hands into my pockets. Half-full cups of coffee sat in front of each man. I made a beeline for the pot.

Matthew's attention refocused on Richard. "Is there anything you can do to get them to change their minds? It sounds like a great area to invest in."

I leaned back against the counter and swallowed slow sips.

"It was," Richard said. "Man, I'd have made a mint. There are a ton of plans for the area. It's going to explode with condos and shopping centers. Fuck." His hands wrenched into fists. "It's gone. I did everything I could. Sometimes someone comes in with a sweeter offer. I know the money shouldn't be an issue, but losing the deal irks me to no end."

"I get that," Matthew said. "You live well, but you aren't all about having money and stuff. It isn't you. You wanted the deal and you lost it. That's the part driving you crazy. I mean…you like to have control, yeah?" Matthew dropped his head and smiled, his eyes on the table.

Richard laughed. "I guess I do." His hands unclenched. He lifted an open palm to caress Matthew's cheek.

"You'll get the next one."

I pushed off the counter and went to them. "He's right. You're not the type to be kept down for long."

"Thanks, Luke." Richard stood and gave me a quick kiss. "You guys want to crash on the couch and watch some TV? We could order pizza later."

"Sounds good." Matthew stood and bounced off toward the living room.

Richard chuckled as he watched him leave. Not an ounce of

tension remained in the big man's body or his laughter. Matthew was good for him. Hell, I was laughing too. He was good for both of us.

We relaxed against one another on the couch. I didn't tense or freak about what it meant to be close without an agenda in mind. I fought the instinct and let my hands wander, let myself enjoy Richard and Matthew for as long as I could.

I was getting used to not being alone. Getting used to them. To wanting. To needing. To the easy way we were together. *Shouldn't that scare me? Shouldn't I be leaving?*

I tried to push away thoughts of my father and what the man had said. And the way I'd found the perfect distraction when I'd gotten home. Most importantly, I tried to avoid that I was referring to the place I'd just moved into as home. Wasn't it temporary?

It didn't matter. None of it mattered.

I had moved in with two men to whom I'd made promises, to whom I'd agreed to be faithful. It was more than I had allowed myself to do since I was nineteen years old.

It was a start.

For once, I was not letting myself or my father scare me away from a good thing.

Chapter Fifteen

Throughout the week, I became a part of an evening routine that had nothing to do with surveillance video feeds or time spent trolling the Haven for someone to spend a half hour with.

Matthew made dinner most nights. I helped finish the food or set the table when I could. After we ate, we'd watch TV, or Richard and I would get some work done on our laptops while Matthew read a book. The nights ended with sex—in the bedroom, the basement, or even on the couch if we couldn't keep our hands off one another before the show ended. We hadn't spent a night together all week that didn't include getting off in one way or another.

Matthew and I had also spent time setting up the spare rooms, unpacking, and rearranging furniture. Matthew even brought over a small television and an Xbox from his mom's place. Richard turned a deep shade of red when he saw it.

"Feeling old?" I asked when we were alone later.

"God, yes. Sometimes I look at him and I think I'm robbing the damn cradle."

"Does it bother you?"

"Not enough to give a shit. Or to give him up."

I couldn't argue with him. I'd never cared about the age difference between myself and any other man. Then again, I hadn't had a relationship with anyone since I was nineteen. When it came to casual fucks, as long as they were legal, I didn't care. And I wasn't about to let it start bothering me. Not when it might have meant Matthew was too young for me.

While he worked on his room, I fixed the other one up to serve as my office. I also wanted to include a bed, in case I needed to sleep alone at some point. I didn't want to mention anything to Richard, so I lived with the room as it was. Things were going well with the arrangement, and I didn't want to disrupt the flow we had going or anger or disappoint them in any way.

I'd taken to giving their feelings considerable amounts of thought. Which I guess made sense when so much of my usual life had vanished, and I was left with all sorts of free time.

It was easy to let go of my obsession with my stalkers. Not because my father said he wouldn't send his men. I didn't believe he'd tell the truth. It was more the diversion of Matthew and Richard and my unexpected enjoyment of our temporary living situation that had me relaxed.

After work on Friday night, I wasn't the least bit concerned with sex clubs, hidden cameras, or fathers. I stepped into the house and headed straight for the kitchen. Matthew sat at the counter leaning over Richard's laptop, his iPod clipped to his pants, headphones in his ears. A low beat of music a generation below my style was audible from the tiny speakers. Not a surprise. When I was in high school, he was in the first grade. I stepped close behind him and glanced at the screen. Shopping for more video games. Richard would love that.

I leaned in and pressed my lips to his ear. "Hey, smells good."

Matthew flashed me a smile. "Thanks." He removed the headphones. "It's a pasta dish. Sort of like gourmet pizza with pasta on it and fresh basil and mozzarella. I found the recipe online. I've never made it before."

"Sounds good. Where's Richard?"

"He said he'd be late."

I sat next to him and gestured at the computer. "Shopping?"

"Yeah. Richard said I could use his laptop to get online, check my e-mail."

"Buying a new game?"

He stared at the screen. "I got a gift card from my mom. For my birthday."

"When was your birthday?"

He lowered his gaze and ran a finger over the touch pad. "When we had our date."

"You should've said."

"Nah. It's just a birthday." His head snapped in my direction. "Hey, don't tell Richard."

"Why?"

"I think it might make him feel bad he missed it. But we barely knew each other, you know?"

"Okay. Next year, though, I'll have to tell him when it comes around again. Then he'll know he missed it anyway."

Matthew's eyes went huge. He bit at his bottom lip and lifted a hand to touch my face.

What the hell? I kept making promises to him I wasn't sure I'd ever be able to keep.

I kissed him. "Happy birthday, Matthew."

"Thanks." He swiped a finger over my lower lip.

I wanted to get closer, touch him more. I stood. "I think I'll use the time to catch up on some work."

"Okay." Matthew stood and stepped around the counter to turn the stove's heat down. "This'll keep until Richard gets home."

His hand brushed my thigh as he moved by me again. Goose bumps rose up. My pants scraped the sensitized skin.

I snaked a hand in his and pulled him back to me. He tasted like basil and tomatoes. I nibbled his lips, his tongue. He was the perfect appetizer.

I savored my way to the flesh of his neck. He dug his heel into my calf and dragged me closer to him. I didn't want to let go. I wanted to taste everything. I wanted to bend him over the counter face first and sink into him until he screamed my name, until he understood how much I wanted to be with him.

I wrenched my hands away from him. "I'm gonna head upstairs."

He whimpered and pouted.

"That was a taste," I said. "Let's wait on the main course for Richard, huh?"

He licked his lips. "Oh, okay. Good idea."

I laughed and brushed a hand over his ass. I headed to the stairs and shook my head. What had come over me? Teasing him, touching him was a delight, an addiction. He was always so damn responsive and eager.

I booted my laptop and flipped open my cell to make a call I'd put off all week.

"Hi, Walter."

"I was wondering when I'd hear from you. You're lucky I know Richard's reputation. How's it going? And where are you calling me from?"

"I'm at home—I mean Richard's." I winced.

"Ah. It's going that well?"

"Yeah, so far."

"Really?"

"Did you have such little faith in me?"

"No. I thought you might have lacked the faith in yourself."

I leaned back in the chair and propped my feet on the desk. "Yeah, I think I did. It's been better than I expected, but I didn't expect much."

"Honestly, I'm surprised you're still there. It sounds like you're trying."

"I think I am."

"Will you be staying?"

"For a while."

"And your father?"

"He called me the other day. I met him for lunch."

"Met him? In person?"

"He asked, and I wanted to know what he's up to."

"And?"

"He said he's going to stop sending his men but wouldn't tell me why. He threatened me, said I should leave town. He said the press was going to figure things out, start making my life miserable."

"Sounds like he might be the one who's being threatened. Maybe a reporter already knows about you and the club and is blackmailing him."

"Could be. He was nervous, unreasonable."

"You believe him? About his men following you?"

"I don't know. Since I moved here last week, I haven't seen anyone. I'm still careful, but it's liberating in a way. Not having the cameras, not trying so damn hard to keep him in the dark."

"You still be careful. Be on the lookout for him in ways that have nothing to do with being followed. He'll lie to the media if he has to."

"Yeah, well, I've never been concerned about my reputation. Not like he is about his."

"Still," Walter said, "it's no fun to have hatred and lies slung at you." He paused. "So it's Friday night and you're *home*. I'm guessing if I'm in the Haven this weekend, I won't see you?"

"Right. We're staying in. Not sure when I'll be back to the club."

He snorted. "I hope it isn't any time soon."

I hoped not either. But my protective instincts, hidden just under the surface, wouldn't let me admit it out loud. Not even to Walter.

We talked for another few minutes, and when we said good-bye, I listened to him laugh yet again about how I wouldn't be at the club.

I hung up and concentrated on work until a knock sounded on the open door an hour later. I gestured for Richard to come in.

"Getting some work done?"

"Yeah." I shut the lid on my laptop and stood. "But I'm done for the night."

"Good, 'cause we better get down to dinner. Matthew said it's been in the oven for a while now."

"He's excited about a new recipe. It wouldn't be fair to make him wait much longer. Although it is fun to watch him bounce around."

"He's amazing, isn't he? Man, I had no idea we'd be getting such a good cook when I asked you guys to stay."

"How could you? What did you really know about us?"

"A few things, but nothing related to cooking." He smirked.

"Oh?"

He stalked closer to me with each word he uttered. "I knew you liked it when I made you beg. You liked it when I told you what to do and when I kept you tied down." His arms wrapped around me.

"Uh-huh."

He whispered in my ear. "You even liked it when I teased and wouldn't let you come until you looked at me." He kissed me.

I wrapped a hand around his neck and crushed his mouth harder against mine. I massaged every part of him I could reach. I loved the strength of his muscles under my fingers. I loved his responses under my hands. I loved his tongue's eagerness as it explored my mouth.

I didn't want to stop touching, stop kissing. I wanted to learn his sweet spots. I wanted to know where my mouth on his body would drive him crazy. I wanted him to throw me up against the wall and take me while I stared into his green eyes.

"I'm glad you're here, Luke. I missed you today."

I tensed.

"You're freaking?" he asked without letting go.

"A little."

"But you aren't leaving?"

"No, I'm not." I relaxed and leaned into him.

"Good. Now, come on." He smacked my ass. "I hear Matthew's cooked this great dish. We'll have to eat before we can get started with what else I'm hungry for." He kissed the end of my nose.

I followed his fine ass down the stairs and tried to convince my dick dinner came first. I'd given it a taste of Richard and Matthew, and it wanted more.

Matthew had gone all out and seated us in the large dining room where we ate one of the most amazing pasta dishes I'd ever had.

Richard hummed with each bite. "This is fabulous, Matthew. Thank you."

"It is," I said.

Matthew sat taller. "Thanks."

"So it's been a week," Richard said. "Everything seems to be going good so far. You guys miss the club?"

"No," Matthew screeched. "I uh…" He clanked his fork onto his plate. "I don't miss it. Not at all."

"I'm glad," Richard said.

"Yeah?" Matthew shifted in his seat. "I've had the best week."

"Me too." I didn't take my eyes off my plate as I said the simple words. Neither man ever left me wishing I had someone new to be with. It was hard to accept, but I wouldn't lie to them. I looked up. Two stunned men stared at me. "What? Have I not been acting like I'm enjoying myself?"

"Yes, you have. I just…" Richard trailed off.

"You admitted it," Matthew said.

"I thought it would have been obvious with every orgasm."

"That was obvious," Richard said. "But what about when we weren't in bed?"

"I've enjoyed your company. I mean…" I sighed and threw my hands in the air. "What do you want me to say?"

Richard got up and crouched next to my chair. He cupped my cheek and forced me to look at him. "The truth."

"I'm not sorry to be here. I've had a great time. Hell, I like you two more than anyone else in my life right now." I squeezed my eyes closed. *Shut up. Shut up.* I looked at Richard again. "There. Happy?"

He swept his palm over my cheek. "Why, yes, I am. I like you, Luke." He glanced over at Matthew. "And you too. I think this whole thing is working out as I hoped it would."

Matthew moaned.

I laughed a quick, unruly chuckle, partly to ease the tension in my chest, and partly because he was making sex noises and we were only talking.

I guess we'd said enough, or too much depending on one's point of view. Richard pulled me to him and kissed me, slow and gentle. It didn't take long for Matthew to kneel next to Richard and join us.

I lost all coherent thought with each kiss. The intensity built, need burning through every touch, every lingering caress of lips and hands.

I stripped Matthew of his clothes and took off my own while Richard got undressed. I grabbed Matthew and led him to the other end of the long table. I kissed him and laid him on his back. His legs splayed out on either side of me. Fuck if that didn't look like the best invitation. No other man I'd ever been with was as ready for me as Matthew.

I licked at his neck, chest, stomach, and inner thighs. I worshipped his body, enjoyed the smell of him, learned every inch of him. I worked my way to his balls and sucked on them in turn while I stroked his cock with my hand.

He writhed beneath me, his head twisting from side to side on the table. His hands dug into my hair, rubbed my neck. My heavy cock arched up toward the edge of the table. I was careful with my movements to protect it but wished like hell I could get some friction, wished I could feel Richard behind me.

But he had left the room. I knew when he came back, though. Thick, slick fingers ran along my ass and pressed into me.

I rocked back. Wanting more. Needing to feel the burn, needing to feel his dick stretch me. "I'm ready. Need you inside me. Now."

He continued to move his fingers and handed me a condom over my shoulder. Thank God. I was only half certain I'd have stopped myself from lowering my mouth over Matthew's erection. It called to me.

I rolled the condom on him and took his prick in my mouth. A few teases later and Richard plunged into me. I reached back and grabbed a hold of one of his thick thighs slamming against me, the power there like a goddamn steamroller.

Richard groaned at my touch and drove into me harder than he'd done before. This wasn't a slow, gentle fuck. He was banging the shit out of me, and I was taking Matthew deep, swallowing him down the back of my throat.

His moans and shrills sounded as loud as his fists when they banged the table every time my throat muscles massaged his cock. Had no one ever deep throated him before? It was a technique I'd mastered over years of nameless fucking. I was glad to use the skill on him.

When Matthew came, he threw his head back. His shoulders slammed into the table, and he arched his back.

Richard stilled. "Damn, Matthew. Love the way you move and sound." He started thrusting again, and after a few more shoves, he screamed my name.

I shot with one touch of my hand to my dick before Richard finished shuddering in my ass. I melted onto the table, my forehead on Matthew's thigh.

Matthew patted my head with a sluggish hand. "Jesus fucking Christ, Luke. That was…wow. No one's ever…wow." And there was his laugh.

Richard settled on my back. "Now there's something we could never have done in the dining room at the club."

Matthew chuckled again. His body shook with each laugh.

With Richard on me and Matthew under me, any thoughts about the club or any other place I could have been brought out my own laughter.

Richard stood and smacked my ass. "Come on, boys, let's hit the bed. We're getting too old for falling asleep on the dining room table. Well, Luke and I are."

"Hey." I stood and used a napkin to clean up the table. I laughed again and promised myself I'd get it better in the morning.

Matthew huffed as he lifted himself onto his elbows and gawked at Richard. "You aren't old. Not with a body like yours."

Richard bent over him. "Thanks, kid. I happen to be quite fond of your bod as well." He reached out and tickled Matthew's ribs.

Matthew wiggled and laughed, rolling them around until he was straddled over Richard, returning the tickles.

I bent for my clothes. "I'm taking a shower before bed." I headed for the stairs. "You guys coming?"

Matthew gasped, and a moment later, Richard hauled ass up the stairs past me with Matthew over his shoulder. I ran after them. No way in hell could we have spent a similar night in the dining room at the Haven.

And I was damn glad I wasn't there.

But that feeling couldn't last.

Could it?

Chapter Sixteen

I entered Amy's Café and spotted Mark Summers talking on his cell at a booth near the rear exit. He looked identical to his online photo. He also looked like a reporter—someone who had everyone sized up and knew more than he ever let on. I approached the table but hung back a few steps to give him time to end his call.

He mouthed my name and I nodded. He gestured me forward and clicked off his phone. "Sorry. The wife."

I nodded again and took a seat.

He watched me with intense interest. "You're not married?"

If he didn't know at least that much, then maybe he wasn't the reporter I wanted to talk to. "This isn't an interview," I said. "I'll tell you what I want you to know. And anything I say is off the record until I give the okay."

He tucked the cell phone into his bag. "That would sort of make this a huge waste of my time."

"Join the club. It's off the record for now, or you don't get to hear anything."

He set his bag on the empty seat beside him and leaned back. "Okay."

I waited a moment so when I spoke again, we were both clear who was leading the conversation. "I'm gay. And I'm living with two men. And they're not my roommates."

He stared at me.

I stared back. "Not what you expected?"

"You know, you're father's a hero to a lot of people. He's worked hard to stabilize the economy. To help people find jobs. To—"

"I've read the stories." I glanced out the nearby window at the bustle of men and women in business attire rushing by, cell phone in one hand, coffee in the other, and not a single one of them paying attention to any other person in the crowd. Lunch hour in the business district. My words were barely a whisper. I wasn't sure if he heard me. "He's not a hero to everyone."

Summers didn't talk again until my gaze returned to him. "His public views on gay rights are the one area where he's been criticized. But hell, even the gay press glosses over that."

I nodded.

He seemed to be sizing me up as much as I had him via my online searches. "No one's that good," he said. "You know that, right?"

"That's why I'm here. I figure you've got something on him."

"I might. You don't expect me to trust you with it, do you?"

"Didn't think so."

He eyed me for another minute and then spoke again. "Let me ask you this: did your father tell you much about his life before politics?"

"He's been in politics all my life."

"But before that? Before he was married?"

"He was in college." My father's college years were the one thing he did talk to me about. He talked about the fraternity, his classes, told me what a great place it was to "try out" different women. That conversation had been one of the reasons I wanted to come out to him. He kept telling me how important it was for me to find the right girl. He said college was the best place to find out what you liked. The irony of that was never lost on me. From the moment I met Tim, I knew he was the man for me.

"Did you know he didn't go to his graduation ceremony?" Summers asked.

I scrutinized him. He was waiting for me to take the bait, maybe seeing if I wanted to follow his threads. "You're pointing me toward something. Why?"

He shrugged. The expression didn't seem natural on him. "Stories get killed all the time. It'd be a shame for this one to get buried." He grabbed his bag, plopped it on the table, and looked inside as if there was something he wanted to take out and show me. He removed his empty hand and set it on top of the bag. "He's done a good job of keeping you a secret. People know he has a son. There've been a few rumors that you're not on speaking terms, but nothing about your sexual orientation." He smiled.

"I take it my being gay is going to make it into your story? Or perhaps my current living arrangement will?"

His smile grew. Then he dialed it back and stilled his expression. "There seems to be a lot about your father you don't know."

I was about to ask what when he spoke again.

"I've got a few details to nail down. It might take some time. You think it over and let me know if I can run with it."

Run with what?

Summers already assumed I'd go through with it. Which I would. I had no issues telling the world I was gay. I had issues with my father knowing anything about Richard or Matthew. But I'd just opened that door. I'd given a crumb to a reporter who wanted to find the entire gingerbread house.

He grabbed his bag and stood.

"He's that newsworthy?" I asked.

Summers laughed as he walked away.

* * * *

"Hey, guys. I'm home." I kicked the door shut with my foot. "Sorry I'm late. I got movies."

The sound effects of Matthew's favorite game, *Call of Duty*, filtered down the stairs. I dropped off the DVDs and my laptop bag in the foyer and headed up.

Richard and Matthew were sitting on the floor in Matthew's room, both fixated on the TV. Richard was clicking away on a game controller, tilting it from side to side, and Matthew was laughing his ass off. I leaned on the doorframe and watched them.

A loud explosion blasted from the TV's speakers, and Richard threw the controller on the floor. "Damn thing's broken."

"No," Matthew said. "You suck."

Richard rolled over and pressed himself on top of Matthew. "That's right. And you're pretty damn lucky I do."

That had Matthew laughing again.

Richard stood. "Hey, Luke. Get us a good movie?" He crowded me against the door and kissed me.

Matthew came to us. He ran his hand over my ass. His fingers twined with Richard's. "You guys ready to eat?"

Richard gave me one last smoldering kiss and rocked our bodies together.

While we ate, he talked about his plans for a new development project he had his eye on. I was glad to be around for the aftereffects of the excitement and thrill he got from his work. I cleared my plate faster, the anticipation building with each glance at him. Matthew smiled and squirmed through the meal, animated in a new way. Richard's business success had a positive effect on all of us.

When the food was gone, Matthew retrieved some papers from the kitchen counter. He bounced into his seat and slid a sheet over to Richard. "It came in the mail today."

Richard unfolded the paper and concentrated for a minute. A smile formed, and he met Matthew's gaze. He passed the paper over to me without breaking the stare.

Matthew's test results. Negative.

Matthew slid a sealed envelope to each of us. Richard opened his, scanned over the results, and smiled again. He handed his paper to me. His results were the same. I passed it to Matthew.

That left me.

I flipped the envelope over and over in my hand. How many times had I been tested? How many times had the results been important to me and no one else? I opened it and slipped the paper out.

A knot formed in my stomach. I unfolded the sheet and read it over.

My heart thudded in my chest, drummed in my ears, filling the quiet. What the hell was I going to say?

I forced myself to look at them. Richard's brow was furrowed. Matthew's mouth hung open.

"I'm not ready."

Richard grabbed my hand. "But you're okay?"

"Oh…yeah. Results say I'm good."

He squeezed my hand and sank back in his chair. Matthew lowered his eyelids and released the breath he'd been holding.

Worry. I might not have seen it often, but I knew it on someone's face. Worried about me. "I'm sorry. I'm…I can't yet."

"That's fair," Richard said. "It's only been a couple of weeks."

"Yeah," Matthew said. "It won't be any good until we're all ready." He stood and stepped around the table. He straddled my thighs and settled onto my lap. His hands cupped my face, and he kissed me. A sweet, luxurious kiss unlike any he'd ever given me. "You're okay. That's what matters." He kissed me again. And again. "You're okay."

Richard knelt behind him. "He's right. Your health is what matters."

Matthew nipped at my neck. His legs squeezed, and he rocked over my lap. The swell of his dick mashed against my abdomen. I wrapped my arms around him and moved with him.

A moment later, Richard slipped a condom into my hand.

For a brief moment, I wanted to throw it on the floor and give into the ache of knowing what it would feel like when Richard's cock filled me with his spunk and Matthew's mouth swallowed my cum.

The moment passed before I could act on the foolish inspiration. Matthew and Richard were standing and kissing. I nudged them toward the stairs as they held on to each other. Fucking them with condoms was nothing to shy away from.

It was something to relish. Every night.

I wouldn't let myself lose that. Not yet.

Chapter Seventeen

"Holy shit. You look like your father."

Roger Vance stood in the doorway of his home gawking at me. With that one sentence, I already hated the guy. He wasn't going to make my Christmas card list—if I had one of those.

I turned on what charm I could muster where an old friend of my father's was concerned. "Thanks for taking the time to see me."

He gestured for me to step inside. "No problem." I slid in past him. He stood holding the door open, staring at me, not moving a muscle. He shook his head and shut the door. "Sorry. It's just such a blast from the past. I could be looking at John."

"You're not."

"I hear ya. Come on in. Wanna drink?"

He led me to a kitchen. The room was small, and the counters were overflowing with cereal boxes, cans of Mountain Dew, and appliances like those indoor George Foreman grills sold at Walmart. Not a single inch of bare counter space remained.

He grabbed a couple of beers from the fridge. "Beer okay?"

"Thanks."

He sat on a stool at a butcher block island in the center of the room. "Have a seat. Sorry about the mess." He gestured to a nearby kitchen table. It was covered in a disarray of placemats, stacks of opened mail, a Hannah Montana backpack, and a pair of soccer cleats with mud caked to the soles. "Kids, you know?"

"Sure."

"Our grandkids have been living here for a couple of years now. Since their mom took off. You got any kids? Is Johnathan Moore a grandfather?"

"No. I'm not married."

"Oh. He'd like that."

"What? That I'm single?"

"Nah. I meant grandkids. Only guy I knew in college who used to talk about his future in terms of a wife, a house, kids, the whole nine yards." He swallowed a mouthful of beer. "I remember the night he met Elizabeth. He came into Uptown—that's this bar we used to hang out at—and he just announced it to me and Phil. Said he'd met the woman he was going to marry." Roger Vance laughed as he stared down at a frying pan with what smelled like bacon grease congealing in the bottom. "He said it just like that. They hadn't even had a date yet. John always did know what he wanted, and things always seemed to work out the way he wanted them to. But marriage? We thought he was crazy."

I took a swig of the beer in my hand. No way could I keep a straight face through that.

Vance's attention was back on me. "I was at your parents' wedding. Such a nice gal, Elizabeth. I knew he was right then. I knew they'd end up together for the long haul." He paused and watched me like I was supposed to say something.

I nodded and tried for another smile.

"So, you're putting together a shindig for them?"

"Yeah. The next one's their thirty-fifth."

"Thirty-five years. Damn. I gotta tell ya when I got your call I was freaked. I thought maybe something happened to him. And I was getting *the call*, you know."

"Sorry."

He waved his hand through the air. "Nah. Don't worry about it. It's not like we kept in touch. I just—well, I didn't wanna get that call. Not about John. I'm glad it's a good thing. A party."

"It's a ways off but I wanted to start getting stuff together. See if I could locate some old friends, gather some stories. I'd like to put together a DVD. I got stuck when I started with college and when they met. I don't know anyone from then. Yours was the first name I came across. You and my dad were in a picture together in the senior yearbook."

"Yeah? Your dad and I were close. Not as close as he and Danny or Phil. But we were all good friends. The five of us. Right off the bat our freshman year when we took Intro to Psych."

"Five?"

"The four of us guys and Maria. Although, she was like one of the guys. Except she talked way too much." He laughed again and took another drink of his beer, swallowing half of it in one lift of the bottle. "I haven't seen any of them in years. How's your dad doing? Oh, can that. He's great, I bet. I catch him on C-SPAN. I read the papers. I always knew he'd land near the top."

I wasn't so sure my father had landed yet. "He's doing well."

"Good. I didn't come from money like a lot of the other guys, but he never treated me like it mattered." Vance stared at the bacon-grease-filled frying pan again. "Boy, those were some good times. And your dad was—well, I'll avoid the details since you're his son, huh? Let's just say college is the time to live it up, and your dad sure was a good guy to have around."

I bet.

"You thinking about inviting the old gang?" he asked. "There was the five of us, but your dad had a lot of friends. It'd be a kick to see everyone. And I've got stories. Loads."

"I was hoping you could give me some names. Round out the invite list."

He recited a list of names as they came to him, and I jotted them down. My hand cramped, and I'd had two more beers by the time he stopped throwing out names and telling me anecdotes about one party after another.

I pointed to the list of names. "Which of these were the three other close friends you mentioned?"

"Maria Lammon."

I circled her name and looked up at him when he didn't say anything more.

He sighed. "Phillip Meade and Danny Conner. But they won't be on that list. Danny passed away the night before we graduated." The sadness started in his eyes and worked its way down his body, overwhelming him like the kid had died just last week.

"I'm sorry."

"It was a long time ago."

"I couldn't find any photos of my dad's graduation. Is that why he wasn't there?"

He nodded. "None of us went. Your dad never mentioned Danny?"

"No."

"They were close. Danny was a quiet kid, small. Your dad looked after him. Hell, we all did. Danny was the same age as us, but we all sorta thought of him like a little brother."

"How did he die?"

Vance pinched the bridge of his nose. "Drug overdose. I wasn't there that night. I always felt bad about that."

"What was he on?"

"I don't know—I don't remember. It's not like he was some big drug user. It was a rare thing for him to even drink all that much. I'm sure I knew at the time what it was." He rushed to say the rest. "If you're curious about Danny, you should talk to Maria. She's a talker. At least she was back then. I don't think I've seen her since, well, since your parents' wedding. God, I'm getting old."

"And what about Phillip Meade?"

"He passed away. Five years ago now. Heart attack." Vance collected our empty beer bottles and tossed them into a container under the kitchen sink. He kept his back to me and stared out the window. "I read it in the paper. Went to the funeral and everything. Thought maybe I'd see Maria or John there. Didn't see either of them, though." He faced me. "Funny how life goes. I thought we'd always be friends."

"Life doesn't always work out the way we think it will," I said.

"Tell me about it."

* * * *

"I've dropped the story." Summers sounded annoyed that I'd bothered him with my call.

After talking to Roger Vance, I was convinced I was on the right track. I phoned Summers during the forty-five minute cab drive back to Richard's.

"Why?" I asked. The chatter of his office masked the silence on the line as I waited for him to explain.

"There wasn't much there, I'm afraid. I thought I was onto something, but I couldn't find anything in his past worthy of a story. My editors wanted me off it. I've got bigger fish to fry. Your father…he appears to be exactly who we've been led to believe he is."

Sure. "Can you tell me what your story was about?"

"It was more of a hunch. It didn't get me much of anything. I'm sorry I led you to believe it was more. It's how I work interviews. People will share more information when they think you don't need what they've got to tell you. Listen, I've got to run. Sorry for the waste of time and all that."

My father got to him. He could get to anyone. "Can you tell me one thing? Were you looking into the death of Danny Conner?"

Click.

That was an answer. Was it the one I wanted?

Chapter Eighteen

"Can I fuck you tonight?"

Richard stood still. He stared at Matthew, his eyes wide, his hands at his sides, not a muscle moving on his large body.

It was another Saturday night, and we'd spent it eating pizza and enjoying Matthew's new video game. After he'd beaten us for the third game in a row, I distracted him with kisses. For a man who never kissed much, I was addicted to it.

Richard joined us in no time. We removed clothes, ran hands over skin, and crashed our bodies together. The floor of Matthew's room was looking good to me when Richard suggested we move to the basement and asked us what he always did.

I wanted them to tie me to the bench and bend me over for a hard fuck. Then Matthew asked if he could top Richard, turning the larger man into a silent statue.

Matthew tapped at a leg of the bench with his foot. His shoulders fell. Regret worked its way down his body through every muscle. How could he think Richard didn't want him? One look at Richard's face said it all.

I pressed against Matthew's back and whispered in his ear. "I think you made him speechless, but I think that's a yes."

"God, yes," Richard said. "I guess...I thought maybe you'd changed your mind. You haven't mentioned it since the club. I didn't want to push you."

"I want to," Matthew said, the words almost a shout.

Richard reached out, and Matthew went to him. They held tight as they stared at each other. Richard ran a thumb over the other man's cheek. "Let's get Luke tied up first, huh?"

"Yeah."

"You go get him ready. I'll get the rope."

I sat on the bench, and Matthew came to me. He straddled my hips. His balls met my skin as he lowered himself onto me. He sucked on my neck, licking, grinding, moving, teasing, until Richard brought two sections of rope to him.

He stood and took the ropes. He worked them around my wrists and through the handholds while Richard stood at the far end of the bench, his eyes on me.

I'd let him watch all night if it's what he needed from me. I ached to fulfill their every sexual wish—be for them what they were to me. Even if it meant Richard wouldn't be touching me.

Matthew finished securing my arms. I could barely feel the rope around my wrists. "Tighter."

He reached for the rope again.

"No, Matthew," Richard said. "The ropes are fine. Leave them." His head jerked from side to side. "Luke, stop asking us to hurt you."

"No. I don't want to hurt. Want to feel it."

He knelt beside me. "You'll feel it. You'll feel my mouth on your body, on your cock. You'll feel me inside you. And after you've come, you'll feel me on top of you as Matthew fucks me."

"Uh-huh. Please."

Matthew knelt at my other side. "You're gonna feel both our mouths on you." He kissed me, gave me so much to feel.

Richard rolled a condom on me. When it came to sucking, with no other distractions, he could give as good as Matthew. He switched between quick lunges and slow sucks on the crown of my dick. Matthew kissed me, tugged my nipples, and sucked on skin everywhere.

As promised, I felt it all. They were everywhere. All over me.

When I shot into the condom, the desire for Richard to swallow me down his throat, to lick me clean, to taste every last drop instead of throwing it in the trash overcame me.

Before I regained my composure, Richard stood and rolled me over. The ropes crossed above my head. He slicked me with his fingers and replaced them with his cock after only the time it took him to get the condom on. Relaxed, my body didn't fight him. He sank into me, and I felt him deep. The ropes tightened as I shoved back. He was giving me the fuck I wanted—the fuck I'd asked for. And it didn't seem to end.

Hard again, I groaned and lowered my head to rest on my arms. My tired body ached in the best way.

My second orgasm built, and my stomach muscles tightened. When my ass clenched around Richard's cock as I shot, he came with a loud cry.

He straightened before his body had stilled, and he flipped me over onto my back. He stood between my legs and stripped the condom from his prick, keeping his cock interested with a slow stroke. I'd never seen him stay hard before. Matthew was on the floor beside me, his own need apparent in his uneven breaths.

Richard's raspy voice sounded loud in the small room. "You two drive me crazy with your need, your begging, your openness. I've never known anyone who can give so much, take so much, from a single moment." He stroked himself faster. "I can't get enough of you. Can't stand to think about you leaving."

Matthew gasped.

"C'mere, kid. I want you inside me."

Matthew straddled my body and kissed Richard. His ass was on display before me, and I wanted a taste. I lifted my head and tugged at the restraints, but I couldn't get close enough. "Fuck."

Matthew swung around and knelt beside me again. "Please, Luke, can I untie you? You can touch Richard while I…"

"Yeah. I'll touch him while you fuck him."

Matthew ran his hands up each arm and untied me.

True to my word, I touched, stroked, caressed, and kissed Richard while Matthew enjoyed his ass for the first time. Breathless cries escaped both men as they savored each other in a new way. I loved them moving over my body. And even though I didn't come, it connected me to them in a way fucking them didn't.

Matthew screamed Richard's name over and over. His hips slammed one last time.

Richard groaned and clung to me as he came. "Thank you. God, thank you, Matthew. Loved having you inside me."

Matthew fell onto Richard. "Uh-huh."

"I think you wore him out," I said. "Keep it up and he might not want to stay."

Richard's body tensed over mine.

"No." Matthew's hands patted my arm then Richard's. "Wanna stay. Not going. Staying."

A tightness in my chest untangled. "Yeah? I guess we're all staying, then."

Richard's body relaxed over mine. "You're not looking for a new place?"

"I haven't since I got here."

"Good."

"You want us to stay?"

He raised his head off my chest. "I do."

Matthew's hand reached around Richard and found my face. He petted my cheek. "Staying."

Richard cleared his throat and spoke louder. "This is how we should spend our Saturday nights. No cooking, no work, some games, and then sex to make Matthew scream like that again."

Matthew shifted to the side and latched on to Richard. He buried his face in the man's neck. Richard returned the embrace. That was a cuddle if I ever saw one. What would it feel like to be wrapped up in them? To be held? *I don't want to know. Do I?*

I ignored the reaction and settled in, trying not to think about how long they thought I meant by staying. Or how long I'd meant when I'd said it.

Chapter Nineteen

Maria Lammon was a hyperactive ball of energy. I got a headache just watching her hands flail through the air as she drank her coffee, ate an orange cranberry muffin, and told me how glad she was to get my call, all without stopping for a breath.

"Thanks for agreeing to help me out," I said and sipped my own coffee from the disposable cup, feeling exposed in the middle of the highbrow coffee shop. It was not my kind of place. More along the lines of my father's taste. His office was nearby. Did he ever fetch his own coffee or lunch, or did some staffer always bring it to him? Would I look up and find him watching me talk to his old college friend?

"Oh, please," she said. "Even after all these years, there isn't much I wouldn't do for your father. Which means you, my dear, can ask me for pretty much anything." She flashed a smile, tore off another piece of muffin, and flung it into her mouth. "Tell me what I can do to help with this party."

Did my father have some sort of admiration elixir he used on people? Or was there more to her relationship with him? More than friendship perhaps? Maria looked years younger than her age. Her primped dark hair, manicured fingernails, and an absence of any serious wrinkles indicated a woman who had spent a lifetime giving thought to her appearance. She had to have been even more beautiful at the age of twenty-two. And she came from money. That much I knew from my online search the day before. Just my father's type.

"As I said on the phone, I'm trying to locate some old friends to invite. I was able to find some of my mom's but got stuck on my dad." I pulled the handwritten list from my pocket. "I met with Roger Vance, and he gave me your name and all these others."

She took the list in one hand and her coffee in the other. Her eyes crinkled at the corners as her smile widened. "Roger Vance. How is he?"

"Fine. He was helpful." I pointed to the list. "I had no other names but his when I started."

She looked over the list, nodding and smiling as she read certain names. "He did better than I would've thought he'd do. He wasn't all that observant." She pulled out a pen and started circling names and scratching off others, adding a couple of new ones to the end of the list, tapping the pen to her lips as she thought of more, all the while guzzling down the coffee. "There. Not sure how big your party'll be, but I'd start with the ones I circled." She handed me the list. "It should be fun to see everyone. We had some great times back then."

I sipped my coffee again and tried to appear casual. "Roger seemed real fond of my dad. I take it you all were close?"

"Oh yeah." She dropped the pen next to her half-eaten muffin, but her gaze lingered on it as she continued talking. Her body hadn't been so still since we'd first sat down. "It breaks my heart sometimes how easy it was to lose touch. But after Danny..." She shook her head and glanced at her coffee. She took a couple of quick sips.

"I heard about that. I'm sorry."

Her eyes met mine. "Did your dad talk about him much? Back then he wouldn't—well, he just sort of shut down after Danny's death."

"I didn't know anything about him until the other day."

"I figured."

"Can I ask what happened? Roger said it was an overdose?"

"Cocaine."

"Roger couldn't remember what he'd taken."

She set her coffee down, practically dropping it. It splashed up and out the small drinking hole. She didn't notice. "Really? That's weird." Her voice rose as she continued. "The night of the funeral, we all went to Uptown and got plastered, drinking to Danny. I heard him talking to Phil. He said he felt responsible. That he knew about the coke, knew about Danny's *problem*." She paused and spoke more to herself next. "Maybe he doesn't want to remember."

"Danny Conner had a drug problem, then?"

"No. No, it wasn't like that. He just got sad sometimes, needed a pickup. It was the '70s, you know. Danny was...emotional. He seemed happy that day though. Everyone was happy then, glad to be graduating. I didn't even know he had anything with him that night. He usually had it in that old pocket watch he carried, inside the back of the case."

"You were there that night?"

"Yeah. We all were. I think Roger was working. He got there…after."

"That had to be hard."

She nodded and resumed her earlier emphatic hand gestures. "It was a big party, night before graduation and all. No one was all that sober. I'll never forget that woman's scream. She found him on the floor in the bathroom. Phil, John, and I rushed in when we heard it was Danny. He was convulsing. I've never been so scared." She sat back hard, her chair sliding with the force. "Oh, you don't want to hear any of this."

"It's okay. I feel bad…for my dad."

She shook her head. "I'd never seen John like that. He kept screaming Danny's name and trying to help him until the paramedics got there. Then he grabbed Danny's pocket watch and jumped into the bathtub to give them room to work. I couldn't see around the paramedics so I watched John's face for any sign that Danny'd be okay. John just stood in the tub, clutching that watch against his chest, his eyes on Danny, his body rocking. I'd never seen him like that." She looked my way. "He's kinda the always-got-it-together type." She laughed but it wasn't a happy sound. "I think he took Danny's death harder than any of us."

Why? Was there more to my father and Danny Conner's relationship than anyone was willing to share?

"Danny was alone when it happened?" I asked.

"Yeah. I guess he went to the bathroom and did a line. Took too much or something." She waved her hand through the air like the why or how of it was inconsequential. To her, it probably had been.

"Uh, how long?"

"For Danny? I think they pronounced him on the way. By the time we got to the hospital, it was over. He never regained consciousness. Doctors said it was a fatal dose. Even if we had found him sooner, I don't think there was anything they could've done for him."

"I'm sorry."

"Thanks. Like I said, I think it made it hard for all of us to be together after that. But"—she smiled at me, her eyes crinkling up again—"it's been a long time. I'd love to see your father again." She plucked off another piece of muffin and waved it in the air. "What else can I do to help with this party of yours?"

I asked her a few more questions, and she chatted about my father's campus political career and a camping trip they all took for spring break one year.

When the last of her stories wound down, I said, "Thanks again for taking the time to help me."

"You're welcome. Sorry I couldn't find that album. It had a lot of good pictures—oh, and all the newspaper stories. Damn, I wish I could find it. I kept every article your dad and Phil were ever in. Did I tell you Phil was captain of the track team? That book's gotta be in my attic. I'd never have thrown it out."

"That's okay."

She popped the last piece of muffin in her mouth. "Nonsense. Let me take another look when I get some time. I know it's there somewhere. Give me your address and I'll send you copies of anything I find." She pulled out a datebook and jotted down the address I gave her. She asked the next question in the quietest voice she'd used yet, still writing as she spoke. "Is your father happy?"

Is he? "I think so."

"Good."

When I stood to leave, she gave me a hug, clinging to me for a moment. "I'm glad I got to meet you."

I glanced around the crowded shop as she held me.

She took a step back and smiled at me before she left in a flurry of movement, her purse, her hair, her arms whirling about as I watched her leave.

* * * *

"Hey, something smells good," I said as I stepped into the kitchen.

Matthew looked good too. He wore a ragged pair of jeans and a plain white T-shirt and moved to a tune from his iPod as he finished making dinner. He hadn't shaved, and the bit of dark stubble looked sexy on him. I couldn't wait to feel the scrape of facial hair all over my body.

"Hi, Luke." He smiled and removed his headphones. He came to me as though he had nothing else he'd rather do.

It'd been a few weeks since the night in the basement when he topped Richard. We worked. We played. We got to know one another. Matthew and Richard talked more than I did, but I offered what I could, mostly about my work.

On the weekends, Richard would cook, or we'd order in to give Matthew a break in the kitchen. He kept reminding Matthew he didn't need to cook all the time, but it seemed to please Matthew. And he had a knack for it. I wasn't complaining.

He also spent a few hours each day doing laundry and all sorts of domestic chores. Richard tried to put a stop to it early on. He told Matthew not to touch any laundry but his own.

It didn't last long. My dirty clothes were cleaned, folded, and put away two days later.

Richard began another protest one night at dinner, but I gave him a stern look to let it go once I saw the crushed look on Matthew's face.

I still spent Saturdays at work, but I left earlier and earlier each weekend in order to get home to the best sex ever. Yet it was more than that. I was having the time of my life with them. The constant stress and panic were gone, the obsession over my father absent along with them.

We spent Saturdays being lazy, eating pizza, and watching movies like *The Terminator*, *Aliens*, and *The Matrix*, which Matthew called "the classics." I was certain he hadn't seen a movie released before the '80s, forget anything in black and white. The night would always end in the basement. Sometimes I'd be tied up. Sometimes I wasn't.

And every day after work, I rushed to the kitchen, to Matthew's waiting arms and kisses, to the scents of the finest food I'd ever had.

"You like the smell?" Matthew asked. He covered my mouth in an eager kiss.

"Yeah, I'm hungry. What is it?"

He grabbed my hand and shoved it down the front of his jeans. He wasn't wearing underwear, and his cock was leaking like crazy. "It's me."

I couldn't move. "Matthew."

He buried his face in my neck and grabbed my ass. That snapped me out of it. I began a slow stroke, and his hips drove forward.

The front door opened and slammed shut. Keys jingled and scraped their way across a hard surface, then clanked as they fell. Richard charged past the kitchen doorway and kept going. His shoes smacked each step hard.

Matthew's hands tightened on me. "Something's wrong."

"Will the food keep?"

"Yeah. I'll warm it later."

We hurried up the stairs and found Richard in the shower, the bathroom filled with steam. I flipped on the overhead vent, and we undressed, neither of us saying a word. I opened the shower door. Richard was leaning against the ceramic tiles, his head tilted back, his body half under the water as if he hadn't had the energy to make it all the way in. The raised scar on his chest was pale against the red, heated skin surrounding it.

I reached in and wrapped my hand around his neck. His eyes opened at my touch.

"C'mere," I said.

He groaned and moved forward. He crushed his mouth against mine. He didn't give me a chance to join him under the water. He stepped out of the shower, not letting go of me. His body shook. His hands dug into my hips and yanked me against him. His cock swelled and came to life as our tongues fought. Matthew's lips found his neck, and Richard groaned louder. I stepped back.

Richard's arms snaked around Matthew. He drove their bodies together with urgency. The big hands forced Matthew's hips to move faster. Their mouths opened wider. They drove their tongues deeper.

I fetched a condom from the medicine cabinet and settled on my knees next to them. I licked at Richard's hip and delighted in the taste of his skin. The position of my head must have given Matthew a clue. He shifted around behind Richard and sank to his knees.

I rolled the condom on Richard, licked his length, and swirled the tip of his cock. I felt him harden more. Not the way I felt him harden in my hand. In my mouth, every suck and flick caused a different reaction from him. I understood what he liked best when he was in my mouth. I loved sucking his dick. It was tough to take him in far, but the stretch of my mouth, the tight fit, and the way he pulsed as I scrubbed my tongue along the underside triggered a twitch in my ass and sent my own cock barreling toward desperate need.

I knew the moment Matthew's mouth met his ass. Richard's legs spread wider, and his begging transformed into whimpers. He rocked between us. "Oh God. I need this. Need you two. Your hands. Your mouths on me."

His hands coiled through my hair. At first, he petted. Then he tugged me farther onto him. I relaxed my throat and took him in. My hands seized his hips and encouraged his thrusts until he came.

"Thank you. Oh God. Thank you."

His dick slipped from my mouth, and I helped him with the rubber. His shaking legs buckled. He collapsed and landed on his hands and knees.

"Fuck me, kid?" The words were a croak instead of his usual strong voice.

Matthew's eyes shot open wide. His hand stilled on his own prick. "Uh, yeah."

Richard spent the next few minutes on his hands and knees with Matthew pumping into him. Richard's hand sped over his dick as soon as it was erect again.

I put off touching myself as long as I could.

"Luke, c'mere," Matthew said. "Stand over Richard."

He always did have the best ideas. I got a rubber on and straddled Richard's back. I held my cock to Matthew's mouth and brushed it across his bottom lip. He opened and took me in. No matter what else he was doing, no one gave head the way he did.

The small room filled with moans, mine and Richard's, sounding loud for two men. I didn't last long, and Matthew came soon after me. Richard's hand flew faster over his own cock. He hollered, and his cum splashed onto the floor.

He fell forward. "Shit. These tiles hurt my knees." His sated, giddy laughter had Matthew and me laughing with him. He rolled over and lay on his back, a forearm draped over his eyes, a loose grin on his lips.

Matthew sat on the edge of the tub. "Wanna talk about it?"

"Don't," I said. "He's smiling now."

"Thanks, kid," Richard said. "Just get tired of people and their opinions of me and how I live my life." He sat up. "There's something I'd like to ask you both. Why don't we talk over dinner? It may not be as big a deal as I'm making it out to be."

"I can have the food heated up in a jiff." Matthew hopped into the shower and rinsed off. He had the table ready by the time Richard and I made it to the kitchen.

We were finishing eating when Richard brought it up again. "A friend of mine's throwing a dinner party this weekend. He has a few clients who might be willing to invest in my latest project." He took a last bite of his food and shoved his plate aside. "I'd like to bring someone with me."

"Someone?" Matthew said.

Richard rolled his eyes. "One of you."

I grabbed his and Matthew's plates and stacked them on top of mine. "You're out at work?"

He met my stare. "I don't advertise, but I don't hide who I am. Most people I've done business with know. But I've never brought two men anywhere. Might be difficult for people to understand."

"That's an understatement," I said. "Being gay is hard enough for people to accept. Add in the two of us…" I waved a hand through the air as I searched for the right words. "That might cost you."

"I was thinking the same thing. I hate the thought of keeping one of you out, but honestly, I don't want to go alone. When Doug asked me if I wanted to bring someone, I told him the truth about you guys, and he was a jackass. Pissed me off. He's been my friend for a long time." He paused. "It isn't fair to ask, but—"

I interrupted with, "The kid should go."

Matthew sat taller. "Me?"

I picked up the stack of plates and carried them to the sink. I rinsed the top dish until every ounce of food and possibly some of the dish's color had washed away, then swung the dishwasher open and stuffed the plate inside. This living together thing, being exclusive with them, was breaking all my rules. No way was I going to a party as a boyfriend, partner, or whatever the fuck Richard would tell everyone.

I turned around in time to see Matthew shake his head.

"What?" Richard asked.

"It wouldn't be right for me to go. I mean...you two look like you make sense together. You and me..." He shook his head again.

"Why the hell would you say that?"

"Have you seen you? I'm not old enough, not sophisticated, not...people would buy the two of you together, but..." He picked at the edge of a thumbnail. "Not me and you."

I crossed the room and dropped into the chair next to him. "Matthew, that's bullshit."

"He's right," Richard said. "And even if people think you're too young for me or whatever, do you think I give a shit? Don't you know what I see in you?"

Matthew stared at the opposite wall. "I have no idea."

Richard seized his face in his hands. "You are energetic, determined, caring, considerate, sexy—"

"Addictive, beautiful," I added.

"That's right," Richard said.

Matthew stared at him for another shocked moment before he looked my way. "You mean all that?"

"I do."

"We do," Richard said.

"No one's ever treated me with respect the way you do."

I hauled Matthew onto my lap, unable to keep away. "You deserve it." I peppered him with kisses, over his cheeks, his jawline, the corners of each eye, showering him with affection. My subconscious told me the gestures were absurd, but I ignored it.

Richard slid into the chair next to us. "You'll come with me?"

Matthew leaned his forehead against Richard's. "Yeah, I will."

Delight spread through me. Not because I didn't have to go to the party with Richard, but because we'd shown Matthew he mattered. Shown him he was worth something to us.

The rest of the evening progressed with laughs and excited bounces from Matthew as we watched *Close Encounters of the Third Kind*. And by the time Richard Dreyfuss sculpted his mound of mashed potatoes, Matthew had given up sitting by himself. He practically leaped out of his chair, landing on the couch between Richard and me. We ended the night with a slow, leisurely fuck that sent Matthew into a deep sleep.

I smiled as I lay in bed beside him. I'd helped to put him in a good mood.

I liked being someone who could make Matthew feel good about himself and his life.

I liked being someone who mattered.

What I didn't know then was that was the moment I'd gone too far. I'd become important to someone again, which meant I had given my father someone to hurt, someone to take away from me.

Chapter Twenty

On the night Richard and Matthew went to the dinner party, I opted to trade Saturday at the office for Friday night. After I finished most of the analysis for my latest project, I shut my office door and dialed Roger Vance's number.

He seemed quieter than the last time I'd spoken to him, reserved, tired.

I wasn't great at this getting-people-to-talk-to-me business. I figured I'd better get right to it. "I'm starting to put together that DVD and had a question. Thought maybe you could help me make a decision."

"Shoot."

"I thought about including some photos of Danny Conner, but I don't know what my dad'll think. I was wondering, how did he act after Conner's death?"

"How? Sad. Shocked. Like the rest of us." He took a deep breath. "It was a long time ago."

"Nothing odd then? Just the usual grief stuff?" I winced internally at my choice of words. Sometimes, I had no tact. At some point my curiosity was going to come off as rude and offensive. I wished Matthew were there to help me. He'd know how to go about this. But that would mean I'd have to tell them what I was up to. Which would also mean explaining a lot of things I wasn't ready for. I quickly added, "I don't want to offend my dad in some way."

"It was a hard time for all of us." He paused. Was he thinking back, or had I gone too far? "But...there was that thing at Mrs. Conner's house. It was weird and not like John at all."

I leaned forward and propped an elbow on my desk. "What happened?"

"It was at the wake. Danny's mom and John were in the kitchen alone when I heard John yell at her. She'd just lost her only kid, and he was screaming at her. Odd, you know. He was usually so diplomatic. Phil and I went to see what was going on. John was carrying on about a journal that Danny kept. He wanted it, but Danny's mom said she was keeping it. He screamed at her again, saying that Danny would want him to have it. Then he saw us, and that shut him up. He stood there for another minute, breathing heavily, more pissed than I'd ever seen him. Then he stormed out the back door. Phil followed him out with a pack of smokes in hand. Phil always knew how to handle the emotional shit better than I did so I left them alone."

"Did you ask Phil what happened? Why my father argued over the journal?"

"Nah. Never came up again. John was subdued after that. Quiet. Shocked. Like we all were. That night we got pretty wasted, but it was a quiet night. Toasts for Danny and all that. A few laughs about old times. Maria talked most, telling stories of the better days. It was the last time we were all together like that. Until John's wedding."

"And the wedding was the last time you all saw one another?"

"Yeah. As far as I know. Maybe Phil and John were in contact, but I doubt it. Why all the questions? This really about a DVD?"

"Yeah. Plus, I'm curious. My dad never talked about Danny."

"I haven't either. I kinda feel like a shit for that. He was a good kid, and I never gave him much thought. It was just…easier. But he deserved better than that. His mother's probably the only person that remembers him, thinks about him."

He was right. Danny Conner deserved better than the ending he got.

Vance sighed. "Hell, I don't even know if she's still alive. Probably not, huh?"

"Maybe she is. One more question."

"Sure."

"Maria says you knew about Danny's coke problem."

"I wouldn't call it a problem. Jesus. Maria always did worry too damn much. But…yeah, I knew. Listen, I didn't know it had gone that far or I would have said something. I would have tried to stop him. He was just depressed sometimes. He was shy as hell and he had a hard time getting girls to notice him. He was a cute kid, so I never got the why of that. The coke helped him relax. When we got to partying, sometimes he'd do a line or two. He never tried to push it on the rest of us and he seemed to be able to put it down without much trouble."

"Did my father know about Danny using?"

"He had to. We didn't talk about it, but we all knew. Danny had that old watch with him all the time. The case had a flip thingy on the back where he kept the coke." His voice was quiet when he spoke again. "I've been thinking about him a lot since your visit. Wasn't sure I'd like to, but it's been...nice, remembering back on the good times. I think adding his photo's a good idea."

"Yeah. I guess I'll do that."

"You got pictures of Danny, then?"

"Maria has some. She's going to send them to me as soon as she tracks them down."

"Oh. Could you, maybe, send me a copy?"

"Sure."

"Thanks. Someone should remember him, huh?"

* * * *

I opened the front door just after midnight and heard Matthew's purrs and hums and Richard's encouraging words.

"Yes, Matthew, yes. Kid!"

I smirked as I stamped the snow off my shoes and shrugged my coat off. I was just about to head into the living room when a large brown envelope on the hall table caught my eye. It was addressed to me. From Maria Lammon. I wanted to open it, but the moans and grunts were calling to me. I slipped the envelope into my laptop bag and headed in.

They were on the couch with Matthew riding Richard's lap, their bodies crashing together, but both men still dressed and following the rules.

"I spent the night slaving away, and you two get started without me?"

Richard's voice was tight. "Luke, need you. Get over here."

I stripped and made my way to them. Richard worked to get himself and Matthew undressed. I knelt by the couch, and Richard kissed me over Matthew's shoulder, his tongue getting me as ready as they were.

"The party was good, huh?" I whispered in Matthew's ear.

"Yeah, Luke. You should've seen him. All business. Strong. Confident. Sexy as hell."

"He is pretty damn hot."

"Me?" Richard scoffed.

"Yeah," Matthew said in a low purr. "Your body is unbelievable."

"You're good for my ego."

"He's good for both of us," I said.

Matthew faced me. The surprised look turned grateful as he

planted a kiss on my lips. I brought my body close to his and savored the joining of skin on skin and the buildup of arousal.

I reached for a condom, rolled it on Richard, and spread lube over him. I didn't want to let him go, but Matthew was ready. He'd come any moment if I so much as touched his dick.

I moved my hand out of the way, and he sank onto Richard. I slicked my shaft and shoved it into the tight grip of my own hand. I couldn't have stopped myself if I'd wanted to. Not with the way Matthew moved. I timed my movements with the slap of his body onto Richard, my eyes glued to them.

I almost came when Matthew spoke, his voice lower than I'd ever heard. Not his usual cries of pleasure. It was as if he had something to say and he wasn't going to let a moment of sexual release get in the way.

"Richard. Luke. So good to me. So good. Never felt like this. Not about anyone. Ever."

Richard groaned. His body jerked and bucked off the couch as he slammed inside Matthew one last time. The movements sent Matthew and me over with him.

I slumped onto the floor, my forehead pressing into the couch, my chest heaving. When I could move, I crawled onto the couch next to them.

Matthew had his head buried in the big man's neck. Richard stroked his back with a slow, soothing hand. "You okay, Matthew?"

"Yeah."

"What you said…that was…it meant a lot to me. You have no idea what it meant."

"Yeah?"

"Oh, yeah. I've been in a few relationships in my life, but I don't think I've ever felt this much, this fast. Not for anyone. Not as I have for you. Both of you."

I didn't think. I kissed Richard and landed a soft peck on Matthew's shoulder. "Me too."

Matthew sighed.

We sat in silence for a few minutes. I was grateful. I couldn't wrap my head around anything we'd said. I didn't want to have to explain more to either of them.

Not until I could explain it to myself.

Chapter Twenty-One

"Damn, is that all you do is work?" Matthew asked.

I saved the opened file and closed my laptop lid. "Actually, I haven't been working as much as I used to."

"Really?" He flopped onto the couch beside me. "I've never been that focused about anything. Not anything I should've been focused on. Probably why I had such problems in college."

"You seem focused when you're cooking. You seem to like it."

"I have been enjoying it. I never knew it'd be something I'd like to do. Never had a reason to before. My mom always cooked, and when she wasn't home, it seemed like a lot of work for just me."

"I usually made a frozen pizza or brought home takeout." I set the laptop on the coffee table and faced him. "Did you have a nice time at your mom's?"

"I did. She liked the necklace I got her. I wish you had come with me. You shouldn't work on Christmas."

"I had lunch with Walter earlier. I thought you hadn't told your mom about us yet—that there's three of us."

"I haven't. I don't mean to keep things from her. It's different. Not sure what she'll think."

"But she knows you're living with Richard?"

"Yeah. She wants to meet him and see where I'm staying. I told her he's a friend helping me out, that his place is closer to work. I don't think she bought it."

"They say moms know the truth even when their kids try to hide it." My own mother had been clueless about so many things. Maybe she had never been a mother at all.

"It's weird staying here without him. It's not..." Matthew took a deep breath. "I miss him." His eyes scanned the room. They settled on the lighthouse painting over the fireplace. He bit his lower lip. "I'm glad he got to go see his folks, but I can't believe he spent all that money to fly to New York for one day."

"There aren't many people I'd do that for." I couldn't think of one, except maybe— "Can I ask you a personal question?"

"Sure."

"What happened in college?"

"Oh…hey, it's cold in here." He jumped off the couch and fiddled with the thermostat in the hall. He crossed the room without looking at me and sat again.

I shouldn't have asked. I had no experience broaching personal subjects. Apparently, I sucked at it. "You don't have to talk about it. I didn't mean to push."

"No, I want to. I don't have anything to hide from you. Or Richard." Matthew lifted his legs. He settled his feet on the couch, his knees to his chest. He folded his arms around his legs and rested his chin on his kneecaps. "I was never the greatest student in high school. I didn't pay attention to my grades. It was tough being the out gay kid."

"I get that. Figuring out I was gay consumed a lot of my focus in high school."

Matthew nodded. "But when I got to college, I studied. I was doing well. Then I met someone. He wanted me to spend a lot of my time at his place. I skipped class. I never studied. I even stopped eating. He didn't notice or care. He wanted me to be there for what he needed. It was messed up."

He let out a heavy sigh. "It sounds bad when I say it out loud, but it wasn't the worst part. I flunked out of school. I had to move out of the dorm, take a semester off before I could start classes again. I didn't want to go home to my mom's. I wanted to stay with Jake. He said I could move in with him, so I did. My mom was furious. She'd never met him and she knew something was wrong. I was thin, and I didn't smile or laugh anymore."

Matthew without a smile or his laugh churned my stomach. I was glad I hadn't seen him like that. Yet, a part of me wished I'd been there for him. Not as a lover, but as a friend.

He turned his head in my direction and rested his cheek on his knee. "I stopped going to see her. I didn't want to hear anyone tell me he wasn't healthy for me. Then Jake started going out a lot without me. He was still in school, and I worked at a grocery store, trying to make enough money to live on. He had new friends and was losing interest in me. One night when he asked me to go with him to a party, I pulled out all the stops, trying to get him to stay with me, to want me. It was desperate and pathetic, but at the time, I wasn't thinking clearly. Then the college party became a drug-induced orgy. Jake put a line of coke in front of me and asked me to join him in bed with three other guys."

Matthew stared at the opposite wall, an empty look in his eyes. "I did it. All of it. Before then, the worst drug I'd ever tried was a joint, and I only did that once. The cocaine hit me hard, and with all the shots they were pouring down my throat, I was a mess. They did a lot of shit to me. Most of it I don't remember. I just know what Jake told me later. I don't have an issue hooking up with men I don't know." Matthew gave me a smile. Nothing near the grin he usually flashed me. "But going along with the drugs and alcohol, losing control like that, just wasn't me." He shook his head. "I put myself at risk to please him. I had no idea if they used condoms or not. Jake said they did, but I got tested at the free clinic like once a month for the next two years. I was kinda freaked."

"Shit, Matthew. I'm sorry." I wanted to kill this motherfucker named Jake.

He shrugged. "I'm okay. I mean it's been four years. It isn't a big deal. I know people who've gotten into more trouble. It just wasn't my finest hour. Losing myself. Falling so hard, I didn't even know how to be me anymore. I moved out the next day and went home to my mom's. She kept hugging me and stuffing food in my mouth." He laughed.

It was almost a giggle. Almost.

"Two months later, I joined the club. I felt safe at the Haven. The men there are serious about playing safe and not doing stuff their partners don't want done. And there's never any drugs on site. I haven't had sex with anyone but club members since."

"It sounds like you made smart choices once you got out."

He met my stare and grinned. "Thanks. One of the first things I liked about Richard was when he asked us what we wanted in bed."

"God, I love that. It drives me crazy every single time."

"Uh-huh." Matthew let go of his legs and turned. He dropped his feet to the floor. "It's like he wants to please us so much he doesn't bother with assumptions. He wants to know what will make us come harder than anything else. He can be controlling—which I also love— but he always wants to give us what we need."

I hooked an arm over the back of the couch. "When we're fucking, he takes me to places where I feel relaxed. Alive."

"Yeah." Matthew laid a palm on the cushion between us. "He always works to make it so damn good, but it's combined with care."

"Right from the beginning, I've loved watching you two. He touches you with a gentleness I don't have a clue how to show." I'd lost the ability to keep my thoughts from spilling out. Matthew did that to me.

"You do, Luke. The two of you can fuck me senseless, but at the same time, I've never felt more secure, more cared for than when I'm with him. Or you."

"I do...care for you." It surprised the shit out of me the words didn't literally get stuck in my throat. But he'd shared a piece of himself, and he deserved to hear my truth, even the one I hid from myself.

"I care about you too." He inched closer and placed a hand over my chest. "I want this to work more than I've wanted anything."

His eyes met mine, and the pure affection and passion in them didn't frighten me in the least. I ran a hand over the dark waves of his hair. We didn't rush to meet. We lingered, expelled several breaths on each other's lips before finally, slowly coming together.

The kiss was drawn out and sensual, a physical culmination of raw emotions I wasn't used to. We held on to each other instead of stroking or petting. We said more with our bodies than I could have put into words. More than I could have given him with anything other than a physical moment. So I showed him all I could. It was the least he deserved.

When Matthew pulled back, he said, "Richard's not like most men. To take this chance with us. To risk everything. It's rare. The way he goes with his instincts and trusts."

"I don't know what he saw in me, but I'm beginning to understand how fortunate I am."

"He saw you. You may not have thought you wanted this, but I think you needed us."

"I think I did."

He kissed me again, then stood and offered me a hand. "Let's tackle his fine body when he gets home. Let him make us feel relaxed, alive."

I smiled, content in the knowledge Matthew understood what I'd meant. He'd been there with me.

Chapter Twenty-Two

"Fuck this."

I slammed my laptop lid shut without an ounce of worry I might have damaged the damn thing.

My latest program, a simple time-card application for a chain of regional pet stores, kept generating errors, and after an hour reviewing lines of code, I gave up on trying to figure it out.

Something was seriously bothering me, and it had nothing to do with work.

It'd been a month since Richard and Matthew had attended one of Richard's work parties, and they were out together again. Without me.

I ditched my laptop on the coffee table and cursed at it again. I stretched out on the couch. Did I really want to be with them? Did it bother me to be left out?

Hell, yes.

I didn't want to give the admission much thought. Instead, I reached for my laptop bag and pulled out the brown envelope. I had looked at the pictures and photocopies from Maria Lammon too many times over the past few weeks, but I couldn't seem to stop myself.

The first time I opened the envelope, I flipped through the pictures as fast as I could, as though my father could see me via the printed images of him thirty-five years earlier.

I took a closer look as I went through them for what had to be the twentieth time. The relaxed, smiling images of my dad couldn't be the same man I'd grown up with. I never saw him smile, not like that.

I reached into my laptop bag and pulled out another envelope, one I'd held onto for years. I'd gone in search of it after first getting Maria's package. The photo of Tim and me had been taken at a dorm Halloween party, the day after we had sex for the first time. I had a goofy smile on my face, a match to the one on Tim's. We were pictured with five other guys, all of us holding up our middle fingers in salute to the photographer. I couldn't remember the names of the other guys in the photo. I rarely allowed myself the melodrama of looking at the only picture I had of myself in college, the only picture I had of Tim.

I held the photo next to the one of my father—two young college men. It was unnerving how much we looked alike. Weren't my mother's genes supposed to factor in there somewhere?

I set the pictures down and picked up the photocopied newspaper articles. Most were from the university newspaper, but a few were from the local city paper. Like the first one on the pile. A note was attached to the front.

> *Not something for your DVD, but I thought you might like to read the article. Maria.*

I pulled off the sticky note and reread the story.

COLLEGE STUDENT OVERDOSES AT GRADUATION PARTY

> *Local college student Daniel Conner was found unconscious in a bathroom at an undisclosed residence on May 11. He had been attending a graduation party and was alone in the bathroom when he ingested a fatal dose of cocaine just prior to his discovery. A friend of the deceased, Johnathan Moore, tried to revive Conner until paramedics arrived on the scene. Conner was pronounced dead at 1:28 a.m. just after his arrival at Memorial Hospital. Police have ruled the incident an accidental overdose.*

Five sentences. You'd think describing the end of a young man's life would take a few more words than that.

I pictured Matthew snorting a line of blow, having shot after shot forced down his throat. If he had died that night, would his newspaper story have read the same way?

I folded the paper in half and shoved it back into the envelope. I picked up the photos again, pausing at the one Maria had marked with another sticky note.

> *The shorter man in the middle is Danny Conner.*

Just a kid. He looked younger than Matthew. He also looked happy, one arm draped across the shoulders of a younger version of Roger Vance, the other arm around my father.

What led Mark Summers to my father's college years and the death of Danny Conner? And if I was right and my father had something to do with his death, the real question was why? Why would Johnathan Moore risk his future? Maybe he didn't kill Conner, but maybe the time he spent trying to revive him wasn't as helpful as it could have been. Perhaps Conner knew something my father wanted to keep quiet. Something Conner had written in his journal.

If I wanted answers, I'd have to find that journal. Roger Vance may have been correct in assuming Mrs. Conner was deceased. What then?

I stared into Danny Conner's eyes. *Was my father really your friend?*

I turned to another picture. Three men, the same pose, but the third man standing beside my father wasn't Roger Vance. My dad had one arm around Conner's shoulders and the other around the new man. Phillip Meade? Danny Conner didn't seem nearly as happy as in the last photo. He still had a smile, but it was subtle, a little sad the way it didn't quite curve his lips. I studied my father. The look in his eyes reminded me of the time he'd held a gun to my face. Was this where it started? Was this when he mutated into the vicious, hard man I knew?

I couldn't look away. I studied his slight, cocky smile, the way the university sweatshirt he wore bunched up on the arm he had around Phillip Meade, the way his jeans fit his frame too well. I pulled the photo closer and sat up. A small, curved metal object stuck out the top of his left pocket. A pocket watch?

I swiped the phone off the coffee table and dialed Maria Lammon's number.

"Oh, hi, Luke. Did you get the pictures I sent?"

"Yeah. I'm just now getting everything together. I wondered if you could help me identify someone."

"Sure. Let me just get the album out so I know what you're looking at." She was gone a minute. The more I looked at the object stuck in my father's jeans, the more convinced I became it was Danny Conner's watch.

When Maria came back on, I described the photo.

"Got it," she said. "Oh, that's a good one. John was so handsome. He's still the most attractive man I know in real life—you know, from seeing him on TV."

I ignored her comments and got to the point. "I know Danny Conner. The other guy next to my father?"

"That's Phil. I remember taking this picture. It's…it's the last one. Three hours later, Danny was gone."

Bingo. Might as well go for broke.

"You said Danny had the coke in a silver pocket watch." Not that she'd told me it was silver. "Is that it in my father's pocket?"

Silence.

"You still there?"

"That sure looks like it. But…Danny always had it. I think it belonged to his father. Why would John have it?"

"He picked it up that night, right?"

"But that was after. That part I remember. I told him later he should give it to the police or Danny's mom. He yelled at me to mind my own business. I'll never forget that. John never yelled at me. I think that's when I knew things were never going to be the same again. He was spending most of his time with Elizabeth and less and less with us. When he did get with any of us, it was always one-on-one. We just never were the same gang again."

"You sure this was the night Conner died?"

"Definitely. I got the film developed months after the funeral. I remember sitting there crying as I flipped through the pictures. This was that night." She paused. "Maybe Danny dropped it and John picked it up." She was talking to herself. I let her continue. "Maybe he…well, he had to have given it back to Danny before we started playing pool. They were gone for a while before that."

"Gone?"

"Yeah. Danny and John disappeared for half an hour. Then John came back and started a game of pool. Danny was in the bathroom. And then—why wouldn't John have said anything about the watch? At least to me."

"Maybe he and Danny argued?"

"Argued? Danny? No. He looked up to John. I think they were off trying to get Danny to make a play for someone. John was always helping him out with girls. It explained the coke. You know, like maybe he had gotten shot down again and needed a pickup. I think he got shot down a lot. He never wanted to talk about his love life. Which was a shame. He was so good looking, so sweet."

"Did you ever ask my dad what happened? Where they were?"

"No. After he yelled at that cop, no one wanted to push him into talking about that night."

"What cop?"

"The one that questioned us before we left for the hospital. John got so mad at him. Well, we all did. He kept hinting that Danny was suicidal, that there was something wrong with him, which wasn't true."

"What did he say to my dad?"

"They were in the other room, so I didn't hear. I didn't know what it was about until your dad's wedding. Phil, Roger, and I were seated together at the reception. We ended up talking about Danny. I mentioned that stupid cop, and Phil told us what happened. The cop called Danny a fag. Which was stupid. Danny was shy. Quiet. He wasn't gay. The cop was just an ass, you know. John never did stand for anyone talking shit about Danny."

I stared at the photo again. The pieces were coming together, clicking in place like hitting the right numbers in a combination lock. Danny Conner was gay. I had no doubt.

Had he made a play for someone that night like Maria suggested? For my father?

I finally found my voice. "Thanks again for the pictures."

"No problem. You let me know if I can help with anything else. I can't wait to see John."

Too bad for her, I had no plans to put together any sort of celebration where my father was concerned. Perhaps I'd celebrate when I had him out of my life for good.

The front door opened as I hung up the phone.

I tucked the pictures in my laptop bag. "Hey. Have fun?"

"No." Richard stepped into the living room. "People shouldn't invest money when they don't have a clue what the hell they're doing."

"Nobody liked your investment plan?"

"Nobody would listen to me. I've never had such a shitty response."

Matthew slid past Richard and headed toward the other end of the couch. He never looked my way. Before I could say anything to him, Richard yanked me off the couch and into his arms.

"It doesn't matter," he said. "Missed you tonight."

"Yeah? I uh…kinda wish I'd gone with you."

His eyes lit up, and the frustration vanished. He dipped his head and kissed my neck.

I glanced at Matthew. He sat on the end of the couch, his gaze fixated on the floor. Richard rubbed his erection against my hip and whimpered a low groan.

"You want something?" I asked.

"You know I do. Been thinking about it all night. Matthew looked damn good. Could barely keep my hands off him."

"He is pretty irresistible." I expected to hear a sign of appreciation from Matthew. He offered nothing.

Richard kissed me. He tasted odd, different, but I couldn't put it all together before his mouth was gone. He stepped backward and tugged me with him. "Come on, kid. Let's go to bed."

"You two go ahead. I'm gonna watch some TV." Matthew dived forward, fumbled for the remote, and slumped onto the couch again, curling up in the corner.

Richard's hands tightened on my waist. "Matthew?"

"It's fine. Really. I know we have a deal. You guys can maybe find something to do so you don't break the deal, right?" He waved us off with a quick gesture of his arm.

Richard didn't make a move to leave.

"I don't feel well. Don't make a big deal about it."

Richard released me and went to him. He laid the back of his hand against Matthew's forehead. "Are you okay?"

Matthew pushed the big hand away. "Yeah. Jeez, don't worry so much. Just don't feel well enough to get off. Okay?"

Richard sat in the chair opposite Matthew. The physical distance between them unnerved me. I wanted to go to bed and forget all about it.

The television sound was muted, but Matthew stared at the screen and nothing else. A tampon commercial—including a 3-D animation on the effective absorption power as compared to a competitor's product—came on, and Matthew kept watching it like it was the most interesting thing he'd ever seen. I sat next to him. He shifted a few inches closer to me, then stopped as if he'd moved out of instinct before he could remind himself he wasn't up for anything.

Richard spoke in a soothing tone. "What's wrong?"

Matthew gave up on the TV and hung his head. "I can't be with you tonight. I'm sorry."

"Can't be with us or with me?"

"With you."

Richard's mouth gaped open. "Why?"

Matthew fixated on the television again. "You had two glasses of whiskey and two beers."

"Shit. I didn't think about it. I usually have a few drinks. That's why I take a cab."

"You didn't drink last time."

"I didn't. I wasn't sure how long we'd stay. It was hard leaving

Luke behind. But tonight...I was pissed no one wanted to work with me. I thought since we weren't going to be home right away—I don't know what the hell I was thinking. I didn't mean to break my promise. I do things a certain way, act a certain way, when I'm working. I didn't think." He stood and took a step toward the couch.

Matthew flinched.

Richard sank back into the chair. "I'd never hurt you."

"You can't trust people when they're drinking. They aren't the same, even when they love you. My dad used to..." He shrugged. "It doesn't matter. I can't be with you when you drink."

So there it was. His own fucking father. If it hadn't been for men like Richard and Walter who got along with their dads, I'd have concluded fatherhood made men evil.

"Oh God." Richard raked a hand through his hair.

How much had Matthew's father hurt him? And how the hell could anyone think of hurting him? Pain stabbed at my chest and clamped down around my lungs. It wasn't the pain of my own life.

"You can trust me," Richard said. "I would never hurt you."

Matthew stared at the floor again.

"Look at me," I said. Matthew's eyes lifted. "You know he'd never hurt you. Not Richard."

"I know that." Matthew faced Richard. "I know that. God, I'm sorry. It's..." His Adam's apple bobbed as he gulped down the rest of his words. He threw his hands over his face.

Without thinking, I gathered him in my arms and held him. There were no tears, no sobs, nothing to signal he was upset at all but the way he held on to me.

Richard strode across the room and dropped to his knees. He petted Matthew's hair. "I won't drink again. I swear I won't." He rested his forehead against Matthew's temple. "I would never hurt you."

Matthew let go of me and wrapped his arms around Richard's neck. "I know."

Richard pulled him off the couch and onto his lap. He captured Matthew's face in his hands. "Please come to bed with me and Luke."

I couldn't stop myself—and I didn't want to. I slid off the couch and held Matthew between us. He had to know he was still safe with us, with Richard. I didn't want him to lose that.

Richard's mouth covered Matthew's in a soft kiss. "Let me make love to you."

"Yes," Matthew said.

I stroked his back, and he turned to me. "Let both of us."

He gasped and nodded.

Richard led the smaller man up the stairs, and I followed. The significance of the moment increased with each step.

In the bedroom, we undressed with the bed separating us. Our breathing deepened as need and longing increased with the toss of each article of clothing, each look exchanged. Richard went to Matthew. He made more promises as he laid him down, kissed him, caressed him, made love to him. They came together like nothing I'd ever seen before.

"I won't hurt you," Richard said. "No matter what, Matthew. It isn't who I am." He spoke with each movement into Matthew's body.

"I know. Know I can trust you. God, you're good to me."

They drifted together, in and out, up and down, their gazes locked, their bodies connected, each showing the other how much he meant his words.

Richard's thrusts lost the sensual rhythm moments before he came. One shudder followed another until his strong body stilled. Matthew continued to stroke himself.

Richard leaned over him. "Stop, kid. Don't come."

Matthew froze. He gripped the base of his cock and squeezed. His brow furrowed with confusion and frustration.

Richard kissed him. Then he rolled to the side. "Luke."

"Yeah," Matthew said. "I need you, Luke. Please."

I fetched a condom, grateful I hadn't touched myself yet. My hands trembled as I opened the wrapper. I tried to roll it on my erection, and my fingers slipped. What Matthew and I were about to do went beyond fucking. Beyond anything we'd done before.

Richard took the condom from me. He wrapped a large hand around my cock, stroked once, and rolled the rubber down. I shot him a grateful look.

Matthew slid under me, as lithe as ever despite his heightened need. I wanted to show him he could trust me. His gaze locked on mine, intent, serious. With him still stretched from Richard's prick, I slid in easily and we came together, our bodies locked.

"That's it, Luke," Richard whispered. "Make love to him. Show him he can trust us."

How the hell do I do that? I didn't know, but I had to try. I grasped Matthew's cock in my hand and brought him along with me.

"Luke." Nothing sounded better than my name in his moans. "Trust you. Trust this. Need this. It's huge. Being made love to by the two of you." His hand touched the side of my face. "Better...than without you."

"Better," I said. My release struck fast, and his followed.

I rolled off, and for the first time after sex, I pulled my lover to me. I wanted to keep contact with him. Matthew pressed his lips against my neck and hummed with each breath.

Richard curled around his other side and cleared his throat. "Uh, your uh...your father used to hit you?" Despite the stiffness of his tone, Richard's hand rubbed over Matthew's back in a slow caress.

"Yeah. When he drank. The rest of the time, he treated me good. He'd take me to the movies or play video games with me. It made it all the harder to take the pain, see the bruises, the blood. He and my mom divorced when I was in high school. He left and I never saw him again."

I held him tighter to me. "I'm sorry."

"I've dealt with it. Really, I have. I just have issues with people drinking around me. God. I'm sorry I made such a big deal about this. It's stupid."

"It is a big deal," Richard said. "I never meant to—"

Matthew rolled over and wrapped himself around Richard. "I know."

Their mouths connected. I let them have a moment together, and then I moved in and kissed Matthew, not able to keep away from him.

His kiss confirmed what I'd known for a while now. He needed us—needed me. I'd never been more significant to anyone in my life. My chest tightened in a wave of anxiety.

I'd never be able to live up to it.

Even with that outcome confidently settled in my mind, I wanted to try. For Matthew. For Richard. And for myself.

For the first time since I was nineteen, I had made love to another man, and I didn't want it to end.

Chapter Twenty-Three

"We need to talk," Richard said.

I poured a cup of coffee and leaned back against the counter. "Okay."

"Matthew and I got our new test results back." They were sitting at the kitchen table. Matthew didn't glance up from the cup he held tight in his hands.

"Yeah?" I'd found mine sitting on my desk the night before.

"We both tested negative. Again."

Matthew lifted his head. His dark eyes asked the question I didn't want to answer.

"I did too."

"I'm glad," Richard said. "Any thoughts on what we should do next?"

I forgot I still held the cup, and it slipped from my fingers. I gripped it before it fell and set it on the counter. "I'm not ready."

"The second tests were because of you. We didn't have an issue giving that to you. Matthew and I are ready. Hell, we were ready last time. We know we've all been careful in the past."

I crossed the room and sat beside Matthew. "I wish I could tell you I'm ready to throw the damn things in the trash. Hell, I want to. But it's a huge thing for me. It goes against everything I've ever promised myself. It's a chance I said I'd never take for anyone."

"I understand that," Matthew said with a nod.

I gave him an appreciative smile.

"I understand it too." Richard spun his coffee cup with his index finger and thumb. It twirled and twirled until he palmed the cup. The coffee splashed around without spilling. He cleared his throat. "My partner, Gregg, left me last year. He wanted things I couldn't give him. At first, I tried. We went back to the club a few times. We played, used ropes, handcuffs, but it wasn't enough. He wanted other men to join us. I couldn't give him that.

"I came home one day to find him on the couch waiting, all his shit packed and stacked by the door. He said it was over. I wasn't what he needed. After he walked out, I couldn't live in our house anymore. The next day, I went out and bought this place." Richard's gaze met mine. "I understand the fear of trusting someone, letting him into parts of your life where no one else can get to. I understand how all of this scares you. But here's the thing: I don't think it's because you don't believe we're safe at this moment. It's because you don't trust we won't fuck someone else, then come home and fuck you."

I stood. The back of my knees smacked the chair and shoved it away from the table. "That's not true."

Richard lifted a hand. "Let me finish. We're not saying we're gonna go bare without you. Not even for blowjobs. It's all of us or nothing. We agreed. What we want to figure out is how to get you to trust us. Trust is more important than the damn rubbers."

"I trust you."

Richard spun his cup again and shook his head. "I thought we were showing each other that the night Matthew and I came home from the last party. But maybe you weren't a part of it."

How could he say that? I'd been there with them. I'd shown Matthew I wanted him to trust me—that I could be trusted. Maybe I didn't trust *them*. Did I think they would betray me?

"No, he was with us," Matthew said, his gaze still on the table.

"I was." My head throbbed. I massaged my temples as I tried to wrap my mind around thought after thought. Why didn't I want to do what Richard and Matthew were ready for?

I wandered through the kitchen and fetched my cup. I poured the coffee down the drain and set the cup in the sink. What was I afraid of?

I opened the refrigerator, grabbed a bottle of water, and downed half the contents. Did I trust them? Did I think they'd hurt me?

I tapped the refrigerator door closed and sat at the table again. Both men were watching me.

I hadn't ever taken inventory of my emotional state, let alone verbalized it. I breathed deep and let the words flow as I made contact with them. "I think I trust you won't do anything to hurt me. Shit. I'm afraid I'll mess up. What if I can't make this work? What if I run? What if I make a mistake?" *What if my father comes looking for me with more than angry threats? What if he shows you who I am? What if it's like Tim all over again?*

"We all make mistakes," Richard whispered, his eyes on his coffee again.

"You don't."

His head jerked up. "You think I don't make mistakes? I make them all the time. Hell, the first month you were here, I figured I was fucking this up and you were going to leave. I was fucking up your lives. His life. I drank around Matthew. After promising I wouldn't. I was in my own head, and I didn't think about him and what he needed. I've fucked up plenty."

Matthew ran the tips of his fingers over Richard's hand, and the two let the touch linger for a moment. Richard returned his attention to me. "I trust you, Luke. If you want to have sex with someone other than us, you'll tell us. If for some reason you can't tell us before, you'll tell us as soon as you can. You wouldn't put us at risk. You're candid with us. You always have been. But in all honesty, I don't think you want anyone else."

"I don't."

"Then as long as you feel that way, I think we're safe to get rid of the rubbers."

"You won't hurt us," Matthew said. "If something changes, you'll tell us."

Richard leaned back in his chair. "You think it over, Luke. You have to be sure. I just wanted to talk about it. Let you know you can trust us."

"I trust you." I stood and hauled Richard out of his chair. His green eyes studied me. I skimmed my hands over his biceps and followed the curves with the pads of my fingers. "I trust you. I'll think it over, okay?"

Richard flashed the hint of a smile before he met my lips with his.

The intensity of the kiss built. He held my head firm to him, plastered his body to mine. His taste, his touch was everywhere in my mouth. Would I ever break free of the kiss? Would I ever get another breath that didn't taste like him? And did I care?

Matthew tugged my hips backward. "Come on, you two. Not on the table again. That hurt my back." He faked a groan and slipped out of the kitchen laughing.

Richard shook his head and chuckled as he followed Matthew.

We made our way upstairs and into bed. I kissed Richard again while Matthew explored our bodies with his tongue. The warmth of his mouth and the sound of his licking and sucking drove me crazy.

Richard rocked against me, his hard cock leaking over my hip. I slid my hand over his ass, ran my fingers along his crease. He twitched with my touch.

"Luke." He lurched for the nightstand, rolled back, and handed me a condom.

I tore it open and stared at it.

I wasn't conflicted. Or unsure.

I wanted it.

I wanted them.

I flung the condom in the general vicinity of the trash.

Richard grabbed my arm. "Are you sure?"

"Yes." A broad smile hit my lips.

"You have to be sure," Matthew said.

"I am. I have been. I didn't want to let myself admit it, but it's the truth."

Richard leaned over me. The kiss was wild. His tongue went deep. His teeth bit at my lips. God, I wanted him. I wanted inside him with nothing else in the way.

His entire body shook.

I jerked back. "Are you okay?"

"Yes. How should we do this? Our first time and all."

"I don't know. Matthew, what do you want first?" I glanced over Richard's shoulder. Matthew lay on his back, staring at the ceiling. His chest heaved with each shallow breath. "What's wrong?"

Richard flipped over.

Matthew wouldn't look at us. "I've never done this before."

"Good," I said. "You had to be safe. You still want to? 'Cause I'm beginning to think I'm the least nervous one, and that's saying something."

Matthew pushed up onto his elbows. "Yeah. Yeah. I want to. It's…it's…wow. We're really going to do this."

Richard barreled over onto him and used his thighs and hips to spread the smaller man's legs apart. Matthew wrapped his limbs around Richard.

"We are," Richard said. "Gonna feel me inside you. Gonna feel my heat when I come in your ass. Luke and I, we'll be the only ones to fill you like that."

"God, yes. I can't remember wanting anything more."

I joined them. We kissed and petted, rubbed and caressed until we couldn't wait any longer. Richard chanted words of appreciation and pleasure when his dick made contact with Matthew's body. I watched them for a moment, entranced by their bodies connecting, by the slide of Richard in and out of Matthew.

I slicked my dick and bent over them. I slid inside Richard and nearly came from the sheer pleasure of his tight heat surrounding me.

I held the skin of his shoulder blade between my teeth and concentrated on fending off my orgasm for as long as I could—and I hadn't even moved yet.

I drew back and pressed in. *My God.* The drag of his heat over the crown of my dick had me ready to go off. I thrust in again. And again. I wanted him to know I was there, inside him, to know I wanted this.

Pleasure flooded my shaft. It spread to my thighs, down my legs, and up my abdomen. I didn't want it to end. I wanted to stay buried in him until morning.

Richard's ass went tight around me as he groaned and came. Matthew cried out. "Richard, yes. Yes. Feel you. Love this."

My body lost all finesse, coherent thought long gone as I came. We collapsed in a heap on the bed, exhaling heavy breaths on one another's skin.

Matthew laughed and untangled his way out from under Richard. He sat up and tugged on my arm. "C'mon."

I lifted my head. "What? Jesus, Matthew, lie down for a few minutes. Enjoy the afterglow."

"I am enjoying it." He got off the bed and tugged on me again. He reached for Richard and yanked. "C'mon, guys."

"Where we going, kid?" Richard asked.

"To take a shower. I wanna suck you both off, back-to-back."

"Tonight?" I yawned with the word.

Matthew stilled, his eyes wide. "Of course tonight."

Richard shot out of bed and smacked my ass. "You heard him, Luke. Get the hell up. Matthew's gonna have himself a taste test." He dragged me off the bed.

"I'm up." I ran past Richard. "First one in gets his mouth for round one."

"You ass. You were faking that sleepy after-orgasm shit."

I turned on the shower and stepped in. Matthew followed me and crowded me against the wall, kissing me like we hadn't fucked in weeks, like getting a taste of me meant more to him than anything.

Richard stepped in and ran his hands all over us in a slow wash. The cool tickle of the soap bubbles he left behind slid down my skin. I ached for more of his warm touch, for Matthew's hot mouth.

"This shower isn't big enough for this," Richard said. "We should get in the tub."

Matthew shook his head. He watched my mouth. "I can't hold my breath that long under water."

I chuckled, but the sound left me in a gasp when Matthew dropped to his knees and pumped my cock to life. His full, wet lips wrapped around the crown of my dick, and my head hit the wall behind me.

The moment Matthew's tongue pushed at my slit, I lost control and almost came. His licks and sucks were more intense without the condom. And he hadn't taken my shaft all the way in yet.

I'd never last long.

Nothing had ever felt so hot and wet and tight around my dick. It was better than the first time he blew me at the Haven. Better than any other blowjob I'd ever had.

My stomach muscles tightened. I bent over him, and an explosive release I didn't think was left in me surged through my cock and balls. I gripped at his shoulders as tremor after tremor assailed my body. I may have stopped breathing for a minute or two. Matthew swallowed my cum and licked every drop off his lips.

He didn't even pause. He slid over and swiped his tongue up Richard's length.

"Fucking hell, Matthew!" Richard reached down and held his head. His fingers threaded through the dark hair.

I laid a hand on his chest. His pecs jumped as his body flexed and jerked under Matthew's attention. The uneven skin of his scar tingled the pads of my fingers. I gripped at his flesh, wanting him to feel me too.

When Matthew finally finished and came in my hand, his hair stuck to his forehead—damp from water and sweat—his lips swollen and his face flushed, he looked delectable. I kissed him and took a taste of Richard from his mouth, enjoying the flavor of someone else's cum for the first time in fifteen years.

We spent the next three nights exploring all the ways we could come inside one another. They were the best three days I'd ever spent with anyone.

And when Richard's cock pulsed in my mouth and Matthew's did the same in my ass, it felt right, perfect.

It didn't make me nervous. The time had come to trust someone again. To move on. To live a different life. Why the hell had I waited so long?

And how could I keep it all from ending?

Chapter Twenty-Four

The front door opened and slammed shut.

I paused the movie trailer on my laptop. I hadn't been able to focus long enough to pick out an actual movie to rent. I just kept watching one two-minute clip after another until I was certain I knew the pitch for every damn movie ever made.

Both Matthew and Richard had been working a lot. I was fidgety and bored. It annoyed me how little I liked being home alone. What had happened to the guy who liked his privacy? The guy who never needed anyone to eat dinner with, to talk about his day with, or to just sit and watch a damn movie with?

I was also on edge because my search for Abigail Conner hadn't gone all that well. She had died ten years earlier. Widowed at twenty-five, she had never remarried. I was unable to find who her home and personal effects had been left to. I imagined Danny Conner's college journal had long ago been lost to a landfill.

"Hey, Richard," I called out. "Thought you were going to be late."

A loud thud echoed from the hall. A repeat of the same sound followed. Shoes smacking the wall after they were kicked off.

"Fuck."

Matthew.

But the tone sounded wrong. More pissed off, frustrated.

I got off the couch. "Kid?"

Matthew hurried past the open archway. He made it halfway up the stairs by the time I stepped into the hall.

"Matthew?"

He hesitated for a moment, his back to me, his hands clenched into fists, and then he started up again. I froze for ten seconds, then sprinted after him. My feet caught the stairs two at a time. I glimpsed the side of his face before he slammed the door to his room shut.

"Matthew, what's wrong?" *Broken. I sound broken. And worried.*

And about to panic. I knocked. "Did I do something? Did something happen?"

The door's lock clicked in place. My mouth fell open. I raised my hand to the doorknob and turned. Sure enough, he'd locked me out.

I leaned against the wall and slid until my ass hit the hall floor. I raced through the past few days. What could I have done to hurt his feelings?

Nothing.

A loud thud echoed in the silence.

I jumped up and banged on the door. "Matthew, are you okay?"

"Leave me alone."

I slumped back to the floor.

I'd wait.

Wait for Matthew to come out.

Or Richard to come home.

Or for me to land on the perfect words to get him to open the goddamn door.

* * * *

The front door opened an hour later. My head smacked back against the wall, and I let out a long breath. I hadn't been able to move from the floor next to Matthew's door, the sounds of *Call of Duty* filling the quiet until he turned it off and the deafening silence began.

After a few minutes, Richard came up the stairs. "What's going on?" He sat next to me. "Are you okay?" He gripped my biceps and turned me to face him. "Are you sick?"

"Something's wrong with Matthew." I waved my hand toward the closed door. "I knocked and called for him, but he won't answer me or come out. I think something happened to him."

Richard looked at the door. "What happened?"

"How the hell should I know? He came home and ran to his room. I knocked and asked him what happened. He locked the door and told me to leave him alone. He was upset, pissed even."

"Pissed? Jesus. I've never seen him angry, let alone pissed off."

"He played his Xbox for a while, but it's been quiet since then. Every once in a while I hear him curse or slam something."

"Shit."

"Yeah. Not like him at all. You know me. I don't know how to handle these kinds of things. I've been trying to think of what to say."

I banged my head on the wall again.

Richard slid his hand behind my head and rubbed. "And?"

I shrugged. "I couldn't even get him to open the damn door. I don't know what's wrong and even if I did, I don't know how to make people feel better, or what to say."

"But you can listen. You've been doing that. Maybe that's all he needs. For us to be here and—"

Glass shattered behind the closed door.

Richard sprang to his feet and knocked. "Matthew? What's going on? Did you hurt yourself?"

Nothing.

The color drained from Richard's face. "Open the door."

Nothing.

I stood, ready to slam my weight against the door, which would hurt. The interior doors of Richard's town house weren't the cheap shit I'd had at every place I'd ever rented.

Richard sucked in a breath and opened his mouth.

The door flew open.

Matthew didn't make eye contact with either of us. "I'm okay. Jeez. I just need to be alone. Is that all right?" He swung the door closed, but Richard's hand stopped it.

Matthew let go and threw his hands up in the air. "I got fired. Okay? When I went on my break, my register came up short. My new asshole boss confronted me. Right in front of the other guys and the *customers*. He said he knew I did it. He said he was right about me and my kind. I lost my temper. I screamed at him. And got fired!"

Richard placed a hand on the smaller man's shoulder. "Shit. You didn't deserve that. It wasn't your fault."

"I wouldn't steal. I wouldn't. That homophobic asshole was just looking for an excuse."

Every muscle in my body wanted to move in and hold the man. What did Richard want to do?

He spoke, his voice tight but soft. "No, you wouldn't. We're here to listen, if you'd like to talk about it."

Matthew shook his head. He stared at the floor again. "Not like this. I get worked up when I feel like I'm failing. I don't want to be around anyone like this. Not you guys."

Richard gave a nod. "Okay. We'll be downstairs when you're ready to talk." He gave Matthew's arm one last squeeze and turned away.

"No, it's not okay." The words came out more pissed than I intended.

Richard spun around.

Matthew's gaze rose from the floor. There was anger and fear and hope in those dark eyes.

Why couldn't I walk away? If I wanted time alone, I wouldn't want them to bother me. Why couldn't I give the same to Matthew?

"We'll be here when you're ready," Richard said. He looped his hand around my arm and encouraged me to move with him.

I stood my ground.

"Give him space," Richard added. "He'll come down later."

No. Matthew needed one thing to feel better. I reached out, settled a hand at the back of his head, and brought his mouth to mine.

He held still for a moment. Then he kissed me back. His arms snaked tight around me, and he fed me everything he could with his kiss. A bolt of desire shot through me as he pressed his groin to me. His dick firmed more with each roll of his hips. He humped at me again and again, strong, powerful stabs of body against body.

Richard's arms circled my waist. He pulled Matthew and me into the hall. "In our room." His voice was low, desire beneath the trepidation.

With his help, we made it to the bedroom and undressed. Matthew wouldn't let go of me. His mouth gave mine no reprieve. He needed me, needed us. He needed to feel alive.

If nothing else, I could give him that.

I wrestled his body to the edge of the bed and flung us down, pushing hard against him. I sucked and bit at his neck. I twisted a nipple until the point felt sharp to the tough flesh of my fingers.

He bucked underneath me with unrestrained force.

I knew what to do.

I got on my hands and knees. "Fuck me?"

"Luke. Yes." His hands never left me. His body trembled.

I reached around and gripped his forearm. "It's okay, Matthew. We're gonna make you feel better."

"Yes," he said, and a desperate moan followed.

Richard retrieved lube from the nightstand. He slicked Matthew's shaft, then my ass. He held Matthew's hips with gentle hands as he lined him up. I lowered my head.

Matthew plunged into me. There was no finesse or grace about him. His movements were sloppy and forceful. His dick slipped out of me more than once, and each time he groaned, grabbed himself, and shoved inside me again. He had never been so fierce with anal sex before. My ass was glad it'd been getting a lot of play lately.

Richard stretched out beside us and placed a hand on Matthew's hip. Only after Matthew climaxed did Richard wrap a hand around his own neglected erection. I came as I watched his large hand work in a quick jerk.

Matthew collapsed onto my back. "Thank you."

Richard drew the smaller man into his arms and held him. His lips lingered over the pale skin at Matthew's temple.

I pressed close on Matthew's other side. Together we'd make him feel safe.

* * * *

I awoke the next morning with Matthew snug against me. He looked peaceful. I buried my nose in his dark hair, breathed in his scent—the spice, the faint mint that somehow always lingered—and enjoyed the man in my arms.

But it was early, and Richard's empty side of the bed nagged at me. I hurried in the shower and descended the stairs.

Richard stood in the darkened kitchen, leaning against the sink. The dim stove light reached the top half of his face. His eyes glowed like a cat on the prowl at night, caught in the beam of a car's headlights. They glared at me. Already dressed for the day, he held a coffee cup in his hand.

He stalked to the table and yanked out a chair.

I poured a cup of coffee and sat across from him. I didn't shy away from confrontations. I'd done nothing wrong.

He didn't speak until I swallowed the last of my coffee. I wasn't a shy man, but I also wasn't a man who liked to talk about anything involving emotions. And whatever he thought I'd done wrong had everything to do with the emotional state of the man I left sleeping upstairs.

"He told you about that asshole from college? Jake?"

"He did," I said.

Richard removed his hand from the cup and leaned back in his chair. He crossed his strong arms in front of him. His stare pierced me so long I almost started to speak, and then he continued. "He told me after he talked to you. I don't think he liked the idea of one of us knowing personal shit about him without the other knowing too."

"Makes sense. He said he didn't want to keep anything from us."

"That's why I brought it up. He's the kind of man who needs to get things out in the open. He needs to talk them through, get them off his chest."

"I'm not blind."

"You weren't seeing so clearly last night." He stared at me, his arms still crossed, his body still. "After he told me about that fucker, I noticed a difference in him. He seemed more connected to us, more relaxed, more open, both in and out of bed." Richard drummed his fingers on his biceps, the muscle in a state of permanent flex. "I won't let you push him away from us."

"What the hell do you think I've done wrong?"

"You can't just let him fuck you and make all the bad shit disappear."

"Really?"

He surged forward. His hands smacked the tabletop. "No, you can't."

I shook my head. "He's up there sleeping. He looks pretty blissed out to me."

"And in an hour, when you and I are off to work and he wakes up alone, what then? I don't think he'll be feeling all that blissed out. He'll be feeling like shit, and he won't know what to do about it. If we'd talked last night, maybe he could have gotten past it, thought about his next step while we were there to listen and support him, remind him how good he is. Now, today, he'll sit here feeling like a loser, a failure." Richard stood and scooped up his empty cup. He dropped it into the sink. I heard the glass crack on contact. He didn't flinch. "I hope you have a good day, Luke." He walked out. The front door opened and slammed shut.

Shit. Not likely.

Sure enough, every time I turned around, I pictured Matthew curled up on the couch, flipping through TV channels, not knowing what else to do. By the end of the day, I seriously considered going home and sitting on him until he talked about it—whether I wanted to hear it or not.

Though I was pretty sure I did want to hear it. I sat in the hallway for over an hour the night before trying to figure out how to get him to talk to me. I'd wanted to know what was wrong. I'd wanted to be there for him.

Richard was right. We should have waited and listened.

That meant I had making up to do—with both men.

Chapter Twenty-Five

When I finally made it home, I dashed for the kitchen. I longed to see Matthew bounce around the room as he made dinner, his iPod on his belt, a smile on his face.

I wasn't awarded that vision.

The room was dark. The aroma of spices and fresh herbs didn't linger in the air. Pots and pans didn't cover the stovetop. I couldn't find one hint he'd even been in the room. Richard's broken coffee cup still lay in the sink.

I sank into a chair.

Solid footsteps sounded behind me.

"Where is he?" I asked.

"He left a note. He went to his mom's for dinner." Richard sat beside me. He reached out and took my hand in his. "I was angry, but I didn't handle it right."

"You wanted to make sure he'd be okay. You care about him. I get that."

"I care about you too."

"I know. I care about you. And him."

Richard caressed the back of my hand with his thumb. "I know that's hard for you to say. I know it isn't something you want to feel, but—"

"No, it is. At first, it wasn't. Not at all. But now…I wanted him to talk to me last night. I just couldn't leave him alone. I had to do something."

He kissed me. Strong coffee flavored his mouth. He usually didn't drink more than a cup or two in the morning. He probably needed the caffeine. His side of the bed had barely looked slept in.

The heat of his strong body and the passion of the kiss made me dizzy fast, made the familiar tightness in my pants return. He could get me hard no matter what else I felt.

I'd get the man off and send him to bed. It was the least I could do.

Richard jerked back. "I want you both to move in with me, permanently."

It took a moment for my swimming head to shake off the desire. "Stay?"

"Stay. Indefinitely. Stop pretending you'll be looking for an apartment at some point. Move all your stuff here. No talk of this place as mine anymore. It'll be ours."

I didn't say anything.

"I know this is a huge thing for you."

I stared at my hands. No tensing. No freaking. No desire to run. "Okay."

"What?"

I looked up at him. Hopeful green eyes gazed back at me.

"It may not seem like it, but I'm trying. I want to stay here. I want to make this work." *I want to believe nothing will make me leave. Not me. Not my father.*

Richard flung himself at me. The force sent me sailing over the side of the chair. I landed on my back with him on top of me.

"Oh God. Luke, are you okay?"

"Yeah. Ow. I think so." I laughed and rubbed the back of my head.

His fingers explored my scalp.

I brushed his hands away. "I'm fine."

He smiled at me, and his lips covered mine again. He rolled us around on the floor, tickling my sides. I laughed more, letting the ease and comfort wash over me.

I attempted a dodge of his movements. My hips and ass wiggled, but his solid body pinned me in place. He unbuttoned the top of my pants and slid a hand in. I was still laughing as he grasped my dick.

He didn't relent with his hand or his mouth. I thrashed my hips into his touch. He knew how to work me with his big fist. I could smell my own need.

My hands grazed his bulge as I went for his pants, and he groaned. I lowered the zipper, pushed down his underwear, and released the red, swollen prick. As it always did, his cock firmed more with my touch. I considered taking him in my mouth, but his next words stopped me in my tracks.

"God, Luke. I need to fuck you."

I stilled. "Maybe we should leave the clothes on."

Richard threw his head back and laughed. "I'd hope I can have at least some control." I stroked his cock. His eyes rolled back and he pumped his hips. "Uh…okay. Let's leave the clothes on, but let me at your dick."

He undid my pants and lay on top of me. We rocked in swift jabs, sliding our dicks together, and came fast. We lay on the kitchen floor, breathless, our shirts lifted, our stomachs slick with our spunk, and our spent cocks lying free.

Some goddamn humping, and it was one of the best fucks of my life.

Richard reached for a kitchen towel and wiped us clean before he fell back onto the floor beside me. "Shit, never thought you'd say yes."

"Me neither. When you first asked us to stay, I thought I'd be moving to Walter's after two days."

He rolled onto his side and propped his head on a bent arm. "That was my fear. It only grew the more I got to know you. At first I didn't want to see you leave before you gave us a try. Then I didn't want to see you go because I didn't think I could take you walking out on us."

I pushed him over and straddled his hips. I drove my lips, my body, my hands against him, letting him feel me, showing him I had no intention of leaving.

I swept my hands under his shirt. I'd never get over the addiction of his skin. My fingers brushed over the scarred flesh. "How'd you get this?"

A laugh rushed out of him. It was almost Matthew's giggle. It took a moment before he could form words. "Matthew asked me that the first week you were here."

"I never said I was one for heart-to-hearts."

He lifted a hand to my face. "I never asked you to be." His fingers stroked my cheek. He dropped his hand and snaked it under his shirt to the edge of the scar by his nipple. "Some homophobic asswipes attacked me at a college party. One of them had a knife."

"Oh God." I unbuttoned his shirt and ran my fingers through the blond chest hair, over the firm pectoral muscles. His flesh jumped. Small bumps rose up. The color of his tan skin darkened. My fingertips examined the raised line of flesh.

He sucked in a sharp breath. "Luke."

I traced the scar to his underarm and back.

"I've never liked anyone touching me there but you."

Heat rose in my cheeks. "It was bad?"

"I was in the hospital for a week. I lost a lot of blood, and there was an infection. It was full of dirt and glass from the beer bottles. They dragged me pretty far."

"What happened?"

"I've never hidden who I prefer to sleep with. My junior year I lived in a frat house on campus. Some of the brothers didn't like knowing a gay guy slept in the same house they did. They wanted me out, and beating the shit out of me was their best plan. I lost the fight."

"That's hard to imagine."

"It was me against five. I knew I'd never win. Not when I saw the knife. But I couldn't back away. I couldn't let them push me around." He laid a hand over mine. "No one bothered me again. The rest of the fraternity respected me for fighting—for staying when it would have been easier to leave." He moved our combined hands along the scar until my palm lay over his heart. "They sent me to a plastic surgeon, but I didn't want it fixed. I wanted the scar."

"Why?"

"To remind me no matter where I go in life, someone could always have an issue with me. For whatever reason. Because I'm well-off. Because I'm opinionated. Because I'm gay. I can't let people get in my way or I'll never succeed. I'll never get what I want."

"What do you want, Richard?"

"Right now? I want you to move in with me."

"I want that too."

We stared for several moments, watching each other's eyes and lips. When the kiss finally came, he met me halfway, and the slow touch said more than the words we'd just exchanged. We didn't make it about anything more than being together—about saying what words couldn't.

We eventually let go, adjusted our clothes, and got off the floor.

Richard righted the chairs and took a seat. "I have to check in with Matthew when he gets home. See if he wants to talk. Maybe help him figure out what he wants to do next."

"Yeah."

"Will you be there with us?"

"Sure. But when the talking's done, can we fuck the shit out of him again?"

"Yeah. We're guys after all." He winked.

I had missed that calm confidence. I didn't like being the reason he'd been upset. He deserved better. He gave Matthew and me a place to stay. He deserved the truth.

I sat across from him. "I don't want you to take this the wrong way, but I don't want anyone knowing I'm living here."

The pleased expression vanished, replaced by a creased forehead and a frown.

"I don't tell people where I'm living. Work never even has my address. I gave them Walter's."

"Why?"

I sucked in a deep breath. "My father." Easier to say than I expected. "I don't want him to know. I move around, never stay in one place too long, and he spends a lot of time and money to find me. His way of tormenting me."

"Why would he want to hurt you?"

"I think he'd do anything to change me. But since he can't, he's been trying to control me, to get me to live the way he wants. I don't think he considers me a son anymore. I'm a challenge for him." I shrugged. "I'd rather he didn't know. It's less complicated."

"Okay. I won't tell anyone if that's what you want."

"Thanks."

"If you need help with anything, if there's any trouble, you'll tell me?"

I wanted to say I'd handle things on my own, but that would bother Richard. As much as I wanted to keep my father away from them, I couldn't let my own fears hurt either of them.

"I will."

* * * *

Richard and I settled in to watch a movie and were halfway through it when Matthew came home and headed for the kitchen. Richard flicked off the TV, and we trailed in after him.

He was bent over with his head in the fridge.

Richard smirked and groped his ass. "Hey."

Matthew stood, a bottled water in his hand. "Oh, hi guys. Thought I heard the TV. Anything good on?"

Richard sat at the table. "No. How was dinner?"

Matthew sipped his water and sat. "Good. I feel bad I haven't told her about us. About Luke. She wants to see where I'm staying and meet you. I've been putting it off. She knows something's up. Most of my stuff's still at her place. I'm scared she's not going to forgive me for keeping this from her."

I sat next to Richard and eyed him.

"Speaking of that, Luke and I were talking about making things permanent. You could move your stuff in. Tell your mom about us. Have her over here. We'll set this place up so it belongs to all of us."

The water bottle halted halfway to Matthew's mouth. "Yeah?" He looked at me, those dark eyes unsure, uneasy.

"I'm going to bring over the rest of my stuff from Walter's as soon as I can."

Matthew set the bottle on the table. "You're gonna live here?"

"I thought I already was," I said.

"You know what I mean."

"I want us to live together. Not as a temporary thing, but for real."

Matthew sat taller. "You do?"

I reached across the table and gave his hand a squeeze. "I do."

His fingers looped around mine. "I want to live with both of you."

Richard scooped up Matthew's other hand and kissed his fingers. "Me too."

I gave Matthew's hand a squeeze and sat back. "I'm sorry about your job, but your boss sounded like an asshole."

"He was. But I liked working there—up until they hired him."

Richard took the cue again. "You want to talk about it? Talk about what your plans are?"

"Yeah?" The surprise in his voice tore at my heart. "I've been thinking about going back to school. Last time, I didn't have a clue what I wanted to do, and I messed it all up. I always thought I'd go back." He swallowed a long gulp of his water and cleared his throat. "I need to give up my membership at the club. I don't have the money. I never did, but I needed it before so I made sure I could swing the fee. Now...we aren't going, and I'm not sure when I'll get another job."

"I don't see a need for us to go back," Richard said. "Unless we wanted to play somewhere. But I won't ever want to invite anyone else to join us."

Matthew's unease melted away. He licked his full lips. I wanted to make love to that mouth. Show him how much I wanted to live with him, how much I wanted to be with him.

I had something to say first. "I don't have any reason to go to the club. I guess I see the point of somewhere we can go as a threesome, but as for playing around, I...I don't want to see anyone else touch either of you." My knee bounced and my heel tapped the floor repeatedly.

Richard's hand gripped my thigh, and my leg stilled. No one's simple touch had ever ignited such need. Or such peace.

"Okay, Matthew," Richard said. "Cancel your membership."

Matthew smiled again. Then his expression sobered. He glanced around the kitchen. "Can we talk about living here? How do we split expenses and stuff?"

"Why don't you each give me what you can, and I'll put it toward the bills." Richard looked my way. "You could make it the same as what you were paying for rent and utilities at your old place."

"That wouldn't cover the cost of your water bill. I can swing more."

"We'll work it out. And Matthew, you can wait until you get another job or figure out what your plans are. I want to know what you're paying your mom too, if you still need to help her, so we can factor that in. If you decide to go back to school, I can help with the money for tuition, give you a loan. We can discuss you assisting with the finances after you're done with school."

Matthew set his water on the table. "That's…too much. I can't accept you paying for me to live here and for school. Even a loan. That'd be weird. I need to know I can take care of myself."

"I understand. I've got the money and I want to help."

"Thanks. I…I've gotta figure this out for myself. I keep messing up. For once, stuff was going good. I thought losing this job was me fucking up again. But maybe…"

He stood, grabbed his bottle of water, and guzzled the rest as he meandered through the kitchen. He tossed the empty bottle into the recycling, opened the fridge, and stared inside. We'd just stocked it full of water and soda. What the hell else could he be looking for? I shifted in my seat. Waiting for people to talk was hell. Pure, evil, kill-me-now hell. Impatience boiled over. I was about to scream at him. I jammed my thumb into my thigh over and over. The dull pain distracted me from nothing. On the next jam, my thumb struck Richard's hand. He gripped my fingers and pressed my palm to his thigh.

I breathed more easily. Anything was easier when I was touching his body.

Matthew shut the fridge door and came back to the table. "Maybe I'm supposed to do something else. Go to school. Finally figure out what I want to do with my life. Maybe this time, it was a good thing."

"That's a good way to look at it," I said. "You should move forward, make your life better. Live here with us. Go back to school. Let Richard help you. Let me help you."

"Thank you. For caring. For listening. For wanting to live with me. I'm gonna try. But right now it's uh, kinda late…" He flashed us a teasing grin and cupped his groin as he walked backward. "Wanna go to bed—our bed?"

I couldn't hold back the laugh. "Yes."

Richard stood and pulled me with him, grabbing Matthew before he got too far away. He wrapped his large arms around us. "Welcome home."

We made love with Matthew suspended between us. He cried out one word as he came. "Home." And when he landed on the bed, he laughed. "I'm home."

"We all are," Richard said.

I grunted my sated agreement. Pride like I'd never known before surged through me. Not pride in my work. Not pride in keeping my father and his men at bay. Not pride in my sexual conquests. Pride in who I was becoming. I'd stayed in the kitchen, listened to Matthew, listened to Richard.

My mind and body relaxed in an entirely new way. My thoughts ran free, spilling out of my subconscious in a rush.

I love having sex with them. I love lying in bed with them. I love listening to them talk to each other.

God, I love…no. I couldn't.

I squeezed my eyes shut and tried hard not to think about those three damn words. It took everything I had to breathe, the pure relaxation long gone.

Chapter Twenty-Six

Sleep continued to evade me for the next few nights. I convinced Richard and Matthew to hold off on moving our stuff in, suggesting we should wait until Matthew had a chance to talk with his mother and then rent a small truck to collect everything at once. They agreed, oblivious to my growing discomfort.

What the hell was I afraid of?

Falling in love with someone again? Or losing them?

I'd managed to travel down a slippery path I never thought I'd be able to stay on. I'd found what I'd lost years ago. And not just one man, but two.

But if my father found out, would he make good on his old promise?

I forced the concerns out of my head. I was still there, with them. I had overcome all of my other fears. I relaxed by the fourth day and found myself enjoying the company of both men again.

By the next Friday night, I was enjoying more than Richard's company. Matthew had gone to his mom's again for dinner. Richard and I made it an early night. We sucked each other off, sixty-nine-style, in the middle of the bed, and fell asleep soon after, Richard curled around me, my hand on his hip.

I awoke a few hours later to an empty bed. At first, it didn't seem odd—years of sleeping alone were hard to erase from the memory. Then sleep escaped me, and the peculiarity settled in. The bed wasn't supposed to be empty next to me. Not anymore. Not ever again if I could get up the nerve to order the damn moving truck.

I checked the clock. 1:36 a.m.

Where the hell were they?

I descended two stairs before I heard it: a low moan from the living room.

What the fuck?

They were screwing around without me. Why would they go to the living room? Any time before when two of us awoke wanting something physical together, we stayed in the bed. None of us saw a need to leave the third person out of it.

Or maybe they were doing more. What else would they hide from me? I wasn't surprised they wanted to have sex in the one way we'd agreed not to do outside the three of us. It was going to become a necessity. I didn't think any of us would mind, once we all said yes.

But we had an agreement.

I considered heading back to bed and letting them have their fun, but I wanted them to know they'd been caught. Hell, I might as well get off too.

I swallowed hard and turned the corner, anxious and not just a little bit aroused at what I'd see.

Both men were seated on the couch, fully clothed, Matthew's head on Richard's chest. His dark hair was mussed, and tears clung to his face. Richard spoke low, comforting words. His large hand stroked Matthew's back, smoothing the fabric of his shirt as he petted the smaller man.

I wanted to turn away, climb the stairs, and crawl back into bed.

Fucking I could join in on. Crying and hugging—I didn't know how to handle that.

Richard lifted his head. My heart raced at the concern on his face. *Not good.* Worse than Matthew getting fired. Worse than the night Richard drank with him.

He waved me over.

My legs twitched, wanting to move away from them as if they'd received an autopilot message from my brain. But when Matthew's miserable, tear-filled eyes met mine, I lurched for the couch and dropped to my knees.

"What is it?"

Richard answered. "He told his mom about us. She asked him not to come back. Said she needed some time. Said she's confused, disappointed."

"She doesn't get it, doesn't know why I need this." Matthew's voice cracked. His eyes were bloodshot, his pale skin ashen, his full lips dry. "She's never not accepted me—accepted who I am."

My gut churned. Matthew wasn't supposed to look like that, to sound like that. He was fire and light and bounce. Pain and fear didn't look right on him.

"I was about to tell him I think we should go see her." Richard lifted Matthew's chin. "Help her to understand."

"You will?"

Air filled my lungs when Matthew smiled. But his expression changed as he turned to me.

"We will," I said.

"She might deal better if she got to know you, if she saw us together."

"That's what I'm thinking," Richard said.

I nodded.

Matthew dragged me onto the couch until we lay in a pile with him laughing between us.

* * * *

I adjusted my tie for the third time and inspected it in the bathroom mirror. It still didn't look right. *Fuck it.* Whatever the hell I wore would be the least of her concerns.

I stared at myself in the mirror.

Hello, Mrs. Stewart.

Hi, ma'am. My name is Luke.

It's a pleasure to meet you, ma'am.

I'm one of the two men who likes to stick his dick up your son's ass.

What the hell was she going to think of us?

She had to accept us. I wasn't going to be the reason he lost his family.

"Nervous?" Richard asked from the doorway, his voice low.

"Nah."

"Sure you're not."

My head snapped in his direction. "Aren't you?"

He leaned on the doorjamb and folded his arms. "I have no intention of letting her continue to hurt him."

"It's that simple?"

He stepped into the bathroom and turned me toward him. He worked apart the tie's knot and retied it. "We'll make her see."

"Is everything always so easy for you?"

"This isn't easy. She isn't the first or the last person who's going to give us shit over this. Our bed is too crowded for most people. But she loves Matthew. And he needs her. We'll keep trying until she gets it. I won't give up on this one. Not his mom."

"He's been different, not like him at all. Fidgety and edgy, snippy even."

"He's entitled. But it's not going to continue. Not if we can help it."

I checked my tie in the mirror. Better. "You know, if it was just you and him, she'd have no issues. She'd be thrilled."

"So what?" He wrapped his arms around my waist, and his chin came to rest on my shoulder. "She'll have to get used to it. It isn't ever going to be just me and him."

Ever? Could three men really last?

I reached around and grabbed his ass, bringing him in close.

I sure as hell hoped so.

* * * *

Matthew's mom greeted us with a warm smile at the door of her apartment. She gestured for us to come in and laughed as she moved out of the way for Richard's large frame.

Same laugh. Same smile. Same wavy, dark hair. If I'd seen her on the street, I would have known her as Matthew's mother. All smiles and light and laughter.

Not the greeting of a woman who had issues with us.

"Come here and give your mother a hug." Her voice lilted as she spoke to her son. She wound her arms around Matthew.

"Mom, I'd like you to meet Richard Marshall and Luke Moore."

The small woman dipped her head in an all too familiar gesture. She reached out and shook our hands.

"Nice to meet you, Mrs. Stewart," Richard said.

"Please, call me Lydia." She turned to Matthew. "They are very nice looking, Matty."

I mouthed the nickname, and Matthew rolled his eyes.

Lydia shook her head and giggled. "Come on into the kitchen. Dinner's almost ready. I made iced tea."

The apartment was small and full of knickknacks, mismatched furniture, and half-finished sewing projects, but there was no dust or disorder about the place. The smell of fresh baked sugar cookies and cinnamon candles gave the impression of Christmas morning. Walking through her home made me feel like I'd been wrapped in a warm blanket on a snowy day.

We stepped into the kitchen, a small room with compact appliances, a rollaway dishwasher, and a distressed wood table that filled the open area off to one side. A battered wooden rocker with worn edges and scratches sat against the wall. I took a closer look. Several spindles were broken. If she sat in it, she'd get hurt.

A quilt hung over the back. Probably handmade. My mother had stitched a similar piece throughout my third grade year at St. Mary's

Elementary. The memory was one of the few I let myself keep. She sewed the quilt in our living room while I did my homework on the coffee table. She'd give me cookies and a glass of milk while we worked. When I drank the last of the milk, she'd pour another before I could ask for more and slip me three extra cookies.

"I need to get it repaired." Lydia reached down and brushed her fingertips over the arm of the rocker. "I can't use it like it is now."

"Did you make the quilt?" I asked.

Her smile grew. "I did. For Matty when he was a newborn. He wouldn't go to sleep unless I wrapped him in that quilt and rocked him. We did that every night until he was seven years old."

"Mom," Matthew screeched. He set four plastic glasses on the table with a loud clank. Tea spilled over the tops.

"Shush, Matty. Don't interrupt your mother."

"Yeah, kid," I said. "Don't interrupt your mother."

Matthew stuck his tongue out at me, and that had me laughing. He grabbed a dish towel and set to wiping the mess.

"He was such a good boy. Always told me everything. What he did at school. What his friends were doing. Which kids he liked. It's how I knew he was gay. I couldn't deny it when he never once mentioned a girl." She paused and looked right at me. "Some men don't talk much to their mothers. Not my Matty. When he keeps something from me, it's because it isn't good for him."

Matthew reached for her hand. "Mom, this is good—"

She jerked away and peered into the oven. "Dinner's ready. Have a seat."

Richard patted Matthew on the shoulder and whispered, "We're not giving up."

Lydia puttered around the kitchen and had a huge feast on the table in minutes. A roast, boiled potatoes, asparagus with hollandaise sauce, and homemade applesauce.

"Tell me about yourselves," she said as she dished out the food.

Richard spoke first. He told her about his business, his house, and his family. She asked us our ages and didn't seem bothered by the difference with Matthew's. Richard talked more easily than I, but I did my best to add more than my usual one comment every hour.

Halfway through the meal, the talk dried up, and we finished our food in silence. No one seemed concerned by the quiet but me. I didn't have the social skills to determine if it meant she didn't like us. I threw Richard a concerned glance.

He smiled at me then spoke. "Now I know where Matthew learned how to cook. This is excellent."

"I can see you have a sense of humor. My son has to be the worst cook. I remember one Mother's Day when he made macaroni and cheese from a box. It came out a dark brown color. I had to smile and swallow and try not to gag."

The tension in my chest eased as everyone around the table laughed. I liked hearing about Matthew from someone who'd known him all his life. Someone who knew all his secrets. Someone who loved him.

"Well, he's come a long way," I said. "He makes the best dishes."

"Really?" She set her fork down. "Matty?"

"I...uh..." Matthew placed his napkin on the table. He slid it under the edge of his plate and back out, repeating the action several times until he lowered his hands in his lap. "I took a cooking class."

"When?" she asked.

He dipped his head again and ran a hand through his dark waves. "Um...I started it the Monday after Richard asked us to move in. I wanted to be able to do something...for them."

Richard's mouth dropped open.

I couldn't help myself. I beamed at Matthew. "You're a quick study. I've never had such good food."

Matthew smiled back. It was a nervous and embarrassed smile, but it relaxed me nonetheless.

Richard kissed Matthew's cheek. "You're something else, kid."

Lydia stood and shifted on her feet. She carried empty plates to the kitchen counter. "Why don't you boys head out to the living room? I'll bring in coffee and cookies."

Matthew jumped up. "Mom, let me do the dishes."

She shooed him away. "Nonsense. It doesn't take much work. That's why you bought me the dishwasher last Mother's Day, right? This is my day to treat you and your friends." She patted his ass and pushed him toward the doorway.

Richard made a move to help her, but Matthew gave him a look warning him not to try.

The living room was a treat. Framed pictures of a young Matthew covered every table and shelf in the small room. Matthew in a baseball uniform, a soccer uniform, holding a puppy, dressed in a *Star Wars* Chewbacca costume, wearing a graduation cap and gown for what had to be a kindergarten ceremony.

Richard and I sat on the couch, pointing out various photos to each other.

"Thanks for coming, guys." Matthew settled in an armchair across from us.

"She seems okay with things so far," Richard said. "Maybe she'll have you over next week and everything'll be back to normal."

Matthew's smile faded. He shook his head. "She's still upset. She doesn't like to be rude."

I wanted to ask him what else we could do, but she stepped into the room carrying a tray piled high with cookies, brownies, and coffee cups.

Matthew relieved her of the tray and set it on the coffee table. He passed out the cups and desserts and returned to his seat, munching a cookie. "Thanks, Mom. These are good."

She didn't respond. She stood at the threshold between rooms.

"Mom, come sit and talk with us."

Lydia tucked her hair behind her ear and slid into a chair by her son. She spoke in a quiet voice. "I just don't understand."

"This is what I want, Mom. They're good to me."

She glanced at Richard and me. "My Matty doesn't always make the best decisions." She spoke more to herself than us. "He was with a boy in college who got him into all sorts of trouble."

"Mom!" Matthew shrieked.

She jerked her head in his direction. "That boy used you. You don't always know who to trust."

Richard perched on the edge of the couch, his elbows on his knees, his hands folded together. "I assure you he can trust us. We are not using him."

"Mom, they're good for me. It's not like Jake."

She shook her head, her curly hair swaying in waves. "I want you to be happy. I want you to be loved. But, Matty, why does it have to be both? Why can't you make a choice?"

"I couldn't choose, even if I wanted to. It isn't about one of them. It's about all of us. I'm happy right now, and it's because of that. Because of them." He looked our way before continuing. "When Richard looks at me, I know there isn't anything he wouldn't do for me. I can feel how much he wants me to be with him, live in his home, spend time with him. He needs me. And Luke. He's a strong person. The strongest person I think I've ever met. He's quiet. He holds a lot in. But when he does say something, it means so much more. He's passionate. He always, always tries to make me feel good. About me."

My jaw dropped.

Richard reached for my hand and held it on his lap. He smiled like Matthew had given him keys to a new luxury convertible.

Lydia stared at Matthew for a brief moment, her mouth open, her dark eyes wide. She glanced at a high school graduation picture of him on the table beside her. She picked it up, wiped the spotless glass with a napkin, and set it down again. "How does it work? How do three men live together, communicate with each other?"

Richard didn't give Matthew a chance to answer. "We handle it pretty good, I'd say. At least two of us do." I got a pointed look. "And we're working on Luke. We're not giving up on him."

Matthew nodded. "That's what we're doing, Mom. We're trying to make this work. All of us."

"I care for your son, ma'am." Richard squeezed my hand. "A great deal. I won't hurt him."

She looked my way. "And you?"

I hesitated, but when I settled on the words, I said them to Matthew more than her. "I care about him, and Richard, more than I've let myself care for anybody in a long time. I'll try my best not to let anyone hurt him. Not even myself."

She bit at her bottom lip and tucked her hair back again. "I guess a mother can't ask for more than that. I want you to be happy."

"I am, Mom. This time I really am."

She watched her son for a moment more. Maybe she deemed our words sincere because she stood and dropped a kiss on his head. The light was back in her eyes.

We visited for a while longer and learned a few more tales about Matthew's childhood, including the time he rescued five small puppies from a storm drain. His mom laughed as she relayed the details of how she had to convince a soaking wet, filthy, bright-eyed ten-year-old Matthew they couldn't keep five German shepherds in their two-bedroom apartment.

An hour later, she sent us on our way with hugs and a plate full of cookies. She was a strong force for such a small, quiet woman, and I liked her. Even though she'd upset him, her concern had been out of love for him, and anyone who cared for him ranked high in my book.

"Take care of each other," she said with a wave.

"We will, Mom."

"And, Matty, I expect you here for dinner next week. All of you are welcome anytime."

"Thanks, Mom." Matthew bounced his way to Richard's car.

* * * *

We headed to the bedroom as soon as we got home. Matthew was eager and excited like he hadn't been since the last time he'd gone to his mom's. Naked in a flash, he watched us, silently pleading for us to kiss him, to touch him.

"What do you want, kid?" Richard asked.

"Me?"

"This is your night to celebrate."

Matthew smirked and crawled up the bed. "I want to be inside you, Richard. And have you inside me, Luke."

"Perfect." I followed after him. I loved to hear him vocalize his desires.

"But first, I want Richard to suck me and you to rim me, get me ready." He smiled wide. His dark eyes glowed.

Richard got on the bed. "I do like your ideas, kid."

We situated ourselves until we had plenty of room to work him over.

Richard spoke one last time before he took Matthew's prick into his mouth. "We're gonna make this one to remember, Matthew."

I licked his balls and made my way back. He lifted his legs higher. His body twitched and begged for me. I breathed deep. His musky scent flooded my nostrils. I loved giving him pleasure. He was the most responsive man I'd ever been with. Every touch, every stroke, every lick stood out, made him crazy. And with Richard adoring his cock, we sent Matthew moaning and writhing even faster.

I didn't want to stop, but Matthew was desperate for more. I got on my knees. "On your back, Richard." I slicked my hands and put one on Matthew's cock, the other on Richard's ass. In, out, up, down. Over and over until Matthew thrust into my hand and Richard drove onto my fingers, both wanting more.

I withdrew my hands and slicked my own cock. "C'mere, Matthew."

I helped him onto his knees. Richard spread wide, lifting his legs, and Matthew pushed in. I let him thrust a few times. Then I stilled them and plunged into Matthew's heat, giving him a night he'd remember.

He kept talking, pleading, praising as he rocked between us.

Then he stopped. His body tensed.

Something was wrong.

He caressed Richard's cheek. "Love you." He dropped his hand to the big man's chest. "Richard. I love you." He threw his head onto my shoulder, reached around, and touched my face. "I love you, Luke. Love you both."

I'd never be just another fuck to him. I'd never be just another guy he dated. Tightness welled in my chest. It overwhelmed me. I wanted to come so I could rid my body of the pressure in my balls, if nothing else.

Richard raised a hand to Matthew's face. Then Matthew's hips rocked, and Richard groaned.

I sucked in a breath and thrust, not sure what else I could give him.

Richard came, and I followed, still shooting into Matthew when his body tightened and screams of pleasure poured out of him. It sounded like nothing I'd ever heard from him before. We collapsed together as one, floating, breathing heavily, stuck together, not because of sweat or cum, but because we couldn't let go. I couldn't let go.

Richard shifted out from under us. He wrapped his arms around Matthew. His voice filled with awe. "Matthew?"

"Yeah?"

"I love you too." He pulled back, and they stared at each other. "Almost from the first night I met you."

Matthew gave him a soft, slow kiss.

Then Richard leaned over him and whispered in my ear. "And, don't freak, but I love you too."

The words tumbled around in my head. I could barely speak. "I…I can't…not…"

Richard released his hold on Matthew. He rubbed his hand along my arm. "I know. It's okay."

Matthew kissed me. "I love you and I'll wait."

"We both will," Richard said.

They knew me well, and they accepted me—without judgment or a desire to change me. Would it hurt to tell them? Would it kill me?

"I can't."

Richard slid closer. He pressed his face against my neck and whispered over my skin, "It's okay."

Matthew ran his palm along my chin. "Don't be afraid." He kissed me again, light kisses on my lips, my cheeks, my chin. "Not about this. This should be the easy part."

Young, innocent, and naive. He couldn't understand. Love was never easy.

Yet, it did feel that way with them. Maybe I could—but I'd always trusted my instincts. I was protecting myself for a reason. Even if I didn't want to think about the why of it.

They kissed me again and again until sleep lured us into dreams where love was enough and lovers never left.

If only I didn't have to wake from the dream.

Chapter Twenty-Seven

Matthew snored and repositioned his head on my thigh. I shifted my ass on the couch until my dick lay an inch from his mouth.

I had it bad. Watching the man sleep got me hard.

I ran my palm over his cheek. I couldn't resist the dark hair over pale skin. The two-day-old stubble scratched the heel of my hand. The rest of me wanted to feel the scrape, the tease. My chest, my abs, my balls. Everywhere tingled, ached to feel his face graze over it.

I rested my hand in the waves of his hair. I listened to his soft snores and focused in on the movie again, a new reinvented superhero flick Matthew'd been dying to see. He made it through the first thirty minutes.

Stupid sleeping man—who needed to remember to shave every day and get more sleep at night. He was driving me crazy.

It wouldn't be as bad if Richard would get off his computer and come into the living room. The man hadn't closed a deal in over four months, and he couldn't hide the disappointment or the fact that he was feeling the crunch where his finances were concerned. He worked every chance he got, searched online real estate listings, made calls, pitched project after project. Success accompanied none of it. A tight coil of tension had attached to the man's shoulders. Even when we made love, I could feel it, and nothing Matthew or I did could work out the frustration.

A half hour after Matthew feel asleep, Richard finally made it into the living room. He sat in the chair across from us. I gave up on the movie and left the local news on instead.

I eyed Richard. Would the nonsexual closeness between Matthew and me bother him? He smiled at me and licked his lips in the way that always told me he was aroused. Nothing in his demeanor indicated anything akin to jealousy. We'd handled that avenue of a threesome with few problems. Why was that?

Right then, I didn't care. I returned his stare and stroked a sleeping

Matthew on the back. Richard lifted his hips and slid down the cushion until his ass hung off the edge of the chair. I lowered my gaze to the bulge at the front of his pants.

As soon as he asked me what I wanted, I'd tell him. Me sitting on his dick. My back to his chest. My legs spread wide. Matthew kneeling before me, dragging his mouth over my cock.

Richard's breath came in shallow pants. He had one hand flat across his chest, a T-shirt-covered nipple pinched between two fingers. Without looking away from me, his hand drifted to his crotch and rubbed the erection through his pants. A few strokes later, he unbuttoned the top button. My plan was reforming. I'd watch him masturbate. Tell him how to work himself over. All while I fondled Matthew awake.

I licked at my bottom lip, and Richard moaned. I kept working my lips with my tongue, never looking away from him. I ran my hand down the front of Matthew and pressed my palm against his cock. He let out a low, sleep-filled moan and rolled into the touch.

The light from the television changed as the local news returned from a commercial break. I hadn't been paying attention, but as soon as I heard it, Richard and his erection were gone. My hand on Matthew stilled.

All I could focus on was my father's voice.

"It is too early for me to talk about my plans for the next election. But if I do decide to run for the office of President of the United States, I know the great people of this state will support me in that endeavor." A cacophony of cheers followed. A female reporter spoke. "Some have said the senator's chances of winning the presidential nomination are quite good. His energy bill elevated his popularity above either of the other recent picks."

I clicked off the television.

So that's it.

The air in my lungs thickened. It caught in my throat.

Three men living together. The press would never leave us alone.

Richard's hand stilled with the ring of the telephone. He answered it, and without saying anything more than hello, handed it over to me.

I grabbed the phone with a shaking hand. "Yeah?"

The voice on the line sounded nothing like the polished, professional one from the television. "Did you see the news?"

My hand recoiled from Matthew. I clutched the back of the couch. "Yeah, Dad."

Richard sat and watched me.

"I'm glad you saw it." My father's voice hissed in my ear like a snake warning its prey. "Now maybe you'll understand what I'm up against. Maybe you'll do as I say."

"What do you want from me?"

"I want you to cancel your membership to that God-awful club, and I want you to move back to your own apartment. Living with two men. Really, Luke? Could you have done anything more appalling? You and I both know whatever you've got going with those men isn't serious and it isn't going to last. You'll fuck it up eventually. Like Tim. So end it now." I heard the threat his words didn't say.

"Fuck you, Dad." I hung up the phone and slammed it onto the coffee table.

Matthew stirred. "What's wrong?"

"What is it?" Richard asked.

I shrugged Matthew off me and stood. I swallowed around the lump in my throat. "I just…I can't."

Matthew's wide, sleep-filled eyes stared up at me.

"I need to be alone."

Richard stood and reached out for me.

I held up a hand and backed away. "I need a few minutes alone."

"Okay. Matthew and I'll be here when you're ready."

I staggered out of the living room and hesitated in the hallway. I glanced up the stairs and then at the front door. My decision made, I picked up my keys and headed out.

* * * *

I crept into the house two hours later, numb from the beers—so many I'd lost count. Exactly how I'd wanted to feel when I'd stormed out earlier.

Most of the house was dark, but the hall light they'd left on offered enough illumination for me to do what needed to be done. I staggered into the dark living room and sat on the couch. I dialed the number and held my breath. Air seeped out of my lungs when I heard my mother's voice.

"Mom. It's Luke."

"Oh, Lukas." She sounded close to tears. "You shouldn't call here."

Did she hate me so damn much we couldn't have one conversation every fifteen years? Or was I missing something? Could it be my father was pulling her strings the way he'd been trying to do to me? I couldn't bring myself to ask, though. With that one thought, I'd fostered a hope I hadn't allowed in years, and a part of me didn't want it crushed. Not yet.

"How are you?" she asked in a low whisper.

Another part of me didn't care about her reasons. "Just tell me…is he going to run?"

"He wants to. Can you please do as he asks?"

"I have stayed out of his life. I want him to stay out of mine."

"He's looking for reassurance. If you could just—"

"Does he think he can hide this? Hide me? Hide who I am?"

"Please don't make this harder for him."

The sincerity of her voice disturbed me. "How would I do that? I'm living my own life. I haven't done anything to make life harder or easier for him. And I'm not about to start now." Did he think I'd give them up because he ordered me to? What would he do to get them to hate me?

"Just try to be discreet. I think that's all he can ask of you."

"Discreet? Sure, Mom. I've already told him I won't talk to the press. Tell him to leave me the hell alone."

"I thought he was." She paused. "He says you're living with someone. Is it serious?"

"Well, according to Dad I'm gonna fuck it all up, so what does it matter?" I hung up before she could say another word.

All the ways I could purposely be indiscreet raced through my mind.

They were also the ways I could hurt the two men sleeping upstairs.

I moved into the hall. My father was right about one thing. I was going to hurt them. The longer I stayed, the more it would hurt. Them. Me. Everyone.

If I left, they'd have each other. They wouldn't be alone.

Images of Matthew and Richard living in the house without me flashed before me. Talking, cuddling, laughing, fucking. It was all too much.

I sighed and climbed the stairs.

At the doorway of our room, I stopped, not able to take one more step. Matthew lay on his stomach, the blanket covering his legs, the top of his curved ass peeking out. Richard lay on his side. His large limbs were wrapped around the smaller man's body, the care and devotion between them palpable, even in their sleep.

Tears filled my eyes. For once, I let them fall.

Leaving would hurt. It would nearly kill me. I was man enough to admit that. It'd be worse than my parents. Worse than Tim. Worse than anything.

Matthew shivered. Using the back of my hand, I swiped the tears away and went to the bed. I raised the blanket, and he hummed as the warmth enveloped him. I stripped off my clothes and climbed in next to him.

Sleepy, dark eyes blinked open and widened. "Hey, Luke. Is everything okay?"

Richard stirred and lifted his head.

"Yeah. Fine. I needed some time to myself."

Matthew rolled to his side. "That's okay. We all need our space sometimes. I'm glad you came home. We missed you." He slid over and rested his head on my chest. He slipped his leg over mine.

"I've had a few drinks."

"It's okay. Let me hold you."

"What happened, Luke?" Richard asked, his voice soft, caring. It hurt to hear.

"I don't talk to my father very often, and when I do, he's an asshole. Sorry I took off." It was what I always did. Whenever my father found me.

Matthew swept a palm over my chest, the touch soft, soothing, loving. He lifted his head and kissed me. His lips were warm and his tongue fluid. He wasn't asking for anything. He was comforting me, and the action filled me with sadness. Richard had been right. Matthew could give so much in a single moment.

That wasn't me. All I did was take. And take. And take.

Richard slid close behind Matthew. He cupped my neck with his hand. "You sure you're okay?"

I nodded.

Matthew pressed his lips against my neck, and Richard curled up around him. Together, they looked right, perfect, at peace.

Could whoever's on my chest get the hell off? I needed to breathe.

I should never have gotten between them. I should never have moved in with them. I should have let them walk up the stairs at the Haven alone. Let them love and laugh and live without me.

Richard was asleep again in moments, but Matthew held me close to him. Maybe he sensed the inevitability of what was to come. He still clung to me when he fell asleep.

I lay awake, unsure what I'd do.

Unsure about everything.

* * * *

I showered, dressed, and walked out the door before either of them woke. They were the actions of a coward, but if I stayed to see them, I'd do something I'd regret.

I couldn't concentrate at work, but I sat at my desk for the entire day anyway, unable to make a decision.

I waited until everyone else had gone home before I left. An hour later, I found myself on Walter's couch, drinking down the last of a beer.

He handed me another and sat across from me. I grunted in thanks. The silence stretched out through the second beer.

"Want another?" he asked.

I did. But I had to go back and I didn't want to be drunk around Matthew. I shook my head. "If I need a place to crash for a few days…"

"And here I thought it must be going good if you'd made it this long."

"I can't stay there with my father watching my every move."

Walter took a long pull on his beer. "Sure, it's about your father."

I met his stare. "What else?"

"You're scared."

"Am not." I ran a hand through my hair. "I meant that to sound less juvenile than it did." I stared down the mouth of the empty beer bottle. Was it possible to truly get lost in the bottle? If I kept drinking, would Richard make me leave Matthew? "It's just not a good fit for me."

"Better to get out before what? You start to care?"

"Fuck off." I tossed the bottle onto the coffee table and slammed the door on my way out. The rattling sound that lingered felt good.

* * * *

I walked into the house and heard two muted voices in the kitchen. I strained to hear them.

No hint of anger or pain.

Matthew caught sight of me, and the relief was unmistakable. He moved with trepidation but still came to me as easily as he always did. His hands cupped my face. "You okay?"

"Yeah. My dad just gets to me."

"What made you upset?" Richard asked. "Tell us what your dad said."

"I don't need you fucking worrying all the time and trying to fix everything."

His eyes narrowed. "It's who I am. I won't apologize for it."

"I like it," Matthew said. He sat next to him. "It's nice to know someone cares about me."

"I do."

"I know. Me too." They leaned in and kissed. Easy. Right.

I went for a soda from the fridge. The bottle didn't make it to my lips, though. I mouthed the words more than said them. I tried again. "I can't do this anymore."

"What?" Richard asked.

I set the soda on the counter and spoke louder. "I'm going to find an apartment."

A chair scraped across the tile floor and banged on the wall. Richard towered over the table.

The sludge of the six cups of coffee I drank at work lurched in my stomach. Bile rose in my throat. The taste reached the back of my tongue, and I almost gagged.

Matthew stood beside me in a flash, one hand on my arm, the other on my hip. I didn't want to face him, but his hands insisted.

"No." His voice cracked with the one word.

"I can't watch the two of you get closer and closer and not be a part of it. I can't."

Matthew gripped my forearms. His eyes darted back and forth. "You are part of it."

"It'll be better if I go. You deserve someone who can give you what"—I gestured with my hand between him and Richard—"what you give to each other."

"You give that to us. You are a part of it." He ran his hand from my shoulder to my elbow and back up. The stroke as warm and intimate as it'd been the night we'd showered together at the Haven.

"You don't need me," I said.

"I need you both." Matthew threw his arms around me. "Don't go."

I jerked away and slid down the cabinet. "Oh God. I don't know if I can leave."

Richard crouched in front of me. "But you want to?"

I leaned my head against the cabinet door. "I don't want to, but it's who I am."

"That's bullshit. You're freaking. You're trying to push us away so you don't have to make a decision. So you'll have a reason to run."

I met his green eyes. "Don't let me fuck this up."

He pulled me to his chest and held me firm against him. "I'm not letting you go anywhere. No one's leaving me again." A tremble vibrated his body.

Matthew curled against me, his head on my arm.

We stayed on the kitchen floor for a long while. Close. Silent. Still.

"You'll stay?" Matthew asked. His head lifted. His eyes pleaded.

"I'll try."

His hand moved over my hip. The touch didn't arouse. It comforted.

"Can we go to the basement?" I asked.

Richard stilled the hand on my back. "Let's go up to bed instead."

"No. I want to remember our first night. The way we were before I knew I'd be—I want it to be like that again."

Richard was quiet for a moment. "Okay, Luke. Whatever you need."

"Yeah. Tonight's for you." Matthew smiled, the expression forced and nervous and scared.

If I left, I'd never see his easy, joyful smile again.

I needed to see it one more time.

* * * *

I lay on the bed in the basement, my arms tied to the headboard. Matthew was straddling me, his cock in my mouth. And Richard was buried deep inside me.

It was exactly like the first night—only I didn't feel at ease. I didn't feel alive. Not like I had then.

I needed more.

Matthew's cock pulsed in my mouth. He came with a shriek, and I swallowed, nearly choking at the thought of never tasting him again.

He fell over onto his side. I didn't want him to go. I wanted him hard and in my mouth again. I ached to taste him once more.

Richard pitched forward. His lips brushed mine, the touch soft and gentle and full of love.

I needed more. "Hit me."

He recoiled. "God no. Luke, don't ask for that."

I arched up. I wanted more contact with him. "Want to feel your marks on me long after we're done."

"No. Don't." He moved in me again and showered me with kisses, giving me all of him, loving me. "We're never going to be done."

I turned my head and savored the skin of his neck. I bit down, not a playful tease but a close-to-drawing-blood chomp.

Richard cried out in pain.

"Luke!" Matthew screamed. "Stop. Please."

I released Richard, and he jerked back.

"Punish me."

Rage flooded his eyes. It didn't matter what made him mad. I wanted his anger. I needed it.

"Luke, goddammit. I won't hurt you."

"I want to give in to you. I need you to make it hurt." My begging was fruitless, but I couldn't stop myself.

"It isn't what I want. And I don't want you to want it. Don't ask me to hurt you." Tears pooled in his eyes. He untied one of my wrists, then the other.

"No!" I tried to jerk away.

He held my face in his hands. "I want to make love to you. I think that's what you need. Not this other shit." He kissed me.

I pressed harder against his lips, and he pulled back, keeping his touch soft. Matthew found my neck with his warm lips. His soothing hands covered my body.

I gave in and wrapped around Richard. He didn't plunge. He didn't fuck. He pushed in and out in slow, long thrusts that broke my resolve.

He took my cock in his hand. "Come with me, Luke."

But it wasn't enough. It would never be enough.

* * * *

Cum, sweat, and tears covered my body. Matthew kissed me everywhere, and Richard glided his hand over my chest in a tender caress.

Matthew spoke first. "Are you okay, Luke?"

"I'm fine."

"Talk to us, please." He wrapped his arm around me. Tight. Restraining.

I shrugged him off and sat up. "I said I'm fine. Drop it."

He reached for me again.

I pushed him away. "Get the fuck off me." I scrambled off the bed.

The hurt look on his face stung. But I couldn't take it back or apologize. I fetched my clothes and went for the door. "I've gotta get out of here."

My father was right. Eventually I'd lose them. It'd be better if I left, better if they didn't have to make that choice for me. Better if my father didn't try to either.

I made it up the stairs. Clean, clothed, keys in hand, I was out the door in no time. I walked several blocks before I found a cab. I didn't know if they followed. They weren't there to stop me, and that's what mattered.

There was one place where I'd get what I needed.

And nothing could have stopped me.

* * * *

The cab dropped me off two blocks from my destination. I wanted to take some time to think things through before I got there. But it wasn't enough time. Or maybe it was just right.

I stood at the unmarked door.

This is what I need. What I've been missing.

I scanned my card and stepped into the Haven for the first time in months.

I handed my coat off and strolled to the bar, the scents of the room invading me. A mix of various colognes, musky sweat, cigars, and booze. A bartender I didn't recognize brought me a beer, and I drank it down fast. My stomach clenched. Whether out of anticipation or guilt, I didn't care.

I needed to be there.

I didn't have long to wait. A thigh grazed my leg as someone slid alongside my stool. The man ordered a draft and gave me a long stare. He was tall and large. Almost Richard's size. His hair and eyes were dark like Matthew's.

Don't think about them.

I stared at the man. He stared back. He wanted me.

This is what I need.

"You're Luke, right?"

I nodded, not sure I wanted to know how he knew me or what he'd heard. I needed something specific, and nothing was going to get in the way.

"I've heard you're good," he said. "You have plans for tonight?" He took a long swig of his beer. Sweat clung to the hair around his ears and forehead. Black crescent-shaped residue inhabited the tips of his fingernails. A white powder had seeped into every crevice of the dry, cracked skin on his hands. He smelled of drywall and melted plastic.

A man who worked with his hands. His fingers on my flesh would be rough, calloused. They'd scrape, chafe. They wouldn't caress or console. They wouldn't remind me of anyone.

"I do now," I said.

"Sure you do." He placed a hand on my knee and yanked. My body swung with the stool, and I faced him.

The touch felt wrong—incredibly wrong. I pushed the reaction aside. "What are you into?"

He smirked. "I can be a pretty damn good Dom if you wanna go that route, or we can just fuck. Your call."

He gave my leg a tug. I slid off the stool and stood before him, our bodies close enough that his warmth invaded my space. A shudder worked its way through me. *Desire. This has to be desire.*

I attempted a deep breath. "I want you to tie me up. I need you to hit me. Make me hurt. You do that, then you can fuck me."

The man's Adam's apple jerked as he swallowed. He wanted it.

"Flogger?" he asked.

I nodded.

"Whip?"

I nodded again.

"My hands?"

I moved a few steps away and turned back to him. "Any way you want. I'll give it all over to you."

The man stood. He grasped my arm and dragged me toward the stairs.

Toward the rooms upstairs.

Toward a mistake that would change my life.

Chapter Twenty-Eight

I trudged down the stairs, sat at the bar, and ordered a water. The cool liquid didn't quell the nausea. It increased it. My heartbeat pulsed in my temples, behind my eyes, at the tip of each finger.

I fumbled in my pocket for my cell phone, pulled it out, and stared at it. Another drink of the water, and thirst still stung my throat. I ran my thumb over the buttons on the phone. Without hitting a single one, I slammed it on the bar.

They didn't deserve to get that call.

But they didn't deserve not to either.

I grabbed the phone again and clutched it in a shaking hand.

A large hand stilled my own. I glanced up.

Walter stood beside me. "Call them."

"Can't. I got lax. Led my father right to them. They deserve better."

He cupped my jaw and jerked my face in his direction. "That's bullshit. They deserve to have what they want. You." He took the cell from me. He dialed and handed it back.

Our home phone number filled the display. The bold numbers blurred together.

"Whatever is going on with you, call them, tell them. You don't have to do this alone." He leaned in close. "You deserve to be loved." He left without another word.

I wanted to believe him. I wanted to be more than what my father thought of me. I wanted to hold on to Richard and Matthew and never let go. But would they still want me?

I hit the call button. The low, deep voice that answered didn't sound at all confident.

I couldn't speak.

"Luke?" Richard said. "Where are you?"

"At the club. I—"

"Stay right there. We're on our way."

"Matthew can't—"

"He's with me. They'll let him in. Don't move." Richard hung up.

I clenched the cell phone in my fist. If I so much as moved to set it down, I might be gone when they got there.

* * * *

Richard looked ill. If I hadn't seen him a short while earlier, I'd have thought he spent the last three days with a bad case of the flu. His dark skin had never been so pale. His eyes were dull and packed with a new expression. Fear? Pain? Disappointment?

Matthew didn't look much better. He chewed on his bottom lip and held his hands in front of him, the thumb of one hand rubbing the fingers of the other.

I had done that to them. I turned back toward the bar.

Richard sat next to me, and Matthew moved closer.

"What did you do?" Richard asked.

I swallowed hard. "He said he'd give me—he said he'd hit me."

Richard's fingers dug into the edge of the bar. He stared at the line of liquor bottles in front of the large mirror. "What did you do?"

"I didn't fuck him. I wanted to. God, I almost did. I made it all the way up the stairs and in a room."

Matthew sucked in a quick, ragged breath.

"I didn't touch him or let him touch me. I didn't kiss him. I wanted him to hit me, but I couldn't even let him do that. Once the door closed, I knew I didn't want anything from him."

"Why?" Matthew asked.

"I couldn't. I've made promises to you. And it's more than that—"

"No." He stepped closer. The firm muscles of his abdomen brushed my arm. I ached to feel more of him. "Why did you want him? And not us? Why did you come here?" His body trembled and swayed. His eyes didn't focus on anything. I wanted to reach out to him, steady him, but I couldn't.

"Oh. I—"

Before I could say more, Richard spoke. "What are you afraid of? Don't think. Answer."

"Driving you away. Not being able to stop you from leaving me when I'm not what you want." I clenched my hands into fists, the phone still clutched inside. "I'm messed up when it comes to emotional stuff. When my dad called, I wanted to run—but I didn't know how to leave you."

Richard let go of the bar and swung around. He caught sight of

Matthew. The big man's eyebrows drew in, and concern softened the fear and anger visible on his face. He grabbed Matthew and pulled him close. The smaller man leaned his hip against a thick thigh. His shaking body stilled.

"You need to talk to us," Richard said.

"I talk. I talk to you two more than I've ever talked to anyone. I've given up the way I live to be with you."

"I'm glad you're more open with us than you've ever been, but that's sad, pathetic."

I threw the phone on the bar. "I've given more to you than I have to anyone. What else can I do?"

"You've come far. You've done things you swore you never would. Sleeping with us again after the first night. Moving in with us. Throwing the rubbers in the trash. They were a lot of huge steps for you."

All I could do was nod. Huge steps. Gigantic steps. Walk-on-the-moon-sized steps.

"Matthew and I have been communicating. You've heard us. You've listened. But you haven't talked. Not about anything personal. Not about your dad. Not about why you won't tell anyone where you live."

My words were barely a whisper. I hoped like hell they could hear me over the music and crowd in the bar because repeating it didn't seem an option. "I want to talk to you."

Richard put his arm around me and hauled me against him. "Let's go home. Get in our own bed. You can talk there, just the three of us."

Matthew pressed his lips to my ear. "Please, Luke. Come home."

I met his dark eyes and nodded. Then I did what I'd needed to do since they'd arrived. I took Matthew's face in my hands and kissed him.

"Take me home."

Chapter Twenty-Nine

Matthew held my hand as he led me up the stairs to our bedroom. No one had spoken a word on the ride home, and the silence loomed like a thick fog I couldn't see through. They were going to expect me to fill the quiet, to tell them about my past, to tell them about the day I lost the two most important men in my life before them.

Richard undressed me and then himself while Matthew shed his own clothes. Matthew took my hand in his again and brought me to the bed. The cool sheets triggered a shiver. The blood went cold in my hands and feet.

For once, I sat between them and let them touch me, hold me. My body warmed, but I still shook. Nothing in my life had prepared me for giving more than my body to someone.

When Richard spoke, his voice was stern. "Talk. The truth—all of it. Nothing you say is wrong. Nothing you want to tell us about is wrong. Just be honest."

"I'm always fighting with myself. I work hard to push away who I am—to never let anyone see me, know me." I took a deep breath. "You two are who you are. You don't deceive. You're always truthful." I turned to Matthew. "How do you love so easily?"

His eyes widened. "I don't want to live without it. I don't want to be alone. I want to really know someone. Let him know me. Feel the connection of intimacy…of love. I've ached without it."

Once again, his openness, his ability to let his love flow out of him, amazed me.

I faced Richard. "How did you know this would work? At first you didn't seem to want to be with someone a second time. Then we're on a date, moving in, committing. I don't understand what you saw in us."

"When I went to the club, I wasn't ready to get involved, not after Gregg. I wanted a fuck, nothing more. Then when I met you two, I could see who you were and how much you needed." He gestured to

Matthew. "He needed someone to give him room to find himself and be confident without feeling like he had to be what others wanted him to be. Someone to need him. To accept him as he is. To appreciate him, cherish him."

Matthew stared at Richard for a moment, then shot out of the bed and sprinted for the bathroom.

Richard pitched forward and peered into the small room. "Kid?"

Matthew darted out and threw a box of tissues on the bed. "This has the potential to get all emotional, and we're naked. Tissues are better than sheets."

Richard shook his head and chuckled.

A hyena-like laugh gripped me. My shoulders shuddered, and my eyes filled with moisture, a release of tension hidden beneath the laughter.

Matthew grabbed a tissue and dabbed at my eyes. "See?"

That brought out another laugh from Richard.

My life would never be dull with them.

I breathed deep, and my head struck the headboard. The exhaustion of dealing with emotional shit had settled in every nerve, every muscle. And I hadn't said anything yet. But telling them too much could mean more trouble than I'd ever want to expose them to. No. Telling them wasn't the problem. Staying with them was all that my father cared about. What would he do to keep me away from them?

The laughter died off, and Richard spoke again. "When we talked about trying this, I could see your nervousness, Luke, your reluctance. But when I stopped you at the door and you didn't leave—you sat there shaking—I knew you needed us. Like we needed you." He reached for my hand. "Why were you scared when your dad called? Why did you leave tonight?"

I closed my eyes and let the words flow, let the story I never told surge out of me.

"When my father found out I was gay he stopped talking to me, stopped looking me in the eye, and, I guess, stopped loving me. He hated that I was gay. Hated *me* for it. His work had a lot to do with what people thought of him. He's always been seen as this conservative man. He didn't think he'd survive the scandal of having a gay son. He told me to keep it to myself, asked me not to say anything. I was a kid. I didn't want to hurt him. I did what he asked.

"He told me it was a phase—that I'd get over it. That one great lay with a woman, and I'd forget about my sexual experiments." The last remnants of my earlier chuckles escaped my chest. "My senior year of high school, he offered to buy me a hooker. He couldn't accept it—couldn't accept me. But they were still my parents. They came to my high school graduation. They helped me get into college. They even paid for school at the start. My mom would call me, but I rarely saw my dad once I left for college. He wanted nothing to do with me. I thought we'd ignore each other. I thought he'd leave me alone. I guess I didn't know him.

"My freshman year, I fell in love with my roommate. I'd slept with other boys in high school, but Tim was the first one I cared about, the first one I loved.

"Right before final exams, my father came to my dorm room. I don't know why. It didn't matter. What mattered was what he learned after a few minutes in our room. He looked at Tim and me and knew we were more than roommates. He didn't say a word, just turned and left. Two days later, he came back."

I said the rest and was back at college again, reliving every moment...

* * * *

"Tim. Don't stop."

"No. This will go on, Luke. I won't let it stop."

I opened my eyes at his words. Did he mean them the way they sounded? I didn't get a chance to ask.

The strong scent of a familiar cologne washed over me. At first, my brain couldn't reconcile the vision. It was in such contrast to what my body felt.

But there he was. My father stood next to my nightstand.

I retreated up the bed and dragged Tim with me.

Tim stared down at me, his face contorted in a mix of passion and confusion until he caught sight of my father. His dick slipped out of me, and he scrambled to my side.

My father whirled his arm upward. He jammed a cool metal object against my face. A handgun. The barrel dug into the flesh of my cheek.

"Don't move, son." The smirk of his lips and the rage in his eyes kept me still, not his words. "You"—he tilted his head to Tim—"get dressed. Your parents are waiting downstairs."

"My parents?"

"They want you to come home for the weekend. They need to talk to you."

"I'm not going anywhere without Luke."

My father inched the gun to my temple, scraping my skin, pressing harder. I scurried backward until he had me wedged between the gun and the headboard.

"Stop." Tim got off the bed and grabbed my father's arm. "Don't hurt him."

My father backed up and spun the gun toward Tim. He held the stance for a moment then aimed the gun at me again. "If you don't go downstairs and talk to your parents, things will get painful for Luke. I'm disgusted with what I just saw, and I really don't care what happens to me if I shoot his ass."

Rapid breaths spilled out of Tim. He held up his hands. "Okay. I'll go talk to them. I'll be right back." He threw me a look I took to mean, *I have a plan. Please be careful.* He dressed and came back to the bed. My father scurried closer and shoved the gun in my face again.

Tim reached out and touched my calf. "I'll be right back." He squeezed. "I love you."

I met his gaze. "Love you too."

My father scoffed. The gun jabbed into the hollow of my cheek. My mouth opened in a protective instinct to make room between my face and the gun's barrel. Had my own father not been holding me at gunpoint, I'd have laughed at the realization I looked like I was about to suck someone's cock.

Tim backed to the door, keeping me in his sights as long as he could.

My father watched him. "Close the door behind you."

Tim stepped into the hall and did as instructed.

My father didn't flinch. He didn't speak. He didn't look at me, and I didn't look at him. The cool steel of the gun was our only contact.

Finally, he stepped away. He pointed at a picture frame on Tim's dresser. Tim with his parents. "I take it this is his side of the room?" His back to me, he grabbed a gym bag off the floor and opened Tim's closet.

I shot off the bed and reached for a pair of jeans. "What are you doing?"

"Packing your lover's clothes. He isn't coming back."

"What are you talking about?"

"His parents need him home right now. They believe God has a better life for him than you."

My gaze flew to the door. "But—"

He swung around. "But nothing. I told them I'd send his things."

He smirked, turned his back to me again, and stuffed more clothes into the bag.

I sprinted for the door. I didn't care if he raised the gun. No shot rang out, and I kept going. I took the stairs two at a time to the first floor lobby. No Tim. I went outside and scanned the parking lot. Nothing. I asked around. No one had seen him. I pushed aside the panic and stormed back to our room. I wanted answers.

My father was gone, and so were most of Tim's clothes.

I collapsed onto the bed. What the hell was I going to do? Call the police? Call my mother?

A few hours later, I called Tim's house. No one answered. The next morning, I borrowed a friend's car and drove the four hours there.

When his father opened the door, his first words were, "He's gone."

"Where?"

"He agreed to get some help. Someplace you should go, if you ask me."

"What did you do to him?"

"We didn't do anything to him. You did. He was a good boy before he met you. And the Free Yourself Ex-Gay Ministry is going to remind him of that."

"No. They'll—"

"They'll help him get things straightened out. They'll help him find God's love again. Now, get off my property. And stay away from my son." He slammed the door in my face.

I made it two steps toward the car before I fell to my knees. "Tim." The misery of my own voice terrified me.

The anger and fear and sorrow fought a war as I knelt in the snow-covered front lawn of my lover's old home, gripping the edge of a three-feet-tall stone birdbath. I had no idea how long I stayed there. My jeans were soaked through from my ankles to my knees, and the frigid skin never warmed during the ride back to school. When I made it to the dorm, darkness had descended—over the day, over me, over my life.

Tim would find a way to get in touch with me. Once he had convinced his parents he'd changed, they'd let him come back to school. He'd do whatever they wanted to get away from them, to get back to me.

So I waited.

I went to class. And I waited.

I studied. And I waited.

I got drunk. And I waited.

I got drunk again. And I waited some more.

It took three months before I opened my door to find him standing in the hall. I pulled him into my arms. He returned the embrace, but it didn't feel right.

"God, I missed you," I said and led him to the bed. "Tell me what happened. I know where they sent you."

"I wasn't sure what they told you."

I'd missed him. I wanted to hold him, kiss him.

As soon as my lips touched his, he jerked away. He swiped at his mouth with the back of his hand. His eyes narrowed. "Don't touch me, Luke. Not like that." He leaped across the room and leaned against the wall. "I want to help you, but if you can't stop touching me like that, then there's nothing I can do for you."

I lurched off the bed and gripped his arms. "No. Listen to me." He shrugged off the touch. I let him go. "What they've told you, it isn't the truth."

"You have to see what we did was wrong."

"What we did? We loved each other. No matter what they've told you, they can't take that away from us. Or make it seem disgusting."

"It is disgusting." He slunk along the wall until he could step around me. He walked toward the door but stopped short. "It took me a while to see what we had was never love. Not when we did those things to each other."

"No." My strangled cry startled both of us. "Stop talking like your parents. Come touch me. Kiss me. Make love to me."

"That will never happen again." He shook his head. "He was right. Coming here was a mistake."

"Who was right?"

He opened the door.

My father stood in the hall, a smile plastered on his stoic face. Tim left without looking back at me.

My father stepped inside and shut the door. "Are you done yet? Are you ready to find your way back to a normal life?"

"Why are you doing this?"

"I didn't do this. I merely showed him the options. Do you think if he cared about you, he'd have been turned away from you so easily? It took him, what, three months to learn to hate you? To see you as nothing but a fag that wants him for one thing?"

"No. That's—"

"You start living a decent life or"—he stalked closer to me—"I swear to God I will track you down and take away every lover you ever have. I'll make them see who you are. I'll make them hate you. I'll make your life a living hell."

"Why?" My voice squeaked with the one word. I swallowed and tried to sound stronger. "Why do you hate me?"

He dropped into the desk chair and hung his head in his hands. I wanted to beat on him until he told me why. Until he brought Tim back.

When he lifted his head, his eyes were filled with tears. "There are many things I want, son. Ways I can help make people's lives better. I can do great things with my life. But you…you are the one thing I've done that's going to fuck it all up. Tell me, why should my life suffer because of you?"

"My life has nothing to do with yours."

"That's not how the world works."

"Get the fuck out of here."

"I'm not going anywhere until you make me a few promises."

"No." I shook my head. "I hate you!"

He stood and stepped closer. "I hate what you are." He went for the door. "I warned you." He walked out and slammed the door shut behind him.

Chapter Thirty

A chill raced over my skin as I repeated my father's final words, everything he and Tim had said still powerful enough it slashed at the edges of my heart. I shivered.

Richard pulled me closer against the heat of his body, and a low growl sounded from deep in his chest. Matthew's hands kept moving over me as I heard him fight back tears.

My pain hurt them, pained them. It reminded me yet again the kind of men they were and how lucky I was to have found myself wrapped up in them. They held me tighter, and I let my body relax and warm under their touch.

"I didn't see either of them again. My father's had me followed for years, always wanting to know where I'm living, what I'm doing. It's this constant reminder. I knew Tim left me—said those things to me—because of what they did to him, but I still managed to blame myself. I thought clinging to him, wanting him, loving him, had made him hate me. And my father…he hated me because of who I was. I couldn't change that, couldn't change me.

"But I did change. I loved Tim, and when he was gone, I became bitter, angry. I became someone else. I promised myself certain things and made up the rules I've lived by since then. Tim was the only man I've ever been with more than once. Until you two."

Richard stroked my shoulders and back. "You didn't deserve what either man did to you, none of it. Your dad is a dickhead."

Matthew nodded. "A big dickhead."

"He's the one who's wrong," Richard said. "He's the one who should hurt, not you."

"I know. Logically, I know that." I couldn't bring myself to tell them everything—who my father was, that he had loftier plans than being a senator, that he might have been responsible for another man's death.

If they knew it all, they might ask me to leave. They might not want the kind of trouble a presidential campaign could bring—the kind of trouble my father could bring. Not when the whole world would judge us. Not when my father would hate them.

I was still lying to them. *Why can't I give them everything?*

Richard pulled back to look at me. "What does it mean to you that your father doesn't approve of you being gay?"

"That he's a conservative prick who can't think past his own needs or wants. Fuck. What do you want me to say? That I can't be worthy of his love because I'm sinful and evil in his eyes? That if the people who brought me into this world can hate me, then anyone can hurt me?" I gripped Richard's forearm. "When I let you tie me up, I wish you'd make it hurt more. I want my wrists to chafe. I want the knots to cut into my skin. I need the pain. But since I've met you two, I haven't had enough. I beg you to make it tighter and you won't. I wanted you to hit me. I needed it."

The color drained from Richard's face. "I won't hurt you."

How many times had he said the same words? And every damn time it hurt to hear. "And now you won't tie me up, right?"

"Not when you give me reasons like those. I can't do that to you."

"Shit. I don't think I can be here with the two of you and have you love me. I always wanted a threesome so there'd be more of everything. More touching, more fucking, and more pain when it was over—every time reminding me I could never have anyone more than once, reminding me there'd be more pain the longer I knew someone, the closer I got."

Matthew's hands stilled their caresses. "Have we caused you pain?"

"God, no. It's why I needed something physical. I nearly exploded without it. In the end, the only hurt came from hearing my father tell me what I feared—that I'd lose you. The closer we got, the more I knew I'd lose in the end. I always lose in the end."

Richard gripped my shoulders. He shook me. "Not this time. We aren't letting you destroy us or yourself."

I let my head fall to his shoulder. "But he'll show you. He'll show you who I am."

"We already see you."

Matthew kissed the back of my neck. "And we love you."

I took the soft kisses they planted all over my body and accepted them into my mouth, hungry for them. "I need you. Don't let me leave."

Richard kissed me and wrenched the three of us around until we lay on the bed, my back pressing into the mattress, his body covering mine. "You don't want to leave, and we're not letting you go."

"No," Matthew said. "No one's going. Staying. Together." His mouth explored my neck, my ears, my chin, my lips.

A fire raged inside me. Every touch of tongue, skin, hand, cock sent desire through me. I wanted them, needed them like never before.

Lost in the pleasure, the touches, I didn't worry about returning the affections. I let them consume me, show me everything I'd have missed if I had left, if I had fucked up.

They tortured me with sensations until I couldn't stand it any longer. My control shattered. No one touched me where I craved it most. I needed them to take me, fill me. "Please."

Matthew slid up my body. "Make love to me?"

I ran my hands through his dark hair and brought our mouths together, pleading the words over his lips. "Yes, Matthew. I need to be inside you. You feel amazing around me, under me, like no one before you, ever."

Matthew rolled onto his back and brought me with him.

I reached for Richard and kissed him. "No one fills me like you do. No one makes me feel alive like you do."

He moved closer. "The way you want me, the way you need, you both still drive me as crazy as the first night." He wasn't the only one.

He reached for the lube and handed it to me. I slicked it into Matthew, using extra. I didn't want to touch my dick with it. I wanted Matthew's body to be the next touch to give me pleasure. I raised his legs and leaned over him, ready to enter his body, when Matthew put a hand on my lower abdomen, stopping me. The uncertainty in his dark eyes broke my heart.

"I swear, Matthew, I didn't. I've only been with you two since I moved in here. Hell, since the first night at the club."

His expression relaxed, and his hand moved from my tense stomach muscles to my face. "I believe you. I do. I just needed to hear it again."

"Are you sure?" Richard asked. "You shouldn't let him go bare unless you feel like you can trust him."

"I do trust Luke. And I trust you. If you didn't think he was telling the truth, you wouldn't let him do me like this."

Richard ran a hand along his jaw. "No, I wouldn't."

My arms shook with the despair. I lowered my head and choked out the words. "Can you forgive me?"

Richard lifted my chin with one strong finger. "Already have. You didn't do anything. You stopped yourself. You called us."

"Uh-huh." Matthew rocked his hips, and my cock pushed into him. I groaned. To be so accepted, so wanted, it meant more than having the love of my parents, than having the pain I thought I needed.

I sank the rest of the way into him. Words flowed out of me, ripped through me like a tidal wave I couldn't dream of stopping. "I don't want anyone else to touch me. To fuck. To love me. No one but you."

I rocked in and out of Matthew's body, and after a few thrusts, Richard pushed into me. Perfect, right, simple. Nothing to run from.

And everything to fight for.

Chapter Thirty-One

I awoke the next morning to two warm bodies surrounding me, arms holding me, lips still touching my skin.

I lifted my head and eyed the clock. Late. Not surprising for me, but Richard never slept in. The night before must have exhausted him as much as it had me. Then a thought pressed in through the sleepy haze.

I slipped out of the bed and threw on a pair of jeans. I descended the basement steps and opened the door to the small bedroom.

There were no chains affixed to the bed. No handcuffs. No ropes or ties in the cabinet. The only remaining evidence of the steel loops were the small holes on the walls and floor. The solitary remnant of bondage was the bench. Probably because Matthew loved it. He liked the way it forced us to be close and hold on to one another.

I sat on the bench.

"We're done with the restraints." Richard stood in the doorway. He wore briefs and nothing else. Tension clung to every muscle.

"I think I am too." I glanced around the room again and nodded. "It's done."

He sat next to me and breathed deep. "I'm glad we're in agreement." He looked away for a moment before continuing. "If I had thought you liked getting hit, getting flogged, that you wanted it, got off on it, then I might have done it. I think I would've liked it, knowing it made you hard, knowing you wanted to submit like that."

"Bullshit. That isn't you. Besides, I was asking for all the wrong reasons. I knew you'd say no, even then."

"Maybe you're right. I just…I want to be what you need."

"You are. I always thought letting myself care about someone again would hurt. Not just because I'd lose him, but because caring would be painful." I met his stare. "It isn't. Trying to leave you two. That was…it was impossible."

"As it should be." He bumped his shoulder with mine. "Did telling us about your father help?"

"Yeah. It doesn't feel as big now."

"That's because you have us." Matthew stood where Richard had been a moment before. He walked in and knelt in front of me. "What happened to you isn't a fear you should carry around. Like my dad and Richard's Gregg. They are pains of the past. Not what define our future together. What your father said fifteen years ago doesn't mean shit now."

Said the kid who was eight at the time. How did he get so damn wise? I stroked his face with the back of my hand in a reverent touch. "When Richard talked about us getting together, he worried you were too young, like you hadn't been hurt by life. But you have. You just didn't let it change you. You kept laughing, kept living. You're a strong man, Matthew Stewart. What if I can't be that strong?"

Richard rubbed a hand over my back. "You're here. You're staying with us. You're living. Try and let yourself enjoy it."

"I was enjoying it—you, us, everything—until he called here. I always thought by living by my own rules I wasn't letting him control my life. But until I met you, he controlled everything." I stood. "Well, it's going to stop. I want us to move in here. Right now."

They smiled up at me.

I tugged on an arm of each man. "Let's go enjoy our life."

* * * *

Richard made a few calls and reserved a small moving truck for the next day. He and I skipped out on work, and the three of us spent the day filling the truck, first with the contents of Matthew's old room at his mom's, and then the rest of my stuff from Walter's. We were fierce in our determination to pack, move, and unpack every single item from our separate lives and bring them together. Richard even insisted we rearrange the living room entertainment center so Matthew could set up his Xbox where he'd be able to play it more.

As we went about the move, I could not stop touching them. Every time one of them walked by me with a box in hand, I groped, tickled, patted, caressed. I'd finally found a peace that allowed me to accept them as I'd never done before.

By the end of the day, we were sweaty, grouchy, exhausted, and utterly pleased. We ended the night in the tub with Richard at one end, me at the other, and Matthew stretched out between us.

Despite the exhaustion settling in my bones, I wanted them,

needed them, in any way they'd give me. I lifted a leg and slipped it between Matthew's thighs. The pads of my toes scraped along his flesh. He didn't jerk or startle at my touch. He raised his eyelids and smiled over at me, as at ease with physical contact as ever.

I pondered that as my toes inched toward his balls. His father had been violent with him. The man had taken his penchant for drink and let the numbness and callousness of alcohol give him a reason to beat down his own son. Despite it all, Matthew had managed to grow into a sensual man with a smile on his face and a laugh in his soul. I'd never take him for granted.

The smile on Matthew's face faded, though, as the sincere look of desire and arousal replaced it. He leaned his head back to Richard's shoulder. My foot caressed him, enticed him with a sample of what I wanted for the rest of the short night.

He let out a soft moan.

Richard sighed. "No way, you two. I'm tired."

My smile widened. Matthew's cock grew fuller with each touch. I had no idea my feet were talented when it came to arousing. He moaned louder and shifted in Richard's arms.

"I'm serious," Richard said. "The two of you may not have had a lot of shit, but it still took all damn day."

"Oh, big strong Richard with all those muscles is too tired for sex?" I said.

"For once, I think I might be. And don't give me crap about my muscles. You two didn't carry as much as I did. I still think we could have waited until next weekend and had more time." He had said the same statement four times during the course of the move. He never meant it. Once I'd made my declaration in the basement the day before, none of us could wait one more day.

"Uh-huh," Matthew said. He inched forward and snaked a hand behind his back.

With Matthew's touch, Richard's tense brow relaxed. He tipped his head back to rest on the edge of the tub, his hips moving.

Focused on Richard's reactions, I missed Matthew's other movement until his foot fondled my balls. His explorations had me aching in no time.

"All right," Richard said. "Out of the tub. I want us all touching if we're doing this. And I want to lie down."

"Uh-huh," Matthew said. He was already headed for the lust-filled bewilderment that meant we'd have to help him to the bed.

I removed my foot from his crotch and stood. Richard slipped out from behind him, and Matthew whimpered at the loss.

"C'mon, kid." I helped him to his feet.

He kissed me, devoured me with his hunger. He tasted salty and sweet at the same time. Richard helped us out of the water as Matthew and I kissed. Then Matthew licked along my neck and chest, sucking and nipping his way toward a nipple.

Richard kissed me and rested a hand in Matthew's hair. His kiss was as lethargic and unfocused as Matthew's, but just as delicious. I wrapped my arms around both men and massaged their tired muscles.

Richard tasted down my body. He took my other nipple in his mouth, twisted and flicked it with his lips and tongue, adding to the sensation Matthew gave me on the other side. Then he moved across my chest. Their breath and lips barely touched me as they kissed over and around my skin. The tease was agony.

"Love your touch," I said. "Harder."

As if taunting me, Richard picked up Matthew, took two steps, and shoved him against the wall. Matthew groaned and arched into the touch, wrapping his legs around Richard.

"Get over here, Luke," Richard said. "You started this. Fuck me and the kid into the wall."

His plea and the scene before me immobilized me. The two men slammed against each other, desperate to satiate their need despite the fatigue in their bodies. I grabbed the lube and slicked my fingers as I knelt behind Richard. He spread his thighs, and I reached my hand between his legs to Matthew's ass. I had Matthew grasping at Richard's shoulders, pushing down, riding my touch, begging for more in a hurry. I stood and slid my hand back to Richard. I enjoyed the feel of his balls for a moment then moved along to slick and stroke his crease.

I shoved my fingers into Richard at the moment he entered Matthew. The combined moans fed my blinding hunger. I withdrew. Nothing could have stopped me from taking him, plunging into his heat.

Whether from the physical tiredness of my body or the desire-laden cloud I traveled on, I needed to be inside him, needed to hear him scream with pleasure and hear Matthew's shrill cries as our bodies slapped together. I thrust hard and drove Richard against Matthew.

"Luke!" Richard yelled. "Yes. Fuck me harder."

I wasn't sure I could do anything with more force or accuracy than I already used, but I sure as hell tried. A tiny part of my brain wondered if we were hurting Matthew with our less-than-gentle shoves. His groan confirmed the opposite. He shouted our names in succession as he came over Richard's hand.

Richard followed him with several loud grunts and quick snaps of his hips. Both men collapsed against the wall, and I gave a few more uncoordinated plunges into Richard.

My forehead landed on his back. "Fuck. That was...that was..."

"Unbelievable," Richard said.

Matthew giggled and spoke with a sluggish voice, his legs and arms still wrapped around Richard, his head resting on the wall behind him. "We should move every day."

"No fucking way." Richard groaned as I left him. He held on to Matthew until the man found the floor with his feet.

We made our way to the bedroom, and by the time Richard had the blankets up, Matthew snored between us.

We lay in silence for a few minutes before Richard spoke. "Luke?"

"Huh?"

"Will your dad come after you again? Will he try to hurt you?"

I rolled to face him. "I don't know. Eventually, he'll try to make you leave me. I just don't know how far he'll go."

"Well, nothing he can do will break us up." Richard lifted onto his elbow. With a soft touch, he brushed a few strands of hair off Matthew's forehead. "Will he hurt him?"

"I won't let him."

"You'll tell me? If he contacts you again?"

"I will."

"Okay. Night, Luke."

"Night." If it hadn't been such a long day, I would have confessed the rest.

But it had been a long day. An amazing day. I couldn't find the courage to ruin it.

Chapter Thirty-Two

It took me the entire morning to work up the nerve, but I finally did it. I filled out the change of address papers at work, and for once, I gave the actual address of where I lived. My father already knew. I didn't need to hide that part of my life any longer.

I couldn't let the man destroy everything. He'd already taken enough.

The moment I gave Richard's address as my own, it seemed more official, legitimate, more than playing around in my private life.

I walked into the house after work with a huge grin plastered on my face. Matthew sat at the kitchen counter, flipping through songs on his iPod.

"Hey, Luke." He came to me and offered a soft kiss.

"Hey. Is Richard late?"

"Yeah. He's finishing some calls for another meet-and-greet for his new investment property." He kissed me again. His hands snaked up the sides of my shirt. His touch felt cold, shaky. Not right. "You taste like tea and lemons," he said.

"I splurged today. Coffee this morning and tea this afternoon. I was pretty tired from the move, needed the extra caffeine."

"It was a long day. Last night was intense." He let go of me and sat at the counter. He fiddled with his iPod again.

"Yeah. Something wrong, Matthew?"

His head jerked up. "Nothing. I, uh…I don't feel right about it."

"What? Last night?"

"God, no. I meant Richard's party."

"What about it?"

He hesitated. When the front door opened, he clamped his mouth shut and scurried for the stove.

Richard came into the kitchen and passed out kisses and gropes. He held on to me longer than usual. His hands skidded over my ass, my arms, my hips, my neck, like he couldn't decide where to touch me.

He dropped his hands and moved to the stove.

What the hell was up with them?

Richard helped Matthew bring the food to the table. We ate in silence. I was about to ask what was going on when Richard spoke.

"I'm throwing another investor party. Since I've had a lot of backouts on the Richfield condos, I need to get a few more people lined up." His gaze shifted between Matthew and me before he spoke again. "I want you both to attend the party with me."

Matthew dropped his fork to his plate. "Oh, good. I felt out of sorts about it all day. I mean, I knew you were working out the details, and I didn't know how to bring it up. I don't feel right about it anymore. It isn't just you and me. I don't want to do anything to hurt your business. I thought maybe we could take turns, but I didn't think that would look right either. I can't keep—"

"Matthew," Richard said. "It's okay. If they don't want to do business with me because I'm in love with two gorgeous, amazing men, then fuck them. If nothing else, all the straight women will want to work with me. They'll be so envious and turned on by all the cock I get, they'll be dying to see us together."

I stared at them until my voice worked its way out. "We can't."

Richard leaned back in his chair. "We can. I'm done pretending. I'm done with you thinking you aren't as important to me as Matthew is."

"I don't think that. I know you—" I shifted in my seat. "What are you suggesting? We just show up together wherever you're having the party, the three of us?"

"Yes. But I thought we'd have the party here."

"Great idea." Matthew picked up his fork and waved it in the air. "Might not be such a big deal if we aren't three men walking in together. Then it's our home, and if someone has anything to say we don't like, we throw their asses out."

Richard's eyebrows rose. "Dang, kid."

"What? I think it makes sense. You should only do business with rich people who care more about making money than about what we do in our own bedroom. Or poor people who know how to mind their own business. But then I doubt you'd make much money, so…I'd go with the rich, money-grubbing people."

I laughed, the reaction so extreme my cheeks burned from the stretch. I'd give them whatever they wanted. I'd already taken plenty of risks. One more wouldn't kill me.

"Come on, Luke," Richard said. "Enjoy your life."

"Yeah. I want to. I guess we're coming out. Again."

Matthew bounced in his seat. "This will be better than when I was fifteen. Back then I was only getting an occasional hand job from Curtis Halloway in the art room after school. At least now I'm getting the best sex of my life."

Richard pulled Matthew onto his lap and kissed him. All the tension of earlier melted away. The kisses became needy, horny.

I cleared my throat.

Richard smiled. He whispered in Matthew's ear.

Matthew's eyes shot wide. He stood and headed over to straddle my lap.

"What did he tell you?" I caressed his thighs.

"He said I should make sure you're good and hard before he comes over here to attack us in three minutes." Matthew rocked his hips. His tongue tangled with my own, and he sent my cock into the state Richard had requested.

Richard laughed. It was the last I heard from either of them before I was lost to the sounds of our sexual bliss filling the kitchen. Over the next hour and a half we enjoyed one another through two orgasms apiece. The kitchen table, the tiled floor, and even the countertops had never seen so much activity in one night.

After we admitted the floor was nowhere to sleep, Richard and I cleared the plates, moving around the kitchen naked. Matthew smiled to himself as he wiped the table.

I'd give them whatever they wanted.

* * * *

Everything was ready to go: the caterers and their silver-plated trays, the servers dressed in pristine white shirts and black vests, and the bartender with his portable mahogany bar at one end of the living room.

I just wasn't sure I was.

I expected we'd be somewhat nervous, but I hadn't expected Matthew and Richard to be calm while I paced, bit my fingernails, and fidgeted with my tie like a kid about to leave for his first date.

I should have known. It wasn't like I was used to dating—I hadn't done so in the traditional sense at any time in my life. Years spent obtaining sex from one-night stands at parties, gay bars, and a sex club hadn't prepared me for my level of nervousness. It didn't keep me from wanting to be a part of the night, though.

I adjusted my tie again and stepped into the living room. The bartender was filling a glass with club soda for Richard. He had promised Matthew three times he wouldn't drink anything stronger. Matthew had insisted he was okay with it now, but I knew Richard. As long as he lived, he'd never drink around Matthew again.

When the doorbell rang, my stomach churned and a bitter taste settled in my mouth. I wished I could reach for a glass of anything strong enough to quell my nerves and numb my head. But I was finished drinking around Matthew too. He deserved at least that much from us. Especially since the rest of the guests filling our home would be drinking a shitload of alcohol. Free booze aided most anyone in taking a risk with their money.

The bald, older gentleman who entered had a kind smile and eyes that held a genuine delight to see Matthew and Richard. His gray-haired wife held on to his arm as they stepped inside.

Richard shook hands with the man. "Welcome, Joseph, Margaret. Come in. You remember Matthew?"

"Yes. Nice to see you again." The older man nodded to Matthew, and the two shook hands. His wife gave Richard and Matthew each a kiss on the cheek.

Richard gestured for me to come forward. "Luke, this is Joseph and Margaret Mason. Joe and I are old friends. We worked together when I first moved to the city, and he was my first investor when I started my own business. Joe, this is my other partner, Luke."

The older man reached for my hand, his eyebrows rising in confusion. "Other?" His eyes shot wide as our hands made contact. "Oh...nice to meet you." He regarded Richard, shaking his head. "Two men? Aren't you getting a little old to be playing the field?"

Richard lifted a hand in protest. "Hey, just because the kid here's barely in his twenties doesn't make me old."

"No, it doesn't," Margaret said. "But the two of them here with you does make you far more lucky than most." She winked at him.

Richard's laugh bellowed out of him. "It does." Then he met the Masons' stares with a serious look. "And we're not playing."

Margaret nodded and embraced me before she took Matthew's arm on her way into the living room.

Joseph slapped a hand on my back and gestured for us to follow. "Luke, what do you do for a living?"

And on it went, introduction after introduction. Most were polite, a few gave questionable glances, and one woman gasped when Richard used the word partner, but overall the declaration was tolerated and well received at times. The talk turned to investment business and financial news, and it became apparent the status of their money and what people did for a living were far more important than what we all did in our beds.

After the servers had circulated trays of Gruyère tartlets and coconut-crusted shrimp and the bartender had poured glass after glass of wine, whiskey, and champagne, I relaxed. I mingled my way around the room and overheard Richard talking with Joseph Mason again. I turned away to afford them privacy to discuss their business dealings when I heard my name.

"I saw Luke and Matthew in the kitchen earlier. They looked chummy together."

"Did they?" Richard's tone was casual and not at all alarmed.

"I have to ask: How can you stand seeing them together? Don't you get jealous? I mean they were kissing and holding each other. If I saw my wife with another man, I'd go crazy."

Richard smirked and sipped his drink. "I love them both. It's different." He faced his friend. "You want me to answer truthfully?"

The man's expression changed to one of somber curiosity. "Tell me."

"I like to watch them. Sometimes when I come home from work, they are in the kitchen together, and I stop dead in my tracks. They will be setting the table or doing some other mundane task and the way they move together and touch each other is the most sensual, beautiful thing I've ever witnessed. They are amazing looking, and together they are stunning, but it's more than that. Each has an awareness of himself and his body that blends. I'm a fortunate man to see them together on a daily basis."

I silently gasped. Matthew was sensual, sexy, beautiful. I was nothing of the sort.

Richard continued. "The attraction and affection you see between them—it isn't just about them. Wrapped up in that is me—their feelings for me."

He could not have described it better. It was what I tried not to see when I looked at Matthew and Richard, but it was there. I was there. In them. With them. A part of them. We all fit together in a way we wouldn't if one of us left.

A deluge of guilt slammed into me. What would have happened to them? What would my leaving have done to them?

The doorbell rang again, and I groaned. I couldn't wait to get Richard and Matthew out of their clothes and into bed. It'd been a long night, and with each glance at my lovers, they offered me promises for later.

A man entered, and I spotted his graying hair but little else. It didn't matter, though. With one look, I knew.

I stepped through the crowd toward the door.

Matthew was shaking hands with Walter, the younger man's smile as warm and inviting as ever.

"How did you get an invite?" I asked.

"I have my ways. I was just saying hello to Matthew. I don't think I've ever had the privilege of meeting him before."

Matthew smiled, always happy to see me, even when I'd been within a few feet of him all night. He turned back to Walter. "It's nice to finally meet you. Any friend of Luke's must be someone special." He stepped back. "I'll let you two catch up."

Walter didn't miss the look that lingered between Matthew and me. "Things are going better?"

"They are."

"I'm glad. I do believe I said they'd be good for you."

"They have been. I'm not sure I can explain it." I paused and struggled to find the words. I settled on the truth of the matter. "I've become the man I didn't even know I wanted to be."

He didn't tease any further. He must have deemed me sincere, or perhaps infatuated beyond all reason. He gave me a squeeze on the shoulder, nothing my father ever gave to me. "I owe them my thanks, then. For giving a dear friend a life filled with more than the club. Can I meet your Richard?"

I spotted Richard across the room and made my way to him. He excused himself from the conversation and met me near the bar.

I leaned in. "I have you to thank for this?"

"I wanted you to have a friend here tonight."

"Thank you." I stepped back and gestured to Walter. "Richard, I'd like you to meet Walter Simon."

Walter accepted Richard's outstretched hand. "It's good to meet you."

They already knew of each other from years spent at the club—whether they'd ever talked or not was beside the point. It was a moment for me to claim Richard and Matthew as mine, and the introductions were necessary, for them and for me. Walter was likely the only person of consequence in my life for me to make such introductions to.

Then, as if to mock my postulation, another unexpected guest arrived.

Natural curiosity caused me to turn my head toward the door.

Matthew's small frame was sidestepped by a man of my height, a man with my own last name, a man whom I never wanted to see walk through my front door.

Chapter Thirty-Three

I dashed out of the room, past the caterers in the kitchen, and down the basement steps in search of the privacy of our small playroom.

As soon as I reached the bedroom, the breath rushed out of me. I bent over and gripped the handholds of the bench. Who invited my father? What the hell was he up to? And what did a heart attack feel like anyway?

He hadn't seen me before my hasty departure, but I still feared hearing his voice behind me. When a voice did come, it was a lower, more familiar one.

"Luke, what's wrong?" Richard's warm hand rubbed my back.

I straightened and glared at him. Anger shook my body without my consent. "What is he doing here?"

"Who?" He reached for me.

I shoved his hand away. "My father! He's in the goddamn living room."

"Johnathan Moore? The senator? He's your father?"

I slumped to the bench.

Richard landed with a thud beside me. "I didn't know. You didn't say. Doug came up with a list of investors. If I'd known—"

"This isn't your fault. I should have told you who he was before now."

Richard stood. "He's not staying." He made a move for the door.

"Wait. I don't want you to make a scene. This is your business."

He came back and sat next to me. "I'll never do business with him. Ever."

"I know." I gave him a halfhearted smile. "But there are other people here you need to work with. Let me talk to him. Ask him to leave. He knows I live here. He isn't sincere about working with you. He's up to something."

Richard stood and folded his arms in front of him. "No way. I'm not letting you deal with this on your own."

"I need to do this. You're here with me. And...and it's making me nervous Matthew's up there all alone."

Richard eyed the door, ready to sprint up the stairs. "Are you sure?"

I stood. "He came to scare me into doing what he wants. I want to be the one to tell him to get the fuck out. This is my home, and I want him out."

"All right. Let's get this done."

Financial discussions continued throughout the house. Richard had already pitched his plans to everyone in the room, and the viability of the investment options took priority over politics, sports, or entertainment news.

I made my way through the crowd. My parents stood by the fireplace talking to Joseph and Margaret Mason. I couldn't take my eyes off my mother. She was older, but as beautiful and soft as I remembered her from my teen years. It amazed me she could be so much his ally and still look the part of a loving, mild-mannered woman. How had my father turned her against me? Kept her hating me for fifteen years?

"Is everything okay?" Matthew asked. "Where'd you go?"

Richard stepped beside me. "Luke's father's here."

"What? Here?"

"His father is Senator Johnathan Moore. Luke is going to ask him to leave."

"The one who's going to run for president?"

"That's him," I said.

The man in question turned toward me. His expression hardened, but he recovered quickly and spoke with a smile to the Masons. He gave the couple a nod and stepped toward me. I didn't let him cover the distance between us. I matched his stride and met him in the middle of the room.

"There you are." He spat the words in a near whisper. "I wondered when you'd show your face."

"You're leaving. I know you don't want a scene any more than I do."

He forged a socially acceptable smile that divulged the truth of my statement. "I came to bring you a message. One of those...whatever...you live with was kind enough to invite me." He offered a frown over my shoulder.

I glanced back. Richard and Matthew stood behind me. Both sets of eyes were upon us. No one could miss Richard's strong, dominating presence. "He's my partner, Dad. His name is Richard

Marshall, and if you treat him with anything less than respect, I'll make a scene you'll find most unpleasant."

I caught a brief look of panic before he covered it with his professional mask. "Let's move this to a more private location, shall we? I have something to say, and I won't be leaving until I've said it."

I scoffed. "Fine." I led the way to Richard's office.

Matthew and Richard entered after us and stood along the back wall behind my father. I shut the door and made no attempt to ask either of them to leave.

"I will not have this discussion in front of *them*." His gaze swung between my lovers and me. We had situated ourselves well. He liked to be in the position of power in any room. Forcing him to look back and forth between us would make him edgy, nervous.

I stood behind the large desk with my arms folded. "You will. Or we can go back out to the other room and have it in front of everyone."

He glared at me a moment more, then squared his shoulders.

A quiet knock interrupted our silent stare. I threw my hands up, stalked to the door, and flung it open.

My mother peered into the room.

"You might as well come in too."

She crept to my father's side. "What is going on, Johnathan? You didn't seem surprised to see Luke here." She looked to me. "Is this where you're living?"

"Yes." I pointed to Richard and Matthew. "These are my partners." I left out their names. The moment didn't require a social introduction, but she needed to understand the situation more so than her husband had allowed her to do.

"Oh. I..." She glanced at them. Matthew's gaze met the floor, but Richard didn't withdraw. He crossed his large arms in front of him. His face held a look of fierce determination. She turned back to her husband. "What is going on?"

"I was graciously invited to this party, and I thought I'd take the opportunity to give Luke one more chance to be a man."

I didn't need to see the flinch in Richard's body to know he wanted to confront the man, make a move.

I spoke before he could do either. "If you're asking for the same things you did the other night on the phone, then forget it. I'm not going to the club anymore, but for reasons that are none of your business. I will not give up my membership because you demand it. I'm not giving them up. I've given you every assurance I can. I will not talk to the press. I will not accept any interviews. That's all I can offer you."

"That's not enough." He released the words in a fiery spat. "I should have expected nothing less from you. It was bad enough you were a gay man. We might have been able to spin that. Then you go to that club. You fuck anyone who walks by you so long as he has a dick in his pants. Now you are what? I don't even know what to call this thing you're doing." He gestured to Richard and Matthew. "Living with and fucking two men at the same time. You are beyond disgusting."

I strode across the room until we stood a foot apart. My mother stepped aside, swiping at her tears with the back of her hand.

My father didn't move, but he did flinch. I took satisfaction in it.

"It's a relationship. It's hard enough being two people in a relationship. Hell, it's hard enough trusting enough to be in a relationship at all. A gay relationship is even harder with people like you fighting against us. There's nothing easy about three people together. It's a hell of a lot of hard work. But with them"—I looked to Matthew and Richard—"it's worth it." I met my father's stare. "So fuck you. I've had enough. You will not come in here and speak to me like this. You will not disrespect me. You will not disrespect them. I want you to get the hell out and leave me alone."

My father's mouth gaped open, an expression I'd never seen on the polished man. My mother tugged at his arm. Her face was covered in tears, too many for her to catch.

Richard came to me. He wrapped his arm around my waist and whispered in my ear. "I'm proud of you."

I smiled at the words and the closeness of his body to mine.

My father rolled his eyes and snorted. When he turned back to us, his stare was cold and more calculating than it'd been a moment before. "Would you be proud of him if you knew what he's cost you? What he'll keep costing you if you don't stop this?"

My hands wrenched into fists until my fingers numbed. "What are you talking about?"

My father let a grin build. He took a step closer to Richard. "The lakefront properties you were interested in. I had a good friend of mine make a generous offer. And every deal you've attempted since then hasn't gone well, has it? And every one you try to make from now on will always be met with resistance. It won't matter how many parties you throw or how many calls you make. No one will work with you. My influence reaches far and wide. Don't fuck with me."

"Johnathan, stop. Please." My mother's voice cracked. She shrank back from her husband. Her eyes darted around the room—to me, to my father, to Richard and Matthew. She spun on her heels and fled the office.

My father glared at me a moment longer. Then he walked out the door.

I turned away and stared out the window into the night sky.

Richard wrapped his arms around me and pulled my back to his chest. "This isn't your fault. I don't care what he threatens us with." He kissed my temple. "Stay in here. Matthew and I'll go out and wind this party down. Then we'll talk."

I managed a nod and didn't move as they left the room. I stood at the window and willed my mind to think of nothing until they could return to me. For once, I wanted to talk to them. I needed to.

The office door opened. I waited for their arms to surround me. When they didn't come, I turned.

Walter stood on the other side of the desk, a glass of whiskey in his hand. "Is everything all right?"

"No." Talking must be like diarrhea. Once you get started, you can't turn it off. No matter where. No matter when.

Walter downed a swig of his whiskey and sat across from me. "From the moment I met him, I knew he'd cause trouble for you one day. He's too ambitious not to try and control everything around him."

I lost the ability to stand. My ass hit the chair behind Richard's desk. "You've met my father?"

"When you first told me he was having you followed, I decided to find out why."

"Because he wants me to live the way he tells me to."

"It's more than that. And I think you know it."

"Do I want to hear this?"

"Probably not. But you need to."

I scanned the room. A stapler sat to the right of Richard's phone. I reached for it and turned it over and over in my hands. The top came loose. I lifted it up and stared at the unused line of staples. Small, neat, orderly. Such insignificant things. Where would the offices of the world be without them? People made their livings in factories that produced and shipped staples. The small metal clips paid mortgages and electric bills and college educations. Entire lives revolved around the tiny shreds of wire. Irony carved a notch in my mind.

We give little thought to the world around us unless we force ourselves to see it. The smallest detail has an entire story behind it.

I snapped the stapler shut, returned it to the desk, and collapsed back against the chair. "Okay, tell me."

He knocked back the rest of his whiskey. "You want me to get you a drink first?"

I nodded.

He made a move to get up.

"Wait. I can't. Matthew…he…I can't."

Walter dropped into the chair. "You're in love."

I stared at him.

"That'll anger your father. It'll make matters worse."

"What do you mean?"

"Men like him never know love or compassion. And they hate others who do. All that matters is getting what they think they deserve."

"He's fucking with Richard's business. Because of me. Because he sees me as a threat to his future."

"You have nothing to be ashamed of, Luke. Even if you weren't living here in a committed relationship, you have a right to live your life how you want. Maybe you should consider talking to the press. Tell how he's been harassing you. Get it all out in the open. Then he can't hold it over you anymore. He won't have a reason to threaten you."

"No, he'll hate me for destroying him."

"I'm afraid he already does. You lost your father a long time ago."

"I know. It doesn't hurt like it used to. I want to be rid of him. But he thinks my life matters in terms of his future. I don't think I'll ever be free of him or his ambitions."

"You might be right."

I studied Walter's face. "What did you find out about him?"

The office door opened. Walter gave a quick nod to Matthew and Richard.

Matthew stepped toward me, but Richard reached out and stopped him. "We'll give you two a few minutes."

"Stay," Walter said. "You need to hear this too."

Chapter Thirty-Four

Walter leaned back in the chair. "It's not exactly legal, but I installed surveillance equipment at his office. I figured I'd find out his true motives where you were concerned or, at the least, I'd find something you could use against him. It didn't take long. Every Friday night a man named Barry Fowler arranges for a prostitute to meet your father in his office." Walter stared into the empty glass in his hand. Did he want to say the rest? Did I want to hear it?

Finally, he set the glass on the desk and said, "It's always a different person, but it's always a man."

I couldn't focus on anything. Not Walter. Not Richard. Not Matthew.

I spotted the stapler on the desk and burst into laughter. The vibrations in my chest released a dam and kept my body from seizing under the enormous pressure. I slapped both hands on the desk. My palms stung. I kept laughing. Tears formed at the corners of my eyes.

My entire life with my father sped through my mind. Short snippets of conversations and arguments and the moment he'd taken Tim from me replayed in a mix of unorganized insight. I laughed harder. "Does he suck their cocks? Does he fuck them? Or do they fuck him?" The laugh bellowed out of me. I smacked my hands on the desk again. "No, no. I don't want to know that. God, do I?" I looked up. Richard and Matthew stared at me, eyes wide, brows drawn in close, deep worry lines visible from across the room. I sounded mad, crazed. I knew it.

The laugh slowed and then tapered off after a few more uncontrollable spurts. I met Richard's stare.

I took a deep breath and nodded.

"Go on, Walter," Richard said. "Say the rest."

"Right. This isn't a new development. When you're at his level, paying for sex is a hard thing to hide. He's working so hard to control your actions, but it doesn't seem like he can control his own.

Although, he tries. The rent boys stop for a few months at a time, but it always starts up again." Walter moved to stand beside my chair. "He hates you for being what he can't. I think he's afraid you'll find out and use it against him."

"Why would I ever use being gay against someone? Even my father."

"I hope you can forgive me for not telling you as soon as I found out. I wasn't sure if you'd want to know."

I wiped the tears off my face. "I don't think I was ready to hear or accept this before now. But I needed to."

He gave my shoulder a pat and crossed the room.

"Walter?"

He stopped by the door and faced me.

"Could you check into someone named Danny Conner?"

"Yeah. What am I looking for?"

"He went to college with my father. They were friends. Or maybe they were more. I don't know for sure. But Conner died of a drug overdose the day before their graduation."

"You think your father had something to do with it?" Walter asked.

"I think my father gave him the cocaine that night."

Richard stood taller. His body stiffened.

Walter shook his head. "Why?"

"Maybe Conner was going to out my father. So he gave him some bad shit to shut him up."

Richard stepped closer to the desk. "How did you find this out?"

"A reporter called me, hinting that my father had something in his past he was hiding. I started checking into it."

"Of course he has something to hide," Walter said. "He's gay, and he's paying for sex."

"Maybe it's more than that." Was it? Was I seeing what I wanted to?

Richard leaned over the desk, his palms flat on the surface. "This isn't something you should be digging into."

"Why? If he killed Conner, I need to know. Everyone needs to know."

"I'll look into it," Walter said. "How do you know he had the drugs that night?"

"His friend gave me a picture that was taken three hours before Conner died. Conner's watch with the coke was in my father's pocket."

"Okay. Let me see what I can find out."

"Thanks, Walter." I closed my eyes as Richard and Matthew said their good-byes and walked him to the door.

The truth hit me again, slamming into me as my head hit the chair behind me.

* * * *

Warm hands tugged me out of the office chair. My head landed on Richard's chest. Matthew snuggled in beside me, his arm around my waist.

"I can't believe I never saw it. I should have. His hatred of me…it was too specific, too personal, even if I was his son. There was more there, and I didn't want to see it. I wanted to keep my distance, keep him from feeling at ease about me. I never wanted to give him anything to use against me. If I had no one, nothing important in my life, he couldn't take anything else from me. Now he's hurting you."

"He's not taking me from you," Richard said. "He'll hurt himself by asking too many people to intervene in my business. Eventually it'll get out what he's been doing. I have plenty of money. Plenty of contacts who know me. Let him play his games. In the end, we'll be the ones who come out with our dignity and self-respect intact."

When I didn't speak, Richard pulled back. "Luke?"

"I knew he'd never leave us alone. Walter suggested I go to the press, turn him in for making the threats against us. That doesn't sit right with me. It'll anger him more."

Matthew's arm tightened around me. "I don't want to see him when he's angrier than tonight."

"I'm sorry I didn't tell you about him. I wasn't sure you'd want me to stay, knowing who he is—knowing what we'll be up against."

Matthew kissed me. "I don't care who he is. You're deserving of his love, and he threw you aside. Well, you're ours now, and we're not giving you up."

"I wouldn't let myself destroy this. I'm sure as hell not letting him."

Richard ran his hand up and down my back. "Then stop looking into his past, huh? You think your father had something to do with a man's death, and you poke around. How does that sound like a good idea?"

"I have to know."

"Walter'll let you know if he finds anything." Richard held my face. He forced my eyes upon him. "Matthew and I will make it all go away. Let us take care of you."

I nodded.

They kissed me. Each pressed into my mouth in turn. Their tongues dived in with devotion and determination, with passion and strength. They were giving me more than pleasure of the body. They were feeding me their love.

I let it spread over me like a protective shield—to keep me warm and safe when the storms came.

They removed my clothes and swiped aside everything on the desk. Richard spread me out on my back, giving me a perfect view as they undressed before me.

Richard located some lube and came back to me. He stood between my legs, and his hands spread my thighs apart. Matthew's mouth met mine again. He gave me not a moment's rest from the assault of lips and tongue. He tortured my chest with flicks and sucks and continued down my body, humming and moaning as he adored me with his tongue. I arched off the desk.

The wet heat of Matthew's lips covered my cock as Richard sent a thick finger into me. I moaned, the sound desperate, a little sad. I gripped at the edges of the desk. Richard assaulted me with his fingers until I writhed and begged for more, anxious for him to push in deeper, fill me wider, and for Matthew to take me all the way in his mouth.

Without warning, Richard pulled out. I begged again, pleaded with words they may not have understood. Whatever I said, it made Matthew suck harder, and his mouth took me in farther.

Richard pressed in again. I wasn't sure how much of him was inside me, but he stretched me wide, wider than I'd ever been taken with someone's fingers before.

"More."

He pushed in and spread my legs apart with his body until my thighs burned with the stretch. I was being split open, sucked dry, and it blasted explosions throughout every nerve. My stomach muscles tightened, and my body propelled forward.

"Stop, Matthew," Richard said.

Matthew gave no protest. He withdrew his mouth and hands. Richard slipped his fingers out in a slow drag. I groaned and collapsed back onto the desk.

I lifted my head. "No, no. Don't stop."

Richard held my balls in one hand and squeezed the base of my cock with the other. "Breathe for a minute, Luke. We're gonna make this last. Stretch this out until you can't stand it any longer. Make you come until you're soaring. You'll forget about tonight. Hell, you'll forget where you are."

"Yes. Want all of you. Inside." I threw my head back to the desk. I arched up in a desperate appeal for more. I wanted what Richard promised. I needed it. But I couldn't forget who was giving it to me. I met their eyes.

Matthew kissed me. I tasted the faint remnants of my precum in his mouth. "Love you," he said and kissed me again, filling my mouth with the taste of him and me.

"Matthew," Richard said, "go get us a couple of towels and the large bottle of lube from the bathroom. In the bottom right drawer."

Matthew stared at him for a moment, his eyes wide, his mouth hanging open, and then he was gone.

Richard's eyes never left mine. I couldn't look away.

"We really going to do this, Luke?"

"Yes. I need you. All of you."

Matthew sprinted into the room. He tossed Richard the supplies and stood beside me again. He kissed me once, and then his searing mouth closed over my prick.

Slick fingers entered me until the fullness and stretch of a moment before returned.

"Oh God." The slow torture compelled me to the edge with ease and care. Richard spread the slick of more lube around the entrance to my body. The pressure spiked as he pushed farther into me.

His voice was tense with desire when he spoke. "Oh, Luke. Are you going to take all of it?"

"Yes! All of you."

A large hand stroked over my hip, and a small hand rubbed in circles over my stomach. The wet heat of Matthew's mouth continued to suck my cock with abandon, and his tongue scrubbed along my shaft. He knew how to work me over, but he'd never gone at it with such vigor before. Who knew he could get better?

My name on Richard's tongue was all the warning I needed. The pressure of the stretch intensified, and Richard's hand worked in past the widest point.

Then his entire hand was inside me.

The only man I'd ever trusted enough.

I couldn't see it, but there was no doubt of what he'd done—what we were doing.

"Richard." I wanted him to move, to fuck me with his hand. If we stayed still for one more moment, I might lose my mind. "Richard. I need…anything. Please."

"Luke." He was breathless. "Hang on. Matthew and I—we'll take care of you." If I could have opened my eyes, I was certain I'd have seen tears in his.

His hand moved, and all words were gone. I understood nothing of what they said or what I screamed. I was lost to all things but the two men touching me—inside and out.

I rode the waves of my orgasm far longer than I imagined possible. Matthew swallowed what he could, but even he had to pull off my cock before I finished spurting. He sucked in a deep breath and took me back in his mouth until I went soft. He licked everywhere, tasting all of me.

My body slumped onto the desk, and I was pretty sure I had no clue where I was. But I knew they were there with me.

Matthew patted my stomach. "Oh, man. Luke, he's…all of his hand."

"Going to pull out now," Richard said. "Relax." I tried to follow the instruction, but he sounded far away, and I rolled about in a fog. I heard myself groan, and his hand left me.

He collapsed into the chair behind the desk. I was vaguely aware of Matthew straddling his lap and riding him for what seemed like a few short moments before they both came, grunting each other's names, with my own mixed into their cries.

I wasn't aware of moving from the office upstairs to our bed, but when they snuggled in beside me, I came back to myself and found my voice. The slow drawl of it surprised me. "That was…intense. Thank you."

"You're welcome," Richard said. "But I think I should be thanking you. I've never gone that far with anyone before."

"Me neither."

"I like that." His arms tightened around us. "The kid's next."

Matthew gasped and buried his head in my shoulder. The reaction reminded me of our second night at the Haven when I'd pondered what he'd sound like fucking Richard. I was glad I knew exactly how he sounded buried inside Richard. I was also glad we still had moments to come that could send him into such an overwhelmed state at the mere thought of them.

I'd have vocalized my contemplation, but I couldn't find my voice again, and I didn't care to. I traveled along a current of satiation that wouldn't let me care about much of anything. Not about clubs, parties, or investors. Not about elections, mothers, or fathers.

I only cared about them. The two men who held me between them, with them, in them.

I had Matthew and Richard, and everything else paled in comparison.

Chapter Thirty-Five

"Is he home yet?" Richard asked.

"No," I said. "I thought you were working. Go back to your office."

"Okay. Holler when he gets home."

It was the same conversation we'd had five minutes earlier. And a half hour before that.

Richard poked his head around the corner. "Hey, the spaghetti sauce smells good."

"Thanks." It came from a jar. Unscrewing the lid hadn't been that hard. It tasted okay. Not like Matthew's homemade, though.

"Don't forget to let me know—"

"The minute he gets in."

Richard took off for his office.

I set the plates and silverware on the table. The act of making dinner for them gave me a domestic satisfaction I'd never known in my life. I was happy to fill in for Matthew. I hadn't even gotten pissed when the water boiled over and I caught the towel on fire trying to dry the stove off.

The entire task was a welcome distraction.

After Richard's party, I forced myself to stop thinking about my father or his threats. I didn't want to give him any more power over me than he already had. I had to trust Walter—trust that he'd find something if there was something to find.

And if not?

I wouldn't allow myself to go there.

Whenever my father got around to announcing he'd be running in the election, my life was going to change. Even if my father didn't want to acknowledge me, I was going to be the son of a presidential candidate. A gay son who lived with two men. I couldn't hide from that.

Until then, not thinking about it helped…some. Making spaghetti while Matthew spent the day at a career counseling seminar helped more.

I strained the spaghetti, and it didn't stick. An accomplishment.

The front door opened, and Matthew stepped into the kitchen a moment later. "Hi, Luke."

"Hey, kid. You better go get—"

Richard rushed in and hugged Matthew from behind.

"Never mind," I said with a laugh.

"What did you learn?" Richard asked as I dished out the food.

Matthew took a bite and smiled his approval at me. "This is good."

"It's just fucking spaghetti," Richard said. He threw me an apologetic look.

I waved it off. "I want to hear about it too. C'mon, Matthew."

Matthew ate another bite and set his fork down. "Well, I've been thinking about a degree program for a while now. A man in the field gave a lecture and had a booth setup. It helped me make a decision." He wiped his mouth with his napkin and sat back in his chair. "I want to go back to school, full time, if I can manage. That way I can be done in two years. I can even start the classes in the summer session. From what I heard today, I should be able to get a loan without much trouble." He picked up his fork and ate more.

"You'll take the loan from me," Richard said.

Matthew raised his head. A string of spaghetti hung out the corner of his mouth. He slurped it in. "Are you sure?"

"I'm sure. They'll charge you interest. I won't."

I hid a smile.

"And don't even ask about paying for this place or anything else," he added. "I want you to concentrate on school. I can cover what you give to your mom too."

Matthew dropped his fork. "That's…I can't let you do that."

"Why?"

"I'm not a child."

"I never said you were."

"Jesus, Richard, I have to pay for something." Matthew shoved his chair back and carried his barely eaten dinner to the sink. The plate and silverware clanked on top of the spaghetti pot. Any harder and it would have broken.

The perplexed look on Richard's face almost had me laughing. Except it wasn't funny. "You can't control everything."

He turned the puzzled look on me. "What?"

"Matthew's got to decide this stuff for himself."

"I just want to help."

"I know. I want him to let you help. But it's his decision. If he doesn't feel right about it, then he'll figure something else out."

"But I have the money."

"Everything isn't always that simple."

"Why not?"

"Dammit, do you ever hear yourself?"

"What the hell—"

"Just 'cause we call him kid doesn't mean he's not a man."

Richard jerked back and crossed his arms. "I know exactly what he is. I've had his dick up my ass."

"He's standing right here."

Richard looked up at Matthew, and the two held the stare for several breaths.

Matthew took his seat. "I shouldn't accept it, but I'd appreciate the loan and the help with the bills. I'd like to hold off on getting a job until I get into the swing of things, get a few classes under my belt. I don't want to mess this up. After a few weeks, I'll get a part-time job." He stretched his arm across the table and pressed two fingers over Richard's half-open mouth. "I won't be able to work enough to pay my share of living expenses and go to school. I know that. I can at least pay for groceries or the electricity or the gas bill. Have my own money for books and lunches when I'm at school. And I will pay my mom the same I've been giving her. That part's not up for discussion. I've gotta be the one to help her. By living here with you, you're helping me do that."

Richard kissed Matthew's fingers. "Okay. I like the idea of you taking some time off, though. Get yourself used to the classes. But don't be afraid. You'll do great."

"Thanks." He sat back. "I guess after Jake, I'm afraid I'll lose my focus."

Richard glared at Matthew. His eyebrows drew together to form one line across his forehead.

I put a hand on Matthew's knee. "You learned from the experience. This is important to you. You're taking it seriously. You're letting Richard help you. You're taking it slow instead of piling a bunch of shit on top of yourself. There's no way you're gonna mess up."

He gripped my hand. "Thanks."

"The only thing we'll have to monitor is the sex. You know, Richard can be pretty demanding, and you'll have a lot of studying to do. I'll be glad to keep him occupied for you at any time."

Matthew rolled his eyes and smacked my arm.

Richard snorted. "Me? He's the one who's years younger than us. He's insatiable."

The incredulous expression on Matthew's face had me laughing. I kissed him and wrapped my arm around his shoulders. "So, tell us."

"Tell you what?" He grabbed my fork and ate a bite off my plate.

"Matthew. What are you going to study at school?"

He looked off into the kitchen. "You'll think it's stupid."

"No, we won't."

"I want to be a vet technician."

Richard leaned forward and grinned. "It was the puppies you rescued when you were a kid, wasn't it? The little beasts got to you."

Matthew's gaze returned, lighthearted and happy.

* * * *

"Hey, I ordered Chinese," Richard said as he came into the living room. "Should be here any minute."

I was sitting on the floor against the couch with my laptop open on the coffee table. Matthew had gone to his mom's for dinner, and Richard had been working in his office for the past couple of hours.

The doorbell rang.

"Great timing," I said.

"What can I say? I'm organized." He answered the door.

"Organized is not what I'd call you."

Richard paid for the food and came back in with two bags of takeout in hand. "What would you call me?" He dropped the bags on the table and flopped onto the floor, stretching out on his side.

"Well, since Matthew hates Chinese, and I love it, I'd say someone who's trying to get lucky."

"Could be." He winked and ran his hand up my inner thigh.

Even through the jeans, his hand sent a fire racing through my body, building need and want where thoughts of work had been a moment before.

He lightly passed over my dick and moved down my other leg. I closed my eyes and enjoyed his touch.

"I was thinking about Matthew," he said, still exploring me.

"Wish he was here."

"Me too. But I had an idea. We should get him a laptop as a good luck gift for school. He'll need it for all the papers and research and shit."

I opened my eyes and smiled at him. "Good idea."

"Great. You can pick it out if you don't mind. You'll know more about what to get than I would. Just let me know what you decide on and the cost." He removed his hand from my leg and settled on his back, his arms folded behind his head. "He's telling his mom he's going back to school."

"That's good."

"Yeah, but I think he's afraid of what she'll think about me paying for it."

"You mean about you loaning him the money?" I raised an eyebrow.

"Right."

"He's not gonna accept you paying for it. You know that, right?"

"That's why I said it was a loan."

"That's not what you meant." I swung my legs around and lay beside him. I tickled his underarm. He smirked and returned the playful touches until we were rolling around on the floor.

He gripped my wrists and stilled me. "Let's let him get through school first, and then we'll discuss the money. Okay?"

I leaned over him. "Have I ever thanked you?"

"For what?"

"Asking two strangers to live with you."

He reached up and stroked the side of my face with the back of his fingers.

My breath quickened at the soft caress. I'd fucked a lot of men in my life, but I'd never known such affection. Not even Tim had shown his love for me with his hands the way Richard did. Now…I needed more than the slamming together of bodies. I needed a caress. A touch to my cheek. A hand in my own.

He dropped his hand to his chest. "It was the best decision of my life."

"Knowing what you do now, you'd do it again?" A part of me needed to hear his answer after all my father had done.

"Hell, yes. I'd have asked the first night if I'd known it'd be like this." He smirked. "But you'd never have said yes."

"It was better you got me addicted to your dick first."

He laughed and kissed me with his warm lips. He gripped my ass with one hand, fanned the other across my back, and tugged me in tight. "I remember how you thanked me when you left at the end of our first night."

"I thought I'd lost my mind. You were like no men I'd ever been with."

He rolled me over in a quick flip that knocked the breath from my chest. He flattened his body over mine and kissed me again. The force of it filled me with an ache for more.

"I love you so damn much, Luke Moore."

I held his face in my hands and pressed my forehead to his. "I..."

His eyes scanned mine. His chest heaved with each breath.

"Richard, I—"

He brought a finger to my lips. "Not yet. Not now. He should be here."

I nodded.

We kissed and touched. Neither of us rushed to get off or make the moment about sex when it was about much more.

Eventually, Richard's hands stilled. He cleared his throat.

"What has he done?" I asked. I couldn't look at him.

A large thumb pushed at my chin until my eyes met his. "I like that you know me so well, but it makes it hard to break news to you gently. Sort of irritating in a way."

I rolled us over and straddled his thighs. "I need to know. You're not the one who's hurting me. He is."

"I know." His tongue wet his lips. "Well, he's been busy."

"Great."

"There's some people who don't want to work with me anymore. They were interested before he talked to them."

It was inevitable, but hearing it pissed me off. I had more to lose than ever before. My body shook, and the dread gripped my heart. I collapsed onto his chest.

He ran a hand over my back. "So what if he takes away some business? Big deal. I don't want to see him hurt you like this. It isn't worth it. I have you. That's what matters to me. You and Matthew. We're not letting him come between us. If I lost you that would be..." Richard didn't finish his prediction.

I wrapped my arms tighter around him. "And if he killed his college friend?"

"Let's let Walter deal with that."

"Maybe he'll come after us. You. Matthew."

"I won't live my life in fear. If he's guilty of something, we have to have faith the police will handle it."

"And until then?" I sat up. "I should go."

Richard's hands tightened on my hips. "No." He spat the word out in a curt, definitive tone. He wasn't going to argue with me on that point. "And no more investigating your father. He's dangerous. That's obvious."

"All right."

We held each other, my body draped over his, the Chinese food long forgotten, until Matthew came in the front door.

"Hey," Matthew called out from the hall, his voice tense.

I lifted my head.

"What's wrong?" he asked.

"My father's messing with Richard's business again." And then I saw it in his eyes. The light and fire were muted. "What's wrong with you?"

Richard reacted to my words. He rolled over as I moved off him.

Matthew shifted on his feet, and his body vibrated. Anger. I'd seen it once before.

Richard stood. "Matthew?"

I went to him. "What is it?" I placed a hand on his arm and tried to calm him.

"My mom had a visitor yesterday. He said he was a friend of mine. He told her I was going to hell, said he knew how to make me better, make me see how wrong I've been. He told her about a place where I could get healthy again."

"Goddammit." I headed for the door.

Richard grabbed my arm. "Where do you think you're going?"

"This has to stop."

"Let's give it some time. See what Walter can find out." He steered me to the couch. They sat on either side of me.

Matthew wrapped his arms around me and kissed my cheek. "I'm not going anywhere. Nothing he says or does will make me leave you."

Nothing?

I trusted Matthew, but I'd never trust my father. What could he do to make Matthew leave me? I didn't want to know.

Richard placed a hand on my thigh. "He was at your mom's?" he asked Matthew.

"Not his father. When I asked her what the man looked like, it didn't sound like him. This was someone else. Younger, tall, dark haired. She said he was good-looking, even pleasant at first."

I pulled back from Matthew's embrace. "Fowler. My father's assistant." I waved a hand in the air. "Lackey. Dirty-handed messenger. Call him what you'd like. He works for my father."

Richard snorted. "Makes sense. Send someone else, never get his hands dirty. What did your mom say to him?"

A slow, satisfied smile spread across Matthew's face. "She threw his ass out, of course. She might be small, but she's tough when it comes to people telling her there's something wrong with me. She's a member of PFLAG for God's sake. He had no idea what he was up against." He paused. "It pissed me off is all. I know he was after you with this stunt, but she's my mom. This has nothing to do with her."

"I'm sorry." I feared I'd be saying those words more and more over the coming months, maybe years. The realization pressed heavy on my chest.

My father could not run for president. He didn't deserve it. And we didn't deserve the agony.

Matthew took my face in his hands. "Don't ever apologize for him. You didn't make him who he is. You didn't ask for him to hurt you and everyone else in the process. He can try to get rid of us all he wants. We're not going anywhere."

"That's what I said." Richard kissed Matthew and then me.

Matthew nuzzled my cheek. His eyelashes brushed over my skin. "I love you. It'll be okay. I promise."

All I could say in response was, "I'm afraid of what he'll do next."

Chapter Thirty-Six

I glanced at the printout once more, tucked it in my pocket, and smiled. I hadn't had anything to be excited about since my father's threats came to light. It felt good to think of something positive instead of the anger looming over every other moment.

Matthew's laptop would arrive in one week. I couldn't wait. It should shock the shit out of him.

"Luke."

I glanced up.

Matthew weaved through the crowd on the train, smiling as he made his way to me.

"Hey," I said. "Where were you?"

"I had problems signing up for classes online. I went to the school to get it worked out." He gave me a quick kiss and slipped his hand into mine.

The public display of affection would have bothered me a few months back. But with Matthew, it wasn't the flagrant display I expected it to be. He was subtle and sweet. I accepted his hand in mine.

A man in a business suit sat across from us reading a newspaper. There, on the first page below the fold, was a story about my father's potential presidential bid. The man behind the paper glanced our way. I'd seen that look of disgust too many times in my life.

Matthew gave my hand a squeeze and let go. Subtle and sweet, but not crazy.

It hit me then, how different Matthew would be if being gay wasn't something that could still get the shit kicked out of him—or worse. He'd have been happy to hold my hand the entire ride home. Hatred had turned that impulse into something he had to hide, something he had to remember to hold back on.

Sometimes the world just plain fucking sucked. There was not one thing wrong with Matthew, certainly nothing worth hiding. He didn't deserve any of it.

For once in my life, I wanted to fix things. I wanted to join every group aimed at making the world more tolerable. If the ACLU had given me a call right then, I'd have signed over my savings.

Matthew gave me a smile and I relaxed. He chatted about his classes, showing me the catalog descriptions and times he'd signed up for. He couldn't hold back his enthusiasm, and by the time we walked in the front door, my smile was as wide as his.

"I talked to Richard this morning," he said and set his keys on the hall table. "He's making dinner tonight to wish me luck at school."

"We'll have to think of some way to thank him." I grabbed his ass.

He giggled and strolled down the hall. I followed him, loving his laugh. It called to me.

He stopped in the living room doorway, his laughter cut short. I stepped around him. The room was dark and Richard was slumped in a chair at the far corner, his forearm resting on the arm of the chair, a glass dangling from his fingers.

"Richard?" Matthew's voice hitched.

I crossed the room and knelt next to the chair. "What's wrong?"

He finally lifted his head. He glared at me for a moment before reaching for the bottle of whiskey sitting on the end table. The bottle clanked against the rim of the glass as he poured more of the booze. He was drunk. It wasn't a good look on him.

He finished pouring and said, "Kid, can you give me and Luke a minute alone?"

Matthew stepped closer to the chair. "What's wrong?"

"I'm not planning to stop drinking any time soon, and I don't want you to see me like this."

I grabbed Richard's hand and stilled the glass before it could reach his lips again. "What happened?"

He let me steer the glass away from him. "Matthew, please—"

I set the glass on the coffee table. "He's fine."

"What is it?" Matthew asked as he sat on the arm of the chair.

"I couldn't close the condominium deal."

Matthew laid a hand on Richard's shoulder. "Why?"

Did he have to ask?

"The funds I needed weren't available."

Matthew began a slow rub over Richard's tense muscles. "I thought you said you had enough people on board this time?"

"I did. But some bank transfers I authorized yesterday moved the investors' money into a series of new accounts."

Matthew looked to me then back to Richard. "New accounts?"

"Accounts that have since been closed."

Matthew shook his head. "I don't understand."

"I didn't transfer the money, but someone made it look like I did."

Matthew looked my way again.

I moved to the couch. "This doesn't make any sense. He can't possibly think this is going to work. No one's going to believe you thought you'd get away with a one-day transfer of millions of dollars."

"But they will believe I intentionally inflated property values and lied to my investors. At the same time the funds were stolen, someone bought property in Ellis Park under my company's name."

"Ellis Park?"

"Yeah. Not a neighborhood where investors build high-rise condos. More like low-rent trailer parks." Richard reached for the glass of whiskey but didn't take a drink. "I've seen this kind of thing before. They'll investigate the business, me. I'll lose all my investors. They'll freeze my assets." He finally met my gaze. "We could lose the house."

"There's got to be a way they can track the money."

He shrugged. "Maybe. Maybe not. They aren't going to take my word that I didn't do this. Or that your father—" The ring of the phone cut him off.

Matthew stood. "I'll get it." He didn't move, though. He reached for Richard and forced the other man to look at him. "You aren't going to be in trouble for something you didn't do." He kissed Richard's forehead and left the room.

"Guess 'kid' really does fit him." Richard swallowed the whiskey until the glass was empty.

The phone continued to ring, sounding loud in the dark room.

"Luke! Richard!"

Richard sprang from the chair and, despite his drunken state, made it across the living room in a quick clip. I followed, and we stepped into the dining room where Matthew stood with his back to the wall, staring off to where a lone figure sat across the room.

The phone stopped ringing.

The light was off, and dark shadows fell across the man's face, but as soon as he spoke, I knew who sat at our table.

"Hello, Richard. The senator wanted to thank you for the generous donation to his campaign fund." The revolting tone sounded all too much like my father's. "You have such a lovely home. It's a shame you're going to lose it all." The fingers on one hand tapped the tabletop. I didn't want him touching our furniture, tainting our home. "I'm here with a message. You'll leave these men and live alone or you'll lose them. Those are your only options." He slunk out of the chair, a lion hunting the prey. Light fell on his hard face and cast him in an eerie glimmer. "Make your choice, Luke. Their lives or your dick."

"Get the hell out of my house!" Richard stepped forward, faltering at first, but he seemed to sober more with each step.

Matthew moved to my other side. "He'd really hurt us?"

Fowler smirked. "Not on his own. He has a way of convincing people to do all sorts of things. Just ask Luke's mother."

He was right on that. Somehow my father had convinced her to hate her only child. Did I want to know how?

Fowler continued. "He's going to be a powerful man soon. I'm more than willing to help him succeed. We can make this all go away. A simple bank error. The money will be returned. Everyone will be safe."

"Fuck you." I spat the words. "I'm staying with them. And I'm going to the police." My hands clenched into balls at my sides, fist-sized missiles ready to strike at him.

The smirk never faded as he stepped farther into the light. "You'll embarrass yourself. No one will ever believe you. All you can do is what he's offering. He'll leave them alone if you'll give them up. The reporters are going to follow you, report on everything you do. He wants you living alone and acting the part of the supportive son when they do. You have one week to decide."

"I'm not leaving. You tell him I am not leaving them. Now get out of here!" I lunged at the man. Anger blocked out every other thought, every other reaction or instinct. Richard caught my arm and stopped me from charging ahead with all of the rage finally, powerfully escaping me. I met his pleading eyes.

Fowler's next movement happened fast, and I had trouble understanding what had occurred until he stood behind Matthew. He wrapped an arm around him and raised a knife to the kid's throat.

All I could see were Matthew's eyes—those sweet, loving, cheerful eyes. Only they weren't cheerful, and Matthew wasn't laughing or bouncing. He was frightened and alone. Even with the mere feet between us and him, he was alone in the man's grip. One slight movement of the knife and...

In that moment, I understood hatred.

I hated my father.

I hated this man standing before us.

I hated that my life choices had destroyed Richard's business and had put a knife at Matthew's throat just as surely as if I'd done the deeds myself.

But I wasn't to blame. I hadn't been the one to twist my life with them into evil acts of hatred. I hadn't asked my father to despise my life and fear my choices would undo his.

"Don't hurt him." Richard no longer sounded strong or confident or angry. He sounded small, scared. He knew the damage a blade could do. "Let him go and leave, and we won't call the cops. Just—don't hurt him." He lifted a hand and stepped toward Matthew.

Fowler clenched the knife. The blade grazed along the pale skin. A scratch. A warning.

Richard stilled. "Don't."

The intruder hauled Matthew tighter against him. Seeing Matthew touched by the hands of depravity sent an icy chill through every part of me.

Matthew shook. His hands clutched at the other man's arm.

I had to do something. Anything. I couldn't stand still for one more moment.

They were five feet from me. I could move damn fast, but would it be fast enough?

My eyes connected with Matthew's. He glanced down at his right arm and back to me with a small nod.

I waited for his move. I had to be ready. Richard was still drunk, but he'd do whatever he could to save Matthew. He'd back me up if I needed it.

It went down fast. Matthew elbowed Fowler in the gut. Fowler doubled over, dropping his hand with the knife until it was nowhere near Matthew's exposed throat. Matthew leaped forward.

I was damn proud of him, and I almost didn't move in time.

Almost.

I charged forward and caught our intruder's throat in one hand and his wrist in the other. I gripped tight on both counts, stilling the knife in his hand. I threw my weight at him and shoved him against the wall, slamming the back of his hand into the hard surface over and over until he dropped the knife.

"No one is hurting them. Not my father. Not you. No one."

My hands squeezed his neck harder. Anger and rage flowed out the ends of my fingers as they dug into flesh.

His voice came in a whisper, traveling on the last bit of air. "He can do whatever he likes. He always does."

"Not this time." My fingers dug in deeper and intensified the choke. The man seized my arms. He wrenched back and forth, gasping.

A hand touched my shoulder. "Stop, Luke." Richard stood at my side. "Let him go."

Despite the anger, the fury, the need to end it all, I did what Richard asked.

Fowler stumbled away and fell to his hands and knees. He wheezed and gulped, his body not under his own control. When he could stand, he scurried off like a rat, coughing and sputtering as he went.

My gaze lingered on the open door of our home, and my feet lurched a few steps forward. They weren't ready to let him go. What would I do if I caught up to him?

Chapter Thirty-Seven

I froze, staring at the door where Fowler had made his exit. My thoughts settled on nothing but the intent, determined hatred that had overcome me when I'd seen the knife at Matthew's throat.

Matthew.

I spun around. Richard had toppled over, and Matthew was holding on to him. I rushed to them, and we maneuvered Richard into a chair.

We didn't speak. We didn't move. Our eyes stated the relief we couldn't voice.

I reached a hand out to Matthew and pulled him to my chest. I kissed the dark waves above his ear and wrapped my arms around him. "Are you okay?"

He nodded. The intake of breath was soft, but ragged. "Yes. Should we call the police?"

I breathed in his scent. He smelled sweaty and spicy, like Matthew. He smelled alive.

"I don't know," Richard said. "Not sure they'll believe us. Everyone loves the senator. But that man broke in here and almost hurt you. We could at least call to report him." His pale face couldn't hide his exhaustion. He still smelled of the booze.

"Why don't we get you cleaned up," I said. "Then we'll decide what to do."

"Okay. Go shut and lock the door, kid."

"Right." Matthew sped off, but neither Richard nor I made a move up the steps until he was back at our sides.

"How did he get in?" I asked Richard. "It was locked when we got here."

"I was pissed when I got home." He stared at the closed door. "I don't remember locking it. I'll get the locks changed tomorrow in case he stole a key or something."

"Okay." I moved toward him. "Let's get you up upstairs."

In the bathroom, Richard removed his clothes and climbed into the bathtub. Matthew undressed and settled behind him, letting Richard rest against his chest. He soaped up a washcloth and worked it over the big man's body.

I hadn't seen him hold Richard like that before. My chest tightened as I watched him care in such a physical way.

How could I leave them?

I knelt beside the tub, reeling. My hands felt like they'd spent the entire day clasping onto something and had just recently let go. The stillness of the clenched fists in my lap unnerved me. They didn't seem a part of my own body. I lifted my hands, opening and closing my fingers, trying to release the lingering tension. Only it wasn't possible. The tension was everywhere. My hands fell back to my lap.

"My father's going to destroy your business. He sent Fowler here to threaten your lives."

"It appears so." Richard raised his arm out of the water and clasped my hand. He lifted our entwined fingers onto the smooth edge of the tub.

"He could've killed Matthew."

"I'm okay," Matthew said. The expression in his gaze told me how alive he was.

"For now." I stood and paced. The realization of everything hit me like repeated strikes to a punching bag. "He broke into your home—our home—and attacked Matthew. This is my goddamn family, and he can't do this. I won't let him. I won't let him take anything else from me." I stopped and stared at them. Two smiling men beamed up at me. "What the hell are you so happy about?"

Matthew laid his cheek against Richard's temple. "Did you hear? Family."

"I did. Get over here, Luke."

I sank to my knees beside the tub. Richard pulled me to him. He made love to my mouth, his hands wet and firm on each side of my face.

Matthew petted me—my neck, my back, my chest—all the while repeating one word. "Family."

"Get undressed," Richard said. He turned his head to the side and kissed Matthew. I stood and undressed, never taking my eyes off them. They looked as great together as they did the first night at the Haven when I lay sprawled out before them. Yet, watching them in the bathtub before me was better. More intimate, more significant in our own home.

I wouldn't let my father run me away from them.

I sat beside the tub again.

Richard shook his head. "No, climb in."

I stood in the water and straddled Richard's lap. The sensation of my balls sinking into the hot water sent a shiver of anticipation and need throughout my body.

Richard's mouth met my lips again. I tasted Matthew there.

I rocked my hips, and my cock connected with Richard's. The warm water around my shaft and the pressure of his dick against mine overwhelmed me.

Richard twisted an arm around his own back, taking Matthew in hand. He pitched back and forth, putting more pressure against Matthew's prick and rubbing forward against me, the water slapping at the sides of the tub with his movements.

My hands grasped at his shoulders and dug in, and I rocked faster. He wrapped a large hand around my dick and his. I threw my head back and pushed into the tight embrace, torn between driving into it and letting Richard take control of my pleasure. I clutched at his shoulder harder with one hand and let my other hand wander back for Matthew.

I traced the slight scratch on his neck. I was so close to losing them. I cupped my hand over his cheek and almost said what I'd needed to say since I saw the knife. "Matthew, I..." Words were never my friends. I always said the right things to get a man into bed. Then the right things to get him the hell out. Anything else never crossed my mind. Three words, and I couldn't arrange them into a coherent sentence.

"Luke, I'm okay. We're all okay. Don't..." His breath hitched and he arched into Richard's touch. "Don't worry."

The grip on my cock tightened. A thumb swiped over the head of my prick and brought to life a moan. Richard's body moved with more vigor. His arms pumped faster. Matthew's head slumped back to the edge of the tub.

My body was close to its release, and I could tell by the whimpers and deep breaths from the other men they were right with me. My orgasm hit as soon as the words left my mouth. "Richard. Matthew. Can't lose you."

They moaned in concert through their pleasure.

When our bodies relaxed, Richard wrapped an arm around me and wound the other back around Matthew, holding us close.

I breathed deep and rested my head on his shoulder. Save for our sated breathing, quiet surrounded us. It was soothing to hold on and not think and let the release wash over me.

Matthew's giggle interrupted the quiet. The sound filled the room and eased my soul.

"What's funny?" Richard asked, his voice filled with contentment.

"The water's all cummy." Matthew giggled again.

"Oh, that sounds good," Richard said. "God, I love your laugh."

"Me too," I said.

Whether it was a genuine reaction, or if he did it to please us, Matthew laughed again.

I sighed, and a blissful smile emerged. I buried my face against Richard's neck. I never wanted to leave the bathtub or the men in it.

If life could only be as simple as when we were fucking.

* * * *

A half hour later, we admitted the water was far too cold to tolerate, got out, and dried off. Matthew adjusted the towels until they hung over the rack in an obsessive-compulsive alignment. I understood his delay. I didn't want to leave the refuge of the bathroom either.

Richard sighed. "Bed. We need to talk, and I want to sit down."

We left our clothes on the bathroom floor and moved into the bedroom. Richard climbed into the bed and sat with his back to the headboard. Matthew crawled to his side, and Richard reached his arm out for me. "C'mere, Luke. We're in this together."

I eased onto the bed and into his outstretched arm.

Matthew outlined my cheek and jaw with the back of his hand. "We're in this together."

I shifted out of the embrace, and Matthew followed suit until we all faced one another.

"What do we do now?" Matthew asked. When no one spoke, he lowered his voice. "Maybe we should leave. Move away from him."

Richard cleared his throat. "I've been thinking about that ever since I saw that fucking knife against your skin. Nothing is more important to me than you two. Let's get out of this city, sell the house and my real estate holdings, take what money I have left, and go. If we don't live near him, maybe he'll back off."

The despair built again. It didn't cancel out the anger of earlier. It blended with it, mixing my emotions into a constricting knot. Matthew had signed up for classes, and he had his mom. Richard had his reputation to think of, and his home. I couldn't ask them to leave and hide out somewhere.

"You're gonna lose everything because of me."

"We are not," Richard said. "We're not losing each other or you. That's all we need. We're your family now. Nothing he does to us can change that. But I won't let him harm us. Even if we go to the police, and they investigate, we aren't safe from him. He'd be screwing himself to try something then, but he might do it."

"He'll find us anyway. The minute he said he was running for president, I knew there was nowhere to hide. And even if there was, we are not running away. He's pushed me around my entire life. I have to stop this, once and for all."

Matthew's large eyes lifted. "What're we gonna do?"

"We could play his game," Richard said. "Blackmail him. Walter probably has video of your dad's indiscretions."

"No," I said. "We have done nothing wrong. I'm not going to let either of you get into trouble. We're not sinking to his level." I got on my knees. "We have to turn him in. They'll know it's him if he tries anything. He won't get away with it. Not once we have the police involved. Not once everyone knows he stole all that money for his campaign. Once they know what he did to Danny Conner."

"You think he knows you were looking into that?" Richard asked.

"I'm guessing that's part of why he's doing this."

"Why wouldn't Fowler have said that?"

"'Cause that would mean admitting my father had something to do with the kid's death."

Matthew shifted closer to me. "But so far Walter hasn't been able to find anything."

"Maybe we can't prove what he did to Conner thirty-five years ago, but maybe we can prove he stole that money, that he threatened your lives."

"You don't think he'll want revenge?" Matthew asked.

I sank back onto my heels. "He might. It wouldn't surprise me. But he won't have anyone left to follow his orders. Fowler's going to be in trouble for this too." I shook my head. "I can't live my life afraid of him. I can't run anymore."

"I think we should do whatever you want to do," Matthew said. "Part of me wants to run, but part of me wants him to pay for what he's done to you, to Richard, to us. I'll stand by you if you want to go to the police. I'll stand by you if you want us to leave and never come back."

Richard kissed Matthew and then reached for my hand. "I think if turning him in is what you feel strongly about, then we should do it. Or else you'll regret it later. I can't say I won't be nervous about something happening to either of you, but I'm not one to back away from a fight. And if we fight your father, we're not going to lose." A smile emerged on his face and triggered one on mine.

"Relief washed over me. "Thank you."

"But what proof do we have?" Richard asked. "All we know is what that man downstairs confessed to us. It will be our word against theirs."

I stood, working through what I'd tell the police and how it would sound. I went to the dresser and grabbed a pair of jeans. "I'm going to call Walter. He'll know who we should talk to. I want to get this over with."

Matthew and Richard clambered off the bed and searched for clothes.

"What are you doing?" I asked.

Richard pulled a T-shirt over his head. "You're not doing this alone. You're not going to plan this out without us. We have statements to make to the police too." He walked across the room and kissed me. "Family's in this kind of shit together."

Chapter Thirty-Eight

"No fucking way, Luke. You are not doing this!"

Richard didn't sound like himself. He wasn't talking in his commanding tone. He wasn't being firm, yet caring. He was screaming at me.

"I have to!" I yelled back and sank into a chair. Matthew put his hand on my shoulder, the touch nervous, but solid.

We were in an empty interrogation room on the third floor of the FBI field office, five days after we gave our statements.

Only a couple of the detectives had glared at us like we were crazy when we told them the three of us were in a relationship together. Then, all of them gave us stares of disbelief when I told them my father, the senator, had fraudulently stolen millions from Richard's investment accounts and had threatened to have Matthew and Richard killed if I didn't do as he asked.

Because it involved a US senator, the FBI had taken the allegations seriously and was working the case with the Department of Justice and local authorities. Even the FBI Special Agent in Charge had been involved in the initial layout of evidence. Not that there was much of that. A few sheets of testimony from my lovers and me were all they had to go on—were all that connected my father to any of his crimes.

The FBI said they needed tangible evidence in order to continue with any investigation. They could either question him or I could help them. Neither option was on my top ten list. But the week deadline was almost up, and something had to happen or Richard and Matthew would never be safe. So I agreed to do what had Matthew nervous as hell and Richard pissed off at me.

I agreed to wear a wire and go after a confession from my father.

The plan wasn't a popular one with the FBI either. Even after the warrant had been signed, there was much debate over the planned surveillance. No one wanted to attempt a recording of the presidential hopeful confessing anything more mundane than where he gets his hair cut. In the end, the task force reluctantly came to the conclusion it was the best way to either learn if he had anything to do with the stolen funds and threats, or to eliminate him as a suspect.

In spite of it being what I had to do, the decision was met with resistance from the men in my life, neither wanting me anywhere near my father or his lackey. I shuffled them into the empty interrogation room in hopes of gaining their support. We'd just made it inside when Richard protested the plan, screaming like I'd never heard him do before.

"What other options are there?" I asked when I could speak without raising my voice.

"How about we let the agents do their jobs first? See what they can find out. We just brought this to them. Give it some time. They're trying to track the money."

"They still think you might have stolen it. It's been five days. You know as well as I do, if they bring my father in for questioning, he'll know it was me. He'll think I've defied him. You were right when you said he'd risk it all to come after us. He's that fucking crazy."

Richard's eyebrows rose. "That's supposed to be your argument that it's okay to do this? What do you think he'll do if he catches you wearing a wire?"

"The FBI will be there."

"He won't let you take everything from him."

Matthew stepped close to Richard and placed a hand on his arm. "I don't think you or I've got a say in this."

I laughed at the look Richard gave Matthew. Boy, he liked to have control, and Matthew telling him he couldn't shocked us all.

Matthew rubbed Richard's arm. "This is his chance to show his father what sort of man Luke is. Show him that standing up and fighting mean more than running and hiding. That Luke is more of a man than his father will ever be. We can't keep him from doing this if he needs to. If his father gets away with it, becomes president, he'll blame himself…and us."

Richard met Matthew's gaze. His eyes pleaded for understanding. "I can't. I can't let him do this."

I flew out of the chair. "Let me? Who the hell do you think you are?"

Richard glared at me. "The man who's in love with you." He pointed a finger at me, jabbing it in my face, reminding me of the entire year of verbal abuse I'd received from the ninety-year-old nun at St. Mary's Elementary who was pulled out of retirement to cover my class when Mrs. Slawinski had gone on maternity leave. I wanted to swat his hand away as much as I did hers. I held back. Although I wasn't sure why. I certainly wasn't ten. And he wasn't a nun. He yelled louder. "I won't stand by and watch you try to prove something and get yourself hurt. All so you can stand up to your father." Richard stalked across the room, grabbed a chair, and fell into it. "I don't know if I can keep doing this."

My mouth dropped open. "What?"

"Sit back and watch while you pull away from us."

"I'm not...this has nothing to do with you."

"How do you figure? We're the ones he's threatening. I'm the one whose reputation he's trying to ruin. I'm the one who might end up in jail. Matthew's the one that fucker had a knife to. How does it not involve us?"

"I didn't mean it like that."

"You meant what? I've no say in how we protect ourselves? I think the FBI should handle this. Not you."

"They're the ones asking me to do this."

"Doesn't mean you have to. What if he doesn't confess? What if they get nothing on him? And he knows you were helping them? What do we do then?"

"We'll figure it out."

"I'm not waiting around to find out." He rose and covered the distance between us with two large strides. "If you do this and anything happens to you or Matthew—"

"You'll what?"

He grabbed my collar and jerked me forward. His mouth slammed over mine. It wasn't a kiss. It was a possession. The top dog was showing his fangs.

I crushed my lips against his and hardened the kiss.

He withdrew. "I'll always love you." He turned and walked out. The door slammed shut behind him.

The silence left in his wake gave the moment a finality I didn't care for. Matthew stared at the closed door, his back to me.

"Matthew."

He didn't flinch or face me.

"If he can't understand why I need to do this...if he can't get past it..." I ran my thumb over my bottom lip. I could still feel his saliva there. "I want you to—you should stay with him."

Matthew spun around. "What?"

"We both can't walk out on him and you know it."

"You're not going anywhere."

"He might not forgive me for this."

"He will."

"Not if I'm putting us in jeopardy. Not if I'm putting you in jeopardy."

Matthew shook his head. "No. I—"

"It's going to be okay."

"Luke…" He took one shaky step after another.

I pulled back. "Just go. If he thinks you're not going home with him, it'll destroy him."

"And you think losing you won't?"

"I didn't say—"

Matthew stood in front of me in an instant. He stroked my cheek with an open hand. "What do you want, Luke?"

I leaned into the touch. "Right now? I want you to trust me."

His lips brushed mine. "I do." His hands hauled me against him. Fear was palpable in the kiss, the contact. He asked for my touch, my reassurance. I let him in and gave him everything he asked for, everything we both needed.

When the kiss ended, we held each other in the quiet for a few more moments.

"Matthew, go to him."

He nodded. "Come home when you're done with the planning tonight. I'll have him calmed down by then."

I pressed one last kiss on his lips.

If anyone could get Richard to understand I had to do this, it was Matthew.

Maybe he'd listen.

Maybe I wouldn't lose them.

Maybe my father wouldn't take everything from me this time.

* * * *

Damn. The house was huge.

How the hell had I ended up standing in front of my parents' home in a downpour? The same scared kid I'd been in junior high, afraid to go inside and face the wrath of my father after the nuns had caught me smoking behind the school.

Thunder struck overhead. I jumped and landed in a puddle. The rainwater sloshed above the sides of my shoes, soaking my socks through to the skin.

Maybe if I hadn't spent the last two nights on Walter's couch, and had spent them wrapped up in the arms of the men who said they loved me, I wouldn't have been as nervous. Maybe I'd have felt bolder, more confident, more at ease with wearing a listening device hidden under my shirt in search of a confession to save us all.

It didn't matter if I ever had the chance to sleep with them again, or talk to them again, or even if I ever saw them again. They'd be safe.

I hiked up the many steps that led to my parents' front door. I wanted to hurry, to get it all over with, but my body wouldn't cooperate. My foot slipped on the last step of my ascent, and I slid as if the cement stairs were a slippery slide at a water park. I reached out and clasped the railing before I ended up back on the sidewalk again. No way in hell was I starting the entire trek over.

I trudged the final steps again and surveyed the house. The exterior was brick, not a worn or damaged block in the bunch. Every curtain was drawn closed from the first floor to the third.

I'd never lived there. My parents moved during my sophomore year in college. After my father had made certain Tim couldn't love me anymore, they never invited me for Thanksgiving dinner or the Christmas gift exchange. I never received one phone call or letter. And it'd been fine by me. I hadn't wanted to enter a home where I wasn't welcome, where I wasn't loved like a son deserved to be.

I pushed the doorbell and stashed my hands behind my back. I was about to walk into a hell I had done all I could to avoid.

I expected a maid or some other member of the live-in staff and was surprised when my mother opened the door. Something had changed in her since I'd last seen her at Richard's party. She was still beautiful, but it wasn't as prominent. It was hidden, a remnant of the woman she had been. Her expression was stern, the lines on her face deeper than they should have been for a woman her age. Her eyes were haunted. Misery had settled in.

She wore a brown skirt and a stiff, frumpy blouse. It made her look less feminine than if she'd worn a man's business suit, but at the same time, elegance encased her like it had been painted on. She had her hair pinned back, not a strand out of place, and the poise of her posture was well rehearsed. From an external point of view, she was going to make an excellent first lady.

She looked up at me, and her face brightened. The lines vanished with her smile as if the grin shot collagen into her skin. "Oh, Lukas." She stepped forward onto the porch and closed the door behind her. The smile faded away. "Why are you here? What's wrong?"

"I have an answer for him."

"What did he ask you?"

Was she really that clueless? Or was it all an act? "Can I come in or not?"

She stood still, staring at me for a minute, and then she led me inside. I followed her into a large living room. The decor was an odd mix of modern, Victorian, and Oriental furniture and collectibles. I expected to find museum-style barriers fortifying the perimeter, protecting their priceless furnishings. Low elevator music played from hidden speakers. Who had that shit playing in their house like some sort of department store?

She shuffled across the room and faced me, avoiding my stare. She raised her hands to her blouse, lifted her collar, and pressed it flat in a repeated loop. When her hands finally stilled, she stepped toward me. Her eyes met mine, and she touched my arm in the slightest contact.

I withdrew out of her reach. "Mom, go get him."

"He has a migraine. He's lying down."

I crossed my arms over my chest. "He'll want my answer."

"I'll go see if I can wake him." She crept across the room. The heels of her shoes were silent as she stepped off the rug onto the wood floor.

Something in me didn't want to let her walk out, didn't want to make it easy for her. "Mom."

She stopped, her back to me.

"Do you have any idea who your husband is? What kind of a man he is? What he's done?"

She whirled around, but didn't respond.

"Why would you?" I said. "You don't even know your own son."

She gasped, her voice tense and loud when she spoke again, her arms stiff and straight at her sides. "I may not know the man you've become, Lukas, but I knew the boy you were. I gave birth to you. I held you when you cried at night. I put lotion on your chicken pox and held your hand when you got your vaccinations. I loved you before anyone else knew you." She shook her head and covered her mouth with her hand as if to stop herself from saying more or letting herself release the sobs trapped below the surface. She fled the room.

If she'd just let herself see who he was, the tears would come, of course, but so would the truth. But I learned when Tim left me: some people didn't have it in them. Believing an easy lie was the less difficult path than facing a hard truth.

I forced myself to look away from where she had escaped the room and sorted through what to say to exact a confession from my father. Nerves grappled with determination. I broke out in a cold sweat, and my hands shook.

I couldn't let him see the fear.

I distracted myself by touring the room. Among the vases and paintings and pricey antiques, I spotted several family photographs: a professional portrait of my maternal grandparents who had died when I was in junior high school, a candid shot of my aunt and uncle at a celebration of some sort, and another of my younger cousin holding a birthday cake. Not one picture of me. Not one baby photo. Not one snapshot of me playing T-ball. Not one photograph of me at my high school graduation. It stung to know my entire childhood had meant nothing to them.

I turned away from the last photo. I didn't want to see anymore.

A sewing basket sat next to a chair across the room. The only item besides the photos that signified real people lived there. A reminder of the mother I had as a child. The one who had hand-sewn a bumblebee costume for my school play. The one who had baked me chocolate chip cookies despite the full-time cook on staff. The one I had let myself forget.

I picked up the quilted basket and lifted the lid. Along with the spools of thread and pin cushions, taped to the back of the basket, was a wallet-sized photo. My high school senior portrait.

Part of me wanted to rip the picture from the basket, chase her down, and demand an answer to one question: why?

But I also needed to do what I had come for. I would not let her distract me.

I returned the basket to the floor. A sliver of light from a doorway across the hall caught my eye. I stepped forward and glanced inside. My father's office.

Since the day I could walk, no matter where we lived, that room had been off limits. *Nothing in here you need to see, son.*

I bet.

Chapter Thirty-Nine

I slipped inside my father's office and drew the door shut behind me, wincing when the door's latch caught the metal strike plate and clicked in place.

Richard was going to kill me.

It was a different room than the office my father had during my childhood, but it was identical to how I remembered it. Same stupid leather books he'd never read. Same credenza showcasing autographed photos of him with celebrities and politicians. Same leather swivel chair with polished brass trim. Yet every piece of furniture couldn't have been more than a couple of years old. In the middle of it all was an antique-style wood desk with carved columns and an electronic keypad discreetly positioned near the right-hand set of drawers. Nothing but the best for Johnathan Moore.

I lowered myself into the chair, hesitating a moment before I moved the last few inches to sit. This was my father's throne. His cologne rose up around me. It was all over the chair, the desk, the papers stacked off to the side. The entire room reeked of it.

I tried the top drawer. Locked. As were the drawers on either side. I fingered the keypad. How long until my father walked into the living room and saw I wasn't there? How long until he found me in his private sanctum?

I breathed deep and ran my fingers over the numbers as fast as I could. My mother's birthday. Nope. My father's. No. Their anniversary. No. *What the hell?* I tried my own birthday. Nothing. I entered the only other date that came to mind. May 11, 1974. The day Danny Conner died. A red light on the keypad turned green.

I tugged on the top drawer again and it slid open. Pens, paper clips, empty notepads, the usual suspects. I shut the drawer and tried a couple of others. More office supplies, business cards, and an old datebook. I flipped through the latter but if there was anything of significance, I'd have to take the book with me to give it a more careful look. I put it back and opened the last drawer.

A bottle of whiskey and a glass. I removed both. The bottle was nearly empty. The glass smelled of the liquor. *How often do you need this, Dad?*

I bent to put them back and stopped short. A leather-bound book lay face down in the bottom of the drawer. Sitting near the back was a small jewelry box. I ditched the whiskey and glass on the desk.

The black box was old, the corners crushed in, and the hinge on the lid was loose as if it'd been opened many times over the years. I lifted the lid. A silver pocket watch lay against the blue velvet lining.

I forced myself to set the watch down and turn the book over. There in gold print was a name: "Daniel Lukas Conner."

I stared at the journal. Danny Conner's full name meant nothing and everything at once.

I turned to the first page, and a paper slipped out and fell to the floor. I fetched it and carefully unfolded it, my hands shaking. Fear of being discovered? Or fear of what I was about to discover?

The handwritten letter was dated the day before Danny Conner died.

John,

Happy graduation.

I want you to have my dad's watch. It's the only thing I have that means anything to me. Except for you. I'd be honored if you'd keep it.

I'm sorry for our fight the other night. I'd give anything not to see you hurting like this. I want to be able to tell you all of this in person, but I know you'll argue back. I know you'll give me the same reasons you already have. I know you want a career. A family. A wife. A son. Elizabeth seems like a lovely person, someone who could give you the life you're looking for. I want to be strong enough to walk away for you. But I can't. I love you. I want a life with you. A friendship. A partnership. A life together. I don't understand how you can't. I know how you feel about me. I feel it every time we're together.

> *Please tell me how you can let us go. I need to understand. Don't give me your reasons again, just tell me how you expect us to live without each other. How you expect me to stop loving you.*
>
> *How you can stop loving me.*
>
> *Danny*

I flipped through the book, spotting one passage after another that depicted a year-long love affair between my father and Danny Conner. The last page was dated one week after Conner's death and was penned in my father's handwriting.

> *I'm sorry, Danny. Sorry for what I've done to you, what I had to do. My greatest regret is I never told you the words you needed to hear...I love you. I think I'll love you until I take my last breath.*

The blood rushed out of my head. I felt cold, dizzy. My hands shook more, the words on the paper blurring.

Was it easier to confess your love to a dead man?

I slipped the letter inside the journal and returned everything to the drawer. The FBI needed to be the ones to find it. Not that it proved anything. But a confession would.

I stood. Before moving away from the desk, I reached into the drawer, removed the silver watch from the box, and slipped it into my pocket.

Footsteps sounded somewhere down the hall. I pressed the lock button on the keypad and scrambled for the door. I just made it into the living room when he stepped up behind me. I faced him.

Despite the late hour, and his supposed migraine, my father wore a dark suit, dress shoes, cuff links, and a tie clip. Even in his own home, the man didn't know how to be casual or relaxed.

"I never would have guessed you'd show up here." His voice brimmed with hatred.

"There are things that must be said. Sometimes a man has to say them in person." The fear and anxiety were but a memory. This man was no father to me. I would not let him torment me or anyone else again.

He chuckled, the sound tense, flat, devoid of any joy, the laughter of a man who knew nothing but his own ambitions. "Yes, and sometimes a man must take every precaution." He moved to a nearby table, grabbed the phone, and dialed a single number. "Come into the living room. I need you to check someone." He hung up the phone and crossed his arms over his chest.

I was about to tell him of my refusal to comply with his demands when Fowler entered the room and came at me.

I stumbled backward a few steps and heard my father's empty laughter again. I stilled. I would give neither of them any satisfaction.

Fowler reached out for me. He held a long, black object in his hand. I swung at him and knocked his arm away.

He grasped his forearm. "Fuck. You shit." He lifted the device he carried. "I'm checking you for any weapons or listening devices."

"No. I don't have either." I staggered back. My calves smacked into an ottoman, and I tripped. I caught myself before I fell. I was trapped. A couch sat on one side, my father on the other, and this shithead in front of me.

"Well, I don't think I'll take your word for it." He moved the wand over my feet and worked his way up. My breath quickened. The device made no sound until it passed over my chest.

I squeezed my eyes shut. The rapid beeping gave me away. I opened my eyes and saw the fury in the man's face before me.

My father's voice rang out. "Did you think I wouldn't suspect you'd try to trap me? You're my son after all. You've got intelligence. I'll give that to you."

Fowler threw the wand on the couch and stepped closer. He reached out, tore my shirt open, and yanked the taped listening device off. A few chest hairs ripped away with it. He threw the device on the couch and skimmed his hands down my legs. Once he reached my ankles, he repeated the search up the inside.

"Don't enjoy this too much, you faggot. I don't do this for your enjoyment."

As if I could ever enjoy his touch—the man who had tried to hurt Matthew. His hands were a brush painting and layering evil all over me.

Satisfied I posed no further threat, he stood, gathered the wand and listening device I'd worn, and with a last smirk, left the room.

I stood alone with my father again. I debated walking out the front door. But I couldn't. At least with his discovery of the hidden recording device, my father might talk honestly.

I closed my gaping shirt—there were no more buttons to hold it together—and shifted on my feet. The soaked leather shoes squeaked. The wet socks squished between my toes.

My father stepped closer. He adjusted his tie and tugged the cuffs of his shirtsleeves in a practiced primp.

"Did you get my message, son?"

I snorted at his use of the fatherly endearment. "You know I did. Did you get mine?"

He stalked to the center of the room and spoke as if giving a lecture on a proposed tax bill. "I don't think you understood the choices I laid out for you."

I stepped away from the ottoman but kept my distance from him. "I'm not leaving. You can threaten us all you want. I came here to make sure you understood."

Rage descended. His eyes narrowed. With the storm brewing in him, I should have left. Richard would be furious that I stayed when my father gave me a look like that—that is if I ever got a chance to tell him or Matthew about it.

My father sighed, unclenched his hands, and sat. His voice softened. "Let me ask you this. You love them?"

My throat tightened. A chill crept over the base of my neck.

"Answer me, son. Do you love them? The one who so graciously donated to my campaign and the one who had the knife at his throat. Do you love them?" He screamed the last of his words.

I fended off the sting of tears. "More than anyone in my entire life."

His eyes searched mine. He wasn't trying to understand me. He was trying to get me to understand him. "Well then, I'd have thought the choice to save them would be easy for you. I won't relent, Luke. I need my life and the lives of those around me to be perceived in a certain way if I'm going to move forward with what I want."

"You mean if you're going to con people into electing you president?"

"Making the hard choices has helped me reach every goal I've ever set. I'm not going to stop now. I can do a lot for this country."

I took a step in his direction. "Hard choices? Is that what you call stealing millions of dollars, interfering with Richard's financial investments, and threatening to kill my lovers?"

"Yes! Those weren't easy decisions for me. You think being a man with my ambitions is easy?"

I took another step. My hands clenched, ached to lash out. I refrained. I was the better man. "But you did it. You stole from investors—people who live in this country you supposedly serve. And you threatened to hurt people, to hurt someone I care about."

His face reddened and his jaw clenched. "I'll do more than hurt them. If you could have just done as I'd asked. If you could have only pretended to be a good son, then none of this would have happened. You have never worked for anything in your life. You have never committed to anything more than yourself. You go from man to man and do what feels good to you. You don't know about making difficult decisions and devoting yourself to anything."

This wasn't just about getting me to do what he wanted. He was punishing me for who I was. I staggered backward and slumped into a chair. I stared at the floor, but I didn't see the Oriental rug for long. I saw a smiling dark-haired kid and bright green eyes filled with compassion. When I spoke again, a quiet, childlike voice slipped out. "You'll really kill them if I don't do what you want?"

"No."

I lifted my head and stared at him. "Then your threats are empty, meaningless to me."

"I won't kill them because if you don't agree to my terms right here, right now, you'll never leave this house." The twisted grin that spread over his lips and the angry, wrinkled flesh around his eyes were not the look a father should ever give his son. He reached inside his suit jacket.

I'd seen the gun before, of course. Fifteen years earlier.

I was a different man then. He wouldn't get the frightened reaction he once did.

"Didn't you know we had a break-in tonight? While my son was visiting. The grieving father makes for a much better image than a perverted son who prostitutes himself at a sex club, selling himself for his own sick pleasure."

A laugh escaped me. The sound pierced the silence left by my father's threat. Richard had been right. Why was that funny? The man fretted and cared like no one I ever knew, but that wasn't what caused the odd laughter. The entire situation was too damned unbelievable, and the realization my father thought murder was his ticket to the White House and that he'd rather kill me than see me live my own life caused the tension-relieving laughter to bubble up and out of my mouth.

He gripped an arm of the chair and rose, holding the gun steady. "Stop fucking laughing. Do you find this amusing?"

I shook my head. The laughter abated somewhat. "No, none of it's funny. If you kill me, what makes you think Richard and Matthew won't be able to convince the police of all you've done?"

The resulting grin painted the perfect picture of a madman. "The police chief and I have always had a good relationship when it came to protecting our citizens. He will not allow you or your depraved friends to destroy me with lies. There's no proof, nothing to connect me to anything. Why the hell would they believe a couple of disgusting men like them? I've seen what they've done to you. I have pictures. I've seen them fucking you on your goddamn dining room table, sucking your cock and licking your ass. They are perverts. They are not people anyone will ever listen to."

Pictures? From inside our home? While I ignorantly went about falling for Matthew and Richard, my father had sent his man into our lives. And I had done nothing to stop it.

I'd heard the confession the FBI wanted, but I needed more. I rose from the chair, ignored the gun, and kept talking.

"Tell me about Danny Conner, Dad."

His face paled. "How—"

"I know all about your lover. I know you killed him." I pulled the watch from my pocket and held out my hand. The watch sat on my flattened palm, shining and pristine despite its age. It felt heavy, as if the weight of my father's lies was tucked inside.

He shook his head, moving the gun from side to side with him, his eyes on the watch. "What?"

"You had his watch that night. You gave him the cocaine. Was there something in it?"

"No. I...I gave him his watch back because I couldn't keep it."

"You put the coke in it!"

"Yes. But...I had to tell him it was over. I knew I'd break his heart. I wanted to ease his pain. I didn't want him to be lonely, to be sad. I-I didn't want to hurt him. Oh, God. But I did...I..."

"Killed him."

"No! I hurt him when I told him we had to end it. He was fine before then. He was high, but he was fine. He said he wanted some time alone. I left him in the bathroom and—I loved him. I didn't want him to die. I didn't want him to kill himself like that. I knew the moment I saw him on the floor that he'd done it to himself."

A part of me hadn't wanted to admit the possibility existed that Conner had committed suicide. I'd never trust my father, but at that moment, I knew he was right. Whether he did it or not to hurt my father, Danny Conner had done the worst thing he could to his lover. He'd left him with a lifetime of guilt.

My father looked at the gun. He twisted his hand until the gun lay flat like the watch in my own hand. He stared at it as if he couldn't figure out how it had gotten there. "Oh, God. He'd hate me. He'd hate who I've become."

I took a step toward him.

He shoved the barrel of the gun my way again. "Don't move!" His hand trembled. He jammed the gun in the air. "I cannot give up after everything I've done to get here. Don't you see that? I can't have lost everything for nothing."

"But you have." I gave up on the gun and looked at my father. "You can't control everything. You don't know everything."

He glared at me and raised the gun higher. "What are you talking about?"

"I'm talking about how you'll never be president." I took a step closer. "You'll never be anything ever again." Another step. "Including my father." Step. His finger twitched over the gun's trigger.

I removed the small listening device from behind my ear. I let the smile of victory tell him what I held.

"You aren't the only one with connections. My friend Walter owns this wonderful technology company. They create all sorts of gadgets, undetectable shit to pick up the smallest sounds. He has a few friends in the police force himself, as well as the FBI. Would you like to meet them?"

That was the prearranged signal to let the agents know I was ready on my end. If they'd gotten what they needed, it wouldn't take long. If I could keep him distracted long enough...

His nervous gaze darted around the room. The fingers holding the gun squeezed around the handle.

Please don't let them lose me like this.

I fixated on the gun's barrel. One more step.

My hand rose before I'd decided what to do. At an inch from the gun, I met his stare again. A swell of tears filled his eyes. Mine met a similar fate.

I covered the last fragment of space between my fingers and the gun in a slow creep. I gripped the barrel and lowered it.

My father let his hand move. If he'd wanted to, he could have fought me on it, kept the gun pointed at me. And of course, he could have fired.

The gun dropped lower and lower. His shoulders slumped, and the furious, determined look disappeared, replaced with a vacant one.

When he spoke, his voice was neutral and possessed no emotion. "The moment I saw you fucking that boy in your dorm room I changed. That's when I lost everything."

"No. It was when you took away every ounce of love from yourself that you lost it all."

He blinked. A lone tear fell to his lapel. "Danny." The misery of that whispered name sounded all too familiar.

The FBI forced their way into the house from every possible angle. My father recoiled two steps before they were upon him. They collected the gun and wrapped handcuffs around his wrists. His head hung low as they read him his rights and hauled him toward the door. Two other officers escorted Barry Fowler out behind my father.

An agent talked to my mother in the hallway. She nodded as the man spoke, but she never looked away from me. Tears overflowed with each blink of her eyes. When the agent stopped speaking, he led her out of the house.

I stared at the open door.

Sweat clung to me everywhere. I felt dirty, grimy, sick. I wanted to go home, jump in the shower, and wash it all away. I wanted to crawl into bed and sleep until morning.

Was I welcome?

A soft hand landed on my shoulder. Walter stood beside me.

"No matter what you were expecting, it isn't supposed to feel good to help get your own father arrested. But this isn't your fault. He has to live with the choices he made."

"I guess we all do."

"Move past this and live your life." He gave me a slight shove toward the door. "Your men are waiting in an unmarked van down the street. I suggest you go to them. They were quite insufferable. The FBI let them listen in, and I think that made it worse."

"They came?"

"They called me last night. I arranged it so they could be here."

I cringed. Knowing they'd heard it all was a relief, but they'd heard my father's threat to kill me. I pictured three FBI agents holding Richard back from storming into the house.

I gave Walter a nod and made my way to the door. I stopped short of leaving. "Thank you. For everything."

"I told you they'd be good for you."

"Asshole."

"Yeah. But I'm your friend. I'll only be an ass in ways that won't hurt you. You can count on it."

"I will."

The rain had stopped, and the dark sky had lightened with the passing of the storm. A droplet of rainwater dripped onto my head. I glanced up. Another drop leaked from the gutter above my parents' stoop and hit my forehead. I wiped it away with the back of my hand and descended the steps.

Several police cruisers and unmarked vehicles lined the street. Traffic was blocked off. News vans and camera crews were setting up. Police officers and FBI agents were filing around the yard, moving in and out of the house, searching for any evidence to substantiate my father's confession. Their work wouldn't be over any time soon.

But it all felt over for me. Finished.

I had shoveled the last bit of dirt over my relationship with my parents.

Chapter Forty

I spotted a van with dark windows a few houses down the street. Would Richard be as angry as he'd been in the FBI offices? Would he be able to forgive me for taking on my father?

The back door swung open, and Matthew and Richard leaped onto the sidewalk.

I stopped a few feet from them. Richard's green eyes held my stare.

We didn't move. We didn't speak.

I had done what I needed to, but I wanted nothing more than to go to him, to go home with them, to make love to them.

Matthew's gaze swung between us. I couldn't look at him. Even if I couldn't read Richard's expression, it would all be visible on Matthew's face. I'd see how they had spent the last two days—if they'd spent them talking or arguing, angry or afraid. I'd see how close I was to losing them.

Richard moved fast and grabbed a hold of me before I could take one step to meet him.

He crushed me against his chest. "I'm sorry." His breath flowed through my hair with his words. "I never should've left. I'm an ass when I don't get what I want."

I wrapped my arms around him. "You're just figuring this out?"

Matthew laughed. He stepped closer and slipped his arms around us. His dark eyes lit up, delight shining in them again.

Richard huffed. "I didn't really figure it out."

"No?"

"Not on my own. Matthew's pretty smart. He explained a few things to me."

I gave Matthew a kiss. "Thank you."

"You two are the most stubborn men. If I wasn't here—"

Richard cut him off with a kiss. "Don't even say that." Then he planted a long, slow one on me. "Come on, Luke. Let's go home."

I relaxed into their embrace, the fear, the anxiety, the anger washing away.

A car drove by, my mother watching us from the backseat. What was that look? Anger? Criticism? Sadness?

It didn't matter. I was where I needed to be, and Richard and Matthew had me, held between them.

* * * *

Richard drove home from the FBI field office and broke every speed limit to get there. I sat in the front seat with his hand on my knee. Matthew hadn't bothered with the backseat. He'd climbed in front right after me. He kissed and petted me as Richard drove.

The FBI had kept us at their office for three hours to answer questions and give statements. And I wasn't finished yet. I'd have to return the next day for an interview with an agent from Washington. I didn't care. I was headed home with Richard and Matthew. It was more than I thought I'd have when the day started out.

When we got inside the house, Richard grabbed Matthew and me by the arms and led us upstairs to the bedroom. He pulled me tight against him. Our mouths connected in a scorching kiss. Our tongues wrestled as heat passed between us. I whimpered, the sound lost to his mouth.

"I need you," he said. "To feel you. To love you both."

"Oh God. Me too." Matthew plastered himself to my back. He licked and nipped at the base of my neck. His hard cock pressed against my thigh. I rocked into his touch, my hips unable to remain still between them.

Richard tugged my shirt out of my pants and shoved it off. His strong hands stroked my chest. "Get undressed, Matthew."

Matthew stepped away and began stripping.

Richard's lips traveled across my chest. He dipped his hand inside the front of my jeans, and his fingers moved over the tip of my cock, teasing me. I threw my head back and bucked toward his hand, wanting more, needing more. I threaded my hand through his blond hair as his mouth worked lower and lower.

Matthew's naked body returned behind me. He wound his arms around my waist. He ripped open my jeans and shoved them down past my hips. Richard dropped to his knees, and his lips replaced his hand over the head of my dick.

I gasped. "Oh God. I need this, need you both."

"We're here for you," Matthew whispered.

He worked my jeans off my body and kissed me, his tongue strong and constant in its affection. I shuddered, clutched, rocked into the touches. I needed them to show me I was still there with them.

Between Matthew's kisses and Richard's burning mouth, my body lost control fast. I gripped Richard's shoulders and my legs shook. I didn't want to come yet.

He stilled my hips and pulled off my cock. He kissed my balls and stood. "Get on the bed, Luke."

I didn't want to let go, but I needed more of them. I rolled onto my back and enjoyed the vision before me. Matthew stood on his toes, leaning against Richard's naked, muscular frame. Their mouths were joined in a kiss. It was a sight I'd never tire of seeing.

When they parted, Richard spoke in Matthew's ear. Matthew closed his eyes and whispered back.

Richard took a step away, his legs a little unsteady, adoration shining in his eyes. He turned Matthew around and gave the smaller man a slight shove toward the bed. Matthew laughed and made his way to me.

"What did he tell you?" I asked when he was eye level with me, his body flat atop mine.

"He said..." Matthew kissed me, the connection electric, intense. "I should love you forever."

"Oh." I lowered my gaze.

He put a hand on my chin and lifted my head. "I told him I'll love you both for the rest of my life."

"Matthew." I wrapped my arms around him and slid my hands down his back to the tight curve of his ass. His body drew closer. We touched at every point possible. "You saved me," I said. "You know that? You and Richard. I'd still be lost if you hadn't picked me. When I saw you at the club that first night, the desire was strong. I wanted, needed, to be with you. I still feel that every time I see you." He bit his bottom lip. I kissed him and swiped my tongue over the teeth marks. "Make love to me?"

"Yes." His head dipped and he kissed my neck, his tongue laving my skin. "You were the first man at the club who let me top. Four years, and no one asked. I knew then you were special."

I laid a hand on his cheek. "Kid, you're the one who's special. You and Richard. You let me in even when I tried to run away."

A low chuckle rang out beside us. "I'm glad you haven't forgotten about me."

"Like we could ever forget you." I squeezed the back of Richard's neck and brought his mouth to mine. Full of passion and promise, the kiss solidified how much I could never forget him.

Matthew slid over Richard until he was pressing atop us both. We traded kisses and touches until I pulled away and asked Richard, "What do you want?"

"I want to feel you inside me, and I want Matthew to top us. Let him drive you into me."

Matthew groaned and pushed his pelvis against us.

Richard leaned his forehead on mine. "I think he likes the idea."

"It's a good idea," I said, overcome, the ache in my chest not one of pain or loneliness but a reminder of what they meant to me.

Matthew laughed.

I stared up at him. "I don't think tops giggle."

Richard shook his head. "No, they don't."

Matthew laughed again. I bucked up under him. The move rubbed his balls on my thigh. He quieted his laugh and moaned, his head thrown back. Once I stilled under him, his look turned deliberate. "Get the lube, Richard."

"Such a bossy top." Richard gave Matthew a kiss and rolled to the nightstand.

"On your knees, Luke," Matthew said.

"Oh God." Hearing him take the lead in bed drove me crazy. My body shook as I scrambled onto my knees. He steadied me.

He licked my shoulder and moved lower and lower until his tongue dragged over the top of my crease.

I arched into the contact. "Please, Matthew. More. Need more of you."

Richard settled beside me.

Matthew's tongue left my body. I whimpered, the sound desperate, on edge.

"On your knees, Richard."

Richard didn't hesitate. He knelt beside me. "Kid, you're driving me crazy talking like that."

Matthew moaned. Despite his playful command, he couldn't keep his reactions at bay.

I'd have had it no other way.

He spread my ass open, and he tongued my crease, finally working down and around the most sensitive skin. I cried out as he licked and nipped. He stabbed his tongue into me, and I lost all words. I lowered my head to the bed and rocked backward.

One of his hands left my ass, and I knew where it'd gone as Richard groaned.

I needed Richard's touch. I reached out and grabbed his hand. He met me in a fierce exchange of lips, tongues, and moans. I loved it best when I felt them both.

Matthew thrust his tongue into me one last time. Then slick fingers filled me. His talented digits gave his mouth a run in becoming my favorite way for him to excite me. His fingers, his mouth, his hands, his feet, his dick. Really, any part of him. My desire for them hadn't faded. It had become more personal, more profound, more knowing. We moved together in ways no strangers could have perfected. They pleasured me like no one had ever learned I needed.

"Stop kissing."

Matthew's authoritative demand sent a shiver through my body that landed in my balls. I was loving the performance. His fingers left me in a quick tug, and he swatted our asses—more of a soft tap than a hard slap.

"Richard, on your back. Luke, straddle his legs."

God, I was loving it.

We repositioned ourselves to his liking with Matthew guiding us into place.

He kissed each of us and smiled before steadying his expression again. "Richard, suck Luke until he's good and slick. When he pulls off, Luke, make love to him, show him you're still here."

He knelt behind us and rubbed one hand along my back. With the other, he caressed my balls and the skin behind them. Richard scooted down and did as Matthew ordered. I was lost in the sensations of hands and mouth.

I loved watching my cock slide between Richard's lips, seeing our bodies connected, knowing he wanted me inside his mouth, knowing my dick on his tongue made him harder. He swirled the crown one last time and shimmied up the bed. He lifted his legs, opening for me in such a desperate, needy motion, it made me ache to fill him. I didn't play around. I pushed inside him until his ass met my hips.

He groaned as our bodies came together. "Yes, Luke. I need to feel you. Know you're with us."

"Yes. Still here. In you." The grunts took control of my voice. I thrust in and out of him in a slow torment of pleasure.

I heard a sharp intake of breath behind me, and then a low sob. I forced my body to still and turned to Matthew. He swiped at his eyes.

"Are you okay?"

"Uh-huh. You're beautiful together. I thought we were going to lose this." He sighed. A shaking hand returned to my back.

"I need you. C'mere."

"Yeah." He moved closer. The head of his cock nudged at my hole. "Not such a top when I cry?"

Richard reached over my shoulder and took Matthew's face in his hand. "I love who you are. Never change." With his strong arms, Richard pulled us together, and Matthew's prick slid inside my body.

I groaned as we came together. It was right that I ended up suspended between them after everything I'd been through that day. I needed to be there. Needed to know I was still a part of them.

And as Matthew plunged in and Richard bucked up, I was reminded all my body ever needed was them. I was finished playing at the club, finished searching. I'd found the men I could be myself with, the men who wouldn't let anyone tell them I wasn't worth loving, and the men I wouldn't ever give up—for anyone.

Richard came with a loud grunt. His ass seized the orgasm out of me, and Matthew came along with us.

We collapsed onto Richard in a graceless thump. Our heavy breathing and Matthew's low, sated hums drowned out Richard's exhale.

"I guess it's a good thing Matthew's such a light top if you two are going to keep landing on me."

Matthew laughed. He dropped beside Richard and patted the man's hip. "Sorry."

Richard leaned over to kiss him, and I joined them. It wasn't heated or fancy. It was slow and tender and everything I needed.

I moved off Richard and wriggled to lie between them. They made room and wrapped their arms around me.

The irony of the moment wasn't lost on me. I laughed at the memory of the first night we'd stayed together in the same bed—when they had positioned me between them for a brief moment.

"What's so funny?" Matthew asked, his voice relaxed.

"Nothing. Just thinking of how far I've come since we first stayed here together."

"We've all come a long way," Richard said. "I'm proud of you, Luke. Proud of what you did today. Proud of the man you are—the man you've let us get to know. When I heard your father say he wanted to kill you…I about lost it."

Matthew laughed. "You should've seen it. I had to sit on him to get him to listen to me."

"I imagined as much." I faced Richard. "Thank you for understanding what I had to do."

"Had you gotten yourself killed, I'd never have forgiven you."

"I get that. I like that you worry. Next time, trust me, huh?"

"I'll try."

Matthew wrapped his arms around me. "We'll always support you. Forever." He kissed my cheek and then rolled over and jumped out of the bed.

"Where are you going?"

He started dressing. "To get food. Walter said you haven't been eating."

* * * *

I finished my shower and found them seated in the dining room. Soft candles lit the room. Trays of food covered the table: cubed cheeses and meats, a sliced French baguette, fresh fruits, whipped cream, and various bite-sized cheesecakes.

I sat across from Richard and reached for my napkin. "Where's the silverware?"

Richard snorted. "Told you he'd notice."

"Of course he's gonna notice," Matthew said. "But he doesn't know what we're up to."

"Can't we eat? It all looks great."

"Uh-huh," Matthew said. "But we aren't using forks. We're using our hands."

"Okay." I picked up a grape from the fruit tray and went to pop it in my mouth.

Richard reached across the table and stopped me. "No, Luke. We're using our hands, but there's one rule." He stole the grape from me and raised it to my lips. I opened for him and licked his fingers, loving the game already. "No one can feed himself."

"You do like your rules, don't you?"

Matthew laughed with me, the sound full of joy and life, wiping away a bit of the horrible memories. He didn't act as though being in the dining room bothered him. I hoped I'd be able to sit there one day and not see steel against his skin. Matthew instilled that sort of hope.

"Hey," Richard said, "it's those rules and my pushiness that got us here. Without that, you'd both still be playing at the Haven."

"This feels like…" Matthew trailed off and lowered his head.

Richard cupped the man's chin. "Finish your thought."

"This feels like a haven. Here, just us. You know?" He shifted in his seat.

Richard smiled. "Yeah, that's exactly what it's been like."

I reached for Matthew and held his hand. "Living here with you two has been better than all the nights I spent at the club combined." I snatched a strawberry, dipped it in the whipped cream, and painted it over his lips.

I pulled him into my arms and licked the cream from his mouth and chin. The sweet taste from his skin ruined me for all other desserts. I traced his mouth with my thumb. "I love these lips. Your laugh. Your smile—"

The doorbell rang. Richard groaned. "What now?"

"I'll get it," I said. "It might be the press." I had already decided I'd talk to them, but not in our home.

I answered the door, expecting to see anyone but who stood on the other side.

My mother stared back at me, her eyes sad and hollow but focused on my own.

I was torn between slamming the door in her face and asking her for the truth I needed to hear. I didn't have time to do either. She barreled through the open door and flung her arms around me.

"Oh, Luke. He said he could make the charges go away." Her arms squeezed tighter. "He said he'd get you help if I let you go."

Charges? Help? Fowler had been right. Somehow my father had convinced her to stay away from me. And it didn't sound like he had used the truth.

She released me and wiped the tears from her eyes.

"Come in." I gestured for her to follow. We passed by the dining room with Richard and Matthew gawking at us. She gave them a small smile and a nod but said nothing.

Richard stood. "Ma'am, if you're here to hurt him in any way, you'll leave. He's been through enough. It's time for him to move on."

Her mouth opened, but she clamped it shut before speaking. Couldn't she promise him what he needed to hear?

"It's okay," I said. "I need to hear her out."

Richard stared at her for another moment, then sat.

I continued on to the living room, and she followed. We each settled in a chair. The tension and unease filled the space between us. I said nothing as I watched her.

She stared at the hands on her lap. "You have a nice home."

I nodded my thanks. I had nothing to explain, nothing to apologize for, and nothing to be ashamed of.

She took a deep breath and gave her fingers one last twist. "I knew your father had a problem with you being gay as soon as you told us. I knew he'd think it would hurt him politically. But I had no idea the lengths he'd go to, or I would have left him then." Tears fell onto her cheeks. She swiped at them and continued.

"After you left for college, I found out he was paying men for sex. I asked him for a divorce. That's when he told me about the night you were arrested."

Arrested? I leaned back against the chair and crossed my arms over my chest. This wasn't going to be good.

She spoke again, her voice unsteady. "He said you'd been having unprotected sex with men for drug money. He said he bailed you out of jail and begged you to stop—the drugs and the prostitution. But you wouldn't promise him anything."

The tears gushed, and she didn't even try to catch them. "He wanted you out of our lives and said he'd help you if I agreed not to see you anymore. He said he'd get the charges dropped and keep you enrolled in school. He knew of a rehab program that would take you against your will and keep you there until you were clean. I didn't want you to get sick. I didn't want you to end up dead. I told myself all that mattered was getting you help." She met my shocked stare. "It was all a lie, wasn't it?"

My one-word answer would break her heart more. Yet none of it was my fault, and at least she'd know the whole truth—about her husband, about me.

"Yes."

She dropped her head into her hands and sobbed. I fetched her a tissue and gave her a few minutes before I continued. When she could look at me again, I told her about Tim and how I'd loved him. About how my losing him was the first of my father's attempts to control me.

When I was done, she cried more.

"I knew...I knew in my heart my boy was a good man. A man who could love. I should never have believed him. I should have gone to you."

"Dad helped take Tim from me, and he helped take away my ability to let anyone else in." I glanced up. Richard and Matthew stood in the doorway. "But I've got it back now."

She followed my gaze. "I see that."

I smiled at them. Richard returned the gesture and tilted his head toward the stairs.

"No, stay. I have nothing to hide from you."

He put his arm around Matthew, and they stepped into the room.

My mother watched them move past until they sat on the couch. She looked back at me. "I know I can't come in here and ask for your forgiveness. It isn't that simple. I may not have known everything he was up to, but I let him push you away from us, and I didn't do anything to stop it. I didn't try to talk to you, to help you." She lowered her head. Everything about her radiated shame. It comforted me despite the pain she was feeling.

"Part of me felt betrayed when I learned you were gay. That was something I needed to work through. I didn't. I believed his lies. I let your father's hatred for who you were—and his hatred for himself—taint my own ability to love you and accept you." She raised her head. "I know I can't expect anything. That's not why I'm here. I want to start by apologizing. I am sorry. So sorry, sweetheart. I've let him tell me what to do for a long time. But that's done. You're a good boy—a good man. I heard that when you came to our house. I stood in the hallway and listened to him threaten you."

Knowing she had heard his words—had heard her own husband threaten to kill her son—disturbed me. I felt sorry for her in a way I never thought I would.

She swiped the tissue over her cheeks. "But no matter what horrible things he said to you, you stood proud and didn't falter. You defended yourself and your…boyfriends." She stumbled on the word, but pride surged through me.

"They're more than that, Mom. They're family." I gave Richard and Matthew a wink.

I felt her gaze upon me. I met her stare.

"Oh. Like married?"

Richard laughed. I glanced back in time to catch Matthew cover Richard's mouth with a small hand.

Matthew gave her a charming smile. "Uh, ma'am, your son wasn't always the marrying kind. For him to say family is a big deal to us."

She nodded. When she spoke again, her voice was a low whisper. "I know you might need some time, but if you'd let me, I'd like to get to know them. I'd like to get to know you."

"I'm gay. I'm living with two men. And I've helped to get your husband arrested."

"None of those statements are news to me, son."

Matthew giggled. The sound muffled in short order as I presumed a large hand covered his mouth.

"Mom, I won't be anyone but who I am. If you can handle that, then I'm open to trying to get to know each other again."

Her lower lip quivered, but she held back more tears. "You're a good man, Lukas Moore." She stood and came to me. She brushed at the hair near my temple, reminiscent of my nights as a small boy when she'd tuck me into bed. "Your father lost himself along the way. I pretended it didn't matter. I'm sorry I was blind to who you really are."

I stood and held her in my arms. I let the tears I promised myself I'd never show her come.

She wiped at my eyes and cupped my face in her hands. "Now, before I go, can I meet your boys? Make it more official this time?"

I led her to the couch. Richard and Matthew stood, and they smiled at me with love and affection in their eyes. There was a time when having that expression visible to someone other than the three of us would have bothered me. Not any longer. My mother seeing it was essential and fitting.

"Mom, Richard Marshall."

Richard held out a hand.

For a moment, she seemed hesitant. Then she stepped forward and hugged him. "You're his protector?"

"I try to be."

"It's good for a mother to know her son has someone looking after him. Please take care of him."

"Always."

I wrapped an arm around Matthew. "And this is Matthew Stewart."

She turned and hugged him too. "And you're sweet and lively. I think my Luke needs that in his life."

"And addictive," I said.

"Right," Richard said. "Don't forget addictive." I laughed with him.

Matthew rolled his eyes. She released him and gave his arm a pat before stepping away.

Richard pulled him close and kissed his temple. I was glad to see they weren't holding back in front of my mother. I wouldn't have asked them to do any different, to be anything but themselves.

She sat and fumbled for her purse beside the chair. She removed a new tissue and stabbed at her eyes.

"Is something wrong?"

"Oh, no, no." Her hands fell to her lap. "For once, it's right. You have a family. Jokes, laughter, love. It's all I ever wanted for you. When you told us you were gay, I never thought you'd have any of this. It's nice to see you in your home with your family."

If she could accept them, accept me, then I had a chance at having a mother again. I'd never have a father, but I would have a family. It was more than I ever thought I'd have.

I walked her to the door.

"Will you keep in touch?" she asked.

"I'll try." Remembering to call on Mother's Day or any other day of the year wasn't something I'd had to do in a long time.

"And I'll try to be the mother you deserve." She moved for the open door but stopped short. "I'd like you all to come for dinner. I'm going to move. I can't stay at the house after…" She patted my arm. "Please think about it. I'll call, and you can let me know."

"Thanks for asking. I'll see what the guys say."

She gave me a kiss on the cheek and left. I watched her walk to her car and closed the door after she drove off. My hand gripped the doorknob. I couldn't let go. If I gave up on the death grip, then I might have to let go of everything. The anger. The hatred. The betrayal. Am I ready for that?

Laughter poured out of the living room.

Yeah, I'm ready.

I found Matthew and Richard lying on the couch, kissing, touching, loving on each other.

"I think she likes us," Richard said.

Matthew laughed. "Uh-huh."

I tried to hide my smile. "Get your asses up to the bed, or it's the dining room table all over again."

"God, no." Richard groaned and stood. "Besides, I have a surprise."

Chapter Forty-One

I stepped out of the cab and let the smile build, let the anticipation flow through me. A night out to fill the ache, the burning inside me.

It was exactly what I needed.

Only it wasn't the ache of loneliness or misery. It was the ache of knowing, with everything I was, what I wanted. I had no doubts, no fears, no inhibitions.

I stepped inside and made my way to the bar. With my long absence from the club, there were many men I'd never seen before. Men I'd never been with. I didn't see any of them. I sat and sipped my water. I wasn't in a hurry. The men I'd find were going to give me everything I needed. The Haven never disappointed.

My gaze captured a dark-haired man walking toward the bar. He wore tight leather pants and a loose white dress shirt. There was a spring in his every step, and his wavy hair bounced with him. He was sexy as hell, but what made him all the more appealing were his eyes. They asked for something, begged for it.

I knew what he wanted—what he needed from me—as if he'd spoken the words aloud.

"Hello," he said with a smile as he sat next to me. "Are you available tonight?" His voice was low and husky. I knew he sounded like that when he was aroused, when he was hard and desperate for contact, a touch, a kiss.

I held his gaze. "Yeah. I am."

Dark eyes stared back at me. "Great."

"I'd like us to find another."

His smile grew. "Perfect."

I smirked, unable to keep the grin contained, absolutely adoring him. I stood and moved to a table, and he followed. I couldn't take my eyes off him. He was gorgeous. I was supposed to be searching for another man, but I wasn't concerned. He'd find us. And he'd understand. One look at the man across from me, and he'd know why I couldn't look away.

"The name's Luke."

He laughed, the sound a delight. "Matthew."

We didn't bother with a handshake as we had the first time we'd done the same exchange. If I touched him, everything would progress faster than we'd planned. He must have felt the same because he made no attempt to reach for me.

Instead, he ran a hand through his dark hair. The strands straightened and snapped back, the movement smooth and just how I remembered him doing it when I'd first sat at the same table with him. I delighted in the knowledge I knew exactly how his hand felt wrapped around my prick, how his fingers felt twisted in my hair, how his hands felt all over me.

I breathed deep. Waiting could be hard. Damn hard. Especially when you knew how great it was going to be.

I'd always imagined being with the same men over and over would be too expected, redundant, reliable, complicated. But it was never any of those things. Not with them.

No matter what my preference on any given day, they fit the bill. The passion wasn't fading. Our feelings for one another were driving it forward, building devotion and desire where the initial surges of lust for the strangers they'd been trailed off.

Matthew blushed as if he could hear my thoughts. "How come we've never done this before?"

I laughed as I remembered the same question from a night similar to the one we were reliving, yet so different. I pulled the words of my reply from memory. "Don't know. Seems every time I considered it, you were already with someone else. Guess you're too popular." That got me a smile and eyes that shone at me. He still had a great smile.

He glanced around the room in a quick sweep. His gaze stilled. "Luke, I think we have our third."

I focused my attention across the dining room. The man strolling toward us still took my breath away. The dress slacks and shirt he wore were the same ones I'd seen him in the first time. I pictured the muscular, strong body that lived underneath. There was no part of him I hadn't explored with my eyes, my hands, my mouth, my tongue.

"You two want to be alone?" That voice still did things to me, had me undone with just a few words.

"No," Matthew and I said in unison.

"I didn't think so." He grabbed the back of a chair from the nearest table, swung it around, and sat. "Richard."

I waited for him to reach out and shake Matthew's hand, but he didn't, obviously as concerned about his ability to limit the contact to one handshake as I.

"I'm Matthew."

"You're cute, kid." The stare lingered between them.

Richard looked to me. All thoughts of what I was supposed to say next were lost. Green eyes, the strong lines of his face, and the love I saw there entranced me.

"Uh, Luke. You forgot to tell me your name."

Matthew threw his head back and laughed. The sound settled in my soul.

Richard continued despite my blunder. "Nice to meet you." His eyes met mine again. "What do you want?"

"Right now?" I grinned. "You. Both of you. Forever."

Before I'd met them, I'd been waiting and looking, only I hadn't known what it was I needed.

Sitting in the Haven again with them, I knew.

I stood. We didn't need to determine our wants or desires, our rules or limitations. We already knew one another in a way I'd known no other men in my life. I wanted to hold, kiss, touch, and make love to them. For that we needed to either get our asses home or upstairs in a room.

The rooms upstairs were closer.

I took a step away from the table. Richard reached out and grabbed my hand. His large body slinked up mine as he stood. "Dance with me?"

"I thought—"

"We've got all night."

"What about Matthew?"

Matthew stared up at us, his dark eyes wide, his bottom lip pinched between his teeth.

"This is for him," Richard whispered. "He has a thing for watching us." Richard bent down to him. "Stay here? Watch?"

Matthew's eyes widened. His head bobbed.

Richard ran a hand through Matthew's dark hair as he moved by the table. The same hand found mine, and I went with him.

He chose a spot on the dance floor near the edge of the crowd, keeping Matthew's line of sight clear. He gave Matthew a smile before he turned to me and wrapped his arms around my waist.

I gripped the front of his shirt with both hands. The beat of the music thudded in my chest, or it might have been my heart. He cupped my chin in his hand. I met his eyes and wound my arms around his neck.

Easy. Right. No thought required. We moved as one.

"You've never done this before?" he asked.

"I'm that bad?"

He licked and nipped along my neck to my earlobe. "I like how you move. It was a guess."

"A good one."

He pulled back. "Not with another guy?"

"Not with anyone."

He gripped the back of my neck and whispered in my ear. "I like that there are some things that can be just for us."

Another exploring hand ran over my ass. Not a random guy hitting on me. The touch was too familiar.

I reached behind me, gripped the waistband of his pants, and yanked him around until Matthew pushed between us.

I wrapped an arm around him. "He didn't last long."

"Nope." Richard's open palm rubbed Matthew's cheek. "But that's okay. He's right where he needs to be."

Matthew laughed and pressed closer.

I looked to one, then the other. A freedom I'd never known washed over me. The last remnants of the man I'd forced myself to be for so long were gone. I was free…free from the past…free from my father. All that remained was the truth.

I grabbed Matthew's face in my hands. "Matthew, I love you."

He bit his lip and leaned into me, his arms slipping around my neck, his body shaking against mine. I held on to him until he stilled.

When we let go, I laid a hand on Richard's chest, and he moved closer. His green eyes scanned mine. His chest heaved with each breath.

"I love you."

He buried his face in my neck. Wet drops tickled my skin. His tears.

I held them close and said what my father never could. "I'll love you both until I take my last breath."

ABOUT THE AUTHOR

Sloan Parker writes passionate, dramatic stories about two men (or more) falling in love. She enjoys writing in the fictional world because in fiction you can be anything, do anything—even fall in love for the first time over and over again. Sloan lives in Ohio with her partner and their neurotic cats. Her greatest moments in life are spent with her family, her friends, and her characters.

To contact Sloan, find out about her other books that are available for purchase, and read free stories, visit: www.sloanparker.com. If you'd like to be notified of new releases and get exclusive sneak peeks, be sure to sign up to receive Sloan Parker's newsletter via her website.

OTHER TITLES BY SLOAN PARKER

Breathe
Take Me Home
How to Save a Life (The Haven Book 1)
More Than Just a Good Book
Something to Believe In
I Swear to You
The Break-In
Swept Away
A Lesson in Truth

Made in the USA
Middletown, DE
24 October 2018